~ ♡ BOOKS ~

Gin Blanco has

More praise f
Eleme

VENOM

"Estep has really hit her stride with the gritty and compelling Elemental Assassin series. . . . Fascinating and complex heroine. . . . Brisk pacing and knife-edged danger make this an exciting page-turner."

—*Romantic Times* (Top Pick, 4½ stars)

"Gin is a compelling and complicated character whose story is only made better by the lovable band of merry misfits she calls her family. Definitely, by far, the best fantasy series I've read this year."

—Fresh Fiction

"Each book is just as solid and awesome as its earlier predecessors. . . . Fast-paced urban fantasy adventure."

—Smokin' Hot Books

"Since the first book in the series, I have been entranced by Gin. . . . Every book has been jam-packed with action and mystery, and once I think it can't get any better, *Venom* comes along and proves me completely wrong."

—Literary Escapism

WEB OF LIES

"The second chapter of the first-person Elemental Assassin series is just as hard-edged and compelling as the first. Gin Blanco is a fascinatingly pragmatic character, whose intricate layers are just beginning to unravel."

—*Romantic Times*

"A fantastic sequel in every respect. . . . This second installment is even more steamy, suspenseful, and full of mystery and adventure. Packed with pulse-pounding action and suspense, this urban fantasy truly delivers. Don't miss this series with unique world building and a complex heroine. I'm certainly caught in Estep's web, and look forward to Gin's next adventure."

—SciFiChick.com

"With each Jennifer Estep book I read I'm more in awe of her writing. She always has fresh story lines with well-developed characters. The dual plotlines are each tied up nicely in the end, yet we're left with a delicious cliffhanger that will have me first in line to read the third book in the series. . . . This is a must read for anyone who loves urban fantasy."

—ReadingwithMonie.com

"Jennifer Estep has written one of the best urban fantasy series I've ever read. The action is off the charts, the passion is hot, and her cast of secondary characters is stellar. . . . If you haven't read this series, you are missing out on one heck of a good time!"

—The Romance Dish

SPIDER'S BITE

"Bodies litter the pages of this first entry in Estep's engrossing Elemental Assassin series. . . . Urban fantasy fans will love it."

—Publishers Weekly

"When it comes to work, Estep's newest heroine is brutally efficient and very pragmatic, which gives the new Elemental Assassin series plenty of bite. Shades of gray rule in this world where magic and murder are all too commonplace. The gritty tone of this series gives Estep a chance to walk on the darker side. Kudos to her for the knife-edged suspense!"

—Romantic Times

"The fast pace, clever dialogue, and intriguing heroine help make this new series launch by the author of the Bigtime paranormal romance series one to watch."

—Library Journal

"Electrifying! Jennifer Estep really knows how to weave a fantasy tale that will keep you reading way past your bedtime."

—ReadingwithMonie.com

"Loaded with action and intrigue, the story is strong and exciting. . . . With a knock-out, climactic ending and a surprising twist that I didn't see coming, I was definitely impressed. This dark, urban fantasy series has a promising start."

—SciFiChick.com

"Watch out world, here comes Gin Blanco. Funny, smart, and dead sexy."

—Lilith Saintcrow, author of *Heaven's Spite*

"*Spider's Bite* is a raw, gritty, and compelling walk on the wild side, one that had me hooked from the first page. Jennifer Estep has created a fascinating heroine in the morally ambiguous Gin Blanco—I can't wait to read the next chapter of Gin's story."

—Nalini Singh, *New York Times* bestselling author of *Archangel's Consort*

"I love rooting for the bad guy—especially when she's also the heroine. *Spider's Bite* is a sizzling combination of mystery, magic, and murder. Kudos to Jennifer Estep!"

—Jackie Kessler, author of *Shades of Gray*

"Jennifer Estep is a dark, lyrical, and fresh voice in urban fantasy. Brimming with high-octane-fueled action, labyrinthine conspiracies, and characters who will steal your heart, *Spider's Bite* is an original, fast-paced, tense, and sexy read. Gin is an assassin to die for."

—Adrian Phoenix, author of *Black Heart Loa*

"A sexy and edgy thriller that keeps you turning the pages. In *Spider's Bite,* Jennifer Estep turns up the heat and suspense with Gin Blanco, an assassin whose wit is as sharp as her silverstone knives. . . . Leaves you dying for more."

—Lisa Shearin, national bestselling author of *Con & Conjure*

The Elemental Assassin titles are also available as eBooks

Spider's REVENGE

AN ELEMENTAL ASSASSIN BOOK

JENNIFER ESTEP

POCKET BOOKS

New York   London   Toronto   Sydney   New Delhi

Pocket Books
A Division of Simon & Schuster, Inc.
1230 Avenue of the Americas
New York, NY 10020

This book is a work of fiction. Names, characters, places, and incidents either are products of the author's imagination or are used fictitiously. Any resemblance to actual events or locales or persons, living or dead, is entirely coincidental.

Copyright © 2011 by Jennifer Estep

First Pocket Books paperback edition October 2011

POCKET and colophon are registered trademarks of Simon & Schuster, Inc.

For information about special discounts for bulk purchases, please contact Simon & Schuster Special Sales at 1-866-506-1949 or business@simonandschuster.com.

The Simon & Schuster Speakers Bureau can bring authors to your live event. For more information or to book an event contact the Simon & Schuster Speakers Bureau at 1-866-248-3049 or visit our website at www.simonspeakers.com.

Cover design and illustration by Tony Mauro

Manufactured in the United States of America

10   9   8   7   6   5

ISBN 978-1-4391-9264-1
ISBN 978-1-4391-9266-5 (ebook)

To my mom, grandma, and Andre—for everything.
And to all the readers out there—this one's for you.

ACKNOWLEDGMENTS

Once again, my heartfelt thanks goes to all the folks who help turn my words into a book.

Thanks to my super agent, Annelise Robey, and wonderful editors, Megan McKeever and Lauren McKenna, for all their helpful advice, support, and encouragement.

Thanks to Tony Mauro for designing another fantastic cover.

And finally, a big thanks to all the readers. There are many great books out there and it's always humbling to realize that folks choose to read my books. I'm glad that you are all enjoying Gin and her adventures.

I appreciate you all more than you will ever know.

Happy reading!

Spider's REVENGE

* 1 *

Old habits die hard for assassins.

And I planned on murdering someone before the night was through.

That's what I did. Me. Gin Blanco. The assassin known as the Spider. I killed people, something that I was very, very good at.

Tonight I had my sights set on my most dangerous target ever—Mab Monroe, the Fire elemental who'd murdered my family when I was thirteen.

I'd been plotting the hit for weeks. Where to do it, how to get past security, what weapon to use, how to get away after the fact. Now, on this cold, cold night, I'd finally decided to carry out my deadly plan.

I'd been on the prowl for hours. Three hours, to be exact. Each one spent out in the bitter February frost, including climbing my way up the side of a fifteen-story mansion one icy foot at a time. Hard bits of snow pelted my body as I tried to keep the shrieking wind from tearing me off the side of the building. It wasn't the most comfortable that I'd ever been during one of my hits, but it was necessary.

Too bad Mab knew that I was coming for her.

Oh, I hadn't expected it to be *easy*, but slipping past the massive net of security, first in the snowy woods around Mab's mansion, and then closer to the house itself, was a bit more problematic than I'd expected. The whole area was teeming with the giants that the Fire elemental employed as her personal bodyguards, not to mention nasty land mines and other traps strung through the trees like invisible spiderwebs. Of course, I could have dropped the giants, killing them one by one as I went along, but that would have resulted in the alarm being raised, and the security net tightening that much more.

So instead I'd opted for a silent, nonlethal approach— at least for now. It had taken me an hour to work my way through the woods, then another one to get close enough to the mansion to slither up the stairs to a second-floor balcony and then heave myself up onto part of the roof that sloped down there. After that, things had gotten easier, since there were no sensors, alarms, or giants posted on the roofs that covered the various parts of the massive structure. Not many people bothered with such things above the second floor, since most folks weren't brave or crazy enough to climb any higher, especially on a snowy night like this one.

I wasn't particularly brave or crazy, but I was determined to kill Mab.

A strong gust of wind slapped and then backhanded

the mansion, screaming in my ears and hurling more frozen snow off the eaves and onto me. The chunks punched my body before disappearing over the side of the roof and dropping down into the eerie silver dark of the night.

I grunted at the hard, stinging impacts. As an elemental, I could have used my Stone magic to protect myself, could have tapped into my power and made my skin hard as marble so that the rocklike wads of snow would bounce off my body like bullets off Superman's chest. But elementals can sense when others of their ilk are using their powers, and I didn't want to give Mab any hint that I was here.

At least, not before I'd killed her.

By this point, I'd worked my way up to the sixth floor, where the mansion's blueprints had indicated there was a particularly large dining room. According to some chatter that my foster brother, Finnegan Lane, had picked up from his various spies, Mab was hosting a fancy dinner party this evening. Finn hadn't been able to determine what the party was for or even who had been invited, but that didn't much matter. Mab was getting dead tonight—I didn't care who was in the room with her.

I'd been in position for more than an hour now, outside the dining room window, lying flat on a part of the roof that plateaued before sloping down at a severe angle and dropping away to the ground far below. The blowing snow and murky shadows, combined with the glare of the lights inside, made me all but invisible to anyone looking out through the window.

But really, the worst part of the night wasn't the guards,

the cold, the snow, or even the icy, treacherous climb—it was having to listen to the stones around me.

People's emotions, actions, and feelings sink into their environment over time, especially into the stone around them. As a Stone elemental, I could hear those emotional vibrations in whatever form the element took around me, from loose pebbles underfoot to the brick of a building to a marble sculpture. The sounds, the murmurs, the whispers that reverberated through the stones let me know what had happened in a particular spot, what sorts of people had been there, and all the dark, ugly, twisted things that they'd done in the meantime—or who might be lurking around in the here and now, trying to get the drop on me.

Fire, heat, pain, death. That's what the stones of Mab's mansion murmured of, punctuated by sly, smirking, confident whispers of power and money—both things that the Fire elemental had in abundance. But the most disturbing thing, the sound that made me grind my teeth, was the cackling of maniacal madness that rippled through the gray stones. Wave after wave of it, as though the rock had somehow been tortured until it was just as broken, burned, and dead as Mab's many victims.

After a minute of listening to the stones' insane, wailing cries, I'd blocked out the damned disturbing noise and had gotten on with more important matters, like checking my weapons. As always, I carried five silverstone knives—one up either sleeve, one against the small of my back, and two more tucked into my boots. The knives were my weapons of choice on most jobs because they were sharp, strong, and almost unbreakable. Just like me.

But Mab was a Fire elemental, which meant that she could create, control, and manipulate fire the same way that I could stone. And Mab wasn't just any *mere* Fire elemental—she was rumored to have more raw magic, more raw power, than any elemental born in the last five hundred years. She could easily fry me alive with her magic before I got close enough to even think about plunging my silverstone knives into her burning black heart.

I'd decided to play it smart and keep a healthy distance between us, just in case things didn't work out exactly as I'd planned tonight. So I'd brought another weapon along with me—a crossbow. It looked like your typical crossbow—heavy, substantial, deadly—made even more so by the rifle scope that I'd mounted above the trigger and the six-inch-long, barbed bolt already in firing position. Since it was made out of silverstone, a particularly tough magical metal, the bolt would rip through anything it came into contact with—glass, stone, flesh, bones.

The crossbow currently sat on the window ledge, with the barb pointing inside. I'd been in firing position for more than fifteen minutes, and all I had to do to release the deadly bolt was pull the trigger.

Good thing, as people were starting to arrive for dinner.

The black velvet drapes had been drawn to either side of the window, letting me see into the dining room. Closing the drapes was something else most folks didn't bother with above the second floor. Sloppy, sloppy, sloppy of Mab's bodyguards not to see to a pesky little detail like that.

I'd actually been inside Mab's mansion once before,

when I'd been stalking another target a few months ago, and the dining room before me was just as opulent as I remembered the rest of the house being. The room was a hundred feet wide, with a ceiling that soared high above it. Gold and silver leaf glinted in elaborate patterns on the ceiling, while several chandeliers dropped down from it and glistened like jewel-colored dewdrops above a polished ebony table. Four dozen place settings of fine china covered the table, along with matching flatware. Silver buckets filled with ice, champagne, and other expensive liquors were spaced down both sides of the table, so that everyone could have easy access to the booze.

For the last ten minutes, tuxedo-clad giants moved through the area, bringing in plates, napkins, liquor, and everything else that might be needed. My gaze drifted over to a buffet table that had been set up on the far side of the room. Mab and her guests were dining on lobster tonight, among other delicacies.

Finally, one of the giants opened the double doors at the end of the room, bowed his head, and held out his arm, ushering the guests inside. Time to get the party started, in more ways than one.

Most of the guests drifted in one by one, although a few were coupled up in groups of two or more. Men and women. Old, young, fat, thin, black, white, Hispanic, dwarves, giants, vampires. There was more variety to the crowd than I'd expected. Usually, all of Mab's business associates looked the same—middle-aged men with more money than common sense and all the greedy, twisted appetites to match.

But these people were different. Oh, they all looked

like I'd thought they would—dressed to the nines in tuxedos and evening gowns, with expensive jewels, perfect makeup, and coiffed hair to match. But they didn't act like I'd thought they would. They didn't mingle, they didn't start drinking and eating, and perhaps most telling, they didn't even bother talking to each other. Instead, all the singles, couples, and tight-knit groups stayed to themselves, leaving several feet of distance in between each of them. Curious. Most curious indeed.

Through the rifle scope, my eye went from one face to another, trying to get a sense of exactly who Mab had invited to her shindig and why they were acting so strangely. I might not care what their names were or how much money they had, but I did want to know if any of them fancied themselves tough guys who might be a threat to me. Not that I was planning on sticking around after I took out Mab, but it never hurt to be prepared. Fletcher Lane, the old man who had been my mentor, had taught me that, among many other deadly things.

Despite their tuxedos, gowns, and glittering jewels, every single one of the men and women had a tense, coiled, predatory air about them, and they all gave each other the same flat, hard stare, as if they were all competing for the same prize and would do anything to get it. A few of them actually eyed the silverware, as if they were thinking about picking up the knives, spoons, and forks, and thinning out the crowd a bit before the show got started.

I frowned. Mab did business with all sorts of unsavory characters, but something about the people inside the dining room bothered me. Maybe because they all reminded me . . . of me. Gin Blanco. The Spider.

Before I had time to think that thought through, the double doors opened again, and Mab Monroe stepped into the room.

The Fire elemental strolled through the tense crowd until she reached the middle of the dining room. Everyone turned to stare at her, and what little conversation there had been stopped, like a radio that had been turned off midsong. Like her guests, Mab had dressed up for the evening, in a long, sea-green gown that complemented her pale skin. Her coppery red hair was piled on top of her head, each artfully arranged strand dripping down the sides of her face like so much blood. But the most striking thing about Mab was her eyes—two bottomless black pools that seemed to suck up all the available light in the room instead of reflecting it back. Even the bright chandeliers overhead appeared to dim as she passed underneath them.

The severe V in the front of Mab's gown showed off her creamy décolletage, as well as the necklace she wore. A flat gold circle encased the Fire elemental's neck, accentuated by a ruby set into the middle of the design. Several dozen wavy golden rays surrounded the gem, and the intricate diamond cutting on the metal caught the light and reflected it back, making it look like the rays were flickering.

The flamboyant ruby-and-gold design was much more than just a mere necklace—it was a rune. A sunburst. The symbol for fire. Mab's personal rune, used by her alone. Runes were how elementals and other magic types in Ashland identified themselves, their families, their power, their alliances, and even their businesses to others.

I had a rune too. A small circle surrounded by eight thin rays. A spider rune. The symbol for patience and my assassin name. Actually, I had two runes—one branded into either palm. The marks had been put there by Mab the night she'd murdered my family. That's when the Fire elemental had tortured me by duct-taping a silverstone medallion shaped like the spider rune in between my hands and then superheating the metal with her magic until it had melted into my flesh, marking me forever.

The sight of Mab and her flashing sunburst necklace made the spider rune scars on my palms itch and burn, the way they always did whenever I was around the Fire elemental, but I didn't move from my position. Didn't rub my hands together to make the uncomfortable sensation go away. Didn't let out a tense sigh. Hell, I didn't even blink.

Killing Mab was much more important than the memories that filled my mind or the pain that they brought me, even now, seventeen years after the fact. Now was not the time to be sentimental or sloppy. Not when I had a chance to kill the bitch, to finally end our family feud once and for all.

Inside the dining room, Mab turned in a circle, her black eyes roaming over her guests, sizing them up just like I had.

"I'm glad to see that you all could make it."

The Fire elemental's voice was low, soft, and silky, with just a hint of a rasp to it. Still, despite her gentle tone, a clear undercurrent of power and authority crackled in Mab's words.

Thanks to Finn and his ability to get his hands on

absolutely anything, I'd opened the dining room window earlier and fastened a small bug inside underneath the windowsill. The bug's receiver, which I'd stuck in my ear several minutes ago, let me hear Mab loud and clear.

"I wasn't sure exactly how many of you would show up on such short notice," Mab continued. "But I'm most pleased by the turnout."

I frowned. Turnout? What was the Fire elemental up to, and who were these mysterious people that she'd invited to her mansion? I had a funny feeling they weren't the tame businessmen and businesswomen that I'd expected to find.

A woman stepped forward, separating herself from the pack. She wore an evening gown like all the others, but the garment was just a bit too big for her thin, wiry body. The fabric was slick and cheap, and the mint green color was faded, as though she'd been wearing the dress for years, pulling it out of the depths of her closet for special occasions just like this one. She had to be seventy if she was a day, and her skin had the dark, nut brown look of someone who'd spent her entire life outdoors, working under the burning sun. Her gray hair had been pulled back into a tight bun, which set off her sharp, angular face, and her eyes were a pale, washed-out blue.

The woman was one of those who'd come in with someone else. A young girl of about sixteen stood off to her right, dressed in a low-rent pink gown with a poofy ballerina skirt, which made it look like a prom dress. The girl was as light as the woman was dark, with long, molasses-colored hair shot through with honey-blond highlights. Her hazel eyes were wide and innocent in her lean, almost gaunt face, and the girl kept glancing from side to side, obviously awed by all the lavish furnishings.

"Well, there was really no choice in the matter, Mab." The woman's voice was low, pleasant, friendly even, as though she were talking to some stranger on the street and not the most dangerous person in Ashland. "Not with the generous payout that you were offering. I'm surprised that more people didn't show up to try to collect."

The others in the room nodded their agreement. My eyes narrowed. Payout, for what? And how were they going to collect? Was this some kind of business deal? Or something else . . . something more sinister? Something to do with the Spider perhaps?

It wasn't out of the realm of possibility. Not too long ago, Mab had hired an assassin named Elektra LaFleur to come to Ashland, hunt me down, and kill me. Of course, I'd taken care of LaFleur instead. Still, ever since then, I'd been waiting for the Fire elemental to do something, anything, to try to find the Spider again. Mab wasn't the type of person to give up, especially when I'd been offing her men, thwarting her best-laid plans, and generally thumbing my nose at her for months.

But everything had been quiet since I'd killed LaFleur in the city's old train yard. Even Finn and his many spies hadn't heard a whisper of what Mab might be planning, which worried me more than if I knew that the Fire elemental had dispatched every man at her disposal to track me down.

Somehow, though, I felt that the quiet was about to end tonight—in a big, big way.

"And you would be?" Mab asked, staring down her nose at her guest.

The other woman bowed her head respectfully, although she never took her eyes off the Fire elemental. "Ruth Gentry, at your service."

"Ah, yes, Gentry. Well, I appreciate your honesty," Mab said, returning the thin woman's pleasant tone. "You have a stellar reputation, as does everyone else in the room. Which, of course, is why I asked you all here tonight."

The Fire elemental had piqued my curiosity with her strange words, and I paused, wanting to find out exactly who the mystery people were. Curiosity was often an emotion that got the best of me, but for once, I forced it aside. I was here to do one thing—kill Mab. Everything else could wait.

"I hope you all had a pleasant journey," Mab said, looking at her guests. "As you can see, we'll be dining on the various dishes that my chef has prepared . . ."

I tuned out the Fire elemental and lifted my eye away from the rifle scope. Slowly, I reached forward until my fingers closed around a tiny, clear, almost invisible suction cup on the window in front of me. I gently pulled on the cup, and a small circular piece slid out of the window. A glass cutter was among the tools I'd brought with me tonight, tucked away in the zippered pocket on my silverstone vest. Earlier, I'd used it to carve an opening in the window. I wanted a clear shot at Mab and not one that might be distorted by my crossbow bolt punching through the glass.

I put the glass down beside me on the snowy roof. Then I slid my crossbow forward, until the tip of it, the end with the bolt, just protruded through the hole in the window—aimed right at Mab.

One of Mab's giant bodyguards, who was pulling double duty as a waiter tonight, came over to stand beside her, as though he had an important message for her. The Fire elemental ignored him and kept talking to her guests about how they'd discuss business after dinner. Too bad she wasn't going to even make it to the soup course.

I waited a few seconds to be sure that the giant wasn't going to interrupt or step in front of Mab, then scooted forward even more and put my eye next to the rifle scope once more. The Fire elemental wasn't that far away from me, maybe fifty feet, but the scope gave me a crystal clear view of her face.

I aimed for her right eye, which looked blacker than ink. I'd only get one shot at her, and I didn't want to waste it on a chest wound that might not put her down for good. Mab might have more magic than any other elemental in Ashland, but even she wouldn't be able to survive a crossbow bolt through her eye, especially since the silverstone projectile would keep on going until it blasted out of the back of her skull. Hard to recover when half your brain matter was missing.

Despite all the people I'd killed over the years, all the blood I'd spilled, all the sudden, violent, brutal deaths I'd caused, my finger trembled just a bit as I set it on the crossbow's trigger. My heart raced in my chest, picking up speed with every single beat, and a bead of sweat trickled down the side of my face, despite the cold. I drew in a breath, trying to calm my nerves and quiet myself. Trying to go to that cold, dark, hard place that I'd been to so many times before—the shelter that had gotten me through so many terrible times in my life.

Because this was the hit that truly, finally mattered. For my murdered family, for my baby sister, Bria, for me. It wouldn't make things right, it wouldn't erase all the horrible things I'd suffered through or the equally bad ones I'd done myself, but killing Mab would keep the people I loved safe. And I hoped it would bring me some kind of peace too.

I hadn't been able to stop Mab years ago, when she'd murdered my mother and older sister, but I could kill her now. Everything I'd ever done—living on the streets, becoming an assassin, honing my deadly skills—had been leading up to this one moment, this final confrontation.

I let out my breath and pulled the trigger.

❖ 2 ❖

The softest snick sounded, and the barbed bolt zipped through the dining room on its deadly collision course with Mab's eye.

Too bad I missed.

At the last possible second, at the very last *instant,* the giant who'd been standing beside Mab got tired of waiting and bent down in front of her, his melon-size head obscuring her face. The crossbow bolt punched through his left temple and out the other side of his skull, missing Mab entirely, before slamming into the wall behind him. The projectile stopped there, quivering from the force of its violent journey, blood and brain matter sluicing off it like water.

For a moment, I just lay there on the snowy roof and cursed luck, that fickle, fickle bitch who'd screwed me over again—tonight, when it had mattered the most. Damn and double damn. And then some. All around me, the gray stones of the mansion cackled with insanity, as if they were pleased that their mistress was still alive. Fucking luck. Fucking stones. Fucking everything.

I'd missed. I'd had my shot at Mab, taken it, and I'd *missed*.

Some assassin I was. My mentor and foster father, Fletcher Lane, would have given me a sad, pointed look with his rheumy green eyes and shaken his head, telling me without a single word that I should have known better. That I should have waited just a few seconds more or at least until the giant had moved away from Mab for good. I was the Spider, after all. My rune was the symbol for patience, one of the defining emotions of my career, of my whole *existence*. But for once, I'd ignored Fletcher's teachings. No, tonight I'd been stupid, impatient, sloppy even, and it had cost me—maybe everything.

Nothing happened inside the dining room for half a second. Then the giant toppled forward, slammed into Mab, and sent them both crashing to the floor. I cursed again, because now there was no way that I could get to the Fire elemental. Hell, I couldn't even *see* her, since she was trapped underneath the giant's seven-foot-tall body.

Another second ticked by, and it finally registered in everyone's brain what had happened. That someone had just taken a shot at Mab—in her own mansion.

Instead of screaming like normal businessmen and businesswomen would have, the majority of the people inside dropped to the floor. A few reached for the silverware that they'd been eyeing earlier, their hands curving around the knives, spoons, and forks with surprising familiarity. I also noticed that Ruth Gentry, the woman who'd spoken to Mab, had draped herself over the young girl she was with, protecting her from potential harm. How considerate.

I took all this in on the move. Even though I'd missed Mab, I had something even more important to think about right now—getting out of here. My hands were already slapping another silverstone bolt into the crossbow, even as I scrambled to my feet.

"The window!" someone inside said. "That bolt came in through the window."

"Of course it came in through the window," Mab's muffled voice jumped into the mix. One of her arms flapped at the giant's body on top of her. "Get her, you fools!"

Everyone froze for another moment, looking first at each other, then at the window. A breeze gusted through the hole that I'd cut into the glass, making the black velvet drapes flutter together like a bat's delicate wings.

"Now!" Mab roared.

My cue to leave. With one collective thought, the guests in the dining room scrambled to their feet and raced toward the window. There was a bit of a logjam as they slammed into each other, jockeying for position, knives and forks slashing like daggers across whoever was in range.

The infighting gave me a few more precious seconds to get the hell out of Dodge. The crossbow still in my hands, I sprinted across the snow-covered roof. My boots slipped on the ice, but instead of fighting the wicked slide, I leaned into it, using my weight and momentum to propel myself forward that much more. I needed to leave the dining room area, and I'd take whatever help I could get, even if it was only a few measly inches.

The roof stretched out flat for about thirty feet before it dropped away into the darkness. I paused at the edge, twisted around, and fired my crossbow back up at the mansion. This silverstone bolt, shaped like a grappling hook with two hundred feet of climbing rope attached to the end, punched through a stone balcony two stories above my head before catching on one of the railings.

I dropped the crossbow, unlooped the rest of the rope from its position around my waist, and threw it over the side of the roof. The thin, black ribbon of it drowned in the darkness below. I gave a quick tug on the rope, checking to see if the grappling hook was anchored securely. Didn't much matter though, because I didn't have time for another shot. Already I could hear glass smashing behind me, as the men and women who'd been in the dining room continued their hot pursuit.

So I grabbed hold of the rope, drew in a breath, and stepped off the roof.

The wind screamed in my ears as I fell the hundred feet to the earth below. There was no time to be subtle or cautious, not now, so I let myself free-fall. I reached for my Stone magic, pulling the cool power up through my veins and pouring it out onto my hands, hardening my skin there so that the thin rope wouldn't shred my flesh as I slid down it. Just before I hit the ground, I reached for even more of my Stone magic, pushing the power outward into my arms, legs, chest, and head, making them all as hard and solid as the stones of the mansion around me.

I didn't have time to slow down, and my body punched through the layers of icy snow before slamming into the frozen ground. I grunted at the hard, bruising impact, but thanks to my Stone magic, my swan dive didn't do any real, lasting damage. I was already rolling, rolling, rolling, churning through the snow, before using my momentum to pull myself back up onto my feet.

I'd taken only two steps when a thin scream sounded, growing louder and sharper with each second, like a train's whiny whistle. I looked up just in time to see the body plummeting toward me. I dived out of the way, and a man splattered onto the ground where I'd been standing. Looked like someone had misjudged the ice on the roof in his haste to get to me and had paid the price for it. The blood and brains splashed across the snow reminded me of the pale pink color of the girl's prom dress, but I didn't give the man more than a passing glance as I rolled back up onto my feet once more.

Because now it was time to run—for my life.

It didn't take long for the alarm to be raised. I wasn't even halfway across the wide, white expanse of the lawn before lights snapped on inside the mansion. One by one, they winked on, like dominos tumbling over each other, each bright blaze taking more and more of the precious darkness with it. Footsteps scraped, scratched, and scuffled on the mansion's stairs and balconies above my head, but I was more concerned with the ones that crunched into the snow on the ground behind me. The cracking sounds made me think of bones breaking—my own, if I didn't get out of here.

"Security alert! Security alert!" a mechanized voice boomed.

The alarm sounded five more times before someone shut it off, but hoarse shouts immediately replaced the blaring, distorted voice. The giants who made up the bulk of Mab's security force had been alerted to my presence and were on the hunt. I could hear their startled, angry bellows even above the *thump-thump-thump* of my quick footsteps in the snow.

"She's here! The Spider's here!"

"She tried to kill Mab!"

"Find the bitch! No matter what it takes! She won't get away this time!"

I'd at least hoped to make it into the woods before Mab sent every single one of her giants after me, but luck had never, ever been my friend.

Still, I didn't slow down, not even for an instant. Now that they knew I was here, the giants would rush in from all directions, trying to trap me in their security net. If they did that, if the web tightened around me, I was dead. Right now, speed was preferable to stealth—

Crack! Crack! Crack! Crack!

Bullets thunked into the snow behind me, sending up cold, icy sprays that pelted my legs and back, but I kept running, my eyes locked onto the shadow-strewn tree line up ahead.

Since it had been snowing for the last week, and Mab's mansion was as frozen and frosted as the rest of Ashland, I'd forgone my usual black assassin clothes—boots, pants, sweater, vest, ski mask—in favor of light gray ones to help me blend in better with the soft shadows. But movement was still movement, and the giants were aiming at anything bigger than a squirrel skittering through the snow tonight.

Still, unless there was a sniper perched somewhere on the grounds with the world's best aim, I wasn't too worried about getting dead from the giants' shooting. Most people couldn't hit what they were aiming at in broad daylight, much less drop a moving target at night, when the snow and shadows painted the landscape in murky shades of gray. Even if someone did manage to hit me, they wouldn't do any real damage. I was still holding on to my Stone magic, still using it to harden my skin, which meant that any bullet that did come my way would just bounce off my body and keep right on going—

The fist came out of nowhere.

I'd just reached the edge of the dense forest when a thick arm swung out of the darkness and the attached fist plowed into my face. The hard, sharp blow rocked me back, and my feet slid out from under me. I stumbled into a tree, hitting it so hard that a few ice-covered pine cones popped off their brittle branches and pinged me in the head. I fell to one knee, the snow soaking through my heavy cargo pants and the many layers that I had on underneath them.

But more important than my discomfort was that the attack took me by surprise. So much so that my hold on my Stone magic slipped, and my skin reverted back to its normal texture—and vulnerability—once more. Which meant that I could now be injured by bullets, fists, or whatever other dangers came my way. Plenty to go around tonight.

"Wow, I thought you'd be tougher to take down than that," a man rumbled and stepped out of the shadows to my left. "Kind of disappointing, if you ask me, you not living up to all the hype, Spider."

He was one of Mab's giants, almost seven feet tall with a big, bulky frame that was ghostly pale in the wintry moonlight, thanks to his silver snowsuit. I recognized him—I'd slid past him on my way toward the mansion earlier. He smiled at me, revealing two rows of capped teeth that were even more dazzling than the frosted landscape around us.

I stayed where I was, down on one knee, as though I were still dazed from his hard hit. The giant's grin widened, his hand clenched into a fist once more, and he stepped toward me, ready to knock my head the rest of the way off my shoulders. He didn't see my right hand fall to my side or the glint of metal that suddenly appeared there.

Arrogance will get you, every single time.

As soon as he was in range, I reached up and slammed my silverstone knife into his chest. I drove the blade in as hard and deep as I could before yanking it out and plunging it into him again. The giant needed to get dead—now. I could still hear my other pursuers behind me, racing ever closer to the pine-filled woods and the freedom that they represented.

The giant screamed in pain, telling everyone exactly where we were, and fell to his knees. He reached for me, trying to hold on to me until his buddies could come and watch him die, but I eluded his groping grasp. Normally, I would have moved in for the kill then and slit his throat, but I just didn't have the time—

Crack! Crack! Crack!

More bullets zinged in my direction, thunking into

the trees. Splinters zipped through the air, and the sharp, sticky scent of pine sap burned my nose. I jumped over the wounded giant and darted deeper into the woods, trying to escape the web of death that was slowly tightening around me.

* 3 *

I ran through the forest, leaping over snow-covered logs, stumbling over icy rocks, and shoving through frozen thickets full of sharp, brittle briars. All the while, I held my breath, hoping that my next step wouldn't be my last. That my boots wouldn't slip too badly on the snow and ice, that I wouldn't break my ankle, that I wouldn't make the single misstep that would mean my death.

Making my way over the hidden, treacherous terrain wasn't the only thing that I had to worry about. Man-made traps littered the woods as well as magical trip wires, elemental Fire bombs, and other nasty things just waiting for me to stumble into them so they could blast me off to hell. I moved as fast as I dared, keeping to the path that I'd scouted before and skirting around the traps I'd already found on my way in. I kept my pace quick and steady, but I didn't run blindly, even though the back of my neck itched as though there was a gun pointed right there, right at the sweet spot that would end me.

Paranoia was never a good feeling, especially for an assassin on the run from a botched hit.

And then there were all the giants in the woods, snarling and swarming over everything like wolves tearing into a fresh kill. This time, I didn't bother skirting around them. If they were between me and my escape, then they got cut with my silverstone knives, as hard and deep as I could manage it and still keep moving.

A few of them blocked my path, putting up as much resistance as they could, but I was quicker and far more ruthless. A swipe or two of my knife, and it was over. By the time the giants realized what was happening, they were more concerned about their guts spilling out of their stomachs than trying to stop me. I moved on, another obstacle hurdled, my eyes fixed ahead once more, ready to take care of the next fool stupid enough to step in front of me. I didn't bother checking to see if I'd hurt the guards enough to kill them. The giants didn't matter—only my escape did.

Finally, I managed to put a little distance between myself and my pursuers. The giants' hoarse shouts faded to eerie echoes that rattled through the trees. But just because they weren't as close anymore didn't mean that I was in the clear yet, so I kept moving. I didn't stop, not even for a second. That would be stupid and sloppy, and I'd already been plenty of both tonight.

I still couldn't believe that I'd missed Mab. That I'd *missed* her when I'd had the chance to finish her once and for all—

The click of the gun surprised me.

So did the woman who stepped out of the woods twenty feet ahead of me. Thin, wiry body, gray hair, nut brown skin, pale blue eyes. I recognized her. Ruth Gentry, the woman who'd spoken up during the predinner festivities inside Mab's mansion.

Now she had a revolver leveled at my chest. The gun was a big, old-fashioned piece, with the kind of fancy pearl finish you see in western movies. It glinted in the moonlight through her fingers, looking as bright as a star against the dark, weather-worn quality of her skin.

"That's far enough," Gentry said in the same pleasant voice she'd used with Mab earlier. "Stop right there."

I did as she asked, even though I wasn't particularly scared of her and her revolver. The silverstone in the vest that I had on underneath my gray clothes would catch any projectile that thunked into it. The magical metal was better than Kevlar for blocking bullets. Plus, I could always use my Stone magic to harden my skin once more.

Instead, I stood there, stared at the older woman, and struggled to make sense of things. Like how she'd gotten here ahead of me. I retraced my steps in my head, wondering how I'd been so stupid, so slow, as to let someone cut off my escape route.

The giants and the traps in the woods, I realized. I'd spent far too many precious minutes fighting them and skirting around the magical trip wires, which had let Ruth Gentry get in front of me. And now she was standing between me and my freedom.

My hands tightened around the bloody knives in my

hands, so hard that I could feel the tiny spider runes stamped into the hilts press against the larger scars embedded in my palms. Not for long.

I could tell by the way her blue eyes stayed on mine and her slow, steady steps toward me that this wasn't Gentry's first time facing down someone like me. She wouldn't be arrogant and assume that just because she'd gotten the drop on me she'd won. She wouldn't give me an opening to use my knives—unless I made her.

"How did you know that I'd come this way?" I asked, even as I kept both ears open, listening for sounds of pursuit behind me.

Gentry stopped about ten feet in front of me, the revolver still aimed at my chest. Sometime between my seeing her in the dining room and then again out here, she'd put a heavy coat on over her dress. The wool fabric was just as worn and faded as her gown, and the leather boots on her feet were cracked from age and wear. Still, despite her rather shabby appearance, she'd come to Mab's for a fancy dinner party and had then been prepared enough to tromp through the woods after me on a second's notice. She was a thinker, then, a planner, which made her that much more dangerous.

She smiled, as though she was delighted by my question. "I guessed."

I raised an eyebrow, even though she couldn't see it behind the gray ski mask that covered my face. "You guessed? You must be one hell of a good guesser."

Gentry shrugged. "Oh, that was just something to say. There wasn't much guesswork to it really. This end of the forest offers the quickest, most direct route out to the main road. It's the way I would have come tonight, if I'd been in your shoes."

Her logic and reasoning were spot-on, although I didn't compliment her on them. Instead, I stared at her speckled hand and the easy, familiar way she held her revolver, like it was an old friend she didn't want to let go of. Gentry definitely knew how to use that gun. Her shots wouldn't go wide like the others fired at me earlier tonight—especially not at this short distance.

Gentry gave me a thoughtful look. "I don't think that I would have missed Mab, though. Risky, taking a shot like that when there was someone else that close by. You should have waited, at least a few more seconds. Guy was shifting on his feet. Easy to tell that he wasn't going to keep still much longer."

I shrugged. She was right, but I wasn't going to give the old woman the satisfaction of agreeing with her.

She stared at me, peering closely, as if she could somehow see through my ski mask and get a look at my true self—Gin Blanco. Even more interesting was that Gentry seemed rather hesitant to pull the trigger on her revolver. I didn't know why she hadn't plugged me full of holes yet, or at least tried to, but that hesitation was going to cost her—her life.

Gentry finally came to some sort of decision about whatever she'd been contemplating because she gave me a regretful shake of her head.

"Well," she said. "Why don't you turn around, and we'll start marching the other way back toward the mansion—"

And that's when I made my move.

I turned around like I was going to obey her, then pivoted back the other way and threw myself at the other woman. But Gentry was even smarter than I'd thought, because she'd been expecting the bluff. She got three shots off—a tight kill cluster, all of which caught in the silverstone vest on my chest—before I tackled her and drove her to the ground. The snow cushioned our fall, and Gentry fought back. She tried to club me with the butt of her revolver, but I slapped it away. With my other hand, I brought my silverstone knife up against her neck. Gentry had the good sense to stop before I slit her throat. Something that I was going to do anyway in another minute, two tops.

We lay there on the ground, me on top of her, both of us breathing hard, surrounded by the frosty, foggy cloud of our own exertions. And then, for some reason, Gentry chuckled, as if she was pleased to be an inch away from her own death at the edge of my blade.

"Damn," she drawled, a deep southern twang coloring her voice. "You're just as good as they say you are, Spider. But I'm good at what I do too. Gotta be in this line of work or you don't last long."

My eyes narrowed. "And what line of work would that be—"

Crack! Crack! Crack! Crack!

For the third time tonight, something surprised me when it shouldn't have.

Four bullets sliced through the air. One zipped by my face, so close to my cheek that I could feel the heat radiating off it, before disappearing into the darkness. The other three were a bit more problematic. Two thudded into my left arm, instantly numbing it, while the third slammed into my upper thigh.

The impacts knocked me back, and I hissed with pain. While I was off balance, Gentry got her hands in between us, shoved me away, and scrambled over the ground toward her revolver.

I rolled backward away from Gentry, my body flattening the snowdrifts, before coming up into a low crouch. Ribbons of fire spread out from my wounds, moving downward through my left arm and leg. I gritted my teeth and bit back a snarling curse. Fuck. I hated getting shot.

But I was already pushing away the pain, forcing it to the back of my mind, because I had something else to worry about—where those bullets had come from. My head snapped to the left, backtracking the projectiles' paths.

And that's when I saw the girl.

It was the same girl who'd been with Gentry in the dining room in the mansion, although at some point during the evening, the girl had put a patched, threadbare coat on over her ridiculous pink prom dress. A pair of worn, cracked boots covered her feet. The shoes were identical to the ones that the old woman wore. The girl also happened to have a rifle with a pearl-inlaid stock aimed at my chest, just like Gentry had a moment before. Déjà vu all over again.

"Leave Gentry alone," the girl ground out the words and advanced on me, slow and steady just the way the older woman had.

I cursed again, this time at my own carelessness. I should have remembered that Gentry had been with the girl before and that maybe she would be out here with her now. Still, despite the two-on-one odds, I wasn't done for. Not even close, though I could feel the blood pumping out of the hole in my leg. That wound was definitely the most worrisome.

The girl kept coming at me. I stayed in my low crouch and let my silverstone knife slip out of my right hand. Then I dug my fingers into the snow and closed my hand into a tight fist.

Satisfied that I wasn't going to try to attack her, the girl's hazel eyes flicked to Gentry to check on the other woman, who was still searching for her revolver. The girl was distracted, just for a second, but it was all the opportunity I needed.

I snapped up my hand and hurled my snowball in her direction. The wad of ice hit the girl's rifle, and she shrieked with surprise. She did the smart thing and pulled the trigger again, but I was already up and moving at an angle toward her. The girl turned toward me, but by that point I was too close. I jerked the rifle out of her hand and cold-cocked her in the face with the butt. She dropped like a stone, and I turned the gun around, ready to pull the trigger and shatter that thin, pretty face of hers with a bullet or two—

"Sydney!" Gentry cried out in a low, hoarse voice.

Something in her voice, some tone, some tiny bit of anguish that she couldn't quite hide, made me look over at her instead of pulling the trigger. Gentry had forgotten all about her revolver. Instead, she huddled on her knees. Her gray hair had come loose from its tight bun, and snow crusted her face, but Gentry didn't care. Fear flickered in her pale blue gaze, and she held her brown, wrinkled hands out wide, silently begging me not to kill the girl.

I studied her carefully, but as far as I could tell, this was no sly trick she was trying to pull. Gentry seemed genuinely concerned for Sydney, which was more than warranted, considering that I was about a second away from ending her existence.

I even went so far as to turn back toward the girl, my finger tightening on the rifle's trigger. But then she let out a low moan of pain and stared up at me with her hazel eyes. Deer eyes—doe eyes—wide, liquid, and trembling, glistening with tears, pain, and fear.

Damn and double damn.

Something inside me, some little black shred of my heart, wouldn't let me kill the girl, even if she had just put three bullets into me. Maybe because she reminded me of myself at that age—poor little Genevieve Snow whose family had been so brutally murdered. Maybe because I was exhausted. Maybe because I was suffering from the blood loss already. Or maybe it was because I could hear Fletcher's voice whispering in my ear. *No kids—ever,* the old man seemed to murmur to me, even though he was long dead and cold in his own grave.

I'd ignored the old man's teachings earlier, when I'd hastily pulled the trigger on my crossbow instead of waiting until I had an absolutely clear shot at Mab. I wasn't about to turn my back on Fletcher again, even if he was only a ghost in my head.

Instead of pulling the trigger, I heaved the rifle as far as I could into the trees. The gun hit one of the snow-splattered trunks and clattered off into the night. Gentry just looked at me, mouth agape, as if she couldn't believe that I hadn't gone for the kill shot when I'd had the chance. Part of me couldn't believe it either, but that was the way things were.

Even as an assassin, even as the Spider, I didn't kill innocents—ever. Sure, the girl had shot me, but she couldn't be more than fifteen, sixteen, tops. Still a kid in so many ways.

Gentry crawled across the snow to the girl and held her close, shielding her from me, like she wasn't sure what I was going to do next. Damned if I knew either.

"Next time, sweetheart," I murmured to the girl as I bent down to pick up the knife that I'd dropped. "Keep shooting until you run out of bullets and not a second before."

Gentry and Sydney both stared at me, their eyes identical pools of wariness, shock, and fear.

I skirted around them and disappeared into the snowy trees.

4

Stumbling and bleeding, as well as listening for sounds of pursuit from Gentry, the girl, or whoever else might be following me, I somehow made it to the old, anonymous car I'd stashed in a thicket of trees two miles from the edge of Mab's property. I sank into the driver's seat, cranked the engine, and turned the ancient heater up as high and hot as it would go.

White starbursts exploded in my eyes, and I struggled to blink them away. The girl, Sydney, had been a better shot than I'd given her credit for. The two bullets in my shoulder throbbed and burned with pain, and she'd gotten close to my femoral artery with that last shot to my left thigh. Good for her, bad for me. I'd left a blood trail through the snow that a child could follow. If I hadn't had the car here, I would have been done for, still out floundering in the trees, trying to stay ahead of Mab, her giants, and her dinner guests, two of whom had already taken an unhealthy interest in me. And I was still in the proverbial woods, if I didn't get the leg taken care of soon.

I ripped off my sweat-soaked ski mask, tore the fabric into strips with my silverstone knife, and used the pieces to make a tourniquet for my leg. I tied it off as tight as I could so I wouldn't bleed out before I got to Jo-Jo. At this point, I just hoped that I had enough juice left to drive over to the dwarf's house. But there was no time to think about things or procrastinate, so I threw the car into gear and put my foot on the gas.

As I steered through the trees and pulled back onto the icy road, I reached for my magic again. But not my Stone power. No, this time I grabbed hold of my other magic— my elemental Ice power—and let it fill the lower part of my body, particularly my left thigh. The cold magic flooded my veins, and the wounded area immediately went numb—so numb I couldn't even feel that part of my body anymore. Or, more important, the pain pulsing through my thigh, and the blood pumping out of it with every beat of my heart. I sighed with relief.

For years, my Ice magic had been the weaker of my two abilities, until I'd overcome a block associated with it. Now it was just as strong as my Stone power. Numbing my own limbs so I wouldn't feel pain was one of the recent tricks that I'd learned how to do with my Ice magic—the one that had helped me kill Elektra LaFleur when she'd tried to shock me to death with her electrical power.

LaFleur's magic had been a bit of a fluke, as it wasn't one of the four main areas—Air, Fire, Ice, and Stone— that most elementals were gifted in, that you had to be able to tap into to be considered a true elemental. But magic could take many forms, could manifest in all sorts of strange ways, and many folks were gifted in other areas, offshoots of the four main elements. Like water was an offshoot of Ice, and electricity was one of Air. The mechanics behind it all had never really concerned me. I was just glad I was still alive—and that LaFleur was rotting in whatever shallow, pauper's grave Mab had dumped her in.

I'd only beaten LaFleur because I was the rarest of elementals—someone who could control not only one but two elements. Ice and Stone, in my case. Connected powers, but each with their own unique quirks.

My Stone magic had always been incredibly strong and let me do anything that I wanted to with the element, like hear the whispered vibrations in the rocks around me, make bricks fly out of a solid wall, or even turn my own skin into the equivalent of human marble.

My Ice power was different, in that it actually let me create elemental Ice with my bare hands—Ice that I could turn into all sorts of shapes, like cubes, crystals, and the occasional knife. My Ice magic also let me numb my body so that I would feel no pain, something that I was doing right now just to stay upright. Hell, maybe it would slow the blood loss too. I wasn't familiar with all the ins and outs of this particular trick just yet. Maybe Jo-Jo could tell me more when I got to her.

If I got to her before I bled to death.

It was after midnight now, and the Ashland streets were deserted. Not surprising, given the icy conditions. Ashland was the southern metropolis that sprawled over the rugged corner of the world where the Appalachian Mountains cut through Tennessee, North Carolina, and Virginia. From a distance, Ashland looked like a jewel-toned paradise, surrounded by emerald forests and sapphire rivers with a silver diamond of a city set into the middle of all the sparkling grandeur. But anyone who'd ever spent any time in Ashland knew exactly what kind of violent, gritty place it really was. The horrible, despicable things that only happened on the darkest, dingiest streets in other cities occurred on Ashland's main thoroughfares—often in broad daylight.

The city was divided into two sections—Northtown and Southtown—held together by the rough circle of the downtown area and flanked on either side by suburbs full of soccer moms, spoiled kids, and other middle-class folks. Northtown was the rich part of Ashland, where the city's social, magical, and monetary elite lived, died, and generally tried to screw each other over every which way they could. All sorts of evil lurked inside the sultan-size mansions in Northtown, made even more sinister by the immaculate facades and perfectly groomed lawns. Mab Monroe, of course, lived in the heart of Northtown in the biggest mansion in the city, given the fact that she was the queen bee of the Ashland underworld.

The folks were poorer in Southtown—much, much poorer—but that didn't make them any less dangerous. Vampire hookers, pimps, gangbangers, elemental junkies strung out on their own magic who'd just as soon light you up with their Fire power as spit on you. Those were the people who called Southtown home. Still, I'd always had a begrudging fondness for the area. At least in Southtown you knew exactly what dangers to expect, whereas in Northtown you might go over to someone's house for a friendly cookout and end up with your ribs being the ones basted in the barbecue sauce.

It had been snowing in Ashland for several days straight. The February cold had been so bitter, biting, and unrelenting that what snow fell didn't even begin to melt before the next arctic front blew in and dropped six more inches on top of it. By this point, the snowbanks on either side of the slick roads were taller than most dwarves—topping out at about five feet.

It was hard for me to drive in it, especially considering the absolute shit box of a car that I was in. Twice, the old, worn tires started sliding on the black ice, and it was only by the grace of whatever god was laughing at me that the car didn't slam into one of the trees that lined the road. It also didn't help matters that I could feel myself weakening and my attention wandering as more and more blood pumped out of my thigh. But I forced my hands to grip the steering wheel, the cracked leather digging into the spider rune scars on my palms, and drive on.

I went as fast as I dared, the car tires alternately crunching through or slipping on the snow and ice. Even though there was no one out tonight, it was still slow going, and it took me thirty long, precious minutes to make it to Jo-Jo's.

Jolene "Jo-Jo" Deveraux was a two-hundred-fifty-seven-year-old dwarf with Air elemental magic who used her power to heal people on the sly. She also happened to be my only hope of getting the wound in my thigh to quit gushing blood before I ran out of the fluid altogether.

Like others of her monetary, social, and magically elite

status, Jo-Jo made her home in an upscale Northtown subdivision called Tara Heights. Most of the subdivisions in Ashland had cutesy names like that, almost all of which had a Southern connotation. Like Lee's Lament, another nearby subdivision. For some folks in Ashland, especially the vampires who'd lived through the era, the Civil War would just never, ever be over.

I steered the rattletrap car past the snowbanks that had been plowed up on either side of the subdivision's entrance and made the appropriate turn onto a street marked Magnolia Lane. I started up the hill to Jo-Jo's house, but the tires just wouldn't grip the ice that coated the cobblestone driveway. For a moment, I was afraid that I was going to have to get out and walk—something that I didn't have the strength or blood left for. But finally the squealing, smoking tires caught, probably for the last time in their miserable, rubbery lives, and the car lurched up the driveway.

I crested the hill, and Jo-Jo's house came into view. The three-story, plantation-style structure looked even more elegant in the winter white dark, the layers of snow and ice swirling around it like buttercream frosting. The columns that supported the house only added to the effect, making the whole thing resemble a tiered cake. Normally, I would have enjoyed the ghostly view, but tonight the snow was just another obstacle to plow through.

By this point, I was fading fast. It took me two concentrated tries before I remembered to put the car in park so it wouldn't roll back down the hill. Opening the door, crossing the yard, trudging up the steps that led to the porch that wrapped around the house—all of it took much more effort than it should have. By the time I raised the cloud-shaped door knocker that was Jo-Jo's rune, a symbol of her Air elemental magic, I was cold and clammy with sweat and about to pass out. I rapped on the door as hard as I could, then sagged against the house, smearing blood all over the white paint in abstract, snowflake-like patterns.

I don't know how long I stood there. Seconds passed, maybe minutes, before I heard heavy footsteps on the other side of the door. Even out here on the porch, I still caught a whiff of her Chantilly perfume. I breathed in the scent, comforted by the sweet smell, because I knew that I'd made it. Jo-Jo would work her Air magic once more and heal me the way she always did whenever I showed up at her house late at night an inch away from death.

A moment later, the door opened and a woman appeared. Like everyone else in Ashland on this cold, cold night, Jo-Jo had been bundled up and firmly ensconced in bed. A long-sleeved pink flannel housecoat swathed the dwarf's stocky body from head to toe. Despite the late hour, a string of gravel-size pearls hung around her neck. In Jo-Jo's mind, nothing proclaimed you to be a true southern lady more than a set of real pearls, and she never went anywhere without hers—not even to bed.

The dwarf's bleached blond–white hair had been rolled up tight for the night in pink sponge curlers in a tidy formation that any general would have been proud of. For once, Jo-Jo's middle-aged face was free of makeup, although the fuchsia polish on her toenails glistened in the semidarkness. The dwarf almost always went barefoot at home, even in the dead of winter.

Jo-Jo stuck her head outside, a turtle coming out of her warm, comfortable shell, obviously wondering who could be knocking on her door at this hour. Especially since I wasn't scheduled to be doing anything tonight other than cozying up with my lover, Owen Grayson.

Jo-Jo's eyes, which were almost colorless except for the pinprick of black at their center, widened when she spotted me on the porch—along with the blood that had pooled underneath my left leg.

"Gin?" Jo-Jo asked in a surprised voice. "Is that you?"

"Who else?" I drawled.

And then I collapsed at her feet without another word.

* 5 *

I was somewhat aware of Jo-Jo calling out to her sister, Sophia, and the younger dwarf picking me up and carrying me inside into the beauty salon that took up the back half of Jo-Jo's sprawling house.

The older dwarf made her living as what she called a "drama mama," using her elemental magic on all the southern debutantes, trophy wives, and grand old dames who frequented her popular salon. Cuts, perms, dyeing, waxing, exfoliating. If it had something to do with changing or improving someone's appearance, then the dwarf was an expert on it. And if you really wanted your skin to glow for that special occasion, then you came to Jo-Jo's for one of her signature Air elemental facials.

Cherry red salon chairs, beauty magazines stacked three feet high in places, buckets of makeup, every conceivable shade of pink nail polish. All that and more fought for space in the salon, cluttered together in a cozy way.

Rosco, Jo-Jo's beloved basset hound, snoozed in his wicker basket in the corner. His brown and black ears twitched once, but he didn't wake up at the sound of us entering the salon. Not surprising. If there wasn't food involved or a chance to be petted in the offing, then Rosco wasn't much interested in things.

I peered at the familiar furnishings, but everything seemed like it had a thick fog wrapped over it. Still, the blurry sight of the salon and Rosco comforted me, no matter how much my brain was distorting them right now.

"Put her in the chair," Jo-Jo instructed her sister. "Quickly now. You can see how much blood she's lost."

"A little more than usual," I murmured as Sophia hefted me into position. "Girl got in a lucky shot on me. My own fault, really, for not remembering that she was even there to start with."

"Babbling."

This time, Sophia Deveraux was the one who spoke, in a raspy, broken voice that sounded like she'd spent her entire life smoking cigars, chasing them down with barrels of mountain moonshine, then chugging antifreeze just for kicks. Of course, I knew that she didn't actually do any of those things. Sophia didn't talk much, given her grinding tone, and I'd always wondered what traumatic thing had happened to her to so completely ruin her voice. But I'd never asked. It couldn't be anything good, not with the quiet, bone-deep sorrow that radiated off the dwarf at times. Still, I made the effort to roll my head to the side to look at her.

At a hundred and thirteen, Sophia was still in the

prime of her life, unlike Jo-Jo, who was firmly entrenched in middle age. And that wasn't the only difference between the two dwarven sisters. Jo-Jo was a southern lady through and through with her pearls and pink dresses, whereas Sophia had a fondness for Goth gear.

Tonight, Sophia wore a black terrycloth robe covered with smiling skeletons. Her hair was a short black stain that brushed up against the absolute paleness of her face, which was even more ashen tonight since her lips were free of the crimson or even black lipstick she sometimes wore. At five feet one, Sophia was tall for a dwarf and had a good inch on Jo-Jo. Sophia was also much stronger than her middle-aged sister, and the black fabric of her robe did little to hide her thick, sturdy body.

Jo-Jo, who'd stepped over to the sink to wash her hands, jerked her chin at her sister. "Get a good grip and hold her down. She's lost a lot of blood, so this is going to hurt."

Sophia nodded, moved forward, and put her hands on my shoulders, securing me to the salon chair. The dwarf's grip was so strong, so firm, that it felt as if my entire upper body had been clamped down with a silverstone vise.

"Sorry, Gin," Sophia rasped.

I would have shrugged my shoulders, telling her that it was okay, but my body wouldn't move. Nothing ever did after Sophia got hold of it.

Jo-Jo finished washing her hands, then dragged a free-standing halogen light over to me, angling it down so that it illuminated my body. The dwarf picked up a pair of scissors from a stack of beauty magazines and cut open my cargo pants and other layers, exposing the ugly gunshot wound in my thigh. Despite the makeshift tourniquet that I'd applied, blood still trickled out of the hole in a steady stream.

Jo-Jo tilted her head and studied the wound. Then she pulled another chair over to me, sat down in it, and raised her hand. A buttermilk white glow coated the dwarf's palm, and the same light filled her colorless eyes, as though clouds were drifting through her pale gaze. Her Air magic filled the room, as the dwarf fully embraced her elemental power.

The sudden influx of magic caused the spider rune scars in my palms to itch and burn, just like they always did whenever I was exposed to so much of another elemental's power. That's because the scars were made out of silverstone, a special metal that was highly prized for its ability to absorb all forms of elemental magic.

Although the silverstone had long since hardened in my flesh, it always seemed to me like the metal in my hands actually *hungered* for magic, as if the silverstone were some sort of parasite inside me just waiting for the chance to soak up all the power it could possibly hold— and then some. Having the metal in my hands was what had made it so difficult for me to use my Ice magic. For years, the silverstone had absorbed my power even as I brought it to bear, since Ice and Fire elementals almost always released their magic through their hands. It was only during a recent fight to the death with another Stone elemental that I'd been able to tap into enough of my Ice magic to blast through the blockage. Now, the silverstone scars held my Ice power instead of preventing me from using it.

A few weeks ago, the feel of Jo-Jo's warm, healing Air magic, which was so different from my own cool Ice and Stone power, would have made me grind my teeth together. The dwarf's magic just felt wrong to me, like a pair of shoes that were too tight.

But ever since I'd used my Ice magic to numb my body when I was fighting LaFleur, the feel of the dwarf's magic hadn't bothered me quite as much. Oh, it still annoyed me, still made that primal little voice in the back of my head mutter, but I didn't snarl at the sensation anymore. At least, not as often. Or maybe that was because I knew that Jo-Jo was healing me, not hurting me with her magic like so many others had done over the years.

Jo-Jo leaned forward so that her palm was an inch above the black, bloody hole in my leg. Something hot sizzled to life on the surface of my thigh, the first prick of what morphed into a thousand needles stabbing deeper and deeper into my skin until it felt like my whole leg was on fire.

The sensation was just Jo-Jo using her magic. Air elementals healed people by tapping into all the natural gases in the atmosphere, especially oxygen, and making them circulate through wounds. The dwarf was using her Air power, using the oxygen, to push the bullet out of my thigh, repair all of my broken blood vessels, and pull the ragged edges of my skin back together.

And it hurt like hell.

Even though Jo-Jo was healing me, her magic was still the opposite of mine. Two elements always complemented each other—like Air and Fire—and two elements always opposed each other—like Fire and Ice. The dwarf's Air magic was the opposite of my Ice and Stone magic, and her using that kind of power just felt wrong to me, the same way that my magic would seem strange to any other Air or Fire elemental.

Even if I'd wanted to move, to squirm away from the dwarf, her elemental power, and the hot, invisible, healing needles stabbing me, I couldn't have—not with Sophia's hands clamped down on my shoulders.

So I gave myself over to Jo-Jo's magic, drifting in and out of consciousness while the dwarf worked on me. Sometime later, something thunked into a metal pan— the bullet that Sydney had put into me. A few minutes after that, the needles of pain started dying down in my leg before disappearing. I sighed, my body going limp in the salon chair. Jo-Jo's magic might not bother me as much as it had before, but I was still glad when she stopped using it.

"Leg's done." Jo-Jo's voice seemed distant and far away, even though I knew that she was still right there leaning over me. "Let's get that silverstone vest off her and look at those wounds in her shoulder now."

"Uh-huh." Sophia grunted her agreement.

Hands moved me around, unzipping my silverstone vest and stripping it off me. The snip-snip-snip of scissors sounded again, as Jo-Jo cut through more of my gray layers, and the warm air in the salon swirled against my bare skin.

"Not nearly as bad as the leg wound," the dwarf murmured. "These didn't hit anything too important, at least."

Once again, the feel of the dwarf's Air elemental magic gusted through the room, and the needles started pricking me once more, now centered in my shoulder. But this time, the pain wasn't as intense and didn't last nearly as long. Two more thunks sounded as Jo-Jo used her power to fish the bullets out of my body.

"Good as new," Jo-Jo pronounced a few minutes later.

I didn't feel as good as new. Being healed, even by an Air elemental, took a toll on your body, as you suddenly went from knocking on death's door to being in one piece again. The mind needed some time to play catch-up and realize what was going on. As close as I'd come to dying tonight, I could sleep for the next eight hours and still wake up feeling tired. In fact, I could have drifted off right now, but I forced myself to keep my eyes open.

"Thanks," I murmured.

Despite Jo-Jo's ministrations, my words still slurred a bit, probably from the blood loss.

"You're welcome, darling," Jo-Jo said. "But where's Finn? Why isn't he with you? Why didn't he bring you in?"

"He didn't go with me," I mumbled.

Jo-Jo frowned. "Why not?"

It took some effort, but I raised my head up to look at her. "Because he didn't know that I was going after Mab tonight, and I didn't want him there while I did. I didn't want him there in case things went bad, which they did."

Jo-Jo and Sophia both stilled. They exchanged a glance over my head before the both of them looked back at me again.

"You went after Mab?" Jo-Jo asked in a soft voice.

"Alone?" Sophia rasped.

The scene replayed itself in my mind. My finger squeezing the trigger. The bolt leaving my crossbow on its perfect path toward Mab's black eye. The giant getting in the way at the last possible second.

"I tried," I muttered, my heart twisting with shame at the memory of my failure. "But one of her giant body-guards took the bolt meant for her instead. So I missed her. I *missed* her."

In a tired voice, I told the dwarven sisters everything that had happened tonight. As I finished the story, hot tears scalded my eyes.

"I had her too—dead to rights. She was right there in front of me. All I had to do was pull the trigger, and it would have all been over. No more Mab hunting the Spi-der, no more threats against Bria, no more danger for the people that I love. And I missed. Can you believe that? Me, Gin Blanco, the Spider, supposedly the best assassin around, or at least the best semiretired assassin around, and I missed her. I fucking *missed* her."

Jo-Jo put her hand on my arm. "It's okay, Gin. Every-thing's going to be okay. You'll see."

The dwarf's voice dropped to a low murmur, and once again her eyes took on a faint, milky white glow, as if she wasn't even really looking at me. In addition to her heal-ing magic, Jo-Jo also had a bit of precognition. Most Air elementals did. They could listen to and interpret all the emotions and feelings in the atmosphere the same way that I could hear the ones that had sunk into the stone around me. But where my magic told me of things that had happened in the past, Air elementals got glimpses of things that might be flashes of possible futures. Just another way in which our two elements, our two magics, were the opposite of each other.

But if Jo-Jo said that everything was going to be okay, I believed her. The dwarf had been right about too many things before for me to doubt her now. Her whispered words brought me some much-needed comfort. So much so that I let go of my anger at myself—let go of my shame and my miserable sense of failure. I wanted to ask Jo-Jo about her cryptic words, but I just didn't have the strength left for that. Not tonight. My eyes drifted shut, and I felt myself falling into the darkness once more.

"Wake her?" Sophia rasped in a concerned voice.

"No," Jo-Jo said. "Gin needs her rest now."

Jo-Jo's hand slid through my hair, untangling the snarled brown locks one by one. I might have only imagined it, but I thought that the dwarf leaned down and put her lips close to my ear.

"Don't worry, darling," Jo-Jo murmured. "You'll get another shot at Mab. Sooner than you think."

Comforted, I breathed in. The sweet smell of her perfume was the last thing that I remembered before the world went black.

* 6 *

I woke up the next morning in one of the guest bedrooms
on the second floor of Jo-Jo's house. For a moment, I just
lay there in my warm, soft cocoon, staring up at the swirls
of blue and white in the cloud-covered fresco that decorated the ceiling. Then I started replaying the events of
last night in my mind—again.

Missing Mab. Running through the forest. Stabbing
giants left and right. Facing down Gentry and the girl.
Stumbling through the snow and driving over here to the
salon. Not the best or most successful night that I'd ever
had as the Spider, but I supposed it had turned out all
right in the end.

Because I should have been dead.

Everything that could have gone wrong had. At the very
least, I should have bled out from that gunshot wound in
my thigh. Maybe I would have, if I hadn't tied that tourniquet around my leg and used my Ice magic to numb it.

But what really bothered me were my emotions. I'd been melancholy last night, moody, and frustrated that I hadn't managed to kill Mab. Jo-Jo might have healed my body, but the dwarf hadn't eased my anguish. Even now, the melancholy, the frustration, the sense of failure, gnawed at me, bothersome termites burrowing deeper and deeper into my black heart, chipping away at the coldness there.

I forced my thoughts away from my epic failure. After all, this was another day, as Scarlett O'Hara would say, and here I was, still alive, still breathing, and still determined to do what needed to be done. Jo-Jo had patched me up, made me whole and healthy once more, which meant that I still had a chance to kill Mab—

"Ahem." Someone cleared his throat.

I raised my head and spotted Owen Grayson sitting in a rocking chair at the foot of the bed, an open book in his lap and a mug of coffee on the table beside him.

"I see that you're awake now," he rumbled in his deep voice.

I smiled at him. "Once more, it seems."

Instead of responding to my teasing, rueful smile, Owen put his book aside, crossed his muscled arms over his chest, and speared me with a hard stare. Uh-oh. Someone was not pleased, and I didn't have to guess why. I hadn't told Owen what I was doing last night—especially that I was going after Mab.

Early morning sunlight slanted in through the window, bathing Owen's chiseled features in a pale golden glow. Blue-black hair, violet eyes, slightly crooked nose, a white scar that slashed underneath his chin. Interesting enough features by themselves, but put them all together, and you had one hell of an attractive man.

And the rest of Owen was just as appealing. My gaze drifted over his solid, muscled body. In many ways, he had a dwarf's sturdy physique, although at six feet one, Owen was more than a foot taller than most dwarves. Unlike so many businessmen of his wealth and position, Owen didn't spend hours in the gym to keep his body lean and trim. No, he'd gotten his physique the old-fashioned way—through years of hard, physical labor. He'd started out as a blacksmith, turning one small shop into a vast business empire that had made him one of the wealthiest men in Ashland, even though he was only in his thirties.

Being a blacksmith had been a natural fit for Owen, who had what he considered to be a minor elemental talent for metal. He could manipulate it the same way that I could Stone, since metal was an offshoot of that element. But his talent was anything but small, given the exquisite sculptures and weapons that he created, including the matched set of five silverstone knives he'd given me as a Christmas present. The ones that had my spider rune stamped into their hilts.

But perhaps the thing that most appealed to me about Owen was his personality—and complete acceptance of me. Unlike a previous lover of mine, Owen didn't judge or condemn me for being the Spider. He knew exactly what kind of dark, violent city Ashland was, and he didn't look down on the things I'd done over the years to survive. Mainly, because he'd done some of them himself to protect his younger sister, Eva.

Strong, confident, capable, sexy, caring. Owen was

everything that I'd ever wanted in a lover—everything that I'd ever wanted in my life. Too bad I was too much of an emotional coward to tell him so—or let him know exactly how much I cared about him.

I kept staring at Owen, and he looked right back at me, not saying anything. Up to me to get the ball rolling then.

I sighed. "Okay. Let me have it. I know you're angry. Your eyes are practically glowing with it. Jo-Jo called you, I take it, and told you about my little adventure?"

Owen gave me the hard stare a moment longer before nodding. "She did. What I really want to know is what the hell were you thinking, going after Mab by yourself? We've talked about this, Gin. We've all decided that it's too dangerous."

The *we* in question being myself, Owen, Finn, the Deveraux sisters, and my sister, Detective Bria Coolidge. All of us had a vested interest in seeing Mab dead. We just couldn't figure out how to make it happen without all of us going down in flames with her.

"I know," I snapped. "But I'm tired of hiding from Mab and her minions. I'm tired of worrying what she might do to Bria. I want the bitch dead."

Owen wasn't the only one who was angry. I felt it too, sinking its hot, gnashing teeth into my heart, along with the rest of the emotional termites. Most of it was directed at myself because I'd missed last night. But part of it was because I was scared too—scared of how much it had meant to wake up and see Owen sitting next to my bed. We'd been together for a few months now, but it always surprised me just how very much I cared about him, especially when I'd been so badly burned by a previous lover.

Owen was far more important to me than he realized—so important that it frightened me a little bit. Okay, a whole hell of a lot. Enough to make me want to keep him at arm's length, even though I knew it was too late for that. Too many people that I'd loved over the years had been murdered for me to easily open up my heart to others. My mother, my older sister, Fletcher. All dead and gone before their time—all because of me and my mistakes.

Somehow, Owen had stormed his way into my heart whether I'd wanted him there or not, and now I'd do anything to keep him safe—even sacrifice myself like I almost had last night on my self-imposed quest.

"I don't see why you care so much anyway," I muttered in a harsher, colder voice than I would have liked. "It was my ass on the line last night, not yours. I made sure of that."

Owen's eyes narrowed, his jaw clenched, and his arms tightened across his chest. "Why? Why do I care so much, Gin? Because I—"

He bit off his words, but they hung in the air between us like a ghost, writhing and twisting, just like my heart was right now.

Because I love you. That's what he'd been about to say. The shock of his almost uttering the words drove the air from my lungs. Owen—loved me? Really? Truly? I didn't know what to make of it. I didn't know what to make of anything anymore—especially not the softness for him that had wormed its way down into the deepest, darkest, blackest part of my heart. Into my very *soul,* even. If I hadn't killed it long ago by being the Spider.

Owen looked away and drew in a breath. "Because I care about you, Gin. That's why. I don't want you going off on a suicide mission to try to kill Mab. I'd rather have you alive any day than her dead, even if she did murder your family and my parents."

I wasn't Mab's only victim. Far from it. Part of the reason Owen understood my obsession with killing the Fire elemental was that she'd murdered his parents when he'd been a teenager. Mab had burned Owen's house to the ground because of a gambling debt that his father owed, killing his parents in the process, and leaving him homeless and to fend for himself and his sister, Eva, who'd been little more than a baby then.

"Better me go by myself than drag the rest of you down with me," I pointed out in a quiet voice. "And you know that's what would have happened. Mab is too well protected at her estate for a full-frontal assault. You and Finn both know that. So do Jo-Jo, Sophia, and even Bria. I had to go in by myself. That was the only way I could even get close enough to Mab to take my shot."

I closed my eyes. The anger, melancholy, and frustration welled up in my chest again, until they coated my mouth and throat like bitter, burning acid. "Too bad I blew it and missed."

"I know," Owen said in a gentler tone. "Finn called me this morning. Seems that his phone started ringing last night and hasn't stopped since. All his contacts are buzzing with the news. He was a little upset about it himself. Said he'd catch up with you at the Pork Pit later today."

I groaned. "What Finn really means is that he'll lambaste me six ways from Sunday while he eats a free lunch at the counter."

Some of the anger softened in Owen's violet eyes, and a sly grin lifted up his lips. "Something like that, I imagine."

I groaned again and returned Owen's smile. More of the anger melted out of his gaze, and the tension between us lightened, like a dark cloud being blown away by a stiff gust of wind. For now, anyway.

"I'm sorry," I said. "You know I'm a little irrational where Mab's concerned. I saw an opportunity to take her out, and I couldn't pass it up."

"I know, Gin," Owen said. "I know."

He got up from his rocking chair and came over to the bed. He sat down and opened his arms to me, and I scooted into his embrace. The warmth from his body mixed with my own, and I breathed in, enjoying his rich, earthy scent, which always made me think of metal, if metal could ever have any real smell.

"I hate that she's after you," Owen murmured, his lips against my hair. "But what I hate more is that you went after her alone. That no one was backing you up. Promise me you won't do that again. Okay, Gin? Promise me that the next time you go after Mab, you'll take someone with you. Me, Finn, Sophia. Someone, anyone, to help you."

I could have lied to him. Maybe I should have. Because I had no intention of stopping until Mab was dead—even if she would probably take me down with her. But I didn't want to lie to Owen and ruin this fragile peace between us.

"All right," I said in a wry tone. "The next time I go

after Mab, I'll take a buddy along to hold my knives. Happy?"

"For now," Owen rumbled, tucking me in even closer to his body. "For now."

We sat there on the bed for a long time, just holding each other.

Owen had to get to work, since his business empire didn't run itself, and I had a barbecue restaurant to run, so we made plans to hook up later. But Owen was quieter than usual as he left Jo-Jo's, and I couldn't think of what to say to him without the words coming out wrong. So we left things as they were, unspoken and unresolved, with neither one of us knowing how to deal with the other.

By the time I showered, threw on some spare clothes that I kept at Jo-Jo's, and made my way to the Pork Pit, it was after two o'clock.

The Pork Pit barbecue restaurant was located in downtown Ashland, close to the unofficial Southtown border. It wasn't much to look at, just another hole-in-the-wall, but it was *mine*—my gin joint. The sight of the multicolored neon sign of a pig holding a platter of food over the front door brought a smile to my face. The Pit was the only real home I'd known since Fletcher had taken me in off the streets when I was thirteen. The old man had started the restaurant years ago, and I'd inherited it after his murder last year.

As I walked toward the front door, I brushed my fingers against the battered brick of the restaurant and reached for my Stone magic. As always, slow, sonorous notes rippled through the brick, whispering of the clogged, contented hearts, arteries, and stomachs of so many diners after eating at the restaurant. The familiar whispers soothed away the rest of my frustration. I might have screwed up last night, but I was still alive. I'd plotted more than one murder inside the Pork Pit. I'd go inside and get started on Mab's lickety-split.

I scanned the interior of the Pit through the store-front windows. Clean, but well-worn blue and pink vinyl booths. Matching, faded, peeling pig tracks on the floor that led to the men's and women's restrooms. A counter running along the back wall with an old-fashioned cash register sitting at one end. A battered, blood-covered, framed copy of *Where the Red Fern Grows* by Wilson Rawls hanging on the wall opposite the cash register, along with a faded photo of Fletcher in his younger years. Everything was as it should have been.

The lunch rush was over, and only one person sat at the long counter. I stepped inside, making the bell over the front door chime, and he swiveled around and fixed me with a cold glare.

"It's about time you showed up, Gin," Finn snapped.

Finnegan Lane was just as handsome as Owen, but in a more polished, classical way. Finn wore one of his many power suits, since as an investment banker, he spent most of his daylight hours swindling people out of their money. Today's color choice was royal blue with the faintest houndstooth check pattern running through the expensive cloth, topped off by a silver shirt and blue-and-silver striped tie. Finn's thick, walnut-colored hair was styled just so, and his eyes were as slick, shiny, and green in his ruddy face as the glass of a soda pop bottle.

Finn crossed his arms over his chest and glared at me, much the same way that Owen had done earlier. Time for round two of the Gin Blanco firing squad.

I sighed and walked over to my foster brother. "Let me guess. You want to have a little chat about what happened with Mab last night."

"Why, whatever gave you that idea?" Finn drawled in a deceptively light voice. "Perhaps it was because I was awakened at an *unseemly* hour this morning only to learn that someone tried to kill Mab last night while she was entertaining guests in the main dining room of her mansion. The very part of the mansion that I distinctly remember getting you the blueprints for just last *week*."

Behind the counter, Sophia Deveraux grunted her agreement with Finn's pointed, acidic tone. Today, the Goth dwarf wore a black T-shirt covered with curved, white vampire fangs dripping blood. The crimson color of the blood matched the silverstone-spiked leather collar around her neck, as well as the cuffs on both of her wrists. Her lipstick was a red slash in her pale face, although bits of silver glitter glinted in her black hair.

I sighed. "Look, I'm sorry that I went off the reservation without you, all of you. But we all know that my getting that close to Mab was strictly a solo job. I didn't want either of you to get hurt if I missed."

Sophia grunted again and shrugged her shoulders, while Finn's face softened just a bit. Then he sniffed, and I knew that there would be no sweet-talking him out of his snit. Finn had built up a good bit of righteous indignation, and he was determined to make me suffer through it.

"While we appreciate your concern for our safety, we're a team, Gin," Finn lectured me. "We always have been. You need to remember that because it's the only way that you're going to kill Mab—by all of us working together. Not by your taking off by yourself with no one to watch your back."

I gave my foster brother a noncommittal shrug. "Not much chance of that happening, since I missed her last night. I imagine that she's upped her security considerably since then."

"Mmm."

This time, Finn was the one who was noncommittal. He reached down and took a sip from the mug of chicory coffee sitting on the counter in front of him. The warm, fragrant aroma of the caffeine brew filled my nose, making me think of Finn's father, Fletcher. The old man had drunk the same coffee in the same copious amounts before his murder as his son did. Even now, almost six months later, I still missed Fletcher. Missed seeing the old man leaning behind the counter at the Pork Pit, reading his latest book and telling me about the newest job he'd booked for me as the Spider.

There at the end, right before he was tortured to death by an Air elemental, Fletcher had wanted me to retire, to *live in the daylight a little,* as he had so eloquently called it. After I'd avenged the old man's death, I'd taken his advice and retired from being the Spider. At least, I'd tried to. I wasn't having much success so far. I might not kill people for money anymore, but I'd still managed to get myself into a whole lot of trouble in the meantime. Mostly by trying to help other people, good, innocent folks, deal with certain problems that had only one solution in a city like Ashland—one that involved my silverstone knives and someone losing a whole lot of blood. Permanently.

Finn took another sip of his coffee and stared at me, knowledge glinting in his sly green gaze. I rolled my eyes, walked behind the counter, and pulled a blue work apron on over my jeans and long-sleeved T-shirt.

"Oh, just go ahead and spill it," I said. "You know you want to tell me every little thing that you know about what's going on with Mab since I didn't manage to kill her last night."

A pleased, smirking grin spread over Finn's face. "Why, I thought you'd never ask."

He took another sip of his chicory coffee before he launched into his story.

"So I've had my feelers out all day," he said. "According to my sources, Mab's plenty pissed and some say even scared. Apparently no one's ever gotten that close to putting her lights out for good."

"Fletcher did train me to be the best," I said in a not-so-humble voice.

Finn saluted me with his mug. "That he did, and that you are. Which is why Mab was so understandably shaken up. Well, that and the fact that you blew that giant's brains out all over her face. Apparently Mab was quite the mess."

A cold, hard smile curved my lips. Poor little Mab, covered in blood. I only hoped that next time it would actually be her own.

"Anyway," Finn continued, "rumor has it that she's holed up in her mansion. But the weird thing is that she hasn't brought in any more reinforcements. At least, none that I've heard of."

"What about the people who were there last night? The ones who were having dinner with Mab? Who were they?"

I told my foster brother about everything that had happened, including going up against Ruth Gentry, Sydney, and the other strange characters Mab had invited into her inner sanctum.

"Weird," Finn said. "None of my sources said anything about who the guests were. I'll keep digging and see what I can come up with."

I nodded. If anyone could find out about those people, it was Finn. My foster brother had more spies in more places at his disposal than the CIA.

Finn had already finished a late lunch of a barbecue pork sandwich, baked beans, and coleslaw, and was ready to move on to dessert. So I dished him up a piece of the strawberry pie that I'd made last night before closing, and topped it off with a big scoop of vanilla bean ice cream. The luscious pie had enough sugar in it to lock a person's jaws and make him lapse into a diabetic coma, but Finn had two pieces. Sometimes I thought that all the chicory coffee in his system made Finn immune to sugar, fat, calories, and all the other things us mere mortals had to deal with.

A few more folks trickled in throughout the afternoon, and Sophia and I whipped up their meals, but the restaurant was quiet for the most part. Not surprising, given the weather. Last night's cold temperatures hadn't warmed up any, which meant that there was still plenty of snow and ice outside, with more on the way. Over the past several days, including today, Catalina Vasquez and the rest of the waitstaff had called in to say that they couldn't make it out of their driveways, much less get to the Pit to work their shifts.

Finn's bank had also closed early today because of the weather so he stuck around and worked his sources while he inhaled a third piece of strawberry pie.

Finn hung up his cell phone. "Okay, now I'm interested. Because nobody I've talked to has any idea who those people were at Mab's mansion."

"Nobody?" I frowned. "Nobody knows who those people are?"

Finn shrugged. "Whatever Mab's doing, she's kept a lid on that part of it. So far at least."

I put down the paperback copy of *Medea* that I'd been reading for the latest class I was taking over at Ashland Community College. Reading during lulls in the action at the Pork Pit was another habit that I'd picked up from Fletcher. Auditing classes at the college was a hobby I'd developed on my own, but one the old man had approved of.

My book forgotten, I leaned against the counter. I had no real reason to think there was anything particularly special about the group of people Mab had been entertaining last night—except that Gentry and her girl, Sydney, had tried to kill me.

No, I decided, that wasn't quite right. Gentry hadn't wanted to kill me—she'd wanted to march me back to Mab so the Fire elemental could do it herself. Sydney, though, had been going for the kill shot, but only after she thought that I was going to stiff Gentry. Still, something about the whole thing just didn't add up, and I couldn't figure out what it might be. Had the people at the dinner been brought to Ashland by Mab as reinforcements for her army of giant bodyguards? As spies? Or something else? I didn't know, but I was willing to bet that my ability to keep on breathing would depend on my finding out the answer—fast.

Finn and I sat there and threw out a few ideas, but neither one of us came up with anything that seemed remotely plausible. I was ready to give up, and Finn was ready to leave to see what else he could dig up from his sources, when the bell over the front door chimed again and my baby sister, Bria, walked into the restaurant.

7

Ashland Police Detective Bria Coolidge was a beautiful woman. Or maybe I was just a little biased, since she was my younger sister.

Bria's mane of blond hair, cut into a series of lush, shaggy layers, just skimmed her slim shoulders, while her blue eyes glinted in the soft curves of her face. The frosty air had painted her cheeks a pleasing pink that showed off her skin's perfection. Given the bitter chill outside, Bria wore a long, black wool coat over a pair of black boots, jeans, and a royal blue turtleneck sweater that further brightened her stunning eyes. Her detective's badge glinted a cold gold on her leather belt, right next to the inky blackness of her gun.

My gaze fell to Bria's throat, and the rune necklace hanging there. The one that she always wore—the one I'd never seen her without. A delicate primrose. The symbol for beauty. Bria's rune, the silverstone medallion given to her by our mother, Eira Snow, when she was a little girl. Our older sister, Annabella, had worn an ivy vine around her neck, representing elegance, while our mother's rune had been a snowflake, the symbol for icy calm.

Once upon a time, I'd had a necklace as well—a spider rune, of course. A small circle surrounded by eight thin rays. The symbol for patience. My assassin name. And so much a part of who and what I was.

In a way, I still had my spider rune and, like Bria, never went anywhere without it—because the metal medallion had been melted into my palms by Mab.

The memories of that night swam up in my head and, for a moment, I was back there. Tied down to a chair. Sweat streaming down my face. Choking on the stench of my own charred flesh. The silverstone melting, burning, searing its way into my palms—

My hands tightened into fists, and I felt another piece of metal dig into my skin—a small silverstone ring on my right index finger. The slight sensation was enough to derail my memories, and I dropped my gaze to the ring, latching on to the distraction.

Truth be told, it wasn't much to look at. The ring was completely plain and featureless, except for the tiny spider rune stamped into the middle of the thin band. But to me it was more precious than any diamond because it had been a gift from Bria.

My sister had given me the ring for Christmas. She'd worn it for years as a reminder of me, her big sister, Genevieve Snow. Even now, two more silverstone bands glinted on her left index finger—with runes carved into both surfaces. Snowflakes for our mother, and ivy vines for our older sister. Bria wore the rings every day, along with her primrose rune, as a tribute to them, our lost family.

I pulled my gaze up from the jewelry and looked at Bria. For seventeen years, I'd thought that she was dead, that I'd accidentally killed her. After Mab had tortured me that night, I'd heard Bria scream and thought that the Fire elemental had found the place where I'd hidden her. So I'd lashed out with my Ice and Stone magic to try to escape from the ropes that had held me down, to try to get to Bria before Mab killed her. But I'd used too much magic far too wildly. As a result, I'd collapsed our whole house—and I'd thought that Bria had been crushed to death by the falling stones. A secret guilt that I'd carried with me until just a few months ago when Bria had come back to Ashland.

My sister had been drawn here by a picture of the spider rune scar on my palm that Fletcher had sent her. Just as I'd started looking for her when the old man had arranged to leave me a photo of her from beyond the grave. Fletcher had wanted us to find each other, and we had. But our reunion hadn't exactly been a rosy one. As a detective, Bria had dedicated her whole adult life to being a cop, to helping people, to doing the right thing and making sure that bad guys like me got exactly what they deserved. As the assassin the Spider, all I'd done was kill people for money and contribute to my retirement fund. The two worldviews didn't exactly mesh.

But Bria and I were working through our differences—or at least trying to find some common ground. It had started at Christmas, when I'd saved Bria from getting dead at the hands of LaFleur and had told my sister who

I really was. Bria had been shocked and horrified that her big sister, Genevieve, had grown up to be the Spider, but she was trying to accept me, which is more than I'd dared to hope for.

Now, almost two months later, we weren't exactly best friends, but we weren't enemies either. We had coffee sometimes and tried to talk. But even when we just sat there staring at each other, searching for something to say, I was grateful that my sister was back in my life. I thought that Bria felt the same way. At least, I hoped she did.

Bria wasn't alone. Xavier, the roughly seven-foot-tall giant who was her partner on the force, stepped inside the Pork Pit and shut the door behind him. I knew Xavier well and counted him among my few friends. The giant had helped me out of some tough situations a time or two, and I'd returned the favor a while back by going after Elliot Slater, the sick, twisted bastard who'd been stalking and terrorizing Roslyn Phillips, Xavier's main squeeze. Roslyn had eventually killed Slater, but as the Spider, I'd claimed responsibility for his death to take the heat off her.

The two of them headed over to the counter. I leaned down on my elbows and waited for them. Sophia stood off to my left, peeling potatoes in case anyone else came in this afternoon who had a hankering for the thick, steak-cut French fries that the Pit was famous for, among other things.

"Hey there, baby sister," I said to Bria. "Xavier."

They nodded at me.

"Here for a late lunch?" I asked.

Xavier grinned at me, his teeth flashing like opals

against his onyx-colored skin. "Something like that. Think the owner will give us a break on the price?"

"Oh," I drawled. "She might make an exception for two of Ashland's finest."

They both took off their coats and settled themselves at the counter. Xavier sat down first, forcing Bria to move in between him and Finn or risk being left out of the conversation that was sure to follow. My sister sighed but slid onto the stool.

For his part, Finn was all too happy to swivel around in Bria's direction and give her his most charming, winning, aw-shucks smile.

To say that Finnegan Lane was something of a womanizer was like telling someone that it was a little steamy in the South in the summertime. Old, young, fat, thin, blonde, brunette, bald, toothless, face like a steel trap, Finn didn't care as long as it was breathing, female, and had the breasts to prove it. He wasn't even particular about how perky they were. Finn regarded pesky little things like wedding bands, engagement rings, and jealous, hulking menfolk more as amusing challenges than immovable obstacles that could be hazardous to his health. It always amazed me that some jilted husband hadn't hired me, the Spider, to kill my foster brother long ago. But Finn had his own sort of magic when it came to charming the ladies.

At least, until he'd met Bria.

Finn had laid a hell of a kiss on my sister during a Christmas party at Owen's mansion. The kind of kiss that would make most women melt. Some men too. But Bria wasn't most women. Oh, I could tell that my sister was attracted to Finn. She'd have to be blind not to be. But she was going to make him work for every sly innuendo, every heated look, every steamy kiss. Which, of course, only made Finn pursue her that much harder. So far, though, Bria had proved to be just as wily and elusive as Finn was clever, rebuffing every attempt he made to get close to her.

Still, there was something in Finn's eyes when he looked at Bria, something that made me think that all this effort might be a little more serious than he let on, something I'd never seen before—a touch of fear. Like maybe he was afraid of what he could actually feel for her—of falling for her the way that he'd made so many other women fall for him.

Maybe I should have stepped in and told him to knock it off. Having the two of them at odds didn't exactly make for warm, fuzzy family moments. But for once, a woman was getting the best of Finnegan Lane, and damned if I wasn't enjoying the show.

"Detective," Finn crooned in his most seductive voice. "You're looking smashing, as always."

Bria smiled at him, although as many teeth as she bared, it was more of a warning. "Lane. I see you're as oily and smarmy as ever."

Finn pouted and put his hand over his heart. "Oh, detective, how you—"

"Wound you." Bria finished his sentence and snorted. "If I ever did hurt you, Lane, you'd know it."

Finn raised an eyebrow and turned to look at me. "I see that your sister has the same violent streak that you do, Gin."

I gave him a toothy smile that matched Bria's. "Must run in the family."

Farther down the counter, Sophia let out a soft, raspy laugh. The Goth dwarf enjoyed Finn's discomfort just as much as I did.

Despite Bria's icy attitude, Finn didn't give up. He focused all of his attention on her, as if he were a general and she was just another battle to be won no matter what casualties he might suffer along the way—including the complete and utter loss of his self-respect, pride, and dignity. Bria coolly rebuffed all of his advances, but she wasn't completely immune to his charms. Interest sparked in her gaze whenever she looked at him out of the corner of her eye. Bria enjoyed being chased just as much as Finn liked running after her.

"So, what'll it be?" I asked.

Xavier ordered a double cheeseburger with all the fixings, along with fries and baked beans. Bria opted for the Pork Pit's most excellent grilled cheese sandwich, along with some potato salad and a piece of strawberry pie—the final slice that Finn hadn't managed to scarf down yet.

Sophia and I worked on the food, and the five of us talked back and forth across the counter. The dwarf and I slid the steaming food over to Xavier and Bria, and the two of them spent the next twenty minutes stuffing their faces, while Finn talked enough for everyone. Food, friends, and my sister, all in one place. It was about as good as things could get for me. Almost good enough to let me forget about how I'd botched my hit on Mab last night.

Almost.

Bria and Xavier polished off their food, but instead of saying their good-byes, the two of them lingered in the Pork Pit. It wasn't like either one of them to do that, not while they were on duty, no matter how good the food was. Something was going on.

Bria kept sneaking glances at first me, then Xavier. The giant nodded his shaved head at her, telling her to get on with it. Still, she hesitated. So I decided to make things easy for her, seeing as how the relationship between us hadn't exactly been smooth sailing so far.

"Something on your mind, Bria?" I asked.

Bria looked up, startled by my question. Then a rueful grin spread across her pretty face. "Is it that obvious?"

"Probably not to anyone else but me."

She nodded, accepting my explanation. "Actually, there is another reason that Xavier and I came by the Pit today, other than the food."

Bria drew in a breath and stared at me. "We need your help, Gin."

My sister asking for my help—especially considering the violent, bloody kind of *help* that I specialized in—was a new experience. But I wasn't about to deny her. Anything that Bria asked of me, I would happily give her—and then some. Still, if my sister, the straight arrow, the upstanding detective, had turned to me, the morally bankrupt assassin, for aid, then something really big must be up.

I raised an eyebrow. "Really? You need my help? Who exactly needs killing?"

Bria winced. "It's not—it's not like that. Not like that at all, Gin. I don't want anybody dead."

I stared at her another moment before my gaze cut to Xavier. The giant just shrugged his massive shoulders, telling me that Bria had the lead on this thing, whatever it was.

"So what's up?" I asked. "Why do two such esteemed members of the Ashland po-po need my help? Got a dirty cop you need to bust or something?"

Xavier snorted, with good reason. Besides the giant and Bria, honest cops were rarer than blizzards in the summertime in Ashland. Most members of the police force preferred to take wads of C-notes to look the other way, rather than actually try to solve the many crimes that plagued the city. It was easier, less dangerous, and far more profitable for everyone involved that way. For most folks, the only justice in Ashland was what they made for themselves—with whatever sharp, pointed weapon happened to be nearby.

Bria took a sip of her blackberry lemonade and tapped her left index finger on the counter before reaching down and twisting around the two rings that she wore there. Turn, turn, turn. Twisting the silverstone bands around and around was Bria's tell, something that she did whenever she was thinking hard about a problem. Light pooled in the snowflake and ivy symbols embedded in the metal and flashed the runes back at me.

"It's not that we need your help," she finally said. "It's just that we can't quite figure things out."

"What do you mean?"

Bria looked at me. "I'm sure you've noticed that there's been a bit more crime lately in Ashland than usual."

"Especially for the dead of winter," Xavier chimed

in. "Usually, crime around here goes down the more the snow piles up, since most folks don't want to get out into the cold. Of course, we get a few bums squatting in abandoned buildings over in Southtown, some trash-can fires that get out of control, but that's about it, except for the usual stuff."

By *the usual stuff,* Xavier meant all the domestic disputes, robberies, rapes, gang violence, and assorted murders that took place in the city on a daily basis. From a distance, Ashland might resemble a larger version of Mayberry, but in reality, the city was about as far removed from that quaint Southern ideal as could be. The only whistling folks did in Ashland was after they'd bashed you over the head, ripped your purse off your arm, and were strolling away counting the bills inside.

"Crime around the city has skyrocketed in the past few days," Bria continued. "Bar fights, robberies, beatings, murders. It's like some kind of army has invaded Ashland and is determined to tear up as much stuff as they can."

I frowned, and my mind flashed back to last night and the dinner guests that I'd seen at Mab's mansion. They'd all had a hard edge to them, a sharpness in their faces, and a twitch in their fingers that had marked them as potential dangerous troublemakers. I glanced at Finn, who was staring back at me, the same thought shining in his eyes.

"You think the crime spree has something to do with Mab's guests?" I asked him.

Finn shrugged. "Maybe, maybe not. Although the people that Mab does business with usually have a little more self-control than to go around getting into bar fights."

He had a point, so I waved at Bria, telling her to continue.

"The whole department's been trying to crack down, but no one can figure out what the hell is going on, who these people are, and why they've all suddenly come to Ashland," Bria said.

"Yeah," Xavier agreed. "Normally, we'd at least get a few whispers about what was up. But even the guys on the take don't have a clue—and you'd figure they'd hear something from their sugar daddies so they could cut off some of the problems before they got started."

"So more people are hurting and killing each other," I said. "Around these parts, that happens every time the moon's full. What exactly do you need me for?"

Bria looked at me. "I got a call this morning from one of my sources telling me that he knew what was going on and that it was something big—something that would really shake things up for everyone in the Ashland underworld. I asked him what it was, but he didn't want to talk over the phone. Said it wasn't secure enough. I'm supposed to meet with him tonight."

"I'm sensing a *but* in there."

A smile flitted across her face. "*But* he sounded strange when I talked to him. Like he was really excited about something, and this is the kind of guy who only gets excited when there's a big score to be had. I don't see what angle he's playing by telling me what's up, since I don't pay him for his info. So I told Xavier about it, and he thought that it might be a good idea to talk to you about things."

I looked at Xavier. "Suggesting me as backup? That's not like you."

The giant shrugged. "I thought that it might be prudent, what with everything that's going on with Mab. Especially since someone tried to take out the Fire elemental last night—in her own mansion, no less."

I winced. I hadn't brought up my little trip to Mab's for all sorts of reasons, but mainly because I'd missed the shot. I wasn't supposed to miss—ever. Especially not when the stakes were this high, not when my sister's life hung in the balance, swaying back and forth on the end of a spider's thin, silky thread. Mab wanted Bria dead in the worst kind of way, and I didn't want Bria to think that I couldn't protect her. I supposed that I was still playing the role of the big sister, just like I had when we were kids. Even though at twenty-five and with Ice magic that was almost as strong as my own, Bria could more than take care of herself.

I sighed. "So you guys heard about that, huh?"

"We did," Bria said.

All sorts of emotions clouded her features. Caution, respect, fear, and just a touch of concern. I wondered if that last one was for me or for herself.

Mab was under the mistaken impression that Bria was the Snow sister with both Ice and Stone magic—the girl who Mab had been told would kill the Fire elemental one day. I'd wanted to put the word out to the Ashland underworld that Mab had it all wrong, that the Spider was the one with both Ice and Stone magic. But Bria had pointed out that since the Fire elemental didn't seem to know who the Spider was or what the assassin's connection might be to Bria, it was foolish to give Mab any information that she didn't already have. From past experience, I knew that the Fire elemental wasn't that stupid, sloppy, or clueless, but I'd acceded to my sister's wishes. Bria wanted Mab focused on her and not me—no matter how dangerous it was.

I thought Bria's fatalistic attitude had something to do with the guilt my younger sister felt over how things had gone down that fateful night. Bria had seen Mab torturing me, but instead of trying to help me, she'd panicked and run away. I didn't blame Bria for that, though. She'd only been eight at the time, just a scared kid, the same as me. If she'd tried to stop Mab, she would have been dead too—burned to ash by the Fire elemental's magic. Still, all these years later, Bria felt responsible for things, like it was somehow her fault that Mab had tortured me instead of her.

I looked at Bria, and our eyes locked. So many emotions swam in the depths of our gazes, so many things that we just couldn't say to each other. But one thing was certain—my sister had asked for my help, and I was going to give it to her.

"You want me to come along for backup, I will," I said in a low voice. "Anytime, anyplace. You know that. So where is this little party going to be? Because I'll be there, but with silverstone knives strapped on, instead of bells."

8

"What's this guy's name again?" I asked Finn.

"What?" Finn said, cupping his hand over his ear to try to hear me better over the rocking music. Something he'd done three times in as many minutes whenever I'd tried to talk to him.

I sighed. Another night, another job, another chance to hang out at Northern Aggression.

That's where Finn and I were now, just before midnight, since Bria was meeting her source here. Northern Aggression was the most decadent nightclub in Ashland, a hedonistic den of sin where you could get anything you wanted if you had enough cash, plastic, or other valuable commodity to pay for the delights that waited inside. Sex, drugs, blood, smokes, alcohol. All that and more was available on the nightclub's pleasure-filled menu.

As its name suggested, Northern Aggression was located in Northtown, cozied in among the area's cookie-cutter McMansions and sprawling estates. The city's rich, corporate yuppies had to have somewhere to go after quitting time, and the club serviced all their needs. At Northern Aggression, you could do everything from have a casual drink with the girls to get your rocks off with whichever waiter—or three—caught your eye.

In keeping with the polite veneer that Northtown was so famous for, the outside of the club was surprisingly tame, looking more like a warehouse than anything else. The only thing that suggested there might be something of interest inside was the rune that hung over the entrance—a heart with an arrow through it. Every night, the sign burned first red, then yellow, then orange, inviting folks to come inside and get their freak on.

Once you stepped through the door, the tame, featureless veneer vanished. Crushed red velvet drapes covered the nightclub's walls, while a bamboo floor cushioned the feet of the many dancers. A bar made out of a single long sheet of elemental Ice ran down one wall, the suns and stars carved into the frosty surface glittering underneath the swirling lights. The runes were the symbols for life and joy, respectively, both of which folks in here seemed to have an abundance of tonight. Even if it all was just an alcohol-, smoke-, and sex-filled high.

As if all that wasn't enough to ambush, assault, and overload the senses, the waitstaff took care of the rest. Impossibly buff, beautiful men and women roamed through the crowd, serving up drinks and themselves to interested parties. Most of them were vampires, and all of them were hookers, as denoted by the necklaces they wore, each one with the heart-and-arrow rune of the nightclub dangling off the end of it.

I'd been in the club countless times, but it never failed to dazzle me with its sheer, unapologetic opulence.

That Bria's source had chosen Northern Aggression for the location of their meeting didn't surprise me. Lots of shady deals went down inside the club's private VIP rooms or the ones upstairs that could be rented out for as quick or as long as you liked. From the way my sister had described her source and the mysterious info that he wanted to give her, I doubted that anything tonight would be on the up-and-up.

I picked up my glass of gin and took a swallow. The cold liquor burned its way down my throat before turning into a pleasant heat in the pit of my stomach.

"What?" Finn asked again.

Next to him, Roslyn Phillips nodded her head in understanding. The vampire had no problem hearing me since enhanced senses were one of the many benefits that came along with drinking blood. Normal human blood was enough to give any vamp excellent eyesight and hearing, while those who drank from giants and dwarves received the great strength of those two races. Vampires could even absorb Air, Fire, and other forms of magic if they had access to an elemental's blood. Besides, this was Roslyn's gin joint, her nightclub. She'd had years to grow accustomed to the noise level.

She leaned forward and put her mouth close to his ear. "Gin wants to know the name of Bria's source."

Finn's face cleared, and he held up his martini glass. "After I finish my drink."

I gave him a sour look and sat back in my side of the booth that we were parked in. Instead of pressing the issue, I contented myself with another swig of gin. From past experience, I knew that absolutely nothing could convince Finn to do something before he was good and ready. The man was stubbornly implacable that way.

Across from me, an amused smile lifted Roslyn's lips. She'd been around Finn long enough to appreciate and sympathize with my dilemma, especially since the two of them had been friends with benefits for years, before she'd gotten serious with Xavier a few months ago.

If Bria was beautiful, then Roslyn Phillips was simply extraordinary. Everything about her was exceptional, from the creamy smoothness of her toffee-colored skin to the bright, matching color of her eyes to the way the cut of her sleek black hair framed her stunning features. Her body was just perfection itself, with toned muscles and svelte proportions that would put any supermodel to shame. Tonight, the vamp wore a tight, fitted, scarlet pantsuit that outlined her figure in a way that was somehow sexier than the skimpiest lingerie could be. Lots of hungry eyes strayed in Roslyn's direction, but she was one of the few things not on the club's menu.

Like so many vampires in Ashland, Roslyn had spent a good part of her life hooking on the Southtown streets before she'd saved enough money to become an uptown girl and start Northern Aggression. Vampires pretty much had the corner on the skin trade in Ashland. All vamps needed blood to live, of course, just the way that humans needed food and vitamins. But for some of them, having sex was just as good as downing a pint of O-positive and gave them a great, healthy high. Besides, vamps could live a long time, and prostitution was the world's oldest profession. It was always nice to have a skill to fall back on, especially given these tough economic times.

I finished my drink, pushed the glass aside, and looked at Bria.

My sister sat at the end of the Ice bar, nursing a mojito. She wore the same clothes that she'd had on earlier, although she'd tucked her detective's badge and her gun into her coat pocket. Bria's outfit was chaste compared to the skimpy clothes that the women on the dance floor sported, her demeanor nunlike when contrasted with those who openly made out with or even fucked their paramours in and under the club's booths and tables. But my sister still got her share of attention. Every other minute, some guy would sidle up and offer to buy her a drink, but Bria always shook her head and declined.

I wasn't the only one who noticed Bria's popularity. Finn stared at my sister as well, his mouth tightening as a handsome man wearing a three-piece suit tried to buy her another mojito. Finn grumbled something under his breath.

I hid a grin and continued scanning the area around the bar. Finally, my eyes landed on the woman standing behind it. The Ice elemental responsible for making sure that the bar stayed in one piece for the night, given all the bodies pressed up against it and the accompanying heat that went with them. The elemental's eyes glowed a dim blue as she sent a trickle of her power into the bar. Even across the room, I could feel the cool caress of her magic. It made me want to reach for my own Ice magic—and think about the last time I'd been here at Northern Aggression.

"How are Vinnie and Natasha doing?" I asked Roslyn.

"Good," Roslyn said. "Real good. I hooked Vinnie up with a job tending bar in a club in Savannah. He's liking the warmer weather down there, especially this time of year, and Natasha's doing well in school. Vinnie said to tell you hello, Gin. He said that if you're ever in Savannah, the drinks are on him."

I nodded. Vinnie Volga was the Ice elemental who used to tend bar for Roslyn—until Mab had blackmailed him into spying on the vampire in an effort to find me, the Spider. Mab had had Vinnie's daughter, Natasha, kidnapped and used for leverage, before I'd rescued the girl and saved Vinnie from being beaten to death by Mab's goons. Another good deed that I'd done pro bono. The only ones that seemed to matter these days.

At the bar, Bria shot down the guy in the suit, who moved on to another, easier prospect. Finn nodded his approval.

I arched an eyebrow. "Are you finally ready to get down to business, then?"

"So demanding," Finn said.

I just looked at him.

"Fine, fine," he muttered, pulling out his cell phone and scrolling through a couple of screens.

After a minute, Finn found what he was looking for.

"Bria's source is one Lincoln Jenkins," he said, talking just loud enough so that I could hear him above the pounding music. "Quite the rap sheet he's got. Dozens of arrests for all sorts of petty crimes, most of which have to do with being caught with things that didn't belong to him very close to houses that had just been broken into."

"So he's a thief, then," Roslyn said.

We'd filled the vamp in on why we were staking out the club. A common courtesy among friends. Roslyn knew who I was, of course. We had a history together, stretching back to last year when I'd killed her abusive brother-in-law and then more recently, when I'd helped her take care of Elliot Slater, the giant who'd been stalking and terrorizing her. Even if we hadn't clued Roslyn in on what was happening, Xavier would have kept her in the loop, since he and Roslyn were hot and heavy these days. The giant cop also moonlighted as the club's head bouncer and was currently working the front door, determining who got in past the red velvet rope and who was left standing outside in the cold. Another reason that he'd suggested that Finn and I back up Bria tonight, since he wouldn't be around to help her if things went bad.

Finn sniffed, "If you call boosting radios out of gang-bangers' cars and swiping rhinestone necklaces out of grandma's jewelry box *stealing*. Some of us prefer to work on a larger, more professional scale."

Being an investment banker, con artist, and all-around swindler, Finn had far higher standards than most of the crooks in Ashland—and a much bigger ego. He preferred to rob his clients while wining and dining them rather than holding them up at gunpoint. He was rather fussy that way. His twisted version of snobbery was one of the odd quirks that I loved about my foster brother, although I'd never admit it to him.

Finn also excelled at digging into people and finding out every little thing about them, from where they got their teeth cleaned to how much money they had stashed in their safety deposit box to how many bodies they had buried in their backyards. After Bria had told us when and where she was supposed to meet Lincoln Jenkins, I'd had Finn dig up all the info that he could on the small-time crook.

And, keeping my newfound promise to Owen, I'd called my lover as well and told him that I was backing up Bria tonight. The conversation between us had been stilted and awkward, but Owen had seemed relieved that I didn't have my sights set on Mab again. At least not for tonight. I didn't tell him that I hadn't given up on my plan to kill the Fire elemental. There was no need. Owen knew how badly I wanted her dead, how much I *needed* her dead to keep everyone that I loved safe—

"Jenkins is late," Finn said, cutting into my thoughts. "Ten minutes late, to be exact."

"He's a thief," Roslyn answered. "He probably hocked whatever watch he stole."

Finn snorted his agreement. "Maybe. But if he was so excited and the information that he had was so big, you'd think that he'd be early. Waiting at the bar, smoking a cigarette, drinking a beer, whatever, wanting to get things over with. Instead, he's a no-show, so far at least. Which looks like it's seriously pissing off sweet, sweet Bria."

Sure enough, Bria seemed impatient, tapping her hand on the Ice bar, turning the silverstone rings around on her finger, and continually scanning the crowd—all the obvious signs of a woman being stood up and getting angry about it. Then Bria's hand stilled, and she frowned before reaching down and pulling her cell phone out of her jacket. She held the phone up to her ear, sticking her finger in her opposite one so she could hear the person on the other end. She said a few words, then hung up. Bria didn't look in our direction; she was too smart for that, but a moment later, Finn's cell phone lit up.

He peered at the text message on the screen. "Bria says that Jenkins just called her. He wants to meet outside in the west parking lot. She's going to meet him right now."

This time I frowned. Why would a small-time hood like Jenkins want to meet outside on a night as cold as this one? There was more than enough of a crowd to get lost in, here in the nightclub, where it was nice and warm with lots of booze to consume and eye candy to lust after. I was starting to get a bad, bad feeling about this. Finn looked at me and nodded. He was having the same nagging doubts that I was.

"Roslyn, it's been a pleasure as always, but duty calls," I said, sliding out of the booth and getting to my feet. "If you don't mind, tell Xavier what's up, okay?"

"You need some help?" Roslyn asked, concern tightening her beautiful features as she got to her feet as well.

I shook my head. "Nah. If Finn and I can't handle a simple lowlife like Jenkins and whatever tricks he might have tucked up his crooked sleeves, then it's time for us to find another line of work."

Bria stood up, paid her tab, and headed for the front door. Instead of following her, Finn and I walked behind Roslyn, who opened a door set into the back wall of the club. The vampire madam led us through a series of narrow hallways that made up the outer wall of Northern Aggression—a hollow shell of space that wrapped all the way around the building. The passageways gave Roslyn, her hookers, and the giant bouncers who watched out for them peepholes and access to every part of the building without having to fight their way through the crowd. I'd taken advantage of them as well a few months back when I'd been stalking the people responsible for Fletcher's murder.

Roslyn led us to the back side of the building and opened a door for us. The February cold stung my face, but I welcomed the chill after the overbearing heat of the club. Beside me, Finn shivered and tucked his chin down deeper into his jacket.

Roslyn pointed to the left. "If they're meeting in the west lot, there are a couple of Dumpsters you can hide behind. There's some cracked, broken pavement that needs to be fixed, so we moved the bins over there to keep folks from driving across it and blowing out their tires."

I nodded. "Thanks, Roslyn. For everything."

She nodded back. "I'll go get Xavier," the vampire said and disappeared inside.

Finn and I stayed where we were, both of us reaching into our coat pockets and pulling out black ski masks. Before I'd retired, I'd never worn a mask while working as the Spider. I didn't need to—none of the people who saw my face were ever around to talk about it after the fact. But ever since I'd declared war on Mab, I'd taken to sporting a mask during my nocturnal activities. It was one more little thing that I did to protect my true identity as Gin Blanco—and the lives of everyone I cared about. If Mab found out who I was, the Fire elemental wouldn't be content just hunting me down. She'd kill everyone she could get her hands on who might be close to me.

Finn, Bria, the Deveraux sisters, Owen, even Roslyn and Xavier. I might be rather cavalier about my own life, but I wasn't risking the others like that.

Once I pulled the mask down over my face, I turned to stare at Finn. "You ready to do this?"

"Just like Bonnie and Clyde." He grinned, his teeth a gleaming white against the black fabric. "Although let's try not to get shot to pieces tonight, okay? This coat is imported leather."

I snorted, and the two of us moved off into the darkness.

⁂ ꟼ ⁂

The Dumpsters were crouched at the edge of the west parking lot, just where Roslyn had said they would be. Finn and I slipped behind the metal containers. The stench of sour beer, fried food, and vomit hung over the area like retched fog. I started breathing in through my mouth, even though the cold air burned my throat and lungs. That was still far preferable to the frontal assault on my nose.

"You know, Gin, this would be a perfect place for an ambush," Finn murmured.

He was right. The Dumpsters cordoned this area off from the rest of Northern Aggression, and the parking lot in front of us was deserted. Someone had made an effort to clear away the snow, letting me see several deep, jagged cracks that zigzagged through the pavement. A cluster of snow-covered trees butted up against the far side of the lot. Next to them, a flat piece of land stretched out parallel to the ice-crusted street beyond. Two SUVs were parked out there off to the right. Their owners must have driven them to the club tonight because the tinted windows were clean and defrosted. The music of the club pulsed out here, but the thumping beat was softer than it had been inside. Still, it was more than loud enough to soak up a scream or two.

The bad feeling in my stomach arched up, gaining force, and I palmed one of my silverstone knives.

Footsteps sounded, along with the rustle of clothing, and Bria rounded the building and came into view, heading toward the parking lot. She looked left and right, scanning the scene just as Finn and I had. Bria didn't like what she saw any better. Her mouth flattened into a hard line, and her hand slid into the pocket of her jacket, probably curling around the gun that she had tucked away in there.

From our position behind the Dumpsters, Bria couldn't see us, but she would know that we were here somewhere, ready to back her up. She strolled to the center of the lot and stopped, peering into the gray shadows cast by the ice-crusted trees.

"Lincoln?" she called out. "Are you here?"

No answer.

Bria looked and listened, but nothing moved in the cold night, and only the steady thump-thump-thump of the nightclub's music interrupted the frosty silence.

While we waited for Lincoln Jenkins to show, Finn trained his gaze on Bria, just as he'd been doing inside Northern Aggression. Supposedly, my foster brother had been keeping a watch out for anyone suspicious, anyone who might have an unhealthy interest in Bria or her source, just as Roslyn and I had been doing. But his eyes had rarely left Bria's face inside the club, and he hadn't so much as ogled any of the scantily clad women grooving on the dance floor the way he usually did.

I watched Finn stare at my sister as she paced back and forth across the parking lot. Maybe I should have been jealous. After all, Finn and I had once been an item, way back in the day when we were both teenagers and hadn't known any better. He'd been nineteen, I'd been seventeen, and we'd spent a rather enjoyable summer getting to know each other before we both realized that we were better off as friends than lovers. Over the years, that bond had turned into a brother-sister connection, one that was very important to me. Probably more than Finn knew.

Still, despite my love for him, I wasn't above yanking his chain, and this was definitely a prime moment if ever there was one. The great Finnegan Lane, infamous womanizer, lusting after my sister, who, so far, was giving him more of a chase than he'd ever imagined.

"You don't have to pretend with me, you know," I said in a soft tone, making sure my voice didn't carry beyond our position behind the Dumpsters.

"Pretend about what?" Finn murmured, still staring at Bria through a gap between two of the metal containers.

"That my sister's nothing more than another casual fling to you, another conquest to chase down and have your way with before you move on to the next woman."

It was like I'd flash-frozen him with my Ice magic where he stood. Every muscle in Finn's body locked into place, and he didn't so much as blink or draw in a breath.

Then, slowly, he turned toward me, his green eyes somehow still bright in his handsome face, despite the semi-darkness that shrouded this side of the nightclub.

"And what do you mean by that, pray tell?"

He tried to make his voice light, teasing even, but I could hear the undercurrent of worry that rippled through his words. Finn might think that digging up people's deepest, darkest secrets was all fun and games, but he didn't want anyone to know his true emotions. Not even me. Maybe it was just because he was afraid of what he was feeling—or worse, screwing up my newfound relationship with my sister. I was a little concerned about that myself, but I wasn't going to choose between Finn and Bria.

"Don't play dumb with me, Finn. It doesn't become you." I gave him a mocking stare. "I know that you're into Bria—*really* into her. That you actually *feel* something for her beyond mere lust. I can see it every time you look at her. You think you're pouring on the charm, being smooth and suave, but it's there in your eyes. There's something about her that intrigues you in a way that I think no one has in a long time. Maybe ever."

"*Feelings.*" Finn shuddered and spat out the word. "You know what I think about *them*. Overblown, overwrought emotion does no one any favors. I, for one, am perfectly happy with my mere lust. It's clean, simple, pure even."

I just kept staring at him. Waiting.

Several seconds ticked by before he sighed, shook his head, and dropped his gaze from mine. "You know me too damn well, Gin," Finn grumbled.

I arched an eyebrow. "You bet your sweet ass I do.

Which is why I think this thing is so hilarious. All these years of chasing women, and what happens? You go and fall in love with my sister before you even get her pants off."

Finn sucked in a breath. "Love? Who said anything about *love*? Please, Gin. You know how much I abhor *that* particular word."

Another shudder wracked his body, as though someone had just walked over his grave. But for the first time, I detected just a hint of wistfulness in his tone. I hid a smile. Oh, yeah. Finn had it bad for Bria.

"It's nothing to be ashamed of, admitting that you've finally met your match," I said. "Because Bria is pretty spectacular. Smart, beautiful, tough. You could do a lot worse."

Finn eyed me with suspicion. He might put on a charming facade, but if there was one thing that made him uncomfortable, it was talking about his own emotions. In that way, we were remarkably similar.

"And why are you suddenly okay with me trying to seduce your sister? If I remember correctly, there was a time not too long ago when you told me to take it easy around sweet little Bria."

"That was before I realized that Bria isn't so sweet and little anymore," I said. "Besides, I've seen the way that she looks at you. She's not quite as immune to your charms as she pretends to be."

A slow grin spread across Finn's face. "Really? You shouldn't have told me that, Gin. Because now I'm just going to try that much harder to seal the deal, so to speak. Even if she is your sister."

His tone lightened, as though he'd fully reverted back to the carefree, conniving Finnegan Lane who had seduced most of the female population in Ashland and had his sights set on the stragglers. But the barest trace of emotion flashed in his eyes before he was able to hide it from me—hope.

I shrugged as though it didn't matter to me what Finn did or didn't do with my sister. I wasn't telling my foster brother the real reason I was suddenly on board with the Finn-Bria love train leaving the station—the fact that part of me wanted them to have each other to hold on to. Because when I went after Mab again, I probably wouldn't be around afterward for either one of them to lean on. Better for them to find each other now. Better for them to realize that they could trust each other now, rather than after I was dead and burned to ash by Mab's Fire magic.

"And what about Owen?" Finn asked. "Jo-Jo called me and said that he came over to the salon to check on you. That he was upset you hadn't told him what you were up to regarding Mab. Apparently, I wasn't the only one you left out of the loop last night."

I shifted on my feet. Finn knew me inside and out, which meant that he could put the screws to me just as well as I could to him. But for once, I didn't mind his inquisition. I needed someone to talk to this about all this relationship stuff, especially since I was in new territory here.

"Owen started to tell me that he loved me," I said in a soft voice.

Finn frowned. "What do you mean *started to*?"

I drew in a breath and told him the whole sad story.

About how angry Owen had been with me because I hadn't told him I was going after Mab and how he'd almost let those three little words slip—words that I wasn't sure I was ready to hear yet, much less reciprocate.

"He really does care about you, Gin," Finn said. "I can see it in *his* eyes whenever he looks at you."

"I don't know why. I'm not exactly the stuff that dreams are made of."

"Oh, please," Finn scoffed. "Smart, beautiful, tough. Does that ring a bell? Not only does it describe Bria, but it fits you pretty well, too."

I shrugged. "Maybe. But it doesn't change what I am and everything that I've done."

"I thought that Owen was okay with all of that. With your being the Spider."

"He might be, but I don't want to rub his face in it over and over again. That's just asking for trouble. That's one of the reasons why Donovan Caine left me, if you'll recall," I said, referring to a previous lover of mine.

Finn opened his mouth, probably to analyze my stunted emotional state some more, when I saw something move in the trees.

"Hey," I whispered, cutting him off. "Looks like we've finally got some action."

A man stepped out of the patch of trees and into the parking lot, heading for Bria. From the way that she straightened, the man had to be her source.

Lincoln Jenkins was a short, extremely thin guy with a mop of frizzy blond curls and a wispy, pitiful excuse for a goatee. A diamond stud too big to be real glinted in one of his ears, while a couple of thick, fake gold chains hung around his scrawny neck. The chains bounced against his white T-shirt, which he had on under some kind of puffy, oversize football jacket. Faded jeans sagged against his lean hips, and the tops of the denim pants all but swallowed up his pricey sneakers.

"He looks like some kind of wannabe white trash gangbanger," I said.

"That's the look that all the petty thieves in Ashland are rocking these days," Finn replied.

I frowned. "Well, if Jenkins is so small-time, then why is he claiming to have big-time information about whatever's going down in Ashland?"

"Every squirrel finds an acorn sooner or later," he said. "Even a low-life hood like Jenkins."

Finn kept watching Jenkins, but I looked past the thief, examining the thicket of trees that he'd left behind, the shadows that stretched out around the parking lot, and the street beyond with its two SUVs. It all looked innocent enough, but something about this whole thing felt wrong to me—seriously wrong.

Lincoln Jenkins sidled up to Bria. My sister glared at him.

"You're late," she snapped. "You said you'd be here ten minutes ago. I don't like standing out here in the cold, Lincoln."

"Aw, now, don't be like that. You wouldn't want me to slip and fall in the snow, now would ya?" Despite his gangbanger clothes, Jenkins's voice rasped with a twang that was pure country.

Jenkins might have been talking to Bria, but he wasn't really paying attention to her. Instead, his eyes flicked from side to side, as if he was trying to determine if Bria was alone. After a moment, a sly smile curled his lips. My thumb traced back and forth over the hilt of the knife in my hand. I didn't like the look of his smile. Not one damn bit.

"So what's this information that you have? The thing that you couldn't dare tell me over the phone? What's going on in the Ashland underworld that has everybody so stirred up?" Bria asked, her voice as chilly as the night air.

"Aw, you want to get down to business already? You don't want to ask me how I've been or nothing?"

She sighed. "I know how you've been, Lincoln. Stealing whatever you can get your hands on, despite the straight jobs that you've been offered. The ones that I got for you. The ones that you worked at a few days before quitting and cleaning out the cash register on your way out the door."

Jenkins shrugged, but he didn't deny her claim. "So where's your partner at tonight? You know, the big guy, the giant?"

Bria's face tightened. "He's around."

"Around?" Jenkins cocked his head to one side. "That's funny because I just saw him working the front door of the club."

The thief backed up a step and took his hands out of the pockets of his puffy jacket. Bria tensed, and Finn and I did the same. But instead of coming up with a gun, Jenkins's hands were empty.

"Cold tonight, ain't it?" he said in a cheerful tone.

Jenkins brought his hands up to his face and blew on

them three times, before briskly rubbing them together and repeating the whole sequence.

My eyes narrowed.

Finn had spotted the particular movement too, because he stabbed his finger through the gap between the two Dumpsters.

"Did you see that? That thing that he did with his hands?" Finn asked. "That looked like some kind of signal—"

And that's when the SUVs roared into the parking lot.

✷ 10 ✷

The lights and engines on the two SUVs that I'd noticed earlier immediately cranked to life at Jenkins's signal. The vehicles roared down the icy street before the drivers turned the wheels, bouncing the SUVs up over the curb, through the snow-covered grass, and into the parking lot. For a second, I thought the lead vehicle was going to plow into Bria, but the driver slammed on the brakes, coming to a stop just a few feet in front of her. The other SUV slid in and stopped at an angle as well, trapping Bria and Jenkins between the two vehicles and the Dumpsters that Finn and I were still hiding behind.

"Fuck," I muttered, my bad feeling now confirmed. "It was a setup all along."

"Yeah," Finn whispered, reaching for the gun in his coat pocket. "But for whom? Bria? Or Jenkins? Somebody could want him dead for deciding to spill his guts to her."

"Doesn't much matter," I said. "Because if they so much as touch Bria, then they're all going to get dead. You stay here and cover Bria. If one of them makes a move toward her, you put a bullet in his brain. I'm going around behind them. Maybe they'll talk a little about what they want and who they're working for before we end them."

Finn nodded and moved into a shooting stance. I tightened my grip on my silverstone knife and stepped into the shadows.

The doors of the SUVs opened, and five dwarves spilled out—two from one car and three from the other. Bria stepped away from the men, putting her back to the Dumpsters, and yanked the gun from her pocket. Jenkins stayed where he was, the smirk on his face even wider than before. Yeah, the thief was definitely in on whatever was happening.

The men spread out and formed a semicircle around my sister. Each one carried a gun, but they were too focused on Bria to do the really smart thing—like check and see if she had any backup. Or perhaps Jenkins had already ruled out that possibility for them by making sure Xavier was by the front door of the nightclub, instead of back here with Bria. With the giant out of the picture, the men probably thought that Bria would be easy pickings. Fools. They didn't realize how tough she really was—or that her big sister, Genevieve, was here and would do anything to protect her. *Anything*.

Either way, it was easy enough for me to hopscotch my way from shadow to shadow, circle around the parking lot, and slip up through the trees until I was right behind one of the SUVs. I stopped there, hidden behind the massive vehicle, a silverstone knife in my hand, with another up my sleeve, two more tucked into my boots, and a fifth hidden against the small of my back. Five knives for five guys. No problem.

"Why don't you put the gun down and come along quietly, detective?" one of the dwarves rumbled. A nasal, *New Yawk* accent colored his words, telling me that he was definitely not from around here. "Because I'd really hate to have to shoot you in that pretty face of yours."

Bria stiffened at his tone, her face tight with anger. "Who the hell are you and what do you want? You called me *detective,* so you obviously know that I'm a cop. You really want to do something as stupid as threaten me?"

The man let out a low, evil laugh and looked at his friends, who all snickered in response. For some reason, they thought this was a laugh riot.

I used their laughter and distraction to slide into the shadows next to the second SUV—the one that was closest to Bria. I peered around the edge of the vehicle, studying the men who surrounded my sister.

They reminded me of a set of Russian matryoshka dolls in that they were all more or less carbon copies of each other, with the short, stocky, muscular frames that dwarves always had. None of them was taller than five feet, but their size definitely wasn't relative to their impressive strength. They all had similar features—oily black hair that was slicked back over their foreheads, swarthy skin, and black eyes. Brothers, maybe, or cousins. And they were all dressed alike, in nylon Windbreakers in a variety of bright, neon colors, matching sneakers, and gold chains around their necks. They looked like pint-size extras from some old *Sopranos* episode, as though the dwarven mob had migrated south for the winter. The only thing that would have been worse was if there had been seven of them. Heigh-ho, heigh-ho.

My eyes dropped to the guns in their hands, the ones they had pointed at Bria. Glocks for the most part. The lead guy, the one who'd spoken to Bria, had a snub-nosed revolver. I didn't know who the men were, had never laid eyes on them before, but they still seemed familiar to me. They radiated the same kind of hard, predatory air as the guests did I'd seen at Mab's interrupted dinner party. Which made me all the more curious as to why they'd decided to ambush my sister—and made them all the more likely to die when I found out the answer.

The lead guy, the dwarven don of the group, as it were, gave Bria a grin that was as greasy as his unwashed hair. "Honey, everybody in Ashland knows that you're a cop. That's why we're all so interested in you."

Bria frowned at his words. "What are you talking about? What's the meaning of this?"

The five men laughed again, as if they were all in on some private joke that was just the funniest thing in the world. Real wise guys, this bunch.

"Don" jerked his head at Jenkins, who'd crept back and joined the semicircle of men surrounding my sister. "Why don't you ask him what's going on? After all, he's the reason you came here tonight."

Bria looked at Jenkins, but the informant wasn't daunted by the anger burning in her icy blue gaze. "What's going on, Lincoln? I thought that you had information on what was going down in Ashland. What the hell are you trying to pull?"

"I'm not trying to pull anything," he said. "Except earn myself a cool ten grand for leading my new friends here straight to you."

I frowned. The dwarven mobsters had paid Jenkins ten large to set up a fake meeting with Bria? Why? What for? What did they plan on doing with her?

Bria glared at him. "You sold me out, you son of a bitch."

Jenkins's lips pulled back in a wide grin, revealing the fake gold grill stuck on his teeth. "Sorry, baby, but I got to get paid."

My fingers clenched around the hilt of my knife. The only thing he was getting tonight was dead. Another minute, two tops.

"Why?" Bria snapped, turning her attention to the leader once more. "Why give Lincoln ten grand? I would have been happy to set up my own meeting with you."

Bria's hand tightened on her gun, her knuckles white against the black barrel, telling everyone exactly how that meeting would have ended. Despite the seriousness of the situation, I couldn't help the warm pride that filled me at her bravado. Bria was no more a coward than I was. Still, that gun wouldn't do her much good against five dwarves. Like giants, dwarves were strong enough to take a couple of bullets in the chest and keep coming at you.

"Well," Don said in his thick accent. "It's not exactly *you* that we're after. But we figured that you were the easiest way to get to the person that we really want, so here we are. So quit talking and drop your gun, detective. Or me and my boys will drop you."

I didn't have to imagine the horrible, brutal things that these men would do to Bria if she surrendered. All of them were eyeing her, their cold gazes flicking from her crotch to her chest and back down again, already salivating at the prospect of getting their hands on her. My sister made no move to lower her gun. She was too smart for that. She knew as well as I did what the men had in mind—and that they would swarm over her the second she showed any weakness.

Instead of giving up, I felt the faintest trace of cold power trickle off her, like ice melting in a glass. Bria was an Ice elemental, a magic that she'd inherited from our mother, just as I had. Now my sister was reaching for her power, getting ready to use it against the men. Another weapon to her, just like the gun in her hand—and one that was just as deadly. I'd once stumbled across a giant that Bria had blasted with her magic. He'd looked like a human Popsicle after she'd gotten done with him, and I had no doubt she could do the same thing to the dwarves. The only problem was that she'd get only one of them before the rest overpowered her.

Don must have seen the blue glow that tinged Bria's eyes because his expression hardened with resolve. "I'm going to count to three. After that, my boys are going to put a few rounds in you. And when we have you down on the ground, well, trust me when I say that you won't like what happens next."

Bria didn't say anything, but she kept her gun up and level with Don's chest.

"One," Don said. "Two—"

I didn't wait for *three*. I sprinted out from behind the

SUV, grabbed the man closest to me, buried my hand in his hair, yanked his thick neck back, and cut his throat. Even a dwarf wasn't tough enough to survive a severed carotid artery. The man gurgled out a scream at the sudden, brutal wound, and everyone's head snapped around to see what the noise was all about.

For a moment, no one moved. Then everything happened at once.

Another one of the dwarves swung his gun toward me, apparently to try to shoot me through his dying buddy.

A soft puff-puff of air sounded, and the man hit the ground a second later, already dead from the two bullets that Finn had put through his right eye. I shoved the dwarf that I'd stabbed away from me. He slammed into the side of the SUV and slid to the pavement, twitching violently as his body shut down from the massive trauma it had just received.

"Take care of the bitch with the knife!" Don snapped. "I'll get the cop!"

Don pulled the trigger on his gun. *Crack! Crack!*

Bria threw herself to one side, and the bullets slammed into the Dumpster behind her. My sister rolled across the cracked pavement and came up on one knee, raising her own weapon to fire at Don. Her other hand was outstretched, and a blue light flickered there, as she formed a ball of elemental Ice to fling at him. Even across the parking lot, I could feel the cool caress of Bria's Ice magic calling out to my own.

But the bastard was quicker than she was. He rushed forward and slapped the weapon away before she could put a couple of rounds in his chest. The blow also broke

Bria's concentration, and her hold on her Ice magic slipped, the blue light cascading away in a shower of icy sparks. My sister retaliated by bracing her hands on the pavement and kicking up with her foot. Her boot slammed into Don's knee, and he staggered back, hitting the hood of the SUV. But the dwarf never stopped moving, bobbing, weaving, and gathering himself for another strike at her.

Another puff-puff of air sounded, and Don grunted as two bullets slammed into his left shoulder. A rare miss for Finn, who had no doubt meant to put the bullets through his eye instead, but the dwarf was moving too quickly, too erratically for that. Two more puffs of air hissed out, but by that point, Don had tucked into a tight ball and launched himself back at Bria. The bullets punched through the hood of the SUV, hitting the radiator and making it steam.

Lincoln Jenkins cowered on the right side of the vehicle, hugging the chrome rim like it was a shield that would protect him.

That all happened in the three seconds it took before the other two guys turned and came at me.

They both raised their guns and fired, but not before I used my Stone magic to harden my skin into an impenetrable shell.

Crack! Crack! Crack! Crack!

The bullets pinged off my body and disappeared into the darkness. The dwarves exchanged a puzzled look, wondering what was going on, but I didn't give them any time to recover. I stepped forward, my knife flashing.

I used my blade to slice a path across the closest man's

stomach. He screamed and tried to punch me in the face, using his gun for extra pop. I dodged his awkward blow, palmed a second knife, and buried that one in his heart, twisting and tearing through the thick, hard muscles in his chest to get to it. He screamed again, even as his limbs went limp, and I let him flop to the ground.

The second guy snarled with anger and threw his body into mine, tearing my knives out of my hands and smashing me up against the side of the SUV with his dwarven strength. He raised his gun up to put a couple of bullets into my face, but I grabbed the barrel and shoved the weapon back into his nose, breaking it. The gun slid out of his grasp and clattered to the ground. Blood spattered onto my face, just the way it had a hundred times before. A thousand times before. I grinned. Nothing gushed quite like a broken nose.

But the guy wasn't done for yet. He came at me again, this time trying to wrap his hands around my neck and choke me. I stepped up and sucker-punched him in the throat. He stumbled back, gasping for air, and a silverstone knife from my boot ended the rest of his struggles.

With my two men eliminated, I turned my attention back to Bria and Don, who were still fighting. The two of them rolled back and forth across the pavement, punching each other, although Don didn't even grunt as Bria's blows connected with his chest. Not surprising, given his inherent dwarven toughness. Blood covered both their faces, and I couldn't tell who the majority of it belonged to. No more puffs of air sounded, and I knew that was only because Finn didn't want to risk hitting Bria with a shot meant for Don, not while they were grappling.

Good thing I had my knives for the up-close wet work.

I sprinted over to the two of them, and the second that Don got back on top of Bria, I kicked him off her. The dwarf rolled back before climbing to his feet once more, looking all bright-eyed and bushy-tailed, despite his fight with Bria and the blood soaking the shoulder of his electric blue track suit.

Although I wanted nothing more than to see how badly Bria was injured, I stepped over my sister, putting myself between her and Don. Now that the other dwarves were down, I knew that Finn would come around the Dumpsters and see to her.

"Hey," I snarled. "Why don't you give me a whirl, if you really want to play?"

Don tilted his head from side to side, cracking his neck and considering me and the bloody knife in my hand. "Well, well, looks like I was right after all. The quickest way to get what I want and all the money that goes along with it is the detective here."

And then we danced.

He came at me, and I stepped up to meet him. Don was much better than I'd realized, moving with the speed and grace of a natural-born fighter and someone who'd gotten in a lot of practice along the way. The bastard had the muscled body of a true athlete, despite the cheesy nylon suit and pricey sneakers.

All of which meant that I couldn't immediately plunge my knife into him the way I wanted to. Normally, I tried to avoid this sort of hand-to-hand fight with a dwarf, as Don could do far more damage to me with his fists than I could do to him with mine. But I was still holding on to my Stone magic, still making my skin as hard as marble. His punches would hurt, but they wouldn't completely debilitate me like they would have if I wasn't using my elemental power to shield myself.

We moved back and forth on the cracked concrete, exchanging blow after blow. I punched him in the face. He landed a solid blow to my stomach. I followed with an uppercut to his chin. He turned and snapped his elbow into my chest. We broke apart, both of us bruised and more than a little bloody.

"Not bad for a dead man," I murmured. "Care to tell me what your interest is in the detective before I finish you?"

Don smiled, showing me a mouthful of bloody teeth that looked particularly garish against his swarthy skin. "Nah. What fun would that be?"

Before I could respond, he came at me again, swinging, swinging, swinging hard. I dodged his first two blows, then let the third connect on purpose. His fist thumped into my stomach again, and I crumpled to the ground in front of him. I didn't get up.

But Don wasn't as dumb as he looked because he didn't stop, not buying my ruse. He swung his leg back to kick me in the head and splat out my brains. I didn't give him the chance. As soon as he drew back, I rolled forward and used my knife to sever his femoral artery. Don screamed, but even then he got in another solid blow to my chest before the heel of his sneaker caught in a crack in the pavement, and he fell back. He writhed back and forth on the ground, cursing me and clutching his wounded leg. I stood there and watched him bleed out. It didn't take long, not with the deep, jagged wound that I'd inflicted. When he'd weakened to the point that he was no longer a threat, I leaned over and cut his throat, just to be sure.

"Why don't you leave being tough to me, and I'll let you handle being dead?" I asked in a cold voice.

Don gurgled once, almost in agreement, before his eyes glazed over and he was still.

✦ 11 ✦

Bloody knife still in my hand, I glanced over my shoulder.

Finn had pulled off his ski mask, come around the Dumpsters, and was helping Bria sit up. He gave me a thumbs-up, telling me that Bria would be okay until we could get her to Jo-Jo to be healed. Satisfied, I turned my attention to the last man cowering—Lincoln Jenkins.

It had taken awhile, but the wannabe gangster had finally realized that the tide had turned. He'd come out from his hiding place beside the SUV and stood in front of the vehicle, eyes wide, staring down at the blood, bodies, and carnage that painted the pavement. But before I could slither over there and finish him off, the thin bastard turned and ran. I let out a curse.

"Stay here with Bria!" I shouted to Finn. "I'll get him!"

I had to get him. Jenkins had seen what had gone down here, and he almost certainly had to know that the Spider was responsible. There weren't any other women running around Ashland who were as handy with knives as I was. At least, not to my knowledge. If Jenkins didn't realize this yet, surely he would when he got somewhere safe and calmed down. Now it was my mission to make sure that he never got to that happy place.

Jenkins was quicker than he looked—much, much quicker. Must be from all that time he spent skulking around and transferring ownership of certain items. He took off like a jackrabbit across the snow, and I had to hustle to keep up with him. Despite the fact that I'd used my Stone magic to shield my body, Don had still gotten in a few good licks on me, and I could taste my own coppery blood in my mouth, as well as what felt like a broken rib scraping against my lung.

Jenkins looked back, realized that I was following him, and picked up his pace, crossing the icy street like a speed skater and disappearing into an alley on the other side. I gritted my teeth and forced myself to push the pain away and move faster, run harder. I entered the alley to find that Jenkins had gained ground on me, since the thief was already halfway down the narrow corridor, which was largely clear and free of snow. He looked back again, his eyes wide with terror.

Instead of taking advantage of his natural speed, Jenkins reached out and grabbed one of the trash cans that lined the alley. He slapped the lid off it and turned it over. All sorts of refuse spilled out of the can, and several bottles tink-tink-tinked my way. One by one, he dumped the cans over, putting all sorts of disgusting things between us. Greasy fast-food wrappers, crushed cigarettes, used condoms. The sour stench alone made me gag, but I churned through the garbage, my boots smashing every-thing that was underfoot.

Jenkins thought he was doing the smart thing, but his tactics cost him precious time and slowed him down as well, when he would have been much better off just hot-footing it away from me as fast as his matchstick-thin legs would carry him. Still, he might have made it even tip-ping the cans over, if he'd been a little quicker or I'd been a little less determined.

Or if I didn't have my Ice magic.

We reached a spot in the alley where it was a straight shot for about a hundred feet with no garbage cans in sight. Up ahead, a light burned at the end of the corridor, indicating another street and possible escape for Jenkins. I was determined that the bastard wasn't going to make it that far, not after he'd sold out Bria. But by this point, the pain in my ribs had intensified until it felt like I was stabbing myself in the chest with my own knives, and I could feel myself slowing with every step.

Good thing I didn't have to catch Jenkins—only stop him.

I dropped to one knee, put my hands on the blacktop, and reached for my Ice power. A cold, silver light flick-ered underneath my palms, centered on the spider rune scars there. Snowflake-shaped Ice crystals spread out from my hands, zipping down the alley floor, coating the al-ready frigid concrete faster than I could ever think about moving—and much, much faster than Lincoln Jenkins could ever dream of running.

The frosty, silvery crystals caught up with the petty thief ten feet from the end of the alley. Jenkins hadn't noticed the elemental Ice creeping up on him, and his sneakers squeaked, then slid on the slick sheet. His arms windmilled as he tried to stay upright. Didn't work, never did. A second later, his back smacked onto the cold pavement. His puffy jacket deflated like a popped balloon, and he let out a low groan. I smiled, my expression even colder than the Ice I'd just created.

Still, I approached Jenkins cautiously, just the way that Fletcher had taught me. Just because someone might be down didn't mean that he was out—a trick I'd pulled more than once.

But Jenkins wasn't all that clever, and he must have hit the concrete harder than I'd thought, because he was still moaning when I reached him. I crouched down on my knees and straddled him, putting just enough pressure on his ribs to make it difficult for him to breathe. The thief's eyes widened at the bloody silverstone knife in my hand, and panic tightened his pasty skin. He tried to grab my hand in his, but I slapped his cold, grasping fingers away and shoved the blade up against his scrawny neck.

"Be very, very still, and you just might make it out of this alley alive," I snarled.

It was a lie, but I needed something to break through Jenkins's fear—I needed something to get him to talk, other than the threat of his own imminent demise. My harsh words worked because he nodded his head in a frantic motion, as eager as a puppy to please me. I eased up a little on his ribs, although I kept my knife against his neck, ready to slash open his throat if he so much as twitched wrong. Even lowlifes like Jenkins could get in a lucky shot, and not taking that into account was how people got dead.

"Now," I said in a pleasant tone. "You and I are going to have a little chat about Detective Bria Coolidge. Starting with who those men were and what they wanted with her."

Jenkins stared at me, his hazel eyes dark and sullen in his face. Underneath his wispy goatee, his lips turned down into an exaggerated, almost comical pout.

"You cost me a payday," he whined. "A big one. I was going to get ten grand for turning on that cop."

I didn't tell him that cop happened to be my sister and that he'd just buried himself for the promise of that elusive ten grand. Instead, I cut him. Not deep, but there was enough of a sting in the wound to remind him of what I'd done to the dwarven mobsters in the parking lot—and that I wasn't just some chick with a knife who looked good in black.

"Start talking," I said in a mild voice, digging the silverstone blade a little deeper into his neck. "Or I'll peel the skin from your throat like it's an apple. Now, why did you sell out Detective Coolidge tonight? What did those men want with her—"

"Bounty!" Jenkins screamed, cutting me off. "There's a bounty on the cop! And one on the Spider too!"

My eyes narrowed. A bounty. Another fucking bounty. I should have known, should have guessed. After all, Mab had hired Elektra LaFleur, one of the best assassins around, to come to Ashland to kill me. No, the bounty on my head, on the Spider's head, didn't surprise me. But why would there be a price on Bria? Why now? Had Mab finally gotten tired of knowing that my sister was alive? Did the Fire elemental still think that Bria was the one who was supposedly destined to kill her? The Snow sister with both Ice and Stone magic?

"So Mab wants the Spider and a cop dead. Tell me something that I don't know." I used my knife to make a sawing motion against his neck, slowly drawing the blade through the blood already running down his throat, but not cutting him again just yet. "And tell me quick."

For a second, confusion filled Jenkins's eyes, as if I'd said something wrong.

"What?" I snapped. "What aren't you telling me?"

He started to shake his head, then thought better of it, given the knife. "No, that's not what's going down at all. Sure, Mab wants the Spider dead, but not the cop. She wants the cop brought to her alive."

There was only one reason I could think of that Mab would want Bria captured alive—leverage. To use my sister against me. To flush me out into the open so she could kill us both. So the Fire elemental had figured it out then. She knew that the Spider was really Genevieve Snow—or at least suspected it enough to want to get her hands on Bria to confirm the theory.

Fuck. Just . . . *fuck*. Jenkins's words spread through me like my own elemental Ice had coated the alley floor— cold, swift, uncaring. My heart clenched with dread and fear for my sister, but I didn't let any of what I was feeling show in my hard face. Instead, I dug the blade even deeper into Jenkins's neck, encouraging him to start talking—fast.

"Tell me everything that you know," I growled. "Before my hand slips even more than it already has."

"It was—it was just a job, you know?" he sputtered.

"I've been laying low these past few days, what with all the bounty hunters in town."

"Bounty hunters?"

Jenkins nodded as much as he could, given the knife at his throat. "Yeah, yeah, bounty hunters. Mab's declared open season on the Spider. The last I heard was that Mab was offering five million to whoever brought the Spider to her dead. The number goes up to ten million if you manage to bring her in alive, but everyone would be pretty happy if she was dead. It's not worth the extra risk, ya know? I could spend five million just as easy as I could ten."

I didn't have to encourage him any more. The thief started babbling on then about how dangerous the Spider was and how bounty hunters from all over the country had come to town just to look for her. Well, I supposed that accounted for all the extra fights, murders, and violence recently. Inviting bounty hunters to a city as dark, gritty, and corrupt as Ashland was like splashing gasoline on top of an already roaring fire. Someone was bound to get burned.

I thought about all the hard cases that I'd seen getting ready to dine with Mab last night, and the way Ruth Gentry and Sydney had more or less been trying to take me alive. So that's who they all were then, bounty hunters come to Ashland to collect on the Spider, on me—dead or alive. Mab had definitely upped her game. Before, she'd brought in only LaFleur. Now, she had a whole city of bloodhounds sniffing after me. Despite the situation, I had to give Mab her props. She never did anything halfway.

"And what about the cop? What does Coolidge have to do with the Spider?"

Jenkins blinked, a little taken aback that I'd interrupted his whiny rant. "Nothing, as far as I can tell. But a few days ago, Mab goes and puts a million-dollar bounty on the cop's head. The only thing is that the cop has to be brought in alive. Not dead. So I'm at the bar the other night, and I hear these guys talking about the bounty, and I realize that this cop they're talking about is actually *my* cop. So I mention this to the leader, all casual-like, and he asks me if I want to make some quick cash."

"And I'll bet you said hell yeah."

Even though I was still straddling him, Jenkins managed a not-so-sheepish shrug. "I gotta get paid, you know?"

"Yeah," I said. "I know."

And then I cut his throat.

He didn't have any more to tell me. At least, nothing that I couldn't figure out myself. Jenkins was a small-time hood, a bottom feeder who survived on others' crumbs. He'd pointed the men at Bria and then had stood back and let them do all the dirty work. He just hadn't counted on me and Finn being there and his new friends getting dead.

Maybe I should have let him live. I'd been dealing with creeps like him my whole life, and he was no real threat to me. Maybe I should have let him slink off to whatever dark hole he called home. But he'd set up Bria for a measly ten grand, set her up to be raped, tortured, and whatever else those men had in mind before they turned her over to Mab. Jenkins had almost gotten Bria killed because of his greed, had turned on her even after she'd repeatedly tried to help him. He'd betrayed her, and that was just unacceptable.

Jenkins was nothing if not an opportunistic weasel. If I'd let him live, word would have gotten out about tonight, and, after a while, he'd have started thinking about things—including the mysterious woman with her silverstone knives who'd come out of the darkness just to save Detective Bria Coolidge. Jenkins wasn't completely clueless. He'd have put two and two together and realized that I was the Spider. If not, he'd have blabbed it to someone who would have put it together for him. And then, Bria would have been even more of a target and in even more danger than she already was, which was something that I just couldn't allow.

Besides, I'd never been much for mercy.

So I cut his throat, stood there, and watched until his blood was just as cold and frozen as the alley floor beneath him—and my own black heart.

✲ 12 ✲

When I was sure that Lincoln Jenkins was dead, I pulled off my ski mask and walked back to the parking lot at Northern Aggression.

Finn stood next to Bria, who sat on the bumper of one of the SUVs. My foster brother said something to her, then pulled out the white silk handkerchief from the breast pocket of his suit. He passed the delicate fabric to Bria, who used it to wipe some of the blood off her face. Oh, yeah, Finn had it bad for my sister if he was offering up his precious silk to her.

But they weren't alone.

Sometime while I'd been chasing after Jenkins, Roslyn and Xavier had joined the party. Roslyn stood on the other side of Bria, eyeing the bodies that littered the cracked pavement like loose gravel, her beautiful features puckered with obvious distaste. I couldn't tell if the vamp was bothered by what Finn and I had done to the men or the horrible, clichéd Windbreakers that they wore. Xavier was being more practical. The giant went from body to body, pulling out wallets and cell phones, and scanning through them, trying to find out who the men were. Their names didn't much matter now, since they were all dead.

At the scuff of my footsteps, Finn turned, his gun still in his hand.

"Relax," I said, stepping out of the shadows. "It's just me."

Finn nodded, but he didn't put his gun away. Instead, he kept scanning the area like he expected more goons to pop up out of the snow and try to grab Bria again. Given what Jenkins had told me about Mab's bounty on my sister, it wasn't that much of a stretch.

I looked at Bria, checking her for injuries just the way that Fletcher had always done for me whenever I'd been in a knockdown, drag-out fight. Her face was a mess. A cut above her right eye dripped blood, while another one across her chin did the same. Bruises blackened both her cheeks, further marring her pretty, delicate features, and she had one arm wrapped around her middle, as though a couple of her ribs were broken.

My heart twisted at the damage that had been done to her, at the pain she was suffering. But I also knew that Bria had gotten off easy. Because she was still here with me, instead of being delivered into Mab's fiery hands.

"So what did he say?" Finn asked.

"One of these men talked?" Roslyn asked in a disbelieving tone. "Before he died?"

I shook my head. "Not them. There was one more who ran when things got bloody, but I chased him down. As for what he said, it was nothing good. Mab's put out a five-million-dollar bounty on the Spider's head."

Finn let out a low whistle.

"Oh, the news gets better. The sum goes up to ten million if someone manages to hog-tie me and dump me at Mab's feet—alive."

"Ten million dollars?" Xavier rumbled. The giant was still bent over one of the bodies on the pavement. "No wonder things have been so crazy around here. Every bounty hunter east of the Mississippi would come to Ashland for that kind of money."

I nodded at the dead dwarves. "Apparently, they're already here."

Nobody said anything.

"But there's more, isn't there?" Bria asked. "Something you aren't telling us. Something to do with me. Because these men tonight? They wanted *me,* not you, Gin. So tell us the rest of it."

Bria and I might not have the closest of relationships, but she was starting to pick up on things about me. Like the fact that I would keep secrets if I thought it would protect the people I loved. I didn't know whether to be happy or annoyed with her insight. But there was no getting around her question, not with Finn, Roslyn, and Xavier eyeing me too, wondering what was going on.

I stared at Bria. "Apparently, Mab has realized our familial connection—or at least suspects it—because she's put a bounty on your head as well. One million dollars. The only catch is that you have to be brought in alive. With me, she'll take whatever she can get."

Bria looked at me, her blue eyes dark and thoughtful.

"She wants to use me as bait. To lure you out into the open so she can kill us both."

I shrugged. "That would be my guess. But it's not going to happen. I'm not going to *let* it happen. I promise you that, baby sister."

Anger tightened her battered features. "I don't need you to protect me, Gin. I'm a cop and an Ice elemental, remember? I've been taking care of myself for a long time now. I can handle a few bounty hunters."

I snorted. "This is more than a few bounty hunters. This is every toothless old geezer with a shotgun in the back of his pickup coming to Ashland gunning for us. Me, they haven't got much of a shot at, since I'm so good at being a ghost. But everybody in town knows your name, rank, and serial number, especially since the incident at the train yard right before Christmas. I'm just surprised it took them this long to get up enough gumption to come after a cop."

Bria shifted on the bumper of the SUV. Her bloody lips clamped down, like she was afraid that if she opened them she'd spill her guts about something she wasn't supposed to.

My eyes narrowed. "This is the first time that someone's tried to kidnap you, right? Because I know you would have told me if something like this had happened before."

For a moment, I thought that she wasn't going to answer me. But my cold, accusing gaze weighed down on her, cracking her resolve.

Bria sighed. "There was a guy two days ago when I was getting coffee over at the Cake Walk. He pulled a gun on me as I came out of the restaurant, forced me into a nearby alley, and told me that he was going to take me for a ride."

"What happened?"

Bria shrugged. "I waited until I was sure that there was no one else around who could get hurt, then threw my coffee in the bastard's face and took away his gun. While he was screaming from the pain and the second-degree burns, I cuffed his ass and hauled him down to the station. End of story."

Finn gave my sister a warm, admiring look. "Nice takedown, detective. Even if you should have found another way to do it. Don't you know that you never, ever waste a cup of coffee like that?"

Bria's brows drew together in confusion. She hadn't been around long enough yet to realize the dark, murky depths of Finn's caffeine addiction. She shook her head, pressed his silk handkerchief to the wound above her eye, and turned to look at me.

"And what about Jenkins?" she asked. "I assume that you caught up to him, since you're telling us all this."

There was more that she wanted to ask me. The question burned like a flare in her icy eyes. A lesser woman would have left it at that, especially when dealing with someone like the Spider, even if I was her sister. But Bria wasn't lacking for bravery or anything else in the toughness department.

"Did you kill Jenkins? After you questioned him?"

"Of course I killed him," I said. "He was a threat to you. He'd already sold you out once, and he would have been more than happy to do it again. I couldn't let him walk away. Nobody hurts the people that I care about and gets away with it—*nobody*."

Bria's mouth flattened into a hard line, and more anger iced over her eyes, but she didn't say anything else. She didn't argue with me about how what I'd done had been so wrong. About how I'd just killed someone in cold blood. About how she could have taken care of Jenkins by arresting him and letting him cool his heels in jail. But I could sense her disappointment in me. The chill of it radiated off her, an arctic front blasting me with her cold displeasure.

Finn stepped in between us. "I hate to interrupt this little debriefing, but in case y'all have forgotten, we're standing in a parking lot with several dead bodies. Something that would look a wee bit suspicious to even the most trusting soul. What do you want to do, Gin?"

"Yeah," Xavier chimed in, getting to his feet. "You want me to call it in? You going to leave your rune here for Mab to find?"

After I'd declared war on Mab, I'd started leaving my spider rune at the scenes of my crimes whenever I ambushed and killed the Fire elemental's men. Scratching the rune into the dirt, carving it into the side of a building, even drawing it in blood. I'd done all that and more because I'd wanted Mab to focus all her anger on me, and not think too much about the folks that I'd saved along the way, like Bria and Roslyn, and what their connection to me might be.

"I can do the whole song and dance," Roslyn volunteered. "You know, say that everyone was in the nightclub and no one heard a thing. Just like always."

I stared at the bodies that littered the parking lot. Ten minutes ago, the men had been full of vim and vigor. Now they were nothing, less than nothing, like yesterday's newspaper all crumpled up and thrown away.

"No," I said in a thoughtful voice. "I'm not going to leave my rune behind, and you guys aren't going to call it in. We're going to pretend like this never happened."

Bria frowned. "But why? What's different about tonight?"

"Because Mab has hired subcontractors," I said. "These aren't her men. Not really. But if I leave my rune behind and they realize that I stepped in to protect you, Mab will know that she's right about our connection. She'll tell the bounty hunters, and then there'll be a feeding frenzy, even more so than there is already. No, our friends here are going to disappear quietly. And I know just the Goth dwarf to make it happen."

Thanks to a call from Finn, Sophia Deveraux showed up about fifteen minutes later, driving her classic convertible.

As usual, the Goth dwarf wore black from head to toe. Only tonight, her ensemble consisted of a pair of work boots and long, heavy coveralls. The perfect outfit for disposing of a dead body. Or six in this case. While we'd waited for Sophia to show up, Xavier and I had walked over, retrieved Jenkins's body from the alley, and brought it back here to the parking lot. No need to make the dwarf trudge all that way, especially when the alley was still coated with the slippery elemental Ice that I'd created. She'd be busy enough here as it was.

"As you can see, things got a little more hectic than I expected tonight," I told Sophia.

"Hmph." The dwarf grunted in agreement as she surveyed the bodies.

"You need help with anything?"

Sophia rolled her black eyes and huffed, like I'd just insulted her. I suppose that I had. Like me, Sophia preferred to work alone, and she was damn good at her job. The Goth dwarf had been getting rid of bodies for Fletcher for years before I'd come along and taken over the assassination business from the old man.

Sophia was incredibly strong, even for a dwarf, but what really set her apart was the fact that she had the same elemental Air magic that her sister, Jo-Jo, did. The older dwarf used her magic to heal, but Sophia did something different with hers. In addition to putting blood vessels and broken bones back together, Air magic was also great for tearing them apart—and sandblasting bloodstains, DNA, and brain matter off doors, floors, walls, and wherever else it happened to spatter. Sophia wouldn't bother getting rid of the tacky pools of blood in the parking lot, since the harsh winter elements would soon erode them. But she would take care of the dwarven bounty hunters' bodies for me, disintegrating them with her Air magic and hauling off whatever pieces were left to parts unknown.

"We're going to Jo-Jo's to get Bria patched up," I told Sophia. "See you there?"

"Mmm-hmm," she said in a distracted tone, already pulling on a pair of gloves, probably so she wouldn't ruin her manicure. Her nails gleamed pearl pink in the semi-darkness, the soft, girly color looking decidedly at odds with her stark black coveralls.

"I'll stay with her," Xavier said. "Just in case anyone wonders what she's doing and comes over to investigate."

I nodded. There was a slim chance anyone would venture by at this late hour, at least someone who was still sober and not soused from their time inside Northern Aggression. But if they did, the giant would flash his police badge and send them on their way. Good. Sophia could take care of herself, but it never hurt to have someone around watching your back.

"Thanks," I told the giant. "I owe you one."

Xavier grinned. "Nah, you don't owe me anything. At least not for this. Although I wouldn't be opposed to another free lunch or two. That was one fine meal we had today."

I raised an eyebrow. "Better be careful talking about how good my cooking is. Roslyn might get jealous."

The vampire madam let out a soft laugh. "Oh, I'll freely admit that your cooking is much better than mine, Gin. But I have certain skills you don't, especially in the bedroom. I think that Xavier far prefers those, even over a plate of the Pork Pit's best barbecue."

Roslyn gave Xavier a sly look, and the giant's grin widened.

"Well played, Roslyn," I murmured. "Well played."

Xavier gave Roslyn a hot, lingering look that told me exactly what the two of them would be doing later on. Then the giant moved over to stand by Sophia, who had pulled a measuring tape out of her coveralls to see how many of the bounty hunters' bodies she could squeeze into the trunk of her convertible. Despite its swooping fins and clean lines, the black vehicle always reminded me of a hearse. Tonight, the dwarven mobsters would take their last ride in it.

Roslyn went back inside Northern Aggression to continue circulating through the crowd and keep up appearances. Finn and I helped Bria limp over to his Aston Martin, which was parked in the nightclub's east lot.

Bria and I didn't speak while we rode over to Jo-Jo's house. My sister was still pissed that I'd killed her informant, even though Jenkins had sold her out. Finn tried to fill in the silence, cracking wise and telling a few jokes, but even his antics couldn't defrost the tension between us.

Twenty minutes later, the three of us were in the warm, familiar confines of Jo-Jo's salon. Bria sat in one of the cherry red salon chairs, while Jo-Jo examined her face with a critical eye.

"That's a nasty cut you've got there, darling," the dwarf told Bria. "The bastard walloped you good, didn't he?"

Bria grimaced. "That he did."

Jo-Jo held her palm up close to Bria's face and reached for her Air magic. The dwarf's power filled the salon, once more making the spider rune scars on my palms itch and burn. Jo-Jo leaned forward, and Bria hissed like an angry cat. Not because Jo-Jo was hurting her, but because she could sense the dwarf's Air magic, just like I could—and it felt nothing like our cool Ice magic or even my similar Stone power.

"I don't like the feel of it either," I said in a quiet voice, coming to stand beside her. "The Air magic."

Jo-Jo passed her hand over Bria's face, forcing oxygen into all the cuts that marred her features. I watched while the gash above her eye knit itself together, and the ugly bruising faded from her skin.

Bria gritted her teeth. "It's not the most pleasant sensation, but I'll live."

"Sometimes, it's better if you hold on to something," I said, stretching out my hand. "It helps distract your mind from the pain."

Bria looked at my hand hovering in midair, my fingers curled up; then her blue gaze flicked up to my face. I know what she saw when she looked at me. A woman dressed in black. A woman covered in blood. A killer. A murderer. A monster. No matter how she tried to hide it, Bria couldn't forget who and what I was—and how conflicted she felt about it.

Finally, she sighed and grabbed my hand. Her palm felt cool and soothing against mine. Bria might not like my past as an assassin, might not like my being the Spider now, but she also knew that part of me would always be Genevieve Snow—the big sister she'd loved so much as a child.

"You squeeze as hard as you need to."

Bria just nodded, her hand tightening around mine.

Besides the cuts on her face and a few cracked ribs, my sister wasn't that banged up from grappling with the bounty hunter, so it took Jo-Jo only a few minutes to heal her. Then the dwarf did the same to me, taking care of the injuries that Don had inflicted on me. Afterward, the three of us trooped into the kitchen.

Most people preferred the salon, but the kitchen was my favorite room in the house, maybe because I loved to cook so much. A long, skinny table sliced the kitchen into two pieces, while appliances done in a variety of pastel colors hugged the walls. Fat, fluffy clouds dotted the fresco-painted ceiling like marshmallows. More clouds could be found everywhere you looked, from the pot holders stacked next to the stove to the dishcloths piled beside the sink. Like other elementals, Jo-Jo also used her personal rune—a puffy cloud that symbolized her Air magic—in her decorating scheme.

Finn stood by the counter, having just finished making his thirteenth cup of coffee of the day. As always, the chicory fumes warmed me from the inside out and made me think of his father. I wished that the old man were here tonight. Fletcher would have known exactly what to do about the mess we were in—the mess I'd dragged us all into by declaring war on Mab in the first place.

Finn stared at me with his green eyes. "Any chance of getting something sweet to go with my coffee?" he asked in a hopeful voice.

I arched an eyebrow at him. "You mean all those pieces of strawberry pie that you ate for lunch weren't enough?"

"I'm a growing boy," Finn said in a sincere tone. "I need my vitamins."

Bria snorted. "The only thing that's growing on you, Lane, is your ego."

Finn sidled up to my sister and gave her a dazzling smile. "Well, other things of mine also tend to swell up in your presence, detective."

I rolled my eyes at Finn's attempt at witty banter. Jo-Jo just chuckled, amused by his antics.

Bria returned Finn's smile with a syrupy sweet one of her own. "Oh, really? So it's gone from what, pencil eraser to cocktail sausage by now?"

Finn sputtered and almost spit out a mouthful of coffee. His face flushed, and he glared at Bria. He opened his mouth, probably to come up with some biting retort, but I cut him off.

"Enough," I said. "We have more important things to worry about right now than what you two think of each other and your various appendages. Like what we're going to do about the bounty on your head, Bria."

She shrugged. "I don't see why we have to do anything about it. Now that I know about the bounty, I can protect myself."

"No, you can't." I opened the refrigerator to see what kind of ingredients Jo-Jo had on hand. "Not from every bounty hunter in the city."

"Bounty hunter?" Jo-Jo asked. "What bounty hunter?"

Bria and Finn filled the dwarf in on what had happened at Northern Aggression. The meeting with the informant, the botched kidnapping attempt, what I'd learned from Lincoln Jenkins.

I let their words wash over me while I got out the ingredients for brownies. Flour, eggs, water, baking cocoa, oil. All that and more went into my mixing bowl. Ten minutes later, I slid the brownies into the oven and got started on the thick layer of cream cheese frosting that would turn the brownies from just a mere dessert into something truly spectacular. Powdered sugar, butter, almond extract, and a block of cream cheese filled another bowl. As always, the stirring, the mixing, the careful measuring of ingredients, soothed me. I couldn't control what Mab did, how she came after me, or whom she hired to do her dirty work, but I could make my family a treat to sweeten the bitter times.

Twenty minutes later, just as Finn and Bria were winding down with their story, I took the brownies out of the oven. While I was waiting for them to cool enough to frost them, I grabbed the milk from the fridge, along with several mugs out of the cabinets. One by one, I wrapped my hand around the glasses and reached for my Ice magic. Crystals spread out from my palm and ran up the side of first one mug then another until all the glasses were cold and frosty.

When everything was ready, I cut the frosted brownies, stacked them on a plate, brought the milk and mugs over to the table, and started munching on my late-night snack with the others.

"So what do you want to do, Gin?" Finn asked. "Now that we know exactly who all these crazy people are in Ashland."

I chewed a bite of brownie. Rich and chocolatey, with an extra sugary sweet kick from the cream cheese frosting. Perfect. "See if you can find out more about them—backgrounds, skills, habits. I especially want to know about Ruth Gentry and Sydney, the girl that she has with her. Gentry seems to be the smartest of the bunch so far, which makes her the most dangerous."

Finn nodded. He'd started digging into Gentry earlier today, but Bria's meeting with Jenkins had taken precedence and sidetracked his search.

"What about me?" Bria asked. "What do you want me to do?"

I looked at her. "You're going to call your boss in the morning and tell him that you've had a family emergency and are going out of town."

Bria's eyes narrowed. "You want me to leave Ashland? Because of a few bounty hunters?"

I shook my head. "It's more than a few bounty hunters, Bria. Six guys jumped you tonight, and Mab had a whole dining room full of them at her house. There's got to be at least three or four dozen of them in Ashland by now, all eager to get their hands on you. Leaving town is exactly what they'll expect you to do, which is why you're not going anywhere."

Bria looked at me. "You want me to go into hiding then, don't you?"

I nodded. "I do. I want you in Ashland, close by, somewhere I know that you'll be safe. Someplace that's easy to defend and hard to get into. Someplace where I know every single nook and cranny, so there are no surprises."

"There's only one place that I know of that fits that bill," Finn said.

"Do you mind?" I asked in a quiet voice, staring at my foster brother. "Because, really, it's your house too."

Finn just shrugged. "He left the house to you, Gin. He knew that you'd need it for something like this someday. We both know that."

Bria looked back and forth between us. "What are you talking about? Where is this place?"

I stared at her. "We're talking about Fletcher's house. Baby sister, you're coming home with me tonight."

✳ 13 ✳

Bria argued with me, insisting that she could take care of herself. But I didn't budge, telling her that she was going to hole up in Fletcher's house even if I had to duct-tape her into submission and keep her that way. Still, Bria acquiesced only after I pulled a roll of the gray tape out of one of the kitchen drawers and starting slicing off strips of it with a silverstone knife.

Deep down, Bria knew that staying out of sight was the smartest thing to do—for everyone. But that didn't mean she liked it. Grumbling under her breath about overprotective big sisters, Bria stalked off into the bathroom to try to wash some of the blood out of her clothes.

That left Jo-Jo, Finn, and me alone in the kitchen. When I was sure that Bria was out of earshot, I turned to Finn.

"You know what I have to do now," I said. "I have to kill Mab. The very first chance I get. That's the only way to lift the bounty on Bria's head."

Finn slurped down another mouthful of his chicory coffee. "Yeah, you tried that last night, remember? It didn't work out so good for you."

My lips curled back into a snarl at the memory of my epic failure, but I forced my anger at myself down into the pit of my stomach. "I don't care. Mab *knows*, Finn. She knows that Bria's my sister. That's why she put the bounty on her head. If Mab can't find me herself, then she can use Bria to make me come to her."

Nobody spoke.

I drew in a breath. "So work your contacts, Finn. The second that Mab leaves her mansion, I want to know about it. I don't care where she's going, one of her businesses, out to dinner, even to the fucking mall. Wherever she ends up at, I plan to be there waiting for her, knives ready."

Finn nodded, already pulling his cell phone out of his suit jacket to start making calls. Jo-Jo reached over and took my hand, her fingers warm against my palm.

"It's going to be okay, Gin," the dwarf murmured. "You'll see."

I thought about how close I'd come to losing Bria tonight. How close Mab, her giants, and her bounty hunters had come to nabbing me at her mansion. How many times in the last few months that the Fire elemental or one of her minions had just missed killing me. I didn't say anything, but I squeezed the dwarf's fingers with my own, trying to reassure myself as much as her.

Finn promised to contact every single one of his sources to see what they had to say about the bounty hunters, Mab, and anything else that might be relevant or helpful. Then Bria came back into the kitchen, and I drove the two of us over to Fletcher's house. Sophia had already gotten rid of the old clunker that I'd used to escape from Mab's mansion last night, hauling it off to some junkyard where it belonged. Bria and I had met Finn at Jo-Jo's earlier, and since he'd driven the three of us over to Northern Aggression, I'd left my regular car at the dwarf's house.

Bria and I didn't speak on the ride over, although she grimaced and grabbed the door handle as my silver Benz churned up the driveway. Couldn't blame her for that. The steep, twisting path still rattled my bones every time I drove up it.

My Benz crested the top of the ridge, and Fletcher's house came into view. A lone light burned like a firefly over the front door, dimly outlining the sprawling structure. White clapboard, brown brick, and gray stone joined together to make up the building, along with a tin roof, black shutters, and blue eaves. You couldn't see much of the odd mishmash of styles and materials in the darkness, but I knew the lines and texture of the ramshackle house as well as I knew my own face.

"Home, sweet home," I murmured, stopping the car.

Bria stared out the window, peering into the shadows that covered the yard like puddles of gray ink oozing over the snow. Despite the fact that we'd been getting reacquainted with each other, my sister had never been up to Fletcher's house before. We always met in public places, like the Pork Pit or Northern Aggression, usually with Finn, Xavier, Roslyn, or one of the Deveraux sisters in attendance. Self-imposed chaperones to keep the long, awkward pauses to a minimum.

There were no chaperones, no safety nets tonight, and this place was as personal as it got for me. I'd loved Fletcher like a father, and his house was a natural extension of the old man himself, as much a part of him and his legacy to me as the Pork Pit was.

We got out of the car. It was after three now, but thanks to the snow, a sort of pearl gray twilight softened the cold edges of everything and made it seem lighter than it really was. In front of the house, snow crusted the flat lawn before the ridge fell away into a series of frozen, jagged cliffs. Snow and ice covered the gravel in the driveway as well, but I could still hear the stone's murmurs. Low, steady, and as quiet as the icy landscape around us.

No footprints marred the smoothness of the snow, and no sense of excitement, urgency, or dark desires rippled through the stones under my boots. No one had been near the house tonight. Good. That meant that Mab and her city full of bounty hunters hadn't unearthed my true identity, hadn't discovered that Gin Blanco was really the Spider—yet.

I led Bria over to the front door, which was made out of solid black granite. Thick veins of silverstone also swirled through the hard stone here and in other strategic places around the house, while bars made out of the magical metal covered the windows.

Bria let out a low, appreciative whistle. "I don't think I've ever seen that much silverstone in a single door before. You'd have to have a hell of a lot of magic to bust through that much of it."

"Remember what I said about easily defendable? Well, this is it," I said, unlocking the door and stepping inside.

I flipped on some lights, illuminating the hallway, and toed off my boots. Bria stepped inside and did the same.

"So this is where you live," Bria murmured, staring out at what she could see of the house. "Looks like you've got a lot of rooms in here, a lot of passageways, a lot of places to hide."

She had no idea. So many additions in so many different styles had been tacked on to the house over the years that the whole structure was something of a labyrinth. Rooms joined together, branching off into hallways that doubled back on themselves, led to different parts of the house entirely, or in some cases just dead-ended. Not the kind of place where you wanted to have to search for the bathroom in the dark, much less an assassin like the Spider. Still, the odd, overlapping designs gave me a clear advantage, since I knew the ins and outs of the whole house—and the best way to sneak up and stab someone in the back when she thought that she was creeping up on me instead.

Bria followed me through the house. I gave her a tour of the first floor and told her to make herself at home. My sister didn't say much, but she didn't miss anything either. She examined everything carefully, slowly, lingering on the well-worn, comfortable furniture and all the odd knickknacks that Fletcher had collected. Her face was blank, closed off, and I couldn't tell what conclusions, if any, that she'd drawn.

We wound up in the back of the house in the den, the room that I always migrated to late at night whenever I couldn't sleep and there was something on my mind. Like tonight and the bounty on my sister's head.

I plopped down on the old, plaid sofa and laid my head back, rolling it from side to side to loosen the stiff, tension-filled muscles in my neck. Bria didn't sit down next to me. Instead, she walked to the mantel over the fireplace and the four framed drawings that rested there. Three of the drawings were for an art class that I'd taken at Ashland Community College. My final assignment had been to sketch a series of runes, all with a connected theme.

I'd drawn the runes of my dead family.

The first drawing on the mantel was a snowflake, our mother, Eira's, rune, the symbol for icy calm. The second was a curling ivy vine representing elegance, and our older sister, Annabella. Bria's rune, the primrose, the symbol for beauty, was the third drawing, although my rendering of it wasn't nearly as elegant as the silverstone medallion that she wore around her neck.

The fourth picture was a bit unusual. It wasn't a true rune, not like the others. Instead, the drawing was of the multicolored neon sign that hung outside the entrance to the Pork Pit. An exact rendering of it, right down to the full, heavy platter of food the pig was holding. The barbecue restaurant and Fletcher were one and the same to me. After the old man's murder, I'd decided to honor him the same way I had the rest of my dead family. Hence the drawing.

Bria moved down the mantel, going from one frame to the next, stopping to stare at them all. I couldn't see her face, and I wasn't sure I wanted to. I didn't know that I wanted to see the emotions flashing in her eyes right now. All the anger, longing, and aching regret. The feelings already tightened my chest, tangled threads slowly strangling me from the inside out.

"I always wondered if you remembered me," Bria whispered. "If you remembered mother and Annabella. If you ever thought about them or me or what happened that night. If you ever missed them as much as I did. If you ever missed me as much as I missed you."

She turned to look at me, the memories and sadness blackening her pretty face like ugly bruises. Only these were wounds that would never fade, because I carried the scars with me just like she did—right on my torn, tattered heart.

"You remembered and thought about them just as much as I did."

I tried to smile, but my face felt stiff and frozen. "How could I forget?"

How could anyone forget what had happened that night? Watching my mother and Annabella disappear into balls of elemental Fire, realizing they were dead, then staring down at their ashy remains and trying not to vomit from the charred stench. It wasn't something I'd ever forget, but I didn't tell Bria that. She had her own horrible memories of that night.

I let out a long sigh. As terrible as that night had been, as much as it had scarred me on the inside and out, as much as it had shaped me into who and what I was, into the Spider, there was nothing that I could do about it. Memories never did anyone any good, and weepy sentiment was for fools too weak to suck it up and do what needed to be done.

What mattered now was keeping Bria safe and finding some way for me to get close enough to Mab to turn the Fire elemental into a pincushion with my silverstone knives. Protecting the people that I loved. That's what I had to focus on right now.

"Come on," I said, getting to my feet. "It's been a long day. Let's get you cleaned up, and then I'll show you where your bedroom is."

Once Bria was tucked away for the night in a room down the hall, I took a hot shower to wash Jenkins's blood off me, then crawled into my own bed. I stared at the ceiling and let out another sigh, resigned to what was going to happen now.

Ever since Fletcher's murder, I'd been having dreams. Horrible, horrible dreams. No, that wasn't quite right. The images weren't so much dreams as they were memories of my past. Try as I might, I couldn't stop the dreams from coming, couldn't keep the memories from bubbling up to the surface of my subconscious. Tonight was no exception. Even as I felt myself slipping under into slumber, the colors, sounds, and smells began to flash in front of my eyes . . .

The sound woke me. A murmur of unease that pressed against my temple like a cold washcloth. I concentrated on the sound, staring into the blackness that cloaked my bed. After a moment, I realized that it was the stone of our mansion. Something had upset it. The stones whispered all around me, the mutters growing louder, sharper, and more frantic with every second. Warning of danger . . . danger . . . danger . . .

I frowned. Danger? Here?

I slid out of my soft, warm bed, threw on a fleece robe,

*and stuffed my bare feet into my favorite blue slippers. Then
I eased open the door and peeked outside. Small spotlights
illuminated the hallway. Everything seemed normal. Maybe
the stones were wrong. But I couldn't shake the dread that the
element had stirred in me.*

*My nose twitched, and I realized that the faintest scent
of smoke hung in the air. I drew in another breath, and
the scent intensified, taking on a harsher, bitter stench.
Was the house on fire? That would certainly be enough to
upset the stones.*

*A bit of white fluttered at the end of the hallway, and
I stuck my head farther outside my door. Annabella, my
older sister, crouched in front of the curling, iron banister
that overlooked the main living room on the first floor. Icicles
thicker than my chubby fingers hung off the railing like jagged, misshapen teeth, and my sister's cold breath frosted in the
air, then fluttered to the floor in a shower of snowflakes. Even
at eighteen, Annabella's magic was still wild and uncontrol-
lable, manifesting whenever she was angry or emotional. I
wondered what had bothered her so much now—and why
she was up at two in the morning.*

"Annabella?" I whispered.

*Her head snapped around to me. "Get back in your room,
Genevieve!"*

*Her sharp, hissed tone made the dread in my stomach
swell up, as though I'd somehow swallowed one of the muttering stones. But instead of doing as she asked, I hurried
toward her. A sudden crack made my heart slam up into my
throat. Was that a gunshot?*

*My legs wobbled, and I fell to my knees beside Annabella.
She had the same beautiful blond hair and blue eyes as our*

mother, Eira, and resembled an icy angel in her long, white nightgown.

"What's wrong?" I whispered.

"Men. Inside the mansion," Annabella said. "They've already killed some of the servants."

My eyes widened. "Men? Why? What do they want? Money?"

Annabella shook her head. Either she didn't know or she just didn't want to tell me. But the worry pinching her face was more than enough to scare me. Whoever the men were, whatever they wanted, it couldn't be anything good. Not now, not this late at night.

"Mom heard them breaking in," Annabella said. "She told me to wait here until she came back. She's going to try to stop them."

I nodded, feeling better. Our mother was strong—the strongest elemental that I knew. Her Ice magic would be enough to protect her. Still, I reached for the spider rune that dangled from the chain around my throat. Toying with the small circle was a nervous habit of mine, one that I was trying to break. The silverstone medallion felt cold, smooth, and hard in my hand. I don't know why touching it always comforted me, but it did.

Until the body flew through the air.

The giant slammed into the stone fireplace before rolling off and landing on the floor. The force of his body hitting the fireplace caused the snow globes on the mantel above to wobble and fall. One by one, they slipped off their high, lofty perch and shattered on the stone below, a horrible symphony of sound.

The giant might have cared about all the shards of glass

shredding his skin—if he'd still been alive. I didn't need An-
nabella to tell me that he was dead—and that our mother
had killed him with her magic. Elemental Ice coated the
man's face, an inch thick in some places, giving his features
a strange, bluish tinge. Even his teeth were blue, his mouth
open in a silent scream.

Our mother had used her Ice magic to flash-freeze him.
That was bad enough, but I couldn't help but wonder why
there were giants in the house in the first place. What was
going on? What could they possibly want from us?

A second later, my mother ran into the downstairs room,
stopping just inside the far doorway. My mother whirled
around, and I realized that there was another figure behind
her. The person was standing in the next room over, so all I
could see of her were her hands.

Her bright, burning, flaming hands.

Orange-red flames twitched and danced like merry pup-
pets on the mystery woman's fingertips. I hissed in a breath
and shrank back against Annabella, pressing my body into
hers. A Fire elemental. Of all the magic users, of all the el-
ementals, they were the ones who scared me the most. Their
magic was hot, hungry, and cruel, and nothing at all like the
soft, soothing murmurs of the stones as they sang me to sleep.

My mother's hands began to glow blue-white with her Ice
magic. Eira gathered her strength, her power, her elemental
magic, until it formed a shimmering ball so cold that it made
my teeth chatter, even here, thirty feet above her.

The Fire elemental countered by increasing the flames on
her hands, shooting out her own intense heat. I could feel
it up here too—the hot, pulsing power. And that scared me
more than anything else had so far. The Fire elemental was

strong—just as strong as my mother was—and now they were going to duel.

To the death.

They faced each other, my mother and this abstract pair of burning hands. Then, with one thought, they threw their magic at each other.

The elemental Fire and Ice crashed together. Steam, smoke, and colorful sparks filled the room, the whole house even, making it hard to breathe. Their magic flickered against my skin, each one cracking across my flesh like hot and cold whips. I bit my tongue to keep from screaming at the sensation. I don't know how long they stood there, locked in this deadly battle, their magic warring against each other's.

But the Fire elemental was stronger.

She overcame my mother's magic one slow, agonizing inch at a time. The Fire burning on the ends of her fingertips expanded, getting closer and closer to Eira, evaporating all of the elemental Ice that she managed to form. Sweat and soot covered my mother's beautiful face, and strain tightened her slender neck. Eira wavered just for a second, just for an instant, and her blue eyes flicked up to the banister, first to Annabella, then to me.

"I'm sorry," I thought I saw her mouth to us.

Then her strength, her Ice, her magic, left her, and the elemental Fire swept over her.

One moment, my mother was there. The next, the blackened shell that had been her body crumpled to the floor. Bits of ash flaked off her charred remains at the impact and drifted up to me. Horrid, macabre confetti that settled on my face, my hands, my hair.

I started to scream—and scream—and scream, but Annabella clamped her cold hand over my mouth and shook me. The sharp motion penetrated my shrieking panic.

"Don't scream," she whispered. "Don't you dare scream. Don't make any noise at all. Go get Bria and slip out of the house. Run as fast as you can. I'll slow down the Fire elemental."

"No, Annabella! She'll kill you too!"

I tried to grab my sister's arm, but she evaded me and pounded down the stairs. She made it all the way to our mother's body. Annabella crouched down and started to touch her but thought better of it. Then her head snapped up, and she raised her hands, forming her own ball of Ice.

Once more, I saw a pair of burning hands. Annabella wasn't as strong as our mother had been. She never had a chance. My big sister tried to defend herself, tried to form a shield of solid Ice, but the searing flames roared through her magic like it wasn't even there, slammed into her chest, and ignited her white gown. For a moment, she looked like a candle, pretty, light, blond. And then she was gone. As dead and charred as my mother.

I swallowed my screams and turned away from the horrific sight. Bria. I had to get Bria. We had to get out of the house. We had to hide—hide or die . . .

"Gin! Gin! Wake up!"

I gasped in a breath and sat straight up in bed, like I was Frankenstein's monster that had just been electrified back to life. It took me a moment to realize that someone was holding me. My eyes slowly focused on Bria, who was standing over me, her hands on my shoulders like she'd been trying to shake me awake. I shuddered out an exhalation and came the rest of the way back to myself.

"I'm okay now," I rasped, wiping the cold sweat from my forehead. "Really. You can let go now."

She did as I asked, and I flopped down onto the bed, every part of me weak, limp, shaking, and exhausted. Bria didn't say anything, but I could feel her eyes on me in the darkness.

"So," I murmured. "How loud was I screaming this time?"

"Loud enough to wake me," Bria replied. "I thought that maybe someone had broken into the house. That maybe some of the bounty hunters had tracked us here."

"No, it was just me and my psychosis. I'm sorry that I woke you. Usually, there's no one around to hear me scream."

She was silent for a moment. "What—what were you dreaming about?"

I shrugged. "The usual. The night that our mother and Annabella died. I always see different parts of it, different bits and pieces."

"What did you see tonight?"

I grimaced, even though she couldn't see it in the darkness. "Oh, tonight was a real doozy. I dreamed about watching them die, about seeing them both disappear into balls of flames as Mab's elemental Fire washed over them."

"Oh."

Bria didn't ask me to elaborate on what I'd seen, and I didn't offer to tell her. It was one thing to know that your family had been murdered, to live your whole life with that pain, with that pulsing, hollow ache in your chest. It was another to hear the play-by-play, color commentary from someone who'd been there. From your big sister, who hadn't been able to do a damn thing to save the rest of your family.

I rolled over, turning away from her. Moonlight slipped in through the lace curtains, slicing everything with its silver cracks. That's how I felt right now—cold and cracked and hollow and empty.

"I'm sorry that I woke you, Bria. You can go back to bed now. I'll be fine. I usually never have more than one of those dreams a night," I said. "So go. Try to get some rest."

I waited for her to turn around, close the door behind her, and leave. I waited for the sound of her footsteps to fade away. I waited for the ache of her absence and alienation to fill me once more.

Instead of leaving, Bria lifted up the covers and crawled into bed with me. She hesitated, then scooted over next to me, until we were spooned together. It was something that we used to do when we were little girls. One of us would have a bad dream and would go get into bed with the other. Somehow, the two of us—together—were always able to go back to sleep, with no more bad dreams or nightmares.

It was something that I hadn't thought about in years, but now I remembered all those nights, and I knew that Bria did too. My baby sister moved closer still to me, her arm slipping up and over my waist, hugging me to her just the faintest bit.

"It's okay, Gin," Bria whispered against my damp hair. "I'm here now. We're together now. Somehow, we'll find a way to take down Mab—together. I promise you that."

Tears spilled down my cheeks at her soft, simple words, but I made no move to brush them away. I didn't want her to know that I was crying. I didn't want her to see me like this. Weak, emotional, unbalanced, uncertain. I was the big sister here. Genevieve Snow, Gin Blanco, the Spider. I should be taking care of her, not the other way around.

But all that didn't keep me from reaching down, covering her hand with my own, and giving it a gentle squeeze. Bria snuggled a little closer to me and let out a soft sigh of understanding—and maybe contentment too.

Curled together, we lay there in bed until sleep claimed us once more.

❈ 14 ❈

Bria slept in late the next morning. Not surprising. Being magically healed by Jo-Jo had left her feeling drained, as her mind tried to catch up to the fact that her body was suddenly well again, despite the beating she'd taken from the dwarven bounty hunter last night.

I'd been injured and healed as well, so I felt a little sluggish myself. But I didn't have the luxury of staying in bed, since I still had appearances to keep up and a barbecue restaurant to run. I woke Bria up long enough to get her to promise me that she'd stay put in the house today, then left to go to work.

The day passed by like any other at the Pork Pit. Sophia and I served up hot, steaming barbecue beef and pork sandwiches, along with thick, juicy cheeseburgers, sweet-and-sour coleslaw, baked beans, and more. All the while, a vat of Fletcher's secret barbecue sauce simmered on the back of the stove, flavoring the air with its spicy cumin kick.

People packed into the restaurant, standing three and four deep at the counter during the lunch rush. Everyone wanted a warm meal on such a cold, blustery day, and Catalina Vasquez and the rest of the waitresses who'd made it to work today swiped the plates of food as fast as Sophia and I could dish them up.

Still, despite the crush of bodies, I kept an eye on everyone who came and left the restaurant. Now that I knew exactly who and what I was looking for, I spotted more than a few of the bounty hunters. Men and women with hard, flat features and even harder eyes who watched everyone and everything around them, even while they were stuffing their faces with barbecue. Real rough types, who'd turn on you in a heartbeat if they thought there was any money to be made from the effort. In some ways, bounty hunters were worse than assassins. Assassins only wanted you dead, but bounty hunters were more than happy to deliver you into the hands of your worst enemy—alive—and all the implied tortures that went along with that, as long as they got paid in the end.

I kept a close eye on the bounty hunters who came into the Pork Pit, but none of them paid me any attention that they shouldn't. They were here for the food and nothing else.

I didn't know whether to be flattered or worried.

Finally, around three o'clock, after the daily lunch rush had come and gone, and the crowd had dwindled to only a few diners, the bell over the front door chimed, and Owen stepped inside.

He wore a tailored, navy suit that could be found in the closet of any wealthy Ashland businessman, topped by a long, matching coat. But on Owen, the layers of fabric went from being merely expensive to exquisite, draping over his shoulders just so and highlighting his tall, broad frame. Still, all the worsted wool in the world couldn't hide the strength of his body, the inherent toughness that radiated off him like the faintest flicker of heat from a burning candle. The dark blue color brought out the paleness of his skin, although his cheeks were red and ruddy from the cold. My gaze lingered on his chiseled features—the scar that slashed across his chin, the crooked quirk of his nose, the intense violet of his eyes. All things that made Owen go from merely sexy to heart-stoppingly devastating.

Owen stared at me, and I looked back at him. Emotions sparked and shimmered in the air between us. Heat. Desire. Need. Longing.

After a moment, his lips lifted into a sly, playful grin, and an answering rush of warmth flooded my heart. Owen had forgiven me for going after Mab by myself. He wouldn't have looked at me like that otherwise—not with such heat, not with such hope. The knowledge loosened a thick knot of tension in my stomach that I hadn't even been aware of until right now.

Looked like Finn wasn't the only one around here who had it bad for someone.

I'd called Owen last night while Bria was in the shower and had told him everything that had happened—the meeting at Northern Aggression, Lincoln Jenkins setting up Bria, the bounty hunters. Once again, Owen had been completely understanding of my situation, the way that he always was. I'd never had much in the way of luck, but

I knew that I'd used up every single scrap of good that I had in finding him, a guy who was so at ease with my alternative career and lifestyle.

I just wished that I had the courage to tell him that, to tell him—everything.

But every time I tried to let Owen know exactly how crazy I was about him, something got in the way. Like a bounty being put on Bria's head. My being the Spider and coming home covered in blood. Or simply my own twisted emotions and the fact that while I excelled at killing people, I wasn't so good at letting them get close to me in any way that didn't involve my silverstone knives.

Owen wasn't alone. Finn strolled in behind him, wearing a similar suit and coat, although Finn looked far more at ease and far smarmier in the expensive fabric.

They walked over to the counter and took the two seats closest to the cash register. Owen leaned over, and our lips met. It was a brief, chaste kiss, the casual kind that lovers exchange all the time. But just the faintest touch of his lips on mine filled me with all sorts of wicked, wanton ideas, like telling the waitresses to go home early and letting Sophia mind the restaurant for half an hour or so while Owen and I went into the back and explored the sturdiness of various appliances. Mmm.

Owen must have known what I was thinking because his grin widened, and he gave me a sly, slow wink.

Finn arched an eyebrow. "Do I need to leave you two alone?"

"Maybe," I murmured, surprised at the depth of feeling that Owen stirred in me just by walking into my gin joint. "But since I know that you won't, there's no point in asking."

Finn huffed out his indignation, and I rolled my eyes. Owen just laughed. So did Sophia, who stood behind the counter shredding lettuce for the rest of the day's sandwiches.

"So what are the two of you doing out and about together?" I asked. "Or do I even want to know?"

Finn gave me a smug smile. "Owen's decided to move some of his business interests over to my bank and let me handle them personally."

I looked at Owen. "You know that Finn will do everything in his power to rob you blind, right?"

"Of course," Owen rumbled. "I also happen to know that he'll do everything in his power to do the same to the tax men on my behalf."

Finn pouted, an exaggerated, wounded look on his face, but I just shook my head and chuckled right along with Owen. The two of them ordered, and Sophia and I worked to dish up their food, along with that for the few other people still lingering in the restaurant during this off hour.

Finn requested a burger, piled high with tomato, lettuce, red onion, and thick slabs of Colby-jack cheese, along with steak-cut fries and a triple chocolate milkshake. Owen opted for a barbecue beef sandwich with coleslaw, baked beans, and a side of creamy macaroni salad.

While the two of them ate, I saw to the other customers, fetching food, refilling drinks, bringing over extra napkins. When I was sure that everyone had everything they needed, I nodded my head at Sophia, telling her that she could take off for a while. The dwarf disappeared through the swinging doors that led into the back of the restaurant to join the waitresses who were already in the break room eating their own lunches.

I assumed my usual spot on the stool behind the cash register. Across from me, Owen and Finn continued munching on their food.

"So," I said in a casual voice, leaning my elbows on the counter. "What's the real reason that the two of you came here? Because I know that it just wasn't for the food, no matter how good it is."

They both froze, sandwiches halfway to their mouths, and exchanged a quick, guilty look that confirmed my suspicions. Finn sighed and lowered his half-eaten cheeseburger to his plate.

"Well," he said in a careful tone, not quite looking at me. "There have been some new developments concerning Mab."

"And what would those be, exactly?"

Finn sighed again. "She's actually going to be leaving her estate tonight."

I frowned. "Why the hell would she do that? She should be tucked away in the deepest, darkest part of her mansion and looking for someplace lower to go, given how close I got to her the other night, how close I came to killing her."

Finn shrugged. "Yes, but Ashland society waits for no woman, not even Mab. There's a big shindig tonight, and apparently the party is being held in Mab's honor. Kind of hard to skip out on it, even if everyone knows that you're being hunted by an assassin. And at this point, not showing her face would hurt Mab more than the chance that you could get to her tonight."

I nodded. Mab might have a stranglehold on the crime in the city, but Ashland had plenty of other underworld sharks who were hungry to knock the Fire elemental off her throne—folks like Phillip Kincaid, who owned the *Delta Queen* riverboat casino. Kincaid and various others had started circling around Mab and her organization ever since I'd helped Roslyn kill Elliot Slater, the Fire elemental's giant enforcer, and they'd only grown bolder since then. Finn had even heard reports about Kincaid cutting into Mab's extortion racket, something that he wouldn't have dared to do if she hadn't been distracted by the Spider.

"Besides," Finn continued, "the event has been on her schedule for weeks now, even since before Christmas when you took out LaFleur."

"Maybe it's been on her schedule," I said, "but don't you think it's rather *convenient* that she's sticking her head out of the sand right now? At this exact moment? Especially since her bounty hunters have come up with nothing so far?"

Finn shrugged again. "I thought of all that myself, but you said you wanted to know what Mab was up to. I'm just the messenger."

I looked back and forth between him and Owen. "And you told Owen first, didn't you?"

Finn had the good grace to wince. "Sorry, Gin. But neither one of us wants to see you get killed. So Owen and I made an agreement to save you from yourself."

"Is that so?"

My words were colder and harder than the two-inch-thick icicles hanging off the neon sign outside the Pork

Pit, but they had no effect on Owen and Finn. Instead, my lover and my foster brother stared right back at me, determination burning in their eyes just as much as it did in mine.

I didn't know whether to be pissed or touched. As much as I wanted to take on Mab by myself, as much as I needed to in order to keep everyone else safe, it was still nice to know that there were folks looking out for me. Just as Fletcher would have done if the old man had still been alive.

So I sighed and nodded, telling Finn and Owen that their concern was appreciated, even if I didn't think it was warranted. They both nodded back, and the tension among the three of us eased.

"So give me the details," I asked Finn. "Where is this party going to be and how do I crash it?"

Finn finished his last bite of sandwich, pushed his plate aside, and wiped his hands on a napkin. "That's the weird thing. It actually looks fairly doable. Mab and a couple hundred of her fawning sycophants are going to be at the ballroom at the Five Oaks Country Club, celebrating the season with a winter costume ball. The party starts at eight. I'm told that Mab will make her appearance around nine. And you'll love this, Gin. Guess what she's going as? What her costume is?"

"I have no idea. Satan's mistress, perhaps?"

Finn stared at me. "The Spider."

I blinked, wondering if I'd heard him right, or if he was just joking around, but his green gaze stayed steady and level with my gray one.

"You're telling me," I said in a slow voice, "that Mab is going to this costume party dressed like an assassin?"

Finn nodded. "That's the rumor I've heard."

"And what, do tell, will this particular assassin costume look like?"

He shrugged. "From what I hear, Mab's interpretation will involve lots of skin-tight red leather and knives. Of course, we both know that you prefer to wear black to hide the bloodstains, but Mab's putting her own spin on things."

Cold anger filled me at the Fire elemental's audacity; that she had the nerve to openly mock me in such a fashion, especially after I'd killed so many of her men, especially after the other night, when I'd almost killed *her*. But Mab wasn't doing anything to me that I hadn't already done to her. The Fire elemental was trying to get under my skin just like I'd already wormed my way under hers.

So I put my anger aside, sat there, and thought about things. First, Mab had hired bounty hunters to come to Ashland to flush me out. Then she'd upped the ante and put a bounty on Bria's head. And now, after I'd been a second away from killing her, from ending her miserable existence, she was going to dress up and be seen in public as, well, *me*.

"It's got to be a trap," I murmured. "There's just no other explanation for it."

Owen frowned. "What do you mean?"

I looked at him. "I mean that there's no other reason for Mab to leave the safety of her estate right now, not with her bounty hunters doing her dirty work. And why would she ever want to dress up like me? There's just no reason for it, unless she specifically wants me to know she'll be out in the open. The costume is just her way of mocking me that much more, of making sure I put in an appearance at the ball. She probably put the word out about that herself."

Worry tightened Finn's face. "That's what I'm afraid of too—that it's all just an elaborate trap. But you said you wanted to know what Mab was doing, so there it is."

The three of us fell silent. Owen pushed away his plate as though he'd lost his appetite, even though he hadn't finished his sandwich. Couldn't blame him for that. This whole thing made me sick too, but in a different sort of way.

"Well," I finally said. "If Mab's going to mock me with her little costume, then I should be there in person to see it, don't you think?"

Finn sighed. "Don't even think about it, Gin. The country club will be crawling with Mab's giants and probably some of the bounty hunters too. Slipping onto her estate was bad enough. They didn't know you were coming then. But the country club? They know you'll be tempted to make another run at Mab there tonight."

I shrugged. "So you'll find me a way. You always do."

"I'm going with you," Owen cut in.

This time, I sighed. "Owen—"

"No," he said, staring at me with his violet eyes—eyes that were just as hard, cold, and determined as mine had been a moment ago. "I'm not letting you do this alone, Gin. You promised me that you'd take some backup along the next time you went after Mab. Well, I'm volunteering to be it, no matter how dangerous it is."

I opened my mouth to protest, but he cut me off again.

"Besides, it'll look better anyway, the two of us at the

ball. We're a couple, remember? That's the kind of thing couples do. You're going to need some excuse to be at the ball. You just being Gin Blanco isn't going to cut it. Not this time. Call me crazy, but I don't think your name is on the guest list."

I wanted to argue with his logic—but I couldn't. I just couldn't. He was right. Alone, I'd be spotted sooner rather than later. With Owen, I would at least have a chance to get close to Mab, even if the whole thing was a trap.

So I tried another tactic. "You don't have to do this, Owen," I said in a soft voice. "You don't have to put your-self out there on the hook with me. Think of Eva. Think of how devastated she'd be to lose you."

Owen's face darkened, filling up with stormy emotion. "I'm also thinking of my parents, and how Mab killed them, how she burned them to death in their own house with her Fire magic, just as she did your family, Gin. I'm thinking about all the nights that Eva and I were cold and hungry living on the streets. I've already talked things over with Eva, and she agrees with me. I'm going with you to the country club, and I'm watching your back whether you like it or not."

In that moment, without a doubt, I knew that I loved Owen—loved him with every bent piece and warped shard of my heart, black, brittle, and broken though they might be. The knowledge left me dizzy and breathless, and I had to grip the counter to keep from falling off my stool.

Owen's mouth crooked up into a grin. "Besides," he rumbled, not noticing my reaction to my words, "it'll give you an excuse to wear some sexy little costume, which I will be all too happy to help you slip out of later."

The hot promise in his eyes took away what little breath I had left, and heat exploded in my stomach like fireworks streaking up into the night sky. Mmm. Sounded like a plan to me. Provided, of course, that I managed to slip through the swarm of giants sure to be at the country club. That I could corner Mab in the first place. That I could somehow survive the Fire elemental's incendiary magic. And the dozen or so other things that could go wrong.

But Owen's absolute, unwavering trust in me made me trust in myself. I could do this. I *had* to do this. I had to kill Mab. For me, for Bria, for Owen, for everyone else that I cared about.

"All right," I said, giving in. "You can be my date for the evening. But if things go bad, you are getting the hell out of there—immediately, no matter what I'm doing or how much trouble I'm in. Understand?"

After a moment, Owen nodded.

"As for you," I said, stabbing my finger at Finn. "You will go to Fletcher's house and stay with Bria tonight. Just in case any of our bounty hunters decide to show up there for whatever reason."

Owen going with me to the party would be bad enough. I didn't want Finn in the line of fire too. I couldn't bear it if anything happened to either one of them, but I'd already failed to save Fletcher from being brutally tortured and murdered in this very restaurant. I didn't want Finn to meet the same bad fate that his father had.

Finn grinned at me. "It will be my pleasure to keep tabs on sweet, sweet Bria."

His lecherous tone made me sigh once more. "I do

hope that the two of you can keep your hands off each other, at least until after I kill Mab."

"It will be tough," Finn admitted. "Given how crazy your sister is about me."

I snorted. "You mean given how much she'd like to slap that smug smile off your face."

"Every woman I meet wants to do that at one point or another, but most of them get over it pretty quick," Finn said, dismissing my concern with an airy, arrogant wave of his hand.

I shook my head. Owen laughed, but there was a hollow note in his chuckle, just the way there was in mine. All three of us knew that we were about to undertake the Spider's most dangerous mission yet—to kill Mab Monroe in a room full of people and get away with it. I didn't know if I could do it, if I could kill Mab, but I was sure as hell going to try.

And probably die later on tonight for my trouble.

❖ 15 ❖

Finn and Owen finished their food and left to start getting things ready, but I stayed at the Pork Pit with Sophia. I kept right on working—cooking, dishing up food, waiting tables, wiping them down after customers left. But my mind was already focused on tonight and the things that I would need to do to get close enough to Mab to kill her—and then get away clean afterward. Assuming, of course, that the Fire elemental didn't just blast me straight to hell with her magic. But at this point, I was determined to at least try to think positive.

I recognized what I was doing, of course. The mind-set that I was getting into. It was something Fletcher had taught me—how to leave myself, Gin Blanco, completely behind and morph into the cold, hard entity known as the Spider, whose only desire was getting to her target and whose aim was always deadly and true. Tonight, I knew that I'd need that separation, that mental toughness, more than I ever had before. Especially if I wanted to live to see the dawn.

Around six o'clock, though, I got the first of what would turn out to be many nasty little surprises during the night—when Ruth Gentry and Sydney strolled into the Pork Pit.

The door opened, making the bell chime, and I looked up from my paperback copy of *Medea*. The two of them stepped inside, and Sydney pulled the door shut behind them, cutting off the cold air that blasted into the restaurant. How polite of her.

While the girl fiddled with the door, Gentry's pale blue eyes scanned the Pit, taking in everything from the clean, worn booths to the blue and pink pig tracks that covered the shiny floor. There was nothing overtly threatening in Gentry's gaze, but I got the sense that she was making a mental checklist. Doors, windows, number of people inside, who might make trouble, who might make a good meat shield. It was probably the same little ritual that she did whenever she went somewhere new. Just like I did.

Gentry was the only one of the bounty hunters who'd seen me and lived to tell the tale, but I wasn't worried about being recognized or Gentry identifying my voice. I'd been wearing a ski mask the last time we'd met in the dark, snowy woods that ringed Mab's mansion, and we'd spent more time fighting than talking. Hell, if Gentry could somehow connect that person to Gin Blanco as I was now in my jeans, long-sleeved T-shirt, and blue work apron, then the bounty hunter deserved to nab me. Still, I wasn't going to be so foolish as to not keep an eye on her.

"Code red," I murmured to Sophia, walking past her to get some menus. "Bounty hunters at two o'clock. The ones who winged me the other night."

Sophia grunted, and her black eyes cut in their direction, but the dwarf didn't stop ladling up bowls full of baked beans for the current crop of customers. Still, I knew that Sophia had my back. If Gentry had come here looking for trouble, then the bounty hunter was going to get more of it than she'd ever dreamed of.

Menus in hand, I plastered my best, biggest, friendliest, most charming southern smile on my face and headed toward them. "Hi, there. Y'all want something good and hot to eat?"

Gentry looked at me and the menus in my hand, sizing me up just the way she had the other folks in the Pit. "Sure."

I led the two of them over to one of the booths that looked out through the storefront windows, put the menus down on the table, and stepped back, taking my order pad and pen out of the back pocket of my jeans.

"So, what'll it be?" I asked, as if they were just another pair of anonymous customers who'd walked in off the street instead of a couple of bounty hunters who'd love nothing more than to drag me off by my hair and dump me at Mab's feet.

"I'll have a cheeseburger, fries, and a raspberry lemonade," Gentry said, glancing over the menu.

"The same," the girl said in a soft voice.

I scribbled down their orders, collected the menus, and went to the back counter where Sophia was dishing up the latest order of baked beans.

"Trouble?" the Goth dwarf asked in her raspy, broken voice.

"We'll see. I can handle those two. You keep an eye out for any others who might come strolling in."

She nodded. We fixed their food, and ten minutes later, I put everything on the table in front of them.

Sydney immediately reached for her cheeseburger and sank her teeth into it. She chewed, swallowed, and let out a little sigh of happiness. Despite the bulky sweater that covered her frame, I could see how painfully thin she was. Her big, hazel eyes were sunken into her face, and the high, sharp edges of her cheekbones would have made a model jealous. The girl put down her burger long enough to push her sleeves back, revealing wrist bones that stuck out like doorknobs.

I knew the look and what it meant—that Sydney hadn't been eating well lately. For a while, probably. I wondered exactly what she was doing with Gentry and why the two of them were here in the Pork Pit to start with. I had a feeling that it just wasn't for the food, no matter how much the girl seemed to be enjoying hers.

"Can I ask you a question?" Gentry said, looking up at me instead of digging into her food.

"Sure."

She reached into the pocket of her quilted jacket, which looked just as old and well worn as the dress she'd sported at Mab's dinner party. A lesser woman, a lesser assassin, would have tensed at the suspicious movement, but not me.

Instead of that pearl-handled revolver that I'd seen her with before, Gentry drew a slim piece of paper out of her pocket. She held it out to me, and I took it from her. I wasn't too surprised to see that it was a head-and-shoulders shot of Detective Bria Coolidge, probably taken off the Ashland Police Department's website. So that's what Gentry was doing here, trolling for clues as to Bria's whereabouts. Smart, very, very smart.

"You ever seen that woman in here before?" she asked. "She's a detective. Name's Bria Coolidge. I hear that she likes to come in here with her partner, a giant named Xavier. The two of them usually eat lunch over at the counter, right next to that old cash register of yours."

Damn and double damn. Not only did Gentry know that Bria came in here on a regular basis, but she also knew where my baby sister liked to sit. The bounty hunter had done her homework. So much so that I wondered how much trouble it would be to lure Gentry into the alley behind the restaurant and introduce her to the sharp ends of my silverstone knives. My eyes cut to Sydney, who was still eating her cheeseburger. But then, I'd have the girl to deal with, and that was a line even I wouldn't cross.

I shrugged and handed the photo back to her. "Yeah, she comes in here—her and half the cops on the force. The food happens to be excellent. At least she's a better tipper than most of those other crooked, black-hearted sons of bitches. So what?"

"Has she been in here today?" Gentry asked, her pale blue eyes locked onto my face. "Will she be in tomorrow?"

I arched an eyebrow and gave her an amused look. "Sugar, I've got too many people wanting barbecue on a daily basis to keep up with one person's schedule. But no,

I don't think that she's been in here today, and she probably won't be because we're going to close a little early because of the weather. What's your interest in her, anyway?"

Gentry tucked the picture back into her coat pocket. "No reason."

I gave her a bored look, as though I couldn't have cared less about whatever she was up to, and went back behind the counter. For the next thirty minutes, I went through the motions, seeing to my other customers, refilling drinks, swiping credit cards, giving change. But I kept one eye on Gentry and Sydney.

The bounty hunter looked over everyone in the restaurant in between bites, her eyes moving from one face, one body, to the next in a slow, deliberate way. Sydney was much more interested in her food. The girl wolfed down her cheeseburger and fries in three minutes flat, so Gentry had me bring her another plate of food. Sydney might have gone hungry, but I didn't think that Gentry was the one who had starved her. The girl gave the bounty hunter an adoring, grateful look for ordering her the second burger and made a visible effort to eat it a little slower than she had the first one. A sad, weary smile creased Gentry's face at Sydney's obvious efforts to please her.

The two of them reminded me of Fletcher and the relationship I'd had with the old man when he'd first taken me in. I'd been so grateful to Fletcher for rescuing me from the cold, hard streets that I would have done anything for him—*anything*. Sydney had the same sort of obsessive, fawning gratitude toward Gentry. I wondered why; what bad thing had happened to the girl that Gentry had rescued her from. Maybe Finn could find out for me, since I'd asked him to look into the bounty hunter.

Curiosity. It was what was staying my hand now and keeping me from dragging Gentry into the alley and stabbing her to death. Ah, curiosity. It always got the best of me, even when I should have known better.

I should just have gutted Ruth Gentry where she sat. The bounty hunter had already proven that she was smart and dangerous. Instead of doing something stupid and pointless like staking out the police station or Bria's house, Gentry had thought to come to the Pork Pit instead—a place where my sister was known to hang out. That showed me the bounty hunter was definitely someone to be wary of.

I let Gentry and Sydney finish their meal in peace. Eventually, they came over to the counter to pay up and leave. Somewhere along the way, Gentry had found a toothpick in one of her pockets that she'd stuck in one corner of her mouth, giving her a hillbilly air.

"That was a fine meal," Gentry said, digging into her jeans and coming up with some small, crumpled bills.

The motion pushed back her jacket, and I spied the pearl revolver sitting in a holster on her black leather belt.

"Thanks," I murmured, careful not to stare at the gun. "But I can't take all the credit. Most of it goes to my cook over there."

Gentry's eyes flicked to Sophia, lingering on the spiked, black leather collar around her neck. She tipped her head to the dwarf. "My thanks then."

Sophia just grunted and turned back to the stove.

While I totaled the order and made change, my eyes

strayed to Sydney. She stared at one of the glass cake stands full of sinfully sweet sugar cookies that sat on the counter. Hunger and longing filled her hazel eyes, but she bit her lip and looked away from the treats.

Her small, wistful gaze hurt worse than a knife ripping into my heart.

I remembered feeling that way once upon a time, back when I'd been living on the Ashland streets. I'd spent hours staring in through restaurant windows and longing for all the food I saw inside—food that was hot, clean, and free of the worms and maggots that littered the scraps I'd been eating out of the Dumpsters. Oh yes, I'd stood outside those restaurants, and I'd stared in, hunger twisting my stomach into knots so hard and tight that I thought they would never straighten out again.

Some sort of wild, crazy emotion seized me then, and I put Gentry's change down on the counter. Before I knew quite what I was doing, I'd lifted the glass lid on the stand of cookies, gathered them all up, and dropped them into a white paper bag, which I shoved into the girl's thin chest. Sydney stared down at the pig logo printed on the side of the bag, the longing in her eyes so bright and hard that it took my breath away.

"Take 'em," I said in a thick voice. "We're getting ready to close, and they won't be eaten tonight."

Surprise filled the girl's thin face, followed by a more tremulous emotion—hope. Her hands tightened around the bag, making the paper crack and crinkle. I wondered how long it had been since she'd had something as simple as a cookie. I wondered how long it had been since some-one besides Gentry had done something nice for her. I wondered—I wondered too fucking much. Saw too much of myself in her, in Gentry. They were hunting me, hunting Bria. That made them my enemies, nothing more.

"Can I, Gentry?" the girl asked in a faint, whispered voice, looking over at her mentor. "Please?"

Another sad smile creased Gentry's face, making her look old, small, and tired. "Of course, Sydney. Just remember your manners to the nice lady."

Nice lady? If Gentry only knew that I was the one that she was looking for—that I was the Spider. The wanted assassin who could net her upward of five million dollars. Gentry would snatch those cookies out of Sydney's hands and draw her revolver faster than I could palm one of my silverstone knives.

Sydney beamed at her, then me. "Thank you, ma'am."

"It's Gin," I quipped. "Like the liquor. Not ma'am. I hate it when people call me ma'am."

Sydney mumbled an apology around the cookie that she'd already stuffed into her mouth. I picked up Gentry's change from the counter and passed it over to her. The bounty hunter took it and stared at me, her sharp eyes searching my face for something that only she knew or could even see.

For a moment, I wondered if she'd figured it out. If she realized exactly who I was.

But then, when she didn't draw her revolver, I knew that she hadn't and that she wouldn't. Because how could an assassin like the Spider, a cold-hearted killer, ever do something as good as give food to a hungry girl?

"Thank you, Gin," Gentry said in a soft voice. "For everything."

"No problem," I replied in a mild tone, playing the part of the simple restaurant owner once more. "Y'all come back now."

Gentry gave me a small smile. "We will."

Then she put her arm around Sydney, who was on her third cookie, and the bounty hunter and her apprentice left the Pork Pit.

❖ 16 ❖

"What do you think?" I asked. "Is it too much?"

Finn tilted his head and gave me a critical once-over. "You're dressed up as an ice queen dominatrix. I don't think there *is* such a thing as too much."

I stared at myself in the floor-length mirror that had been set up in the den in Fletcher's house. Trust Finn to perfectly describe my garish getup. I wore a pair of ice blue leather pants that laced all the way up my legs on both sides. A leather bustier done in the same color and trimmed with silver thread covered my chest, pushing my breasts up to new and spectacular heights. A matching collar set with silverstone squares ringed my neck.

A leather jacket covered the bustier, which let me tuck my two usual silverstone knives up my sleeves. I sported another knife against the small of my back, while two more waited in the sides of my stiletto boots.

Jo-Jo had come over a little while ago to do my

makeup, which consisted of rimming my eyes with silver liner and painting my lashes and lips the same cold color. The dwarf had also pulled my chocolate brown hair up into a high, tight ponytail and sprinkled silver glitter over the slicked-back locks. All put together, I looked like I was in the mood for a night of cold sex and frostbitten pain.

"Where did you get all this leather from?" I asked, turning to stare at myself from another angle.

"From Roslyn's stash of costumes at Northern Aggression," Finn said. "Where else would I get such come-hither clothes?"

Since leaving the Pork Pit, Finn had used his various connections to find out that there was a theme to tonight's masquerade ball—Fire and Ice. How ironic. Finn had even managed to get photos emailed to him of what some of the other folks would be wearing in order to help Owen and me blend in. Hence all the leather.

"You look like a completely different person," Bria said from her spot on the couch.

I turned and looked at my baby sister, who had an unreadable expression on her face. After closing down the restaurant, I'd come over to Fletcher's house to tell her what was going on—and exactly what I was up to. Bria hadn't liked it, hadn't liked my making another run at Mab, but there wasn't much she could do about it. Not without getting captured by Gentry or one of the other bounty hunters and making the mess we were in that much worse.

"I don't know. I think I like Gin's costume a lot better than mine," Owen rumbled and stepped into the den.

If I was the ice-queen dominatrix, then Owen was my eager client for the night. He also wore leather pants, although his were black and topped by a jacket and matching vest crisscrossed with silverstone chains. The magical metal clanked with every step he took. The two of us looked like a pair of sexual deviants ready to get our freak on, but according to Finn's info, our costumes would be among the tamer ones at the party.

Owen and I were already late, so I checked my knives one final time, then turned to him.

"You ready?"

Owen nodded. "As I'll ever be."

"We should go then," I murmured.

I looked at Finn, then turned to Bria. My sister hadn't said much while we'd been making plans and getting ready, but worry tightened her face—worry for me. The emotion made my heart twist and soar in my chest all at the same time. Despite what I was, despite all the people that I'd killed, Bria had somehow come to care for me, at least a little bit. It was more than I'd ever dreamed of—and somehow, it made everything that I'd suffered over the years worthwhile.

Bria leaned forward and grabbed my hand. Then, to my surprise, she reached for her Ice magic. For a moment, I wondered what she was doing, but then I felt her cool power trickle into the silverstone ring on my right index finger. Her ring, the one that she'd given me for Christmas. A slender silver band with a spider rune stamped in the middle of it.

Lots of elementals wore jewelry made out of silverstone, since the metal was capable of absorbing and hold-

ing their magic. By wearing pieces of the metal, elementals could have access to an extra influx of power should
they need it. Like, say, if they decided to duel another
elemental, to test their power against the other person's.
It wasn't cheating, not exactly, since everyone did it, but
it was still sneaky.

The two rings on Bria's left index finger hummed with
her Ice magic, as did the primrose rune that she wore
on the chain around her neck. My ring was small and
thin, but the silverstone still soaked up quite a bit of Bria's
power, until it felt like a band of Ice pressing against my
skin. The sensation wasn't an unpleasant one. If anything,
it comforted me to be taking a piece of my sister with me
into battle.

"Thank you for that," I said. "I had been meaning to
store my magic in the ring, but hadn't done it yet. I'm not
one for wearing jewelry."

"I'd noticed that," Bria said in a wry tone. "And I know
that you prefer to use your knives, but you just never
know what you might need. Especially . . . tonight."

I nodded, not sure what to say. I didn't want to offend
my sister or push her farther away, but we both knew
what I was planning to do tonight—kill Mab in cold
blood the way that I had so many other people. Even if
she deserved it for everything she'd done to us, part of
Bria would have preferred to handle the Fire elemental
through legal means, to throw her in jail and let her rot.

Not me. I just wanted Mab dead, and I wasn't picky
about how she got there.

"Just—just be careful, Gin. Okay?" Bria asked, staring
at me.

I squeezed her cold fingers with mine. "I always am, baby sister. I always am."

Thirty minutes later, Owen steered his BMW up the driveway that led to the Five Oaks Country Club, where the masquerade ball was being held. Five Oaks was the snobbiest, most expensive, and highfalutin country club in Ashland, and only the insanely wealthy and powerful were allowed to be members.

I stared out the window at the snow-covered buildings of the club. The last time I'd been here was several months ago when I'd been stalking Alexis James, the Air elemental who'd tortured and murdered Fletcher. Alexis had managed to outmaneuver me that day, taking Finn and Roslyn hostage and escaping before I could kill her. I couldn't afford to be that sloppy tonight, not with Mab, or I'd be the one who wouldn't be leaving the club alive.

"You ready?" Owen asked in a soft voice.

I let out a breath and nodded. "As I'll ever be," I said, echoing his words.

Owen leaned over in the darkness of the car and pressed his lips to mine. For a moment that was all too brief, I just let myself feel—Owen's lips warming mine, the faintest rasp of his stubble against my skin, his fingers sliding down my cheek. I breathed in, letting his rich, earthy scent fill my nose.

And then the kiss ended, and I was the Spider once more.

A valet came and took the car away. After we made note of where he put it, Owen and I strolled inside the country club arm in arm. Owen gave his engraved invitation to the tuxedo-clad vampire manning the interior door. The vamp waved us on, and we stepped into the main ballroom. We moved to one side of the open doors, getting our bearings and watching the ebb and flow of people.

Five massive, circular buildings comprised the Five Oaks Country Club, including the ballroom before us, which covered several thousand feet and towered four stories into the air. Multiple sets of stairs led to the upper levels, each of which featured a balcony that circled the entire ballroom. The walkways made it all the better for the rich snobs to look down on their peers. A glass dome arched high overhead, forming the ceiling. Through the glass, I could just make out the soft curve of the moon. The bright silver sliver peeked through the thin clouds that wisped across the sky like a child playing peek-a-boo. Now you see me, now you don't.

Floor-to-ceiling glass windows lined the back wall of the ballroom, along with doors that led outside. In daylight hours, the sweeping view would show off the club's acorn-shaped swimming pools, several tennis courts, and, of course, the green carpet of the back nine. Tonight, though, only darkness and snow peeped through.

Normally, round tables covered with pale peach linens would have filled the ballroom, each one with the country club's rune—an acorn—stitched in gold thread in the center of the tablecloths and napkins. Since this was a masquerade ball, the decorations had been swapped out accordingly. Long, low settees done in red and black velvet ringed a black-and-white, checkerboard dance floor. Abstract elemental Ice sculptures squatted here and there throughout the ballroom, while more icicles dripped down the walls and clustered together in lieu of actual flowers. Black and crimson pillar candles thicker and taller than my arms burned in the middle of some of the icy arrangements, the flickering flames making the frosted shards glitter like diamonds.

I had to give Finn his props, because he'd been right about our costumes. Owen and I looked practically tame and toothless in our leather, compared to how much skin some of the trophy wives were showing. One woman walked by wearing nothing but a diamond choker and strategically placed bits of elemental Ice—shaped like sharp, curving thorns no less. Another vamp wore several long, fluttering layers of gauzy red silk, although the fabric was far too transparent for the woman to be the chaste angel that her ruby halo proclaimed her to be. I even saw one woman dressed completely in silver spandex. She was supposed to be a superhero, I think. Karma Girl or somebody like that.

We grabbed a couple of drinks at the bar and circulated through the room. To keep up appearances, Owen chatted with all the business types that he knew. I made the appropriate polite noises when called upon, but I scanned the crowd the entire time, looking for my prey for the evening—Mab Monroe.

She appeared about twenty minutes after we did, a little trilling trumpet of fanfare heralding her arrival. Conversation dulled to a low hush at the sound, and all eyes turned to the entrance. A moment later, Mab stepped inside, dressed just as Finn had said she would be.

Dressed as the Spider.

Crimson leather covered the Fire elemental from head to toe, every inch of it molded to her lush, curvy figure, making it seem as though she'd bathed in blood. Maybe she had, given all the other horrible things she'd done.

The leather made Mab's hair look even redder than it really was. Tonight the soft, curling waves reminded me of ribbons of fire swirling around her head. As always, Mab wore her trademark necklace—a large, circular ruby surrounded by several dozen flat, gold, wavy rays. A sunburst. The symbol for fire. Mab's rune.

The Fire elemental turned her head to speak to someone just inside the door. The candlelight glinted off the diamond cutting on the gold, making the rays spark and flash, while the ruby glowed with its own inner fire. But the sunburst wasn't the only symbol that Mab was wearing tonight.

The bitch also had on a spider rune—my rune.

A small circle surrounded by eight thin rays. The symbol was stitched in glossy black thread on the left side of Mab's crimson catsuit—right where her heart would be, if she even had one and not just a gaping maw in her chest.

Mab had taken the costume one step further. A pair of knives glinted in the black leather belt that circled her waist. Truth be told, they were fairly accurate versions of my own weapons—the ones that I wanted to reach for right now.

Anger burned in my heart at her blatant mockery of me, and my vision went red with rage. Once again, just for a second, I let myself feel the emotion, let the anger pump through my veins, let the thumping roar of it drown out everything else.

And then I put it aside—pushed it down into the pit of my stomach where it would continue to smolder but not consume me. This was a trap, after all, and the costume was just another piece of it, something else to lure me in, to make me lose control. To make me careless, something that I would not allow to happen. Not tonight.

So I stared at my enemy again, this time with narrowed eyes and a cold, calm heart.

"Are those real silverstone knives she's wearing?" I murmured to Owen.

He cocked his head to one side, and his violet eyes began to glow ever so slightly. Owen was using his magic, reaching out with his elemental talent for metal.

"They are," he murmured back. "High-end ones too. Made of almost pure silverstone."

We watched as Mab shook hands with a dwarf dressed like a miniature version of Jack Frost.

"What do you want to do, Gin?" Owen asked.

"Nothing," I said. "She's got too many people around her right now, and she's probably expecting me to strike immediately. Let's give her a chance to settle in and get good and bored waiting for me to make my move."

Owen nodded, and we moved off into the crowd.

But Mab wasn't the only enemy that I had here tonight, because she'd brought someone with her—Jonah McAllister.

McAllister was Mab's lawyer, the number-two man in her organization who was responsible for burying the Fire elemental's foes in so much legal red tape that they choked on it. Usually, McAllister wore a suit that was as slick and sharp as he was, but tonight the lawyer had forgone the ball's Fire and Ice theme in favor of dressing up like a pirate. *Yargh*.

A black patch covered one of his cold brown eyes, although he hadn't bothered putting a bandana over his styled coif of thick silver hair. A loose white shirt stretched across his chest, topped off by a red sash that was patterned with Mab's sunburst rune. The shirt and sash tucked into a pair of black breeches, which themselves tucked into a pair of matching boots. McAllister also had a curved scimitar strapped to his waist, made out of the same kind of silverstone as Mab's faux Spider knives, from the looks of it.

Despite his sixty-something years, McAllister's face was as smooth as glass underneath his eye patch. The lawyer was one of those who used Air elemental facials to fight the ravages of time. In fact, he was more vain about keeping his face wrinkle-free than most women.

Jonah McAllister had an active desire to see me dead, ever since I'd killed his son, Jake, a few months ago. Jake had come into the Pork Pit one night and tried to rob my gin joint. When I'd put Jake in his place, he and his father had gotten a little upset about it, threatening to run me out of business, among other, more unpleasant things.

A few days later, Jake had confronted me at a party at Mab's mansion with the intention of raping and murdering me. After he got done spouting his threats, I'd stabbed him to death with one of my knives and left his body in the Fire elemental's bathtub.

As I'd been in disguise at the party, Jonah McAllister had no real proof that I'd killed his son. But since I, as Gin Blanco, was one of the few people who'd ever dared to stand up to his kid, McAllister had rightly assumed that I'd had something to do with Jake's death. He just couldn't prove it. Still, he'd been keeping an eye on me ever since, waiting for his chance to strike.

Maybe if things went well with Mab tonight, I'd take out Jonah too. A little reward to myself for a job well done.

McAllister saw me staring at him. His nostrils flared with anger, and his mouth puckered into a cold frown that didn't register at all on the rest of his tight, ageless face. Since I was on Owen's arm tonight, there was nothing that McAllister could do about my being here, and we both knew it. So I waggled my fingers at him and blew the bastard a kiss. McAllister's mouth pursed that much more, but I didn't care.

Because I was ready to end this—all of this—tonight.

The minutes slipped by and turned into one hour, then two. I kept my attention on Mab as much as I could, waiting for her to separate herself from the crowd and her giant bodyguards who roamed through the room. I counted five of them on the ballroom floor, never moving more than a few feet away from the Fire elemental, looking for anyone suspicious or out of place. Even more giants strolled along the balconies above my head, continually circling the area. Their diligence would have made it impossible for me to station myself on a higher floor and snipe Mab from above, even if I'd managed to somehow sneak a crossbow into the club.

For her part, Mab seemed content to stay in the middle of the crowd and not wander off by herself where I could kill her. Still, I was the Spider, and I was good at being patient. I'd waited seventeen years for this moment. A few more minutes or even a few more hours was nothing in comparison to that.

Just before midnight, though, I finally got my chance.

Jonah turned to speak to someone and then swiveled back toward Mab—hitting her arm and spilling his bourbon all over the front of her crimson catsuit in the process. The liquor soaked into the spider rune on Mab's chest, making the symbol look like an inky stain bleeding over her heart.

The conversation around them froze, as Mab glared at her attorney, her black eyes as cold as the Ice sculptures that decorated the ballroom. Jonah murmured a hasty apology, but Mab was having none of it. The Fire elemental brushed him off with a wave of her hand.

Then she left the ballroom.

Mab stalked through the open double doors and vanished from sight, probably headed toward one of the bathrooms to try to wipe the bourbon off her expensive leather. I waited several seconds, expecting at least one or two of her giant bodyguards to fall in behind her. But none of them did.

"That looked a little too deliberate to me," Owen murmured.

"Oh, yeah," I replied. "It was about as subtle as a sledgehammer to the head. But it means that her men have no clue who I am and that she's tired of waiting for me to show myself. So she's putting herself out there instead, the final bit of bait in the trap, which means that I have to follow. So wish me luck."

"Good luck," Owen said.

He didn't kiss me, not this time, but our eyes locked together. No words were spoken—we didn't need them. I could see the emotions flashing and sparking in Owen's gaze. Worry. Concern. Determination.

Love.

I stared back at him, trying to tell Owen all the things I wanted to say to him, all of the things that I just couldn't find the words for. He nodded once and squeezed my hand, his fingers warming my icy ones.

I squeezed back, then slipped out of the ballroom, heading after Mab.

At last.

❄ 17 ❄

I stepped through the double doors of the ballroom and turned to my right, just as Mab had done. The Fire elemental strolled down the hallway about a hundred feet ahead of me, before coming to a junction and turning right again.

I followed her, although I dawdled, staring at the oil paintings on the walls, the crystal vases with their elaborate arrangements of roses, and anything else that caught my eye. Going straight after the Fire elemental would have tipped my hand, but now I was just another bored costumed character escaping the cloying confines of the ballroom in search of some fresh air. At least, that's the persona that I affected. Whether it would work well enough to get me close to Mab remained to be seen.

Just as I'd suspected, the Fire elemental headed for one of the women's bathrooms, opening the door and disappearing inside. I examined the pattern etched onto a Tiffany lamp before following her.

As befitting the grandiose nature of Five Oaks, the bathroom was just as monstrous and ostentatious as everything else. It was the size of a small house, with a large, formal sitting area that was all velvet couches and gilded mirrors, for ladies of a more delicate nature, should they need a place to rest and refresh their makeup. A few women clustered together in groups on the couches, already gossiping and exchanging catty comments about the night's ball, who had worn what, and who was fucking whom. A swinging door led into the bathroom itself, so that's where I headed.

An expanse of creamy white marble flecked with gold greeted me, along with real gold faucets and all the other nonsensical features that one finds in upscale bathrooms, where people have more money than sense to spend on the finest toilets that their trust funds can buy.

Mab was keeping up her charade rather well, standing at one of the sinks and dabbing at the bourbon stains on her crimson leather with a damp cloth. But there was a watchfulness in her black eyes, a tightness in her face, a stiffness in her whole body that told me she was ready to fry whoever came through the door after her.

So I ignored her.

A woman washed her hands at the sink in between me and Mab, and I didn't have a clear shot at the Fire elemental anyway. I went into one of the stalls, closed the door, and did my lady business, keeping up my charade that I was just another bored bimbo coming in here to use the facilities and get a break from the booze and bullshit that permeated the ballroom. I flushed the toilet, left the stall, and moved over to one of the sinks to wash my hands.

Mab stood in the same spot as before at the long counter, still dabbing at her red leather, still watching everyone who entered the bathroom. Women came and went in groups of ones and twos, a steady stream as befitting the crowd that had turned out for the ball. Mab's black eyes finally turned in my direction, but I opened the tap and soaped up my hands like that was the only thing in the world I was here for. I made my movements small, casual, ordinary, as if I were no more a threat to Mab than a fly on the wall.

I couldn't help but grimace at the irony, though. The last time that I'd been this close to the Fire elemental had been in another bathroom—hers—the night that I'd killed Jake McAllister. I'd been disguised as a blond, busty hooker, one of Roslyn's girls from Northern Aggression, and I'd gone so far as to proposition Mab in order to distract her from finding Jake's body in her bathtub. The Fire elemental had turned me down, with obvious regret, but my ruse had helped me escape.

I wondered which one of us would make it out of here alive tonight.

I kept my face calm, serene, blank, as Mab stared at me. The Fire elemental frowned, as if something about me bothered her, and I wondered if the moment that I'd been waiting so long for was here. If Mab had finally recognized me as the Spider.

Like everyone else in Ashland, Mab knew me as Gin Blanco. In fact, the Fire elemental had been there the night that Jonah McAllister had ordered Elliot Slater to beat me at Ashland Community College to try to find out what I knew about Jake's death. Mab knew exactly who I was and what I looked like as Gin—especially when I was covered with my own blood.

The door swung open again, and two more women stepped inside. After another second of staring at me, the Fire elemental turned her attention to the two women, giving them the same sharp perusal.

I dried my hands, left the bathroom, and stepped out into the hallway. But I didn't go back to the ballroom. If I did that, I would lose whatever chance I might have to kill Mab. The Fire elemental wouldn't expose herself again. Not tonight.

So I meandered down the hallway, my eyes scanning the rooms that branched off either side, looking for a spot for a potential ambush. Mab had been expecting someone to come at her in the bathroom. In those tight quarters, the odds were in her favor—she could easily fry her attacker with her Fire magic before she had time to retreat or mount any kind of defense. It was exactly what I would have done if I'd been in Mab's position.

But maybe luck would finally smile on me, and the Fire elemental would lower her guard and be careless enough to let me take her by surprise on her way back to the ballroom.

More than a few folks moved back and forth in the hallways, going from the ballroom to the bathrooms and back again, or outside for a quick smoke or an even quicker fuck. They were all wrapped up in their own little dramas, so no one saw me slip into a room and close the door almost shut behind me. No lights burned in the chamber, which was a sitting area, but I could still make out the crouching shapes of the thick, heavy furniture. I stayed in the shadows by the door and palmed two of my silverstone knives. Then I waited.

More people came and went in the hallway in front of me, laughing, talking, drinking, gossiping. Normally, I wouldn't have dreamed about doing a hit in a place like this, one that was so open, so exposed, and with so much foot traffic. But I didn't have a choice. Killing Mab was the only way to get the bounty off Bria's head, and I'd be damned if the Fire elemental would ever get her hands on my sister.

I started counting off the seconds in my head. Ten . . . twenty . . . thirty . . . But Mab was being just as patient as I was, because I stood in the shadows five minutes before the bathroom door down the hall opened, and Mab stepped outside. The Fire elemental stopped where she was a moment, surveying the scene around her. Her mouth thinned out into a flat, ugly slash in her face. Whatever she'd expected to happen in the bathroom, the fact that I hadn't taken the bait infuriated her. My hands tightened around my knives. Not for long, though. Not for long.

Mab rapped on the next door down the hallway, and two giants slid outside. Ah, so that's where she'd stashed her backup, in the next room over, ready to come in behind me if I somehow got away from her in the bathroom.

"Anything?" Mab snapped. Her anger made her normally delicate voice rasp almost as badly as Sophia's.

The giants both shook their heads.

"Nothing, ma'am," one of them rumbled. "We've checked everyone on the guest list. There's no one on the grounds who wasn't invited and identified when they came inside. No missing waiters, no extra workers, nothing like that at all. None of the regular staff even called in sick. If the Spider's here, we can't find her."

The Fire elemental glared at her two men. "Incompetent fools," she snarled. "Go check again. The bitch has to be here. She wouldn't pass up a chance like this."

The giants nodded and scurried away to go do their mistress's bidding. They passed my hiding spot and made the turn to go back toward the ballroom.

Mab paced back and forth in the hallway, muttering something under her breath. I imagined it wasn't very complimentary to me, though. A few people started to wander down the hall toward the bathroom, but one look at Mab had them backtracking the way that they'd just come. Good. I didn't need an audience for this.

I stood there and waited, just waited for her to come closer, close enough that I could leap out of the shadows and bury my knife in her back with one swift, fatal blow.

Finally, the Fire elemental dampened down her anger and quit muttering. She turned on her heel and stalked down the hall toward me. My hands tightened around my silverstone knives that much more. Thirty feet. Twenty . . . ten . . . five . . . Mab walked past my hiding spot, not even bothering to glance at the partially closed door.

I drew in a breath, slipped out of the room, and fell in step behind her, gathering my strength for what was to come.

I'd spent years learning how to be quick, quiet, and invisible, so Mab never heard the door open, and she never sensed my creeping up behind her. She was moving quicker than I'd anticipated, but five more steps and I'd be in range. Five more steps, and I could finally kill her.

Four . . . three . . . two . . . one . . . I raised one of my silverstone knives, ready to strike—

And that's when Jonah McAllister rounded the corner and entered the hallway in front of us. He spotted me at once—along with the knives in my hands.

"Behind you!" McAllister yelled.

Fuck. Just—*fuck.*

If I could, I would have slipped back into the shadows. But I was too committed now to turn back or wait for another opportunity. There was nothing else to do but go through with my strike.

McAllister's warning tipped off Mab, and she threw herself to one side. So instead of punching into her back, my knife only nicked her shoulder. Mab hissed with pain, and she went down in a heap on the floor. I started to throw myself on top of her to finish the job with my other knife, but some sense of self-preservation, some subconscious whisper of warning, some sense that it just couldn't be that fucking *easy,* made me pull back at the last second.

Good thing, since her fists burst into flames.

The elemental Fire flickered around her fingers and spread outward, snapping and cracking against her skin. I bobbed and weaved, trying to duck the arcing flames and stab her, but Mab managed to stay just out of arm's—and knife's—reach. Meanwhile, McAllister started bellowing for the giants who'd just left the hallway.

"Guards!" the lawyer roared. "Guards!"

I had maybe fifteen seconds before someone answered

his frantic call, and I planned to make the most of them. This time I didn't hesitate. I reached for my Stone magic, used it to harden my skin, and threw myself on top of Mab, all in one motion, my first silverstone knife slashing through the air again.

Mab saw the movement out of the corner of her eye and rolled away at the last possible second. Again, my knife only scraped along her arm, instead of doing the massive, fatal damage that I so desperately wanted it to do.

But I wasn't done yet—not by a long shot. I propelled myself forward that much more. My body slammed into the Fire elemental's, and we hit the floor again. Mab immediately blasted me with her magic. The hot, hungry flames engulfed my body, forcing me to push back with my Stone magic just to keep from being burned alive. Even then, I could feel the strength of Mab's power—the sheer, raw, all-consuming force of it. I brought all the Stone magic that I had to bear, but her Fire still burned me, cutting through my defenses and making blisters pop out on my skin, searing my flesh one layer at a time.

But I wasn't the only one who felt the effects of Mab's overwhelming power.

Her Fire magic also ignited the carpet underneath our rolling bodies, and more flames and smoke began to fill the hallway. Mab swung her fists at me, and with every blow, red-hot sparks fluttered up into the air like butterflies. The sparks only helped spread the elemental Fire, which leaped up the walls and consumed everything in its path, including the expensive oil paintings and elegant drapes hanging there.

Over and over, we rolled together, with me trying to stab Mab with my silverstone knives and her blasting me with her Fire magic. The threat of my knives distracted and kept her from truly unleashing her elemental power on me, but the flames burning on her fists also blocked me from doing the quick, deadly damage that I wanted.

It was a fucking stalemate.

By this point, other people had noticed what was going on, and hoarse screams and shouts filled the air, along with thick smoke and the blare of a fire alarm. But even that sharp, steady clang-clang-clang couldn't quite drown out the sounds of our guttural snarls. Heavy footsteps also thumped down the hall, making the floor quiver and quake, as Mab's giants ran through the flames toward us.

And I realized that I'd already lost.

I just couldn't get close enough to Mab to stab her with my knives, not without being consumed by her Fire myself. My Stone magic just wasn't strong enough to completely shield me. Maybe I should have used my Ice power as well, but I wanted to have a little bit of magic left in the tank for my getaway. Besides, I'd planned to stab Mab in the back, not confront her. Of course, that plan had gotten shot to hell, like so many of my best-laid ones before it.

Now, with more and more of her giants filling the hallway, my escape route would soon be cut off. I knew what would happen after that. Mab would pin me down and burn me to death, just like she had my mother and older sister before me.

And then she'd go after Bria.

Fletcher had always told me that there was no shame

in retreating, in running away, even if you missed your target. Survival was the only thing that ever really mattered in the end. As long as I was alive, I still had a chance to kill Mab—even if tonight wasn't going to be the night. The old man's wisdom had saved me more than once, and I saw no reason to doubt it now. I just hoped I hadn't waited too long to take his advice.

I snapped up my left hand and punched Mab in the face, even though the action caused me unbelievable pain as her flames licked and burned my skin. Screams, snarls, and curses spewed from my lips like venom. The sharp blow stunned the Fire elemental, and her magic flickered and dimmed just enough for me to roll away from her and get back up on my feet. On the other side of the hallway, Mab did the same, her head whipping around in my direction.

Through the smoke and flames, our eyes locked together. Gray on black. Anger, hate, and loathing burned between us, a living, palpable thing even brighter than the elemental Fire that filled the hallway. I knew the second that Mab recognized me. The Fire intensified on her fists, so hot that it seared my skin all the way across the hallway, even though I was still holding on to my Stone magic to try to protect myself from her power.

"Gin Blanco!" Mab hissed. "I should have known!"

Yeah, she should have. But I didn't have time to trade quips with her, especially since she was drawing back her fist to send a ball of fire at me—one that would end me.

I sprinted down the hallway, heading back toward the bathroom. But that wasn't my goal—the Exit sign at the end of the corridor was. Even as I ran, I could feel Mab gathering more and more of her elemental strength, holding on to more and more of her Fire power. I was moving away from her as fast as I could, but still, her magic chased after me, stabbing my skin like thousands of red-hot needles. She was going to throw everything she had at me, and if I didn't get out of the hallway before she did, I'd be dead.

Up ahead, a giant who I recognized as one of Mab's men stepped out of a room that branched off the corridor. The bodyguard ran straight at me, his long, beefy arms outstretched, like he wanted to crush me in a bear hug. And I saw a way to save myself—the *only* way to save myself from Mab's elemental Fire.

So I let him.

I slammed myself into the giant's body, letting him wrap his arms all the way around me, and then pivoted and spun around as hard as I could. The move surprised the giant, and his feet moved of their own accord, twirling him around and putting his broad back between me and Mab.

A second later, Mab's elemental Fire slammed into him.

The giant screamed as the flames swept over his body. He had no elemental magic, no power of any sort, so there was no way that he could protect himself. Hell, I would have been fried extra-crispy if his body hadn't shielded mine and if I hadn't grabbed hold of my Stone magic once more and used it to turn my body into an impenetrable shell. Even with those pieces of protection in place, Mab's flames still seared my skin, burning, burning, burning.

I screamed right along with the giant.

The flames seemed like they lasted forever, even though they flared out after only a few seconds. I drew in a ragged breath, gagging as the familiar, acrid stench of charred flesh filled my nose. Somehow, I shoved the giant's melted body away from me, even though it disintegrated into smoking ash at my touch. I looked down at the ruined thing that had been a man a second before. The horrible scent of seared skin filled my nose again, and tears streamed down my face from the pain pulsing through my body.

Bitter bile rose in my throat, choking me, but I forced it down and raised my eyes.

Mab was at the other end of the hallway. We just stood there, both of us breathing hard and staring at the other, not quite believing what had just happened. That neither one of us had killed the other.

And then Mab let out a primal, furious scream that made my lips draw back into a matching snarl. I wanted nothing more than to race back down the hallway, throw myself on top of her, and pound her with my fists, just hit her over and over and over again until she was nothing but a smoking red smear on the carpet.

But the elemental Fire flickered to life on Mab's fists again, building and building and building as she prepared to take another shot at me.

I turned and ran, and this time, I didn't stop for anything. My eyes locked on to the Exit sign up ahead, even though I could hear Mab moving behind me, could feel her Fire magic gaining force with every step that we both took.

Mab let out a scream and unleashed her magic at me

again. The elemental flames roared down the hallway toward me with all the force of a supernova.

I forced myself to run faster, to make my legs pump harder, despite the burns and blisters that sent continuous waves of agony through my body. Sweat poured down my face, blurring my vision, and screams of pain slipped from my open lips, but still I ran.

Even though it felt like I was running in place instead of moving forward, I finally reached the end of the hallway and barreled through the double doors. Mab's Fire hit them a second later, blowing out the glass and sending the hot, jagged shards at me. The pieces sliced into my back, even as the force of the blast threw me forward into the snow.

I screamed again, from the pain and frustration of my failure, but there was no time—no time to do anything but keep running. So I forced myself to get to my feet and staggered off as fast as I could into the cold, welcome embrace of the snow.

✳ 18 ✳

I stumbled through the darkness, my boots sending up sprays of snow, not sure where I was going and not caring, as long as it was away from Mab and her elemental Fire.

After about thirty seconds, the cold penetrated my pain, and I snapped back to myself. My hurried, staggered steps had taken me away from the immediate proximity of the ballroom. I risked a glance over my shoulder, wondering if Mab was racing up behind me, flaming fists held high, ready to unleash another blast of magic. But all I saw was the fiery outline of the ballroom. The elemental Fire that Mab had created had already spread to the roof, and a second later, a loud, ear-shattering groan ripped through the building. Sparks, smoke, and ash erupted like a volcano into the night sky as part of the structure caved in on itself. No, Mab wouldn't be coming after me that way. A brief respite, but I'd take what I could get.

My stumbling, sluggish path had taken me out into

the open, into the dead space between the tennis courts and the edge of the golf course. Everyone might be concerned with the fire right now, but it wouldn't be long before Mab rallied her giants to start searching the grounds. If I was still here when that happened, I was dead.

I'd made Owen promise me earlier that he'd slip out of the club and wait by the car while I went after Mab. The plan had been to meet there and get the hell out of Dodge if things didn't go well. I didn't want to be anywhere near the flames pouring out of the building but backtracking and following the curve of the structure was the quickest way to get to Owen. So I made myself turn back, getting as close to the elemental Fire as I dared, and slogged past it. Even from ten feet away, I could still feel Mab's power in the flames, still feel her magic pricking at my skin like red-hot needles. I hissed at the sensation and hurried on.

Another piece of the roof caved in. The smashing roar momentarily drowned out the startled shouts and screams of those who'd been inside the country club. No matter what happened the rest of the night, no one in Ashland would ever forget this party. Fire and Ice ball, indeed. I grimaced at my black humor and kept moving.

Mab had blocked the exit on this side of the building with her last burst of Fire, so I didn't see or pass anyone as I hurried on. A small favor, but luck owed me a little something tonight.

Finally, after what seemed like an eternity but couldn't have been more than five minutes, I rounded the side of the building, and the snow gave way to smooth pavement. Still I kept moving, my heels clacking like talons on the concrete. Already, I could hear the mutters in the stone, low, ugly sounds that whispered of fire, heat, death, destruction. The stone wouldn't forget what had happened here tonight either.

I sprinted through the parking lot as fast as I could, considering my injuries, heading toward the space where the valet had parked Owen's car. Hopefully, he would be there waiting, and we could at least get away clean—

Thwack-thwack-thwack.

The steady sound of fists pummeling flesh dashed that hope. Up ahead, shapes moved back and forth, backlit by the flames. Owen. Mab had raised the alarm, and her giants had found Owen already. My heart twisted in my chest, so hard and tight that I couldn't breathe, but I forced myself to run as fast as I ever had in my entire life—even faster than when I'd been trying to escape Mab's elemental Fire minutes ago. If anything happened to Owen, I'd just—I'd just *crumble* inside. What little there was left of my heart would disintegrate into ash and blow away, leaving nothing behind but aching, bitter emptiness.

I rounded a row of expensive cars and charged ahead, my eyes already locking onto the struggle in front of me and focusing on who my first target would be. Despite my fight with Mab and subsequent stagger through the snow, I'd somehow managed to hold on to my silverstone knives, one in either hand. Good. I didn't want to waste even half a second reaching for them—not while Owen was in danger.

Owen stood fifty feet in front of me, his back to his BMW. He'd gone to his car like we'd planned—he just hadn't gotten to it quite fast enough to drive away. Four giants surrounded him in a loose semicircle, trapping him against the car. I didn't know when the giants had spotted him, but they'd been fighting for a while now, because blood and bruises covered Owen's face like a second skin.

But my lover was determined to take the bastards down with him.

Owen gripped a blacksmith's hammer in his hands. I'd never seen him fight before, and I hadn't spied him putting the hammer in the car earlier. But he used the solid, heavy, black hammer like it was a staff, swinging it first one way, then the other, with easy, deadly skill, his movements as beautiful and graceful as those of any dancer. Two giants already lay crumpled at his feet, their blood shimmering like oil slicks on the pavement. Judging from their caved-in skulls, they wouldn't be getting up anytime soon. Good.

The four giants who were left eased in toward Owen, but a couple of cracks of his hammer against their ribs sent them scurrying back. They all stared at each other, hesitant to step forward and take the full force of Owen's assault. One of the giants was a little bolder or perhaps just a little stupider than the rest because he rushed toward Owen, intending to overpower him with his sheer, brute strength and then let the others pile on. Fool.

Owen waited until the man was in range, then pivoted and swung his hammer in a perfect arc. The metal slammed into the giant's temple. That side of his skull collapsed, and blood squirted out of him like juice from an orange. The giant never made a sound, although his body hit the pavement with an audible thump.

"Come on!" Owen roared. "Come on! Which one of you bastards is next?"

The three remaining giants exchanged uneasy looks, but none of them dared to step up and get their head bashed in like their buddy just had. In that regard, they were smarter than they seemed—but not smart enough to do something as simple as look behind them.

With an angry hiss, I leaped out of the shadows and slammed my knives into the giant closest to me. The blades flashed silver in the firelight just before they ripped into his broad back. One cut, then two, and he was dead. The giant gurgled out a weak scream before he went down, and the others' heads snapped around at the surprise attack from the rear.

I didn't hesitate, and neither did Owen.

He moved forward and slammed his hammer into another giant's knee, before whipping around and plowing his weapon into the man's other knee. The giant howled with pain, staggered back, and did a header onto the pavement. I grabbed his hair, yanked his head back, and cut his throat before letting him flop to the ground once more.

That left only one giant, who started backing away from us, eyes wide with surprise and more than a touch of fear. Normally, I would have charged after him and put him down, but there was no point in it. Not tonight. Not when Mab and Jonah McAllister had both already seen my face and knew that I was the Spider.

Owen tightened his grip on his hammer and started after the giant, but I grabbed his arm and pulled him back toward the car.

"Forget him," I rasped, my throat burning from the effort of talking. "We need to get out of here. Now!"

Owen nodded, and the two of us hopped into the car. He cranked the engine and threw the BMW in reverse. By this point, more people filled the parking lot, taking refuge from the flames that had skipped from one roof to another of the country club's buildings. Most of the people wore dazed, shocked expressions, but there were several of Mab's giants in the mix—men determined to find us, to find *me*.

The giant who'd gotten away from Owen and me waved his arms and screamed at his brethren before pointing in our direction. The other giants got the message and raced forward. Those who had guns raised them up and took aim at Owen's car.

Crack! Crack! Crack!

Bullet after bullet slammed into the vehicle. One splintered the windshield in between us, while the others thudded into the metal hood.

"Go!" I told Owen. "Go!"

He threw the car in gear, stomped on the gas, and roared out of the parking lot. The car raced down the hill and took a turn on two wheels. One of Mab's giants must have gotten the bright idea to alert the man in the guardhouse at the bottom of the hill, because up ahead, I could see the club's iron gates closing. Owen spotted them too and slammed his foot on the gas pedal so hard that I thought he might punch it through the floorboard. He knew as well as I did that getting trapped on the grounds would seal our fate. But for once, luck actually smiled on us, because the BMW shot through the gates just before it was too late. A few sparks flashed into the night air where the iron scraped against the sides of the car, but I didn't care because we were out of the country club and safe—at least for the moment.

But the others weren't. Not by a long shot.

"Phone," I rasped. "I need your phone. Now!"

Keeping one hand on the steering wheel, Owen used the other to dig into his pants pocket and hand me his cell phone. I flipped it open and hit a number that I'd programmed into his speed dial.

"Pick up," I muttered. "Pick up, pick up, pick up."

Just as I was starting to worry that I was already too late, she answered on the fifth ring.

"Hello?" Jo-Jo Deveraux's warm, friendly voice filled my ear, making me want to weep with relief.

But there was no time for that. No time to give in to emotions of any kind. Not now, when Mab finally knew who I was. No doubt, the Fire elemental was already mobilizing her army of giants and bounty hunters. So I said only one word to Jo-Jo.

"Run."

❖ 19 ❖

"Mab?" Jo-Jo asked, her sweet voice sharpening as she heard the tight worry in mine.

"Not dead," I said. "She saw me, Jo-Jo. She knows who I am. So does McAllister. So get Sophia and go to the safe house just like we planned. Right *now*. Owen will go pick up Eva. He'll meet you there. I'm going to call Finn and Bria next."

"Who else do you want me to round up?" the dwarf asked.

I thought about the other people that I'd helped over the last few months, all my friends and even friends of friends. "Tell Xavier and Roslyn, and call Violet and Warren Fox, just to be sure. I don't want anyone left behind that Mab can snatch and use as leverage."

"Got it."

We both hung up.

"What now?" Owen asked, driving away from the

country club as fast as he dared on the slick, snowy road.

I didn't answer him. I was too busy dialing. But instead of picking up like he should have, Finn's cell went to voice mail. I tried again, with the same result. One missed call I could understand, given what a sprawling labyrinth Fletcher's house was, but not two. My stomach flipped over and started tying itself into tiny, worrisome knots.

I tried a third time. Same result. No answer, only voice mail. Why wasn't Finn picking up his phone? He knew what was going down tonight, what was at stake for us—for all of us. Had Mab, her giants, or the bounty hunters gotten to him and Bria already? Maybe, if Mab had put out the call to her minions immediately after our fight at the country club. Now that the Fire elemental knew who I was, Fletcher's house would be one of the first places she'd start looking for me.

The thought that Bria and Finn could already be in trouble—could already be *dead*—made me sick, made me physically ill, but I forced myself to remain calm. To be as calm and rational as I had ever been as the Spider. To remember all of the old man's training over the long years, everything Fletcher had taught me about how to survive and make sure that my enemies didn't. It took a minute, but my breathing slowed, and I felt the cold, hard, unending blackness fill my heart once more. I embraced the cold, welcomed it, reveled in it, even. Because this was the only way I had any hope of living to see the sunrise—and making sure that the people I loved did the same.

"Gin?" Owen asked in a quiet voice, sensing the change in me. "What's wrong?"

"Finn's not answering me," I said. "Which means that something's going on with him and Bria. Either they've both gotten on the other's nerves and killed each other in a fit of rage or something bad is happening at Fletcher's house and they can't answer me. I have to go there, Owen. Right now."

"Okay. I'll take you."

I shook my head. "No. We've got to split up. You need to go get Eva and drive her over to the safe house just like we planned. I'm going after Finn and Bria—alone."

"Gin—"

"I'm not going to make you choose between me and your sister, Owen," I snapped. "I would never, *ever* ask you to do that—not when I know how much your sister means to you. Eva's in danger right now, and you need to get to her. Just like I need to get to Bria and Finn. But we can't be in two places at once, at least not together. Splitting up is our only option. We both know it's true."

Owen turned his head to stare at me in the darkness. After a moment, he let out a loud, vicious curse, and his hands gripped the steering wheel like he wanted to rip it to pieces. He knew I was right, and he didn't like it one bit. I understood his anger, his frustration, because I was feeling it too. So I put my burned, blistered fingers on top of his, trying to soothe him—and myself—in some small way.

"I—I appreciate your concern and the fact that you want to come with me. But we both know that it has to be this way. I would never forgive myself if something happened to Eva because of me. Because of the fact that I missed Mab tonight. I know what it's like to think that your sister is dead, and I don't ever want you to have to go through that pain. I care about you too much for that, Owen."

"I know you do," he said in a soft voice. "And I care about you too, Gin."

"Good. Then pull over into that parking lot."

Owen did as I asked, steering into a lot that fronted one of the many upscale shopping centers that populated this part of Northtown. A few folks had decided not to try to drive home in the snow, because a couple of cars remained in the lot, despite the late hour. Owen parked his BMW next to a late-model sedan.

"What are you going to do?" he asked.

"First of all, I'm going to boost that sedan right there," I said. "Then I'm going to drive over to Fletcher's house, hide the car at the bottom of the hill, and hike my way up to the top of the ridge. If everything looks kosher, I'll go in and get Finn and Bria and see why they weren't answering the phone."

"And if it's not kosher?" Owen asked.

I shrugged. "Then I guess I'll be killing people until it is."

He just nodded, and we fell silent. Both of us bruised and bloody, and me with burns covering my hands and arms. Mab hadn't completely melted my leather jacket with her elemental Fire, but she'd singed the sleeves in places, letting me see the raw, blistered skin that lay underneath. Something else that made me sick. Unfortunately, the night was far from over—for me or Owen.

"I'm sorry, Owen," I said in a low voice, staring at my

burned flesh instead of at him. "So, so sorry. All of this is my fault. If only I hadn't missed Mab tonight. If only I hadn't missed her *again*—"

Tears scalded my eyes, and frustration burned my throat, even harsher than Mab's elemental Fire. Fucking emotion. Something that I didn't need. Not now, not if I wanted to survive—and save the others.

Owen understood what I was feeling because he put his arms around me and pulled me over into his lap. For a moment, I buried my head in his chest, and he rocked me back and forth like a child.

"It's okay, Gin," he whispered against my hair. "Everything is going to be okay. You're going to make it okay. I know that you will. You always do."

His words gave me the strength to blink away my tears, lift up my head, and look at him. Moonlight painted his chiseled face in soft lines and dappled shadows, and I trailed my fingers down his bruised jaw. Owen winced, since he'd taken a couple of the giants' punches there, but he didn't pull away.

I leaned forward and kissed him as hard as I dared, given our mutual injuries. I poured all of my pent-up emotions into the kiss, trying to tell him everything that I felt just by touching his lips to mine, just by pressing my body against his. Trying to tell him how much I cared, even if the words always seemed to get stuck in my throat.

I don't know if it worked, but Owen kissed me back, his arms tightening around me. The familiar heat filled my stomach just by being near him, but there was no time for that. No time at all.

I drew back and stared into his violet eyes, wondering,

as I always did, at the concern that shone there for me and what the hell I'd ever done to deserve it.

"I'll see you at the safe house," I whispered.

"You'd better," he murmured back. "Or I'll come get you myself—no matter what."

Owen called his younger sister, Eva, and told her what was going on. She was at home with her best friend, Violet Fox, and Owen told the two college girls that he'd be there to pick them up as soon as possible. While he did that, I rummaged around in the trunk, pulling out the tins of healing salve I'd gotten from Jo-Jo.

In addition to healing with their hands, Air elementals could also infuse their magic into certain products, like creams and ointments, and give them an extra kick. When Jo-Jo had come over to Fletcher's house earlier to do my makeup, she'd given me several containers of just such an ointment, in case Mab got a few licks in on me before I killed her. I was grateful for the gift.

The lids of the tins all featured Jo-Jo's puffy cloud rune, painted on the tops in a vivid blue. I cracked one of them open, dipped my fingers into the ointment, and slathered it all over my hands and arms. The soothing smell of vanilla wafted up to me, and warm tingles spread throughout the blistered areas, just like they did when Jo-Jo was around in person to work her Air magic on me. I sighed with relief as the pulsing pain of the burns lessened. The ointment wasn't as good as Jo-Jo healing me herself, but it would keep me together long enough for me to get to Fletcher's house and see what trouble waited for me there.

Owen hung up with Eva, and I popped open another

tin and passed it to him. He smeared the ointment onto his face. The salve soaked into his skin, and Jo-Jo's magic made short work of the cuts and bruises that marred his features.

I moved over to the sedan that Owen had parked beside. I didn't bother trying to finesse the lock with a couple of elemental Ice picks. Instead, I used Owen's hammer to smash in one of the back windows, then unlocked the front door, slid inside, and stripped the wires under the dash like Finn had shown me how to do. A few seconds later, the engine purred to life. I climbed out of the car and laid the hammer on the front passenger's seat of Owen's BMW.

By this point, Owen had finished with the salve, and the two of us were ready to get on with things—and split up. We stared at each other across the roof of his car.

"I'll see you soon," Owen said, a hard promise in his voice.

I nodded. "Count on it."

Owen got back into his battered BMW and raced out of the parking lot. I wasn't too worried about his getting to Eva and Violet in time, since his mansion wasn't that far away. Besides, Mab would be focused on me right now and my immediate family—Finn, the Deveraux sisters, and most especially Bria. It wouldn't be long before the Fire elemental sent her men after Owen, but the lapse should give him enough of a head start to get the girls to the safe house.

There was no time to waste, so I slid back into the driver's seat of the sedan and steered the car out of the lot. While I drove toward Fletcher's house, I pulled out the spare cell phone that had been among the supplies in Owen's trunk and dialed Finn's number again. Once more, it went straight to voice mail.

I growled in frustration. Where was *he*? What was happening with him and Bria? When I got my hands on Finn, I was going to find out. And, depending on what kind of shape he was in, I might not ask nicely. Because if Finn and Bria were busy knocking boots instead of not answering my calls telling them that they were in mortal danger, well, I was going to be a little pissed.

In between trying Finn, I also called Jo-Jo back. The dwarf told me she'd managed to reach Xavier and Roslyn, and that the two of them were on their way to the safe house. Roslyn's sister, Lisa, and young niece, Catherine, were out of town visiting relatives, and Jo-Jo told me that Roslyn was calling them and telling them to check into a hotel under an assumed name. Jo-Jo had also managed to reach Warren Fox. The old coot had been reluctant to leave his warm, comfortable bed, but he'd seen the need after the dwarf explained the situation. Warren would meet everyone else at the safe house as soon as he could.

That just left Finn and Bria twisting in the wind—and my stomach tightening into more and more knots.

I drove as fast as I could on the slippery roads and not skid the car into a ditch, but it still took me thirty minutes to reach the road that ran by Fletcher's house. Of course, I could have barreled the stolen vehicle right on up the driveway to the old house itself, if not for the possibility that Mab's giants or bounty hunters were here already. I might not have killed the Fire elemental tonight, but I wasn't going to get dead myself by doing something so reckless. The old man had trained me too well for that.

I pulled the car into a cluster of trees just off the road about a quarter mile from the driveway entrance. Five seconds later, I was out of the vehicle, in the woods, and hiking up the ridge to the house.

It was a long, hard climb, made even more so by the injuries that I'd gotten fighting Mab. Jo-Jo's salve had healed the worst of the burns and blisters, but the ointment had done little to stop the mental and physical exhaustion creeping up on me. I gritted my teeth, shoved the weakness away, and hurried on. Every second I delayed was another second that the Fire elemental had to mobilize her troops and send them here.

Still, I paused every so often, looking, listening, and peering into the gray shadows that cloaked the uneven landscape. Nothing moved in the woods but me, and only the rasp of my breath broke the silence. I reached out with my magic, but the frosty stones buried underneath the layers of snow only sleepily murmured of the ice and cold that had seeped into them, threatening to crack their solid forms. Satisfied, I moved on.

I'd climbed about halfway up the ridge when gunshots shattered the silence.

Crack! Crack! Crack!

The sounds boomed down the slope toward me, each one hammering at my heart and confirming my worst fears. I forced myself to move even faster, to plow even quicker through the snow drifts, until my feet and legs were soaked from the sprays that I kicked up. More shots rang out as I moved, along with hoarse shouts. Both echoed down the ridge to me, making it easy to pinpoint the source. Whatever bad thing was going on, it was happening at the house, which meant that Finn and Bria were in serious trouble.

After about thirty seconds, the gunshots and shouts died down, but the silence didn't soothe me—because the quiet meant that Finn and Bria could already be dead. Once again, I could be too fucking late to save the people that I loved, just as I hadn't been able to reach Fletcher in time to prevent the old man from being tortured and murdered inside the Pork Pit. A fist of fear punched me in the stomach, hitting me hard and stealing my breath, but I kept moving.

It took me another ten minutes to reach the top of the ridge and slide to the edge of the woods. What I saw there in the clearing before me made my heart stop in my chest in a way that nothing else like it had before.

Because bounty hunters surrounded Fletcher's house.

❄ 20 ❄

I'd been expecting the bounty hunters to show up here now that the word was out about who the Spider really was. I just hadn't thought they'd get here so quickly—or that there would be so damn many of them.

A dozen vehicles were haphazardly parked in front of the sprawling structure. The multitude of lights burning inside the house let me see exactly what I was up against. Several of the bounty hunters crouched behind their vehicles, using the open doors as shields. Every single one had their guns out and pointed at the house—or at each other. Half a dozen bodies littered the snowy landscape like forgotten Christmas decorations, blood spilling out from wounds instead of holiday cheer.

There had been one hell of a fight already, probably with the various bounty hunters gunning it out in front of the house to see who got to go inside and capture whatever prize was in there waiting for them. I was grateful for the crowd. The bounty hunters slugging it out with each other in the yard was probably the only reason that they hadn't collectively stormed the house yet and either captured or killed Finn and Bria.

My eyes scanned the ranks. Men, women, young, old, dwarves, giants, even a vampire or two—all with a hard, hungry, predatory set to their shadowy features. I recognized a few of the faces from Mab's dinner party. I couldn't tell if any of the bounty hunters had elemental power, though. No one's eyes glowed in the semidarkness, and I didn't feel any kind of magic stirring in the night air. Some elementals, especially those with considerable juice like Mab, continuously gave off waves of power, like heat radiating off a fire. As an elemental myself, I could sense that constant surge of magic. Even if there had been another elemental in the mix, it didn't much matter. I was going to do whatever the hell I had to in order to save Finn and Bria—if they were even still alive.

One of the bounty hunters let out a low curse and started creeping around the hood of his pickup. He paused and looked over his shoulder. Three more men had taken refuge behind the vehicle. I couldn't tell if they were all part of the same group, but the other three leveled their guns at him, a clear indication that he should go forward—or else. Looked like he'd drawn the short straw tonight.

The man eased out from behind the front of the truck and tiptoed through the snow toward the house, hunching over as much as he could. He stopped and swallowed once, clearly nervous about being out in the open. A minute later, when nothing happened, he straightened. He stood there a moment, his body tense, expecting a shot from somewhere. Maybe from the other bounty hunters, maybe from the house. But it didn't come, and he continued on his slow, careful journey.

I palmed my silverstone knives, my hands tightening around the hilts. Why wasn't someone shooting at him? Fifty more feet, and the bastard would be at the front door. Once he made it up onto the porch, the others would follow in a sudden, violent swarm. Then, if Finn and Bria were still in the house, they'd be found, dragged outside, and hauled off to Mab.

The bounty hunter stopped again in the middle of the yard. Looking a little more sure of himself now, he turned and called out to his buddies behind the pickup truck. "They must finally be out of ammo, boys—"

Crack! Crack! Crack!

Last words he ever said.

Gunfire exploded in one of the downstairs windows of the house, and the bounty hunter dropped to the ground, his brains already blown out onto the snow behind him by the three bullets that had punched through his skull.

A grim smile curved my lips, and the knots in my stomach loosened. The Annie Oakley display told me that Finn was still alive, because my foster brother was the only person I knew who could shoot like that. If he was well enough to hold a gun, that meant Bria was still alive too. Finn would die before he let anything happen to my baby sister, just as I would.

I crouched there in the snow and waited until I was sure that no one else was going to try to bum-rush the house. Then I pulled out my cell phone and dialed Finn's number. This time, this fucking *time,* he finally picked up.

"Where the hell are you, Gin?" Finn growled in my ear.

"Me? You're the one who hasn't been answering the phone," I snapped right back. "What have you been doing? Is Bria okay? How long have the bounty hunters been camped outside of the house?"

Finn let out a tense breath. "Bria's fine. She's right here with me. The bounty hunters have been outside for almost an hour now. As to why I wasn't answering my phone before, Bria and I were, ah, engaged in something else."

I let out a soft curse. I should have known. Finn could never be in the same room with a beautiful woman without trying to seduce her, especially someone like Bria, whom he had some genuine feelings for. I'd always thought that Finn's womanizing ways would get him into trouble one day. I just hadn't realized that it would be this much trouble—and that Bria and I would be caught in the middle of it.

"You mean that the two of you were busy screwing around instead of waiting for my phone call like you were supposed to," I snarled. "What the hell were you thinking, Finn? You know better than that. Fletcher taught you better than that."

I could almost hear him wince through the phone. "I know, Gin. Believe me, I know. The two of us were arguing, I don't even remember about what, but I was texting, and Bria grabbed my phone and threw it across the room. After that, one thing just led to another, and we ended up in one of the downstairs bedrooms . . ."

His voice trailed off in shame, but he didn't have to tell me the rest. I knew what had happened. Finn and Bria had finally given in to their simmering attraction, and the rest of the world had just fallen away—including my mission to kill Mab.

Finn cleared his throat. "Anyway, neither one of us heard your calls. We were right, ah, in the middle of things, when I hear someone roar up the driveway. Then another car, then another car, followed by a series of gunshots. By that point, we're out of bed, looking out the windows, and realizing that we're in deep trouble. The bastards just kept coming, and they surrounded the house before we could slip out the back. Some of them took out each other, but we didn't know how many more of them might show up, so Bria and I got out our guns and settled in to wait for you."

I wanted to scream at Finn for being so sloppy, for being more interested in seducing my sister than keeping her safe. But it took two to tango, and Bria was just as much to blame as he was. They'd both known what was going down tonight, and they'd given in to their emotions instead of staying sharp like they should have.

I could—and would—yell at them later. The most important thing right now was getting Finn and Bria out of the house and away from the bounty hunters.

"All right," I said, my tone a little calmer. "All right. I'm here now, and I'm not leaving without the two of you. We can discuss everything else later."

"Agreed," Finn said, the relief apparent in his voice. "What do you want us to do, Gin?"

I stared out at the assortment of bounty hunters before me. "You made a good choice staying in the house. There's no way you can break through the ring of them. They've got the whole front of the house surrounded, and there's too much ice and snow on the rocks to try to get out the back and rappel down the cliffs. You'll have to use the old tunnel."

Finn knew as well as I did that there was a secret passage in Fletcher's office that led from the house into an underground tunnel. The tunnel snaked under the yard before opening up about a half mile away in the woods—well out of the tight ring of bounty hunters that circled around the house like pioneers on a wagon train heading west.

"I thought of that," Finn said. "But Bria spotted some flashlights in the woods, and I didn't want to risk stepping out of the tunnel and right into a couple of bounty hunters' line of fire."

He'd made the right decision. Fletcher had designed his house to be almost impregnable, and there was enough food, water, and ammo stored inside to last for weeks. But there was also strength in numbers, which the bounty hunters had, and Finn couldn't shoot them all, not if they decided to attack all at once. He and Bria needed to get out of the house as soon as possible.

"All right," I said. "I'll make sure that the tunnel is clear and take care of any stragglers in the woods, then come in and get you. You keep them busy thinking that they've got a couple of shooters still inside. I want them focused on the house as long as possible and not thinking about our escape route. Got it?"

"Got it."

"Good. And answer your fucking phone next time."

"Yes, ma'am," Finn said, actually sounding chastised for once in his life.

I hung up and stuffed the phone back into my jacket pocket. Then I slipped away from my perch at the edge of the woods. I headed deeper into the gloom, skirting around to the west of the house, although I kept the bounty hunters in sight through the screen of trees. If a group of them made a move toward the house, I'd come out of the woods and cut my way through them until I got to Finn and Bria. But the bounty hunters weren't that brave—or stupid. They stayed close to their cars, muttering to each other about how best to get inside the house without getting dead. I took advantage of their inattention, moving quickly and quietly, slipping from tree to tree, shadow to shadow, all the while heading toward the secret tunnel.

Crack! Crack! Crack!

More gunshots rang out, along with something that sounded like rusted metal creaking, although the noise was mostly drowned out by the whine of the bullets. I'd almost reached the entrance when I heard voices—loud voices with a distinctive southern twang. Knives still in my hands, I paused behind a tree and peered around the ice-crusted trunk.

Ahead of me, two women and a man stood in the middle of the woods—right in front of the opening of the tunnel.

Somehow, they'd found it in the snow. They'd even been bright enough to pull back the metal hatch to reveal the dark hole leading down into the ground, which was no doubt the creaking sound that I'd heard. Fuck. I'd wanted to do this quick, clean, and quiet, and get Finn and Bria out of the house before the bounty hunters even realized that they were gone. Probably not going to happen now. Oh, it didn't bother me, the thought of killing the three people in front of me, but it meant more precious seconds wasted, more precious time when Finn and Bria were in danger of being overrun by the other bounty hunters.

"What do you think it is, Liza?" one of the women asked, shining a flashlight into the dark space.

"What do you think it is, Celia? Because it looks like some kind of tunnel to me, genius," Liza sniped.

"See?" The guy grinned. "I told you that an assassin like the Spider was sure to have some sort of escape hatch from that ugly-ass house of hers."

"Yeah, Connor," the first woman, Celia, chimed in again. "But we don't even know that the Spider's in the house. According to that info bulletin that went out, the last time anyone saw her, she was still at the country club."

"Well, someone's in that house, and they're picking off the other hunters like flies," Connor replied. "If the Spider is as good as everyone says she is, then I'm sure that the shooters have plenty of ammo to spare. Besides, did you see all that silverstone in the doors and the matching bars over the windows? They could hold that house for a week. We go through this tunnel here, we can come up in the house behind them and surprise them. They'll never even know what hit them."

The two women stared at the tunnel, then at each other. Liza shrugged.

"Might as well see where it goes," Liza said. "Connor's right—we're not getting in through the front door. At least not until someone gets the bright idea of trying to burn them out. Even then, someone would have to get close to the house to do that. I don't think that whoever is inside is going to let that happen."

No, Finn knew better than to let anyone breach the house, especially anyone carrying a flaming torch or a can of gasoline.

I scanned the rest of the area, but I didn't see any more bounty hunters in the shadows. If I was lucky, these three were the only ones who'd given up on a full-scale frontal assault and had decided to go poking around in the woods. But I doubted it. For one thing, my luck could never be that good. For another, I hadn't noticed Ruth Gentry or Sydney among the crowd circling the house. If the old bounty hunter had received the same kind of bulletin that the others had, she was sure to be lurking around here somewhere with her apprentice in tow.

Right now, though, I had a more immediate problem—the three people in front of me and how to kill them as quickly and quietly as possible.

The man, Connor, had a gun like all the other bounty hunters, but the two women had gone in for more exotic weapons. Celia had a sword strapped to her belt, while a leather whip coiled around Liza's waist. I grimaced. That whip was going to hurt, especially since Mab had already blasted my skin with her Fire magic tonight. Nothing I could about it now, though, which meant that it was time to get on with things—

Crack! Crack! Crack!

Another barrage of shots echoed through the trees, as Finn mowed down whichever fool had been stupid enough to step out from behind his vehicle.

Knives in my hands, I moved forward. By this point, snow crusted my boots an inch thick in places, so my footsteps made little noise. I crept up until I stood at a right angle with the three bounty hunters, who were dickering about who should lead the way into the tunnel. Despite their weapons, none of them wanted to come face-to-face with the Spider in her own house.

They just didn't realize that it was too late for that already. Way too late.

The three bounty hunters continued to mill around the tunnel entrance, still arguing. When it was apparent that they couldn't come to a decision by themselves, they held out their hands and decided to go rock-paper-scissors for it. They slapped their hands together, and I used the noise to tiptoe even closer to them. I stood in the woods and waited, but all three of them picked paper, so they had to do it again.

I rolled my eyes. And these were the people that Mab was promising millions of dollars to if they found, captured, or killed me. At least Elektra LaFleur had been smart and strong enough to be a real challenge. Mab was wasting her money on these amateurs.

Finally, their hands smacked down for the final time, and the two women grinned, because they'd both picked paper again, while Connor had chosen rock, which meant that he'd lost.

"Fine," he grumbled. "I'll go first since you ladies are so afraid to—"

The silverstone knife I'd just thrown sank into his right eye, and he fell to the snow without a sound. For a moment, the two women stood there—stunned—and stared down at their fallen comrade, mouths open, their brains not quite catching on as to what was happening.

And that's when I made my move.

I palmed another knife, darted out of the shelter of the trees, and raced toward them. Connor had been the only one with a gun, which is why I'd dropped him first. My focus was on keeping the noise to a minimum—not letting Connor shoot up the woods and give away my location. Besides, if I couldn't take out two chicks with only a sword and a whip between them, then I wasn't the Spider, wasn't half the assassin Fletcher had trained me to be.

After another second, the women snapped back to reality and realized that there was someone else in the clearing, someone who was an immediate threat to them—me. Celia reached down, fumbling at her sword, trying to get it free of the loop on her belt.

I didn't give her the chance.

My first knife punched into chest, rupturing her heart. Her hot blood painted my hands a steaming crimson, spattering onto the snow like scarlet teardrops. Celia opened her mouth to scream, but I used my second knife to cut her throat before she could utter so much as a whimper. I pushed her dying body away and turned to face the other woman—

Her whip snapped against my neck.

I hissed in pain and staggered back, my blood mixing with that of the other bounty hunters' on the snow. In front of me, Liza flicked her whip over the ground, making it writhe like a rattlesnake. She also backed up out of the range of my knives. Smart. Just not smart enough.

"So you're the Spider," she muttered. "I suppose I should thank you for killing Connor and Celia. Now, I won't have to bother with it—or share the bounty with them."

I gave her a cold, hard smile that was as wintry as the landscape around us. "You're assuming that you're going to live long enough to collect."

Liza returned my smile with one of her own. "Oh, I will, Spider. Don't you worry about that—"

I rushed her, trying to take her by surprise while she was still talking, but the bounty hunter had been expecting the move and raised her whip. I threw myself to one side, but the leather streaked through the air like black lightning. The blow opened up a deep cut on my cheek, burning my skin almost as much as Mab's elemental Fire had. I hissed again.

"What's the matter, Spider?" Liza laughed. "Don't you like the feel of my whip?"

My eyes narrowed, but I didn't say anything. Instead, I began moving to the left, trying to get into her blind spot. But she turned with me, and the two of us circled around and around, like two dogs fighting over a bone that lay between them.

Crack! Crack! Crack! Crack!

Another round of shots rang through the woods. Someone else must have tried to approach the house, and Finn had killed him for his trouble. Still, I knew it wouldn't be too much longer now before the bounty hunters decided to storm the structure en masse. I needed to get Finn and Bria out of there before that happened.

Trying to end things, I darted forward, but the bounty hunter raised her whip again. This time, the weapon cut through my leather bustier and opened a stinging gash on my chest, right above my heart.

"By the time I'm through, you'll have more cuts than any you ever made on one of your hits," Liza crowed, flicking her whip back and forth.

"The hell I will," I snarled.

Too late, the bounty hunter spotted the hard anger in my face. Liza backed up and raised her whip even as I charged her again. The leather sliced through the air toward me, but this time, instead of ducking it, I caught the leather in my hand, even though it opened up another deep cut on my palm.

And I didn't let go.

The bounty hunter tried to jerk her whip out of my grasp, but I used my Ice magic to numb my fist, so I wouldn't feel the whip cutting into my skin. Then I moved toward her, one quick step at a time. Once more, Liza tried to tug the whip out of my grasp. When that didn't work, she turned and started to run.

But by then, it was too late.

My knife sliced into her back, and Liza joined her other two dead friends on the forest floor.

I plodded over and retrieved the knife I'd thrown at Connor, breathing harder than I would have liked. The fight with Mab had taken its toll on me, and I'd just used up the remaining scraps of my magic to defeat the bounty hunter. My heart raced, my lungs burned, and my legs trembled with the effort of just standing upright. Not to mention the blood that dripped out of the fresh cuts on my skin. Right now, I wanted nothing more than to get Jo-Jo to heal me, then crawl into bed and sleep for twelve hours. But I couldn't do that. Not until Bria and Finn were safe, and the three of us were far, far away from here—

A branch creaked somewhere farther back in the forest.

I whirled around, silverstone knives up and at the ready. Looking, listening, straining to see what new danger might be waiting in the dark.

Nothing. I saw and heard nothing.

Maybe it had just been the wind rattling through the trees, a branch collapsing under the weight of the snow, or a wild animal drawn by the smell of fresh blood. But I didn't believe that. Not really, not deep down in my gut where it mattered. Because Gentry was out there somewhere, with Sydney and her rifle. Nothing I could do about it now, though. Getting Finn and Bria out of the house was my first priority. I'd deal with everything else later—including Gentry, should she decide to show herself.

The snow started to fall once more as I ducked down and slid into the tunnel.

* 21 *

Fletcher Lane's escape tunnel reminded me of a coal mine that I'd been in not too long ago—low, squat, and round, with rough, uneven, earthen walls supported by thick wooden beams. The air smelled as old and musty as a dust-covered book long forgotten on a shelf. Dried-up leaves littered the entrance, and they crackled like cellophane under my boots as I moved farther inside.

The leaves gave way to hard-packed dirt, worn smooth and shiny by the tread of countless feet across it over the years. Fletcher had told me that the tunnel had once been used by bootleggers back during Prohibition, a hiding place for them and their mountain moonshine to rest before continuing their journey. Even now, all these years later, the rocks underfoot muttered with worry, tension, and fear of discovery. The on-edge sound matched my own mood perfectly.

I'd picked up one of the bounty hunters' flashlights before stepping inside so it was easy enough for me to make my way down the tunnel. Still, I sidestepped carefully to avoid disturbing the spiderwebs that stretched from one wooden beam to the next like wispy threads of silver silk. If any more of the bounty hunters discovered the tunnel, I didn't want them to realize that I'd been in here—or that I'd taken Finn and Bria out this way.

Ten minutes later, I reached the far end of the tunnel. I walked up a series of steep steps to a heavy metal door and banged on it three times with the flashlight, then three more times, then still three more times—a long-standing signal Fletcher had taught Finn and me should we ever need to get into the house this way.

I'd barely finished tapping on the door when I heard the bolt screech back. A second later, the metal door opened, letting light from the house stream into the tunnel. I shielded my eyes against the glare and looked up to find Bria staring down at me, her gun pointed at my head. She wasn't taking any chances. Good.

"You all right?" I asked.

Bria lowered her weapon and moved to one side so I could climb up out of the trapdoor that was set into the floor of Fletcher's cluttered office, right behind the old man's desk.

"I'm fine," she said.

She looked no worse for wear—despite the fact that she didn't have on a shirt and had just thrown her long wool coat on over a pale pink camisole and a pair of jeans. Her bare feet were stuffed into a pair of my sneakers. A missing shirt and socks. That must have been as far as Finn had gotten to undressing her before the two of them were interrupted.

"Where's Finn?"

"A few rooms over still picking off bounty hunters," Bria said.

"Get him, and let's get out of here," I said. "I had to drop a couple of the more curious ones out in the woods already, and I want to be clear of here before the others start searching the area around the house and find their bodies and the entrance to the tunnel."

Bria nodded and left the room. Fletcher's office stood in one of the front corners of the house, so I eased over to the window and peered out through the curtains and silverstone bars that covered the glass. The bounty hunters still ringed the front of the house.

Every once in a while, one of them would take aim and fire off a couple of shots, even though the bullets did nothing more than catch in the thick, reinforced walls and the slabs of granite that covered the house like an armadillo's layered, protective shell. Still, the bullets pinging into the granite had activated the runes that I'd traced into the stone with my magic. Small, tight, spiral curls— the symbol for protection. In addition to using them as symbols of their magic and allegiances, elementals could also imbue runes with power and make them perform specific functions.

When I'd first moved back into Fletcher's house several months ago, I'd spent hours tracing the runes into every bit of stone that composed the house, watching them shimmer with the silver color of my magic before sinking into the stone. My own personal alarm system. If anyone tried to sneak inside the house, she would trigger the protection runes, and my magic would echo through the granite, rising to a shrill shriek that would rouse me from the deepest, darkest, deadest sleep. Just like it was doing now. I gritted my teeth at the harsh sound of the stone wailing all around me. Yeah, I knew we were in trouble—I didn't need my magic to remind me of it.

Thirty seconds later, Bria entered the office again. Finn followed her inside, a flashlight in his left hand. He clutched a revolver in his right hand and had another stuffed into his waistband. The pockets on his pants bulged with ammo, and he jangled louder than a cowboy sporting a pair of shiny new silver spurs. Finn looked just as disheveled as my sister did. His suit jacket was missing, along with his tie, and his impeccable shirt was mussed and untucked, the tail of it flapping against his pants like a loose tongue.

Finn saw me eyeing his rumpled clothes and exchanged a guilty look with Bria before turning back to me. "Gin, we're both so sorry—" he started.

I held up my hand, cutting him off. "I know you are. Let's just get out of here. Then I can properly scream at the two of you for being so careless, and you can spend the rest of the night apologizing profusely. Deal?"

They both nodded.

"Good. Then let's get out of here."

Flashlight still in hand, I pounded down the steps into the tunnel. Bria followed me, her gun still out. Finn brought up the rear and closed the metal door behind us, this time bolting it from the inside, so that no one from the house could come up behind us in the tunnel—at least not without pounding through the metal and making a hell of a lot of noise doing it.

I moved quickly, despite my lingering aches and pains, and Bria and Finn did the same. Several minutes later, we exited the escape tunnel at the other end, back in the snowy woods. I went first, sliding out and moving off into the trees. Looking, listening, searching for anything that didn't belong, anything out of place, any shadow that hadn't been here before when I'd first gone into the tunnel.

Once more, I didn't see or hear anything, not even the soft fall of the snow as the dime-size flakes fluttered to the ground. Still, a finger of unease crawled up my spine one cold inch at a time. The primitive, predatory, lizard part of my brain knew that something was wrong, but I couldn't pinpoint it, and I didn't have time to stop and think about it. Not when the bounty hunters could charge the house or start searching the woods at any second.

"Come on," I muttered to the others. "It's clear."

Finn and Bria slipped out of the tunnel after me. Finn stopped long enough to shut the door on this end as well, and I had to stop myself from snapping at him for the delay. As precarious as our situation was, even a few seconds could mean the difference between life and death. But even worse than that was the grinding screech that the door made. It echoed through the forest just the way that the gunshots had earlier, only this time, there were no bullets flying through the air to help mask the noise. I would have cursed, if that sound wouldn't have carried as well. If Gentry or any of the other bounty hunters were lurking in the woods, there was no way that they wouldn't have heard such a high, distinctive sound—or come to investigate. Finn winced and hurried over to Bria and me.

"Follow me," I whispered to them. "Stay right behind me no matter what. Quickly now."

They nodded, guns ready. Finn and I turned off our flashlights. We didn't need them. Both of us had been raised in these woods and had spent hours exploring them. Besides, someone might see the bobbing lights, which was a risk I wasn't willing to take. There was more than enough moon and starlight to reflect off the snow and show us the way, not to mention the bright, collective glow from the bounty hunters' cars and the lights still blazing inside the house.

The three of us plowed through the woods, going as fast as we could through the snow and still keep our footing. I took point, putting myself out front, a silverstone knife in either hand, with Bria behind me, and Finn guarding the rear, all three of us looking, watching, listening. Our breaths rasped and frosted in the air like jets leaving vapor trails behind them.

My unease grew, rising up until it matched the wailing shrieks of the stone of Fletcher's house in its piercing intensity, but I shook it off and kept going—

Crack! Crack! Crack!

The gunshots came out of nowhere.

Too late, I realized what it was that I'd been missing before—the sound of the bounty hunters shooting at the house. The loud cracks of bullets zipping through the night had completely vanished. Now I knew why. Some of them had finally gotten smart and invaded the woods—probably drawn by the creak of Finn closing the tunnel door.

One second the three of us were alone in the forest.

The next, figures moved in the trees all around us, like we'd kicked over an anthill and had sent all the biting insects scuttling in our direction, determined to exact what vengeance they could.

"Run!" I told Finn and Bria. "Run!"

We took off. There was no time to be silent or sneaky, and no time to take the bounty hunters out one by one. There were just too many of them, and they rolled over us like waves crashing against a sandy shore. As soon as one bounty hunter went down, another one swept in to take his place. I led the way, with Bria and Finn behind me, firing their guns at our pursuers. I ran as fast as I dared, as fast as I could go and still have them keep up with me, but I still knew that it was too slow—too fucking *slow*.

Faces began to appear in the woods. The bounty hunters' lips were all drawn back into triumphant smiles, while greed made their eyes glint like the predators that they were. Closer and closer they crept, slowly gaining on us. Two giants had moved quicker than the rest and actually managed to get in front of us, stepping out into the path ahead and blocking our escape. Not for long. My hands tightened around my knives.

I barreled into the first giant. My blades sliced one way, then the other, and he went down screaming. But the other bastard stepped up to take his place. Behind me, Bria and Finn had both stopped to reload their guns and take aim at another group of hunters closing in on our left flank.

And that's when Ruth Gentry made her move.

The old, spry bounty hunter darted out of the trees to our right, like a ghost appearing out of thin air. Gentry timed her attack perfectly, popping out of the forest from less than ten feet away. How the hell had she gotten that close to us without my seeing her?

Before I knew what was happening, before I could even think about stopping her, before I could even scream out a fucking *warning,* the old woman was on us. She snuck up on Bria's blind side, grabbing my baby sister by her shag of blond hair. Bria shrieked in surprise and stumbled back but she brought up her elbow, ready to drive it into the stomach of whoever was behind her—

Click.

Gentry's revolver pressed against Bria's temple, and my sister did the only thing that she could—she froze. Finn whirled around, cursed, and raised his own gun, determined to put a bullet through one of Gentry's eyes—

Crack!

A bullet whined out of the trees, kicking up the snow at Finn's feet. This time, everyone froze, even the giant who'd been about to swing at me. I knew who it was, of course. Sydney, Gentry's girl, apprentice, or whoever the hell she was, hidden farther back in the trees with that rifle of hers.

"The next one will go in your head," Gentry said.

She spoke to Finn, but the old woman's gaze never left my face. She recognized me from the Pork Pit. I could tell by the way that her pale eyes narrowed and her lips puckered with thought. Something like sympathy flashed in her face, and she nodded her head at me. Being respectful, the way that you would to an enemy you admired, to someone who maybe wasn't all that different but was on the opposite side from you.

"I'll take care of her as best I can until you come for her," Gentry said, still staring at me. "I owe you that much for sparing Sydney the other night. Now, come on, little lady. We need to get going."

Take care of Bria? What did she mean by that?

Keeping Bria between us and her gun against my sister's temple, Gentry eased my baby sister back into the woods. All around me, the other bounty hunters closed in, their delighted, excited shouts making them sound like a flock of crows cawing in triumph.

But I only had eyes for Bria, and she for me. Across the snowy landscape, our gazes met and held. Desperate gray on agonizing blue.

"Go, Gin!" Bria screamed the words at me. "Leave me!"

Never.

The word burned into my heart like an icy brand, hurting me worse than anything ever had before, including Mab melting my spider rune medallion into my palms. I started forward, thinking to hell with Sydney, her rifle, and the fact that she might put a bullet in my brain, but the giant blocked my path once more. Automatically, I dodged his blows, then brought my knives up, then down, just as I'd done a thousand times before. But even as I cut into him, I knew that it wouldn't be enough—that I just wouldn't be fast enough.

The giant had just started to fall when Gentry and Bria disappeared from sight.

"Bria!" I screamed, trying to get past the dying giant. "Bria!"

I wasn't quick enough. Even as I reached for my baby

sister, more bounty hunters appeared, half a dozen of them running toward Finn and me.

"Come on, Gin!" Finn said, grabbing my arm and pulling me forward. "It's too late! Bria's gone!"

It might have been my imagination, but, for a second, I saw a glimmer of silver through the trees, as the moonlight illuminated the rune necklace Bria always wore. A delicate primrose. Bria's rune. The symbol for beauty.

"Bria!" I screamed again.

Then the falling snow swirled and fell like a curtain between us, and she vanished.

22

I don't really remember much of what happened after that.

Somehow, I got myself under control long enough to stop screaming and start running. Finn covered our backs, exchanging enough shots with the pursuing bounty hunters to keep them from overwhelming us, while I took care of any who were unlucky enough to step into our path. Cut, cut, cut. I went through the motions automatically, my limbs heavy and my mind disconnected from the rest of my body. Nothing could penetrate the fear that cloaked my heart like an icy shroud.

Bria—Bria was *gone,* and it was all my fault. For being so arrogant, for assuming that I could kill Mab. Right now, at this very moment, my sister was being delivered into the Fire elemental's cruel clutches. I'd lost my baby sister to that bitch for the second time in my life. I wanted to curl into a ball and weep at my miserable, miserable failure.

But there was no time for that. There was no time to do anything but cut and run, and cut and run some more.

Somehow, though, Finn and I made it down the steep, snow-covered ridge and back to the sedan that I'd boosted earlier. I was just—out of it, so Finn took charge. He tucked his gun in his waistband alongside his other gun, opened the door, and shoved me into the passenger's seat. At this point, my hands shook so badly from adrenaline, fear, and fatigue that it was all I could do to pull the door shut. My bloody knives slipped from my numb fingers and clattered to the floorboard. I just stared dully at them.

Finn ran around to the other side of the car, slid into the driver's seat, and reached underneath the dash. "Come on, baby," he muttered, bringing the loose wires together. "Start for me."

A second later, the engine roared to life. Finn threw the car in gear, put his foot all the way down on the gas, and swerved back out onto the road.

Not a moment too soon.

In the side mirror, I saw several figures run out into the road behind us.

Crack! Crack! Crack!

Bullets slammed into the car, one of them blowing out the back windshield and spraying us with sharp splinters of glass. Finn hunched down over the wheel, making himself a smaller target, but I didn't even have the energy to do that. Didn't much matter anyway, since Finn rounded a curve, putting us out of sight and out of range of the bounty hunters and their guns.

Finn took the first side road he came to, then another, then another. When he was sure that none of the bounty hunters was on our tail, he made a final turn, one that would take us to the safe house where the others should be waiting. We rode in silence, with me slumped against the window.

Bria—Bria was gone. I'd vowed to keep my sister safe, and I'd been stupid and sloppy enough to let her be captured by a bounty hunter, by Ruth Gentry—a woman who was sure to be taking Bria to Mab this very *second*, with Sydney and her rifle along for backup. And when Mab got her hands on Bria . . .

Hot, sour, bitter bile rose in my throat at the thought of what the Fire elemental would do to my sister, of how she would torture her. Just because she could. My stomach twisted, and it took what little strength I had left to keep from vomiting.

"I'm so sorry, Gin," Finn said. "So fucking sorry. This is all my fault. If I hadn't set my sights on Bria, if I hadn't tried to seduce her tonight, if I hadn't baited her, if I'd just answered my damn phone when you first called . . ."

Finn swallowed the rest of his words, but I could hear the anguish in his voice. Despite his womanizing ways, Finn genuinely cared for Bria. Even more than that, she was part of our makeshift family now. He would have felt the same way if Jo-Jo had been kidnapped or Sophia or me. And I couldn't point the finger of blame at Finn too much. We all made mistakes, we all fucked up from time to time. Not too long ago, one of my screwups had led to my foster brother's almost being killed in the Ashland Rock Quarry. No, I couldn't fault Finn for being himself, for doing what was in his nature. I just couldn't. I'd already lost Bria tonight—I wasn't losing him too.

So I roused myself out of my stupor long enough to lean over and squeeze his cold hand. "If you'd answered my call and tried to leave the house, you might have run into the bounty hunters coming up the driveway and been captured immediately. It's okay. We'll get her back. Bria will be fine. You'll see."

Finn nodded, but we could both hear the hollow echo in my weak, mumbled words.

We headed due west to the suburbs that lay on the far side of Ashland. Given the late hour, falling snow, and treacherous roads, we didn't pass a single car—not one. We'd gotten our clean getaway after all—it had just come too late for Bria.

Twenty minutes later, Finn left the main road. He made a series of turns, finally steering the car into what looked like two ruts leading smack-dab to the middle of nowhere. A mile later, the car broke free of the snow-laden trees, and Finn stopped in front of an enormous log cabin that had been built into the side of this particular ridge.

In the dark, the cabin looked like a stain that had been spilled over the pristine carpet of the white, fluffy snow. No lights burned in the structure, which was flanked by trees, but one of the fins on Sophia's classic convertible peeked around the far side of the building. The Goth dwarf and Jo-Jo had made it here. I just hoped that the others had too.

The cabin was a safe house Fletcher had kept up for years, one of several that the old man had maintained. Now that he was gone, the only people who knew about the place were me, Finn, Owen, and the Deveraux sisters. But that didn't mean there still couldn't be trouble lurking inside—not with all the bounty hunters in the city who were searching for me. So I made myself pick up my bloody knives from the floorboard. Next to me, Finn pulled out one of his guns again. The two of us left the car and approached the house cautiously, sliding from shadow to shadow and watching for any sign of movement behind the curtains.

We'd only gotten halfway across the yard, when the light on the front porch snapped on. Finn and I both dropped into a low crouch, weapons ready. A moment later, the front door creaked open, and Jo-Jo stuck her head outside, no doubt looking for us. Finn and I climbed back to our feet and headed her way. The dwarf spotted us and opened her mouth to call out a greeting. Then she saw there were only two of us—and that Bria wasn't here.

"Gin?" Jo-Jo asked in a soft voice, stepping back to turn on some more lights.

I shook my head and plodded past her inside.

The cabin was exactly what you'd expect to find in this part of Ashland. Large, sprawling, roomy, and filled with rustic, woodsy furniture done in dark, manly shades. Soapstone figures carved into the shapes of various animals crouched on the tables, while paintings of mountains and creeks covered the smooth log walls.

They were all gathered in the downstairs living room, huddled together on the couches and chairs. Xavier and Roslyn held hands on a love seat in front of the windows. Warren Fox sat next to them in an old-fashioned rocking chair. Warren's granddaughter, Violet, perched on one side of another sofa, next to her best friend, Eva Grayson. Sophia stood by herself next to the fireplace, stirring up the flames that flickered there. And finally, there was Owen, already moving toward me, concern flashing in his eyes. Everyone was here, everyone was safe, except for Bria.

The guilt and grief overwhelmed me, and I collapsed in the middle of the floor.

Owen scooped me up, carried me into the next room, and gently laid me down on the bed there. Jo-Jo pushed up the sleeves of her pink flannel housecoat, leaned over, and started working her healing magic on me. I just lay there, staring at the ceiling, for once not even caring that the dwarf's Air magic pricked my skin like hundreds of tiny needles. The discomfort was nothing to what I'd endured at Mab's hands tonight.

It was nothing to what Bria could be suffering this very second.

Owen held my hand as Jo-Jo healed me. I could hear the others talking in low, strained voices out in the main den. Finn would have filled everyone in on what had happened at Fletcher's house. Even now, though he had to be as exhausted as I was, my foster brother would be working the phones, contacting his myriad sources, trying to determine if Bria was still alive or if Mab had killed her on sight. The others would huddle around him, staring at each other and trying to think of some way to help, of some way to rescue Bria, of some way out of this mess. They shouldn't have bothered. Because it was a mess that I'd created, just by being born, just by existing in the same world as Mab, just by breathing—or so it seemed tonight.

A few minutes later, Jo-Jo dropped her hand, and the feel of her Air magic faded away.

"There," the dwarf said in a low voice. "Good as new. I'll give you two a minute to talk."

I nodded, and Jo-Jo left the room. As soon as the door closed, Owen lay down on the bed beside me and drew me into his arms.

"Oh, Gin," he said, his lips pressed against my temple. "I'm sorry. So, so sorry. For you and for Bria."

For a moment, I clung to him, letting him hold me, letting him be the strong one. I closed my eyes and concentrated on the feel of Owen's arms around me, of his smell, that rich scent that always made me think of metal. The warmth from his body heated my own, melting the icy numbness that had gripped me since Gentry had dragged Bria away in the woods. I shuddered in a breath and came back to myself.

And then the moment passed, the way it always did, whether I wanted it to or not.

And I knew it was time to get on with things. Time for me to be the Spider once more. To be the assassin that Fletcher had raised me to be. To do the thing it seemed the old man had been secretly preparing me for all these years.

To finally kill Mab Monroe—or die trying.

Owen seemed to sense my withdrawal because he sat up and pulled me up with him. Emotions filled his face—worry, fear, concern, but most important, acceptance. Owen knew what was coming, what I had to do now as well as I did. Even if he could have, I knew that he wouldn't try to stop me, because if our situations were reversed, and Eva was gone, he would do exactly what I was going to do now to save Bria.

I loved him for it. For letting me be the Spider, for always letting me do what needed to be done, with no judgments, no remorse, and no regrets, even when the price was going to be so very, very high this time—for all of us.

I cupped my hand to Owen's cheek, pulled him over to me, and kissed him once—hard. He returned my kiss, even though I knew that my lips felt like ice against his. We both drew back. He looked at me and nodded. I nodded back, then got up, walked over to the door, and stepped out into the main room.

Everyone snapped to attention as I entered, their eyes full of sympathy and worry for me, for Bria, for all of us. I stared at Finn, who ended his latest phone call and looked at me.

"Gentry and Sydney took Bria straight to Mab's estate," Finn said. "According to my sources, they went through the front gate with her thirty minutes ago."

I nodded. Gentry was nothing if not a professional. The first thing the old woman would do would be to hand Bria over to Mab so no one could snatch my sister out from under her and collect on the bounty. At least Gentry had nabbed Bria and not some sick, twisted bastards like the ones I'd killed at Northern Aggression. Those kinds of bounty hunters would have raped my sister—maybe worse—before turning her over to the Fire elemental. There was some small comfort in that, and right now, I'd take what I could get.

"I need your phone," I said. "And that private number

you got for me. You know the one. She's sure to be waiting for me to make contact, and I think it's time to give her exactly what she wants."

Finn bit his lip, but he nodded. He punched in a number, then handed me the phone.

It rang three times before she picked it up.

"Yes?" her silky voice rasped over the line.

I drew in a breath. "Hello, Mab."

23

Silence.

For a moment, I thought she wouldn't answer me, but then the Fire elemental let out a low, slow laugh that made my hand tighten around the phone until my knuckles cracked. I wanted to break the damn thing—I wanted to break *her*.

"Well, well, well, if it isn't the Spider calling me. Tell me, do you prefer Gin Blanco? Or Genevieve Snow?" Mab sneered. "I'd like to get it right, now that I know exactly who the hell you are."

"It's Gin," I quipped. "Like the fucking liquor. As for who I really am, it certainly took you long enough to put it together, didn't it? The clues were all there. My spider rune, my rescuing Bria over and over again, my declaring war on you. You know, you really should have listened to Jonah McAllister when he wanted to kill me that night at the community college. It would have saved you a lot of trouble."

Mab let out another laugh, a light, high, pleased, pealing sound that made the small, primal voice in the back of my head start muttering. *Enemy, enemy, enemy.*

The Fire elemental's laughter faded away, and her tone hardened once more. "I suggest that you watch your tone," Mab snapped. "Considering as how I've got your dear, sweet sister right here in this very room with me and several of my giants. Men with a particular kind of . . . appetite, if you know what I mean."

I listened as closely as I could, but I didn't hear anything through the phone. Not crying, not whimpering, nothing. Bria wouldn't give the bastards the satisfaction of any of that—not until the pain was just too much to bear. Still, the silence unnerved me. Even if Bria had screamed, at least I would have known that she was still alive. The silence told me nothing—not one damn thing.

But now was not the time to show weakness, because I was dealing with Mab, and there was only one thing that the Fire elemental respected—strength.

"You haven't got a damn thing," I said, letting a mocking tone creep into my words. "Because you haven't got *me.*"

Something in my voice must have registered with Mab, because she paused in her gloating. "And what do you mean by that cryptic statement?"

"You know, for all these years I wondered why you came to our house that night," I said, my voice as hard, cold, and ugly as hers. "Why you murdered my mother and older sister. What the point of it all was. What had we ever done to you? But Elliot Slater was kind enough to tell me before he died. You remember Elliot, don't you,

Mab? The giant was your number-one enforcer, before I blasted his brains out with a shotgun."

Across the room, Roslyn shuddered. We both knew that she'd really killed Slater, but the vampire clamped her lips together and didn't make a sound. Xavier put his arm around Roslyn, hugging her to his chest. I turned away from them, blocking them out, blocking everything out but the sound of Mab's voice and what it might reveal to me.

"And what did Elliot tell you?" the Fire elemental sneered. "What do you think you know, little Genevieve?"

"Why, Elliot told me all about your crazy aunt, what was her name? Oh, yes, *Magda*. Elliot was more than happy to spill his guts to me. He told me all about dear aunt Magda and how she used her Air magic to see the future. How she prophesized that a member of the Snow family would one day kill you—a girl with both Ice and Stone magic."

"So what?" Mab snapped. "Because believe me when I tell you that your precious sister is in no position to do any such thing."

"So this, bitch. Bria isn't the one that you want. She isn't the one with both Ice and Stone magic—I am."

Silence. I didn't know what effect my words had on Mab, and I didn't care. My whole world shrank to what I could hear on the other end of the line, to straining as hard as I could to just hear Bria's voice, a whimper, a murmur, something, anything that would tell me she was still alive—

"You're lying," Mab said. "Lying to keep me from killing your precious sister."

I laughed. "Please. I have no need to lie. Not about

this. How the hell do you think I survived being trapped in that coal mine with Tobias Dawson after the dwarf knocked me out at your party a few months ago? I used my Ice magic to collapse his own mine right on top of his head and then my Stone power to help me find my way out after the fact. That's how. Ask Bria. She'll tell you the same thing. Or better yet, get her to use her magic. Because she only has Ice, not Ice and Stone like I do."

More silence. A swishing sort of noise filled my ear, and it took me a moment to figure out what it was—fabric rubbing together, like Mab was walking across whatever room she was in.

"What kind of magic do you have?" the Fire elemental hissed.

No answer.

My heart twisted in my chest, and I wondered if Mab was just playing a game with me. Why wasn't Bria answering her? Was she in such bad shape already? Was she—was she dead already? That paralyzing, icy numbness began to fill my body again, one cold inch at a time—

"Ice," Bria finally mumbled, her voice sounding faint and far away, so very far away. "I only have Ice magic. Gene—Gin's the one with both Ice and Stone magic."

Relief punched me in the gut, doubling me over. The others stared at me in alarm, and Finn started toward my side, but I waved him off. I couldn't stop the cold tears of relief from streaming down my face, though. Alive—Bria was still alive. Which meant that I still had a chance, however small, however remote, to save her. As long as Bria was still breathing, Jo-Jo could fix whatever damage had been done to her.

More noises sounded, more voices, and then something crackled. Whatever happened, whatever Bria said or did, Mab didn't like it. The Fire elemental hissed out a scream of rage and frustration that was so loud that even the others in the cabin heard it through the phone.

Despite the situation, I smiled. It always felt good to rattle your nemesis.

"Say that I believe you," Mab said, coming back on the line. "How do I know that this isn't some trick? Over these past few months, I've learned a lot of things about you, Spider, one of which is your rather uncanny ability to trick your opponents, to sense their weaknesses and exploit them to your own advantage."

"It's not a trick, Mab," I replied. "Once again, you were just too stupid to make sure that you were targeting the right sister. Sloppy, sloppy, sloppy, letting me keep on breathing all these years."

"I could kill Bria right now for your insolence," she snapped.

"You could, and that would be the end of you—of *everything*. Because there would be nothing left for me—nothing left for me to do but get my revenge on you."

This time, Mab laughed. "Something that you haven't had any success with so far. You've missed me twice already this week."

"True. But if you kill Bria, then I promise you this—I will *destroy* you. No matter how long it takes, no matter what it costs me. I won't sleep, I won't eat. I won't do anything but plot your downfall. I will mow down your men like they're weeds. I'll kill so many of them so viciously, so brutally, so horribly that no one will dare to work for you.

And sooner or later, I'll get you too. We both know that you can't hide in that big, fancy house of yours forever. I almost got you there this week. You really think that you can keep me out forever?"

Mab didn't respond.

"Face it," I said. "Bria's not the one who's a threat to you—I am. Me. Gin Blanco, Genevieve Snow, the little girl that you tortured all those years ago. And if you kill my sister, I will stop at nothing to end your existence. *Nothing*. And by now, you should know exactly how good I am. I'm the Spider, bitch—I'm the best there is."

More silence.

In the cabin, the others stared at me, shock filling their faces at my harsh words—and the fact that I meant every single one of them. My hand tightened around the phone. I turned away from my friends and stared out the window into the dark. I needed to be hard right now, as cold, hard, and unfeeling as winter itself. That was the only way that I was going to buy Bria some more time.

"What are you proposing?" Mab finally asked.

"A simple trade. My life for Bria's."

My friends gasped, but I kept my eyes fixed on the blackness. This was the way it had to be—the way it was always going to be.

Trading myself for Bria was a price that I was willing to pay—a price I'd been paying ever since Mab had duct-taped my own spider rune in between my hands and then superheated it with her Fire magic. Everything that had followed afterward—my thinking that Bria was dead, living on the streets, being taken in by Fletcher, training to be an assassin—all of that had just been leading up to this one, inevitable moment. Maybe it was fate, or maybe it was just my own bad luck, but there was nothing I could do to change the past. All I could do now was try to survive long enough to give Bria a new future.

"And how do I know that this isn't some kind of trick?" Mab repeated.

"You don't," I snapped. "But we both know you want to kill me too badly to turn down a free shot at me. And one more thing—I want Bria there in one piece. That means no rape, no torture, no burning her alive with your Fire magic like you did to the rest of our family."

Mab let out a little chuckle. "I'm afraid it's too late for that last one, Genevieve. Your sister's already screamed quite nicely for me."

For a moment I thought I might lose it. That I might start screaming and never, ever stop. Mab had tortured Bria, had burned my baby sister with her elemental Fire magic. The thing that I'd feared the most had already come to pass, but there was nothing I could about it now, no real way I could help Bria, except by trying to spare her more of the same and keep her alive long enough for me to try to rescue her.

"Then you stop the torture right now."

"Or what?" Mab sneered.

"Or I won't show tomorrow, and you'll spend the rest of your miserable life looking over your shoulder—until I kill you. That's what. You really want to take that chance just so you can get a few hours' amusement out of torturing Bria? Besides, we both know you'd have more fun with me anyway. I didn't break and tell you what you wanted to know when I was a kid. Just think of all the long hours you could work on me this go around, the happiness that would bring you. Bria's a small fish, Mab. I'm the catch of the day—the catch of a *lifetime*. You can either stop torturing Bria and have me, or you can start counting down the days until I kill you. Your choice."

More silence.

Finally, Mab huffed out a sigh of displeasure. "Fine. I won't torture your sister . . . much more."

It was the best I could do, given the circumstances—no matter how much it hurt. No matter how much my heart was breaking for Bria and what she was suffering right now. "Good. So why don't you tell me when and where, and we can get on with things?"

"Tomorrow. Dusk. As for the place, why don't we go back to the beginning?"

My stomach twisted at her nasty tone. "What do you mean?"

"Let's go back to the very beginning, since you seem to be such a fond student of history," Mab said. "Meet me at your old house, Genevieve Snow. The place where I tried to kill you all those years ago. I'm sure you remember where it is. And don't worry. Because this time I plan on succeeding."

I opened my mouth, but for once, Mab hung up on me.

I closed the cell phone and turned to face my friends. If they'd been shocked before, they were simply horrified now—eyes wide, mouths open, faces pinched white with fear for me and what I was about to do.

"What did Mab say?" Finn asked. "Will she go for the trade?"

I handed his phone back to him. "She'll go for it. She wants to kill me too badly not to."

"You're not actually going to go through with it?" Eva piped up from her spot on the couch. "It's suicide, Gin!"

I shrugged. "No more so than any of the other things that I've done over the years."

Roslyn, Xavier, Finn, Eva, Violet, Warren—they all tried to talk me out of it, of course. They listed all the reasons why meeting Mab would result in nothing but my own death, along with Bria's. They ranted and raved up one side and down the other that I was being foolish, stupid even, if I thought that Mab would let either one of us live.

But they didn't change my mind.

If I had to sacrifice myself to save Bria, so be it. I didn't care anymore as long as she was safe. It was all I'd ever wanted since this whole thing had started.

Jo-Jo and Sophia didn't join in the others' protests. Instead, the two dwarven sisters stood still and silent by the fireplace. They both knew that there was no use trying to talk me out of meeting Mab. Hell, maybe Jo-Jo had seen this was what was going to happen, thanks to her Air magic and the precognition that went along with it.

Owen was quiet too, not joining in the Greek chorus. Instead, he slung his arm over my shoulder and stood by my side while the others alternately bullied, threatened, and tried to cajole me into abandoning my plan. I leaned into his body just the smallest bit, letting him take the weight of the moment.

Finally, when the others realized that they weren't going to change my mind, they quit grousing and drifted off to bed. Jo-Jo shepherded the crowd and made sure that everyone had enough pillows, sheets, and blankets for the night. I took a long, hot shower to wash the blood and grime from my body, then grabbed a spare set of pajamas from among the various clothes stashed at the cabin.

Owen and I took the bedroom on the ground floor, while everyone else trooped to the upstairs bedrooms. I wanted to be downstairs, wanted to be the first line of defense, just in case any of the bounty hunters traced us here. The odds of that happening were next to impossible, especially since on paper the cabin was owned by Nick A. Medes, which was one of Fletcher's rock-solid aliases. But Sophia had volunteered to stand watch, just in case. I would have done it myself, except that Jo-Jo bullied me into getting some rest.

I was tired—so tired—but I couldn't sleep. Instead, I paced back and forth across the bedroom, the wooden floorboards creaking under my bare feet. Owen watched me from his position on the bed. He didn't say anything, but his gaze never left my tight face.

"I'm sorry," I said, finally stopping to turn and look at him.

"For what?"

I threw my hands out wide. "For all of this. For the fact that you and Eva are now on the run because of me, because of my being the Spider."

Owen sighed. "There's nothing to be sorry for, Gin. I knew that this was a possibility when we got together. I knew that you were going after Mab, and I knew that it might come to this."

"Yeah," I said, flopping down on the bed beside him. "But it's not exactly what you signed up for, is it?"

Owen shrugged. "Maybe it's not, but I wouldn't trade it—or you—for a second. You know how much I care about you, Gin. You know how much I love you."

He'd finally said the words that I'd been dreading and longing to hear.

And I wanted to say them back to him.

My mouth opened, but the words—the damn *words*—just wouldn't come out. They snagged in my throat, choking me, even as the syllables squeezed my heart like a silverstone vise cranking tighter and tighter. My emotions were just too raw from everything that had happened tonight and all the awful things that might happen tomorrow. I couldn't speak, I couldn't breathe, I couldn't do anything but just feel—feel all the love I had for Owen.

Part of me knew that my gaped-mouth silence was stupid. I should tell Owen how I felt now, tonight, before another second passed. But part of me wanted to wait. When I told Owen I loved him, I wanted the moment to be about him, about us, and what we had—not because Mab was more than likely going to kill me tomorrow.

But try as I might, I just couldn't force out the words. Agony welled up in my aching chest, and a crazy, feverish sort of passion gripped my body. So I did the only thing that I could do—I leaned forward and kissed Owen.

My tongue drove into his mouth, over and over again, even as I started tearing at his clothes. Maybe I couldn't say the words, but I could show Owen how much he meant to me. I needed to—I was *desperate* to.

I didn't want to think tonight. I didn't want to think about the fact that Mab had Bria. That the Fire elemental had already tortured my sister, would torture her even more before the night was through, and that there was nothing I could do to stop it. No way to rescue Bria. No way to break into Mab's mansion without getting myself and everyone else killed in the process. No, I didn't want to think tonight.

But for once, I couldn't bury my emotions, my feelings. Couldn't pretend they didn't exist or that my heart wasn't breaking for Bria, even as it swelled with love for Owen. Everything I'd been through tonight—fighting Mab, feeling her Fire burn me, battling the bounty hunters, losing Bria in the woods—roared up inside me, a tidal wave of emotion that I just couldn't fight any longer. It needed a release—now, before it consumed me.

Owen let out a low growl, wrapped his hand in my hair, and pulled me down on top of him. His tongue met mine, dodging and darting just as fast and hard as mine did, even as we sucked the air out of each other's mouths. Owen raked his teeth across my earlobe before his lips dipped lower, nipping at my neck.

"Mmm," I murmured, feeling my desperation melt into a far more pleasurable form of agony. "You know how much I—I love it when you kiss me there."

"And you know how much I love *you*," he rasped against my neck.

I responded by ripping open the flannel shirt he'd changed into after taking his own shower. The buttons flew everywhere, landing on the wooden floor, but I didn't care. I was already leaning forward, tracing my tongue down his broad, muscled chest. Owen kneaded my back, urging me on, letting me take the lead. But I was feeling too much, too hard, too fast, and my hands shook as I tried to work the button on his jeans, my fingers slipping off the smooth metal.

"Here, let me," he murmured.

Owen popped open the button, then drew down the zipper. He lifted his hips, and I peeled the jeans off him. He wore nothing underneath, and I stopped a moment to admire his muscled body, and his erection that was already waiting for me. I started to lean down and put my mouth on him, but Owen grabbed my arms.

"Not yet," he whispered. "Let me take care of you first."

I didn't have time to protest before Owen rolled me over onto my back. He took a little more care with my borrowed clothes than I had with his, but they disappeared soon enough. Owen's lips scorched a path down my neck before his mouth closed on my right nipple. Over and over, he ran his tongue over the peak before gently scraping his teeth across the tip. He repeated the process on my other nipple until I wanted to scream with pleasure and frustration. I arched up off the bed, already wanting to feel him moving inside me.

Owen had other ideas. His tongue moved from my breasts and dipped into my bellybutton before sliding lower. I opened my legs, and he put his mouth on me, flicking his tongue against me with exquisite precision, ratcheting up my desperate need that much more.

Where he had been gentle, patient even, before, now he became as hard and wild as I had been, his tongue driving deeper and deeper into me, making me thrash and moan beneath him.

"Owen," I rasped, my fingers digging into his shoulders. "Owen."

Finally, just when I thought I couldn't take any more, Owen got up on his knees and pulled me up to him. Our arms locked around each other, and our bodies melded together.

Now we were both out of control—our passion for each other, our desire, our need, burning, burning, burning. Our hands were everywhere, kneading, caressing, stroking, and our tongues dueled back and forth as we moaned into each other's mouths.

Finally, I got the upper hand. I pushed Owen down onto his back, straddling him. I took his hard cock in my hand, thumbing the wet tip before lightly raking my nails down the whole length of him. He shuddered with pleasure under me, his muscles straining.

I reached over, opened the nightstand drawer, and drew out a condom from the box there. Of course, I took my pills, but we also used extra protection for a variety of reasons.

Owen arched an eyebrow. "You're always prepared for everything, aren't you?"

I smiled down at him. "The cabin is nothing if not well stocked."

Using my hand and then my mouth, I teased his cock a little more, until his hands were fisting the sheets just as mine had been a few minutes ago, before I unrolled the condom over his straining shaft.

"Gin," Owen murmured. "My Gin."

"Oh, yes," I said. "You're mine. And I want you—now."

I went up on my knees, then sank down, taking him deep inside me. Owen pulled me down on top of him, and we rocked back and forth, thrusting against each other as hard and fast as we could. Until everything that we'd both been feeling tonight—all the fear and agony and passion and love—exploded inside us like a shower of stars falling from the sky.

❄24❄

The next day dawned all too quickly, bringing with it another round of snow—and most likely my messy death at the hands of Mab Monroe.

Last night had taken its toll on us all, physically and emotionally, which was why everyone was still asleep when I slipped out of Owen's warm arms around ten the next morning.

Everyone except Jo-Jo, that is. The dwarf sat at the kitchen table, wrapped in her pink flannel housecoat and sipping a cup of lavender tea. The fragrant fumes filled the air, making it smell warm and soothing. I breathed in, drawing what comfort I could from this safe, quiet moment. Because all too soon, I knew it would be gone—and perhaps me along with it.

"Shouldn't you be asleep like everyone else?" I asked Jo-Jo, as I opened the kitchen cabinets to see what supplies were on hand for a late breakfast.

"I slept plenty before I spelled Sophia from guard duty," Jo-Jo said. "Now, I'm restless, just like you are."

I grunted. *Restless* wasn't quite the word that I would use to describe my mood. More like *resigned*. I pushed the feeling aside and started pulling ingredients out of the cabinets. Flour, sugar, salt, and all the other nonperishable staples that Fletcher had packed the cabin with. If I was going to go out today, then I wanted a good breakfast to help me along.

"I grabbed fresh milk, berries, butter, and a few other things from my fridge before coming over here last night," Jo-Jo said. "Just in case you were inclined to feel like making breakfast this morning."

I arched an eyebrow. "Got a glimpse of that with your Air magic, did you? Your precognition?"

Jo-Jo grinned.

"Tell me," I murmured, opening the fridge and grabbing the milk. "Did you happen to see whether I manage to kill Mab today before she kills me? Because right now, I'd take any good news I could get."

Instead of answering me, Jo-Jo stared down into her tea, as though she could read something in the leaves in the bottom of the mug. Hell, maybe she could, given her Air magic. After a moment, the dwarf seemed to decide something because she nodded and looked up at me with her clear eyes.

"Did I ever tell you how I first met Fletcher?"

I shook my head and moved over to the counter where I'd placed the rest of the ingredients.

"It was a week after Sophia was kidnapped."

I jerked around in surprise, and the milk almost slipped

from my hands. "Sophia—Sophia was *kidnapped*? When? By whom?"

Jo-Jo's hands tightened around her mug. "It happened almost fifty years ago. There was a sick, sadistic bastard by the name of Harley Grimes. Half giant, half dwarf, and all mean. Grimes and the rest of his clan of miscreants lived way up in the mountains, even farther up than Warren's store, Country Daze. He saw Sophia one day, and he decided that he was going to have her. When I wouldn't give her to him, he came into my salon and took her. Busted up the place, beat me real bad, then beat Sophia when she tried to stop him."

Breakfast forgotten, I slid into the seat across from Jo-Jo.

Jo-Jo's eyes clouded over, like she was reliving that terrible day—the day that her sister had been taken from her. I knew what she must be feeling all too well. The rage, the frustration, the helplessness. They all pulsed through me with every beat of my heart.

"I went after Grimes, of course, but I couldn't find my way up the mountain to his hideout, and I couldn't get past all the booby traps that he had strung through the woods. Besides, my magic is for healing, not killing. But I'd heard stories about someone who could help, who could kill, for the right price."

"The Tin Man," I whispered Fletcher's assassin name.

Jo-Jo nodded. "So I went through the appropriate channels, and I made contact with him. I told Fletcher that if he brought Sophia back I would be his friend for life—that anything I had would be his, including my Air magic. He agreed to my deal and took off after Sophia."

I could almost see the scene unfolding before my eyes. Fletcher, tall, strong, and in his prime as an assassin. Jo-Jo, desperate for her sister's safe return. And Sophia—no, I couldn't picture Sophia. Not as she might have been back then. Before—before her innocence was taken away from her.

"What—what did Grimes do to Sophia?" I asked.

Tears welled up in Jo-Jo's eyes and trickled down her face. "Just about every awful thing that you can imagine. Rape, torture, beatings. He made her into a slave, made her work from sunup until sundown, then come in and warm his bed at night. Grimes and one of his brothers had some Fire magic in them. The two of them would spend hours torturing her with it—burning her, blistering her skin, even making her breathe it in like cigarette smoke."

An odd thought crossed my mind. "Is that—is that why Sophia's voice is the way it is? So raspy and broken? Because Grimes made her breathe in elemental Fire?"

Jo-Jo nodded. "It damaged her vocal cords something fierce. I offered to fix it for her with my Air magic, but she wouldn't let me. She just—wouldn't."

I leaned over and grabbed Jo-Jo's hand, trying to offer her what comfort I could, even though I hadn't even been born when all of this had happened. But so much made sense to me now. Why Fletcher had such a close relationship with the Deveraux sisters, why they'd helped him so much all these years, even why Sophia was the way that she was—moody, withdrawn, broken. My heart ached for the Goth dwarf. My torment at the hands of Mab had been nothing compared to what she'd endured.

Jo-Jo swiped away her tears and continued with her story. "Fletcher kept his word. He went up that mountain, and he did what I asked him to do, what he'd trained himself to do as the Tin Man. It took him two weeks of guerrilla warfare tactics, but he killed a whole passel of Grimes's men and hurt Grimes himself real bad. Fletcher would have killed the bastard, if one of Grimes's men hadn't gutshot Fletcher. He was almost dead when he showed up on my front porch, but Fletcher rescued Sophia and brought her back home to me. And he made sure that Grimes never bothered us again. Every time that bastard came sniffing around, Fletcher let him know exactly what would happen— that Fletcher would finish the job he started and kill Grimes if he didn't stay up there on his damn mountain and leave us alone."

Jo-Jo fell silent, lost in her thoughts once more. Then she looked at me again, a fierce light burning in her pale eyes.

"Fletcher Lane was the finest man that I ever met, and he was certainly the best assassin. But you know what, Gin? Fletcher told me something a few weeks before he died—something about *you*."

"And what would that be?" I asked, even though I wasn't sure I wanted to hear the answer.

Jo-Jo speared me with a hard look. "He told me that you were even better than he was. That you had the kind of cold, iron will that few people have. That you weren't afraid to do what needed to be done. But the most important thing he told me was this—that if anyone could kill Mab, it was you. Don't you see, Gin? It's what he's been preparing you for all these years. It's why he trained you in the first place, it's why he made you into the Spider. So you could do what needed to be done to save your sister, just like he saved mine all those years ago."

Jo-Jo drew in a breath. "That's why I'm telling you this now. If Sophia could survive all the horrible things Grimes did to her, then you can survive Mab too, just like you did when you were a little girl. And I need you to survive, Gin. We all do. We lost Fletcher already. We can't lose you too."

I sat there holding the dwarf's hand, but I wasn't really there with her. Instead, I was with the old man. A thousand images of him flashed through my mind then, from the way he leaned over the counter at the Pork Pit reading his latest book to how he'd always had a hot meal waiting there for me when I'd come back from an assignment.

But mostly, I thought about how Fletcher had always believed in me, how he'd never once wavered in his support of me, how he'd been so patient in teaching me all the things that had helped me survive.

Genevieve Snow, Gin Blanco, the Spider; whatever I called myself, one thing remained the same—Fletcher Lane had fiercely loved me, and I'd loved the old man just as much in return. Enough to follow in his footsteps as an assassin. Enough to avenge his murder. And more than enough to take on this final impossible task of killing Mab Monroe.

"What are you thinking, Gin?" Jo-Jo asked.

A cold smile curved my lips. "I'm thinking that I'll be damned if I'm going to disappoint the old man and rob us both of our revenge on Mab, even if Fletcher isn't around to see it."

By the time the others came down to the kitchen, Jo-Jo and I had both regained our composure, and I'd whipped up enough food to feed an army. Sweet raspberry pancakes, blackberry biscuits, lots of scrambled eggs, piles of sizzling bacon and country-fried ham, creamy peach smoothies. All that and more waited on the kitchen table and surrounding countertops, and the air smelled of all the sugar, spices, and grease that I'd used to create my last supper, as it were.

One by one, they trudged down the stairs and planted themselves in the kitchen. Finn, Xavier, Roslyn, Sophia, Eva, Warren, Violet, and finally Owen. I handed everyone a plate and forced them to eat, chattering inane pleasantries all the while.

"Somebody's had too much sugar this morning," Finn mumbled into his coffee mug, waiting for the chicory fumes to rouse him from his postsleep stupor.

"Nonsense," I declared, mussing his walnut-colored hair. "I haven't had nearly enough yet."

I ate more than anyone else, stuffing down as much food as I could stomach. I'd need the calories and energy boost before the day was through. Everything tasted fine, as long as I didn't think about Bria and how Mab had tortured her last night, could still be torturing her. But there was nothing I could do to help her right now, nothing at all, so I made myself swallow biscuit after biscuit, even if they all plummeted to the bottom of my stomach like lead weights.

Once everyone was finished, I got up and started to wash the dishes, but Warren grabbed the plate out of my right hand, while his granddaughter, Violet, snagged the one out of my left hand.

"You sit right back down, missy," Warren said in his high, thin, reedy voice. "Violet and I will wash the dishes."

The old man hadn't combed his hair yet today, and the wispy white strands stuck up every which way over his forehead. The frizz in his hair matched the fuzzy mess of Violet's blond locks, even though she'd tried to tame hers. A family trait, right along with their dark brown eyes and tan skin that hinted at their Cherokee heritage.

The two of them moved over to the sink. I slipped back into my chair next to Owen, my eyes going to the clock on the wall. High noon already. The hours were ticking down until my meeting with Mab at dusk.

Everyone saw me staring at the clock, and I forced myself to smile.

"Don't look so glum, folks," I quipped. "My funeral isn't officially for six more hours yet."

"What are you going to do, Gin?" Violet asked me, her dark eyes wide behind her black glasses. "About Mab and the meeting tonight?"

I shrugged. "There's nothing to do but go through with things and meet her. I imagine that once I trade myself for Bria, Mab will get on with the business of killing me."

The Fire elemental murdering both Bria and me was far more likely, but I didn't voice that troublesome thought.

"Mab isn't going to kill you—not if we can help it," Owen rumbled, putting his hand on top of mine and squeezing it tight.

I frowned at him. "And what is that supposed to mean?"

Owen looked at the others, then back at me. "It means that while you were cooking breakfast, we had a powwow upstairs. We're all in agreement, Gin. You're not going to meet Mab by yourself. We're going with you—all of us."

I was just—stunned. Simply stunned that my friends would want to do such a thing, that they would even *consider* it. Trying to help me bring down Mab was just crazy on their part. Foolish. Insane. Stupid. Dangerous. Worry tightened my chest. So very, very dangerous.

"You—you can't do that," I protested. "This is between me and Mab. It always has been."

"This is about family, darling," Jo-Jo said in a firm voice. "You're a part of us, a part of all of us, and we aren't losing you without a fight, even if we do have to take on Mab and every single one of her giants."

The others nodded their heads and murmured their agreement. All I could do was stare at them.

Xavier with his massive frame. Beautiful, perfect Roslyn. Crotchedy, cranky Warren. Soft, pink Jo-Jo. Eva and Violet, who were both still so young, still so innocent. Sophia, who had been through more horrors than probably any of us really knew. Finn, with his bright green eyes that always reminded me so much of his father's. And finally Owen, full of that strength and quiet inner confidence that had drawn me to him in the first place.

Eyes hard, mouths set, faces tight. They all radiated the same stubborn determination, as immovable, implacable, and eternal as the mountains themselves. Emotion tightened my throat at their belief in me, that I could actually pull this off, that I could actually kill Mab and save Bria at the same time—even though I knew better deep down inside.

"You don't have to do this," I said in a rough, thick voice. "You all know the risks. Mab won't let me slip through her fingers this time. She'll have an army of men with her to make sure that doesn't happen. Not just her giants, but the bounty hunters too. Folks like Gentry and Sydney. Dangerous people."

"And you're going to have an army of folks with you," Xavier rumbled. "You've helped us all too much for us to abandon you now, Gin. You know that. We all know that. You've put your life on the line for each one of us. Now it's our turn."

One by one, the others all nodded their heads again, as if we were talking about having a spring picnic instead of going up against the deadliest woman in Ashland and all of her men. Didn't they know that all of us taking on Mab was much more dangerous than just me facing the firing squad by myself? If one of them went down in the fight, the others would rush to help that fallen friend. Mab's men would take advantage of their distraction, and then they'd all be lost.

I didn't want to accept their help. It was just too risky. One slip, one mistake, one tiny, minuscule miscalculation, and my friends could all wind up dead. Or worse, Mab could get her hands on them and torture them first before she killed them, just as she was probably doing to Bria right now. I didn't want that. I'd never wanted that. I couldn't fucking *bear* that.

But no one ducked from my searching gaze. No one's

eyes slid away from mine. No one wavered or showed any kind of doubt.

I sighed. "I'm not going to change your minds, am I?"

They all shook their heads.

No, I didn't want to accept my friends' help, didn't want to put them in any more danger than they were already in. But I also knew that having them with me was the only way that Bria might survive this thing. I needed someone there to make sure she made it to safety while I took on Mab. It made me sick, weighing my sister's life against everyone else's, using my friends this way, dragging them all down into the muck with me. But the truth was that I needed all the help I could get right now—and so did Bria.

"All right," I said in a quiet voice. "All right. Since I can't hog-tie all of you—at least not all of you at once— tell me what you're thinking."

A grin creased Finn's handsome face. "I thought you'd never ask."

Finn put his coffee mug down long enough to go upstairs. He came back a minute later with what looked like five reams of paper clutched to his chest. Finn dumped everything onto the kitchen table. Sheets of papers swirled up into the air like snowflakes before settling back onto the table. Photos, maps, old blueprints.

"What is all this?" I asked. "And how many trees did you kill printing it all out?"

"This," Finn said, sweeping his hand out over the mess on the table, "is every scrap of information that I was able to get my hands on concerning your childhood home. Or, at least what's left of it, anyway. Maps, police and aerial photographs, deeds, everything."

With his massive network of spies and other shady sources, as well as his own computer skills, Finn had the uncanny ability to dig up dirt on the saintliest soul. So I imagined that compiling all the info on my old childhood home hadn't been too much of a stretch for him. Still, the effort touched me because I knew that he was trying to give me the tools I needed to survive my confrontation with Mab. It was something his father, Fletcher, would have done, if the old man had still been alive.

"Actually," Finn said, "it wasn't too hard to get the info, since, well, I sort of own the land now."

My head snapped up. "What? What do you mean you *own* the land now?"

Finn winced. "Well, Dad left you quite a bit of money, his house, and the Pork Pit in his last will and testament."

"And . . ."

"And he left me everything else, including all his other real estate holdings. Rental properties, safe houses, and the land where your childhood home was. According to the tax records I found, he bought the land six months after your family was murdered."

I arched an eyebrow. "And you're just now finding out about it?"

Finn shrugged. "You know how paranoid the old man was about paper trails. He knew more about how to fake documents, confuse creditors, and hide assets than even I do. It's been months now, and I'm still trying to sort out which identity he used to purchase what property."

Everything that Finn said made sense. Fletcher had had dozens of identities and aliases, all with the appropriate driver's licenses, bank accounts, and passports to match. Still, I wondered why Fletcher had bought the property in the first place. Had he planned on telling me he knew who I really was? Maybe he'd thought that I'd want the land for sentimental reasons. Or had he known I'd battle Mab there one day? Once again, Fletcher had managed to surprise me from beyond the grave—and leave me wondering at his motives.

"Anyway, we can talk about transferring the ownership later, for a reasonable price, of course. And you can thank me later for digging up the rest of the files, Gin," Finn suggested in a not-so-humble voice.

I rolled my eyes, picked up the closest photograph, and got to work.

For the next half hour, we went through the information page by page, pulling out everything that might be useful. I didn't know much about Finn's methods, especially how he'd gotten his hands on so much data so quickly, but the maps and photographs were better than finding a pirate's buried treasure. Because I began to see that maybe things weren't as completely hopeless as they seemed. At least, not when it came to rescuing Bria.

"This is almost certainly where Mab will be," Finn said, pointing to a small cleared area on one of the photographs and then comparing it side-by-side to a more recent shot of the same spot. "It almost looks like some kind of patio."

I recognized the first, older photograph as being one that the police had taken during their investigation of my family's murder. There was a copy of it in the fat file of information Fletcher had left me on the same gruesome subject. All the photo really showed was a bleak landscape filled with piles of smoldering rubble. I'd looked at the photo a hundred times before, but my stomach still turned over at Finn's words. I recognized the spot—it was the place where I'd hidden Bria, the place where I'd thought she'd died all those long years ago.

The place where she could still die tonight.

My eyes dropped to my right index finger and the small silverstone band there. My spider rune ring. The one that Bria had given me for Christmas. Somehow, I'd forgotten about it during the long, long night. I could feel my sister's Ice magic in the thin band, like a cold string tied around my finger. Forget me not. I reached down and twisted the ring around, just like Bria always did to the ones that she wore. My heart lurched with the movement. If Bria died, this would be all that I'd have left of her—

"Gin?" Owen asked, seeing me stare at the ring.

"It was a courtyard with a garden and a fountain," I said in a soft voice, focusing on the photo once more. "Bria and I used to play out there and in a secret chamber that was hidden in a nearby staircase. I destroyed it all the night that Mab came to call on us when I used my Ice and Stone magic without thinking and collapsed our whole house. Part of the house toppled over into the courtyard, crushing the fountain, the staircase, and everything else that was there."

Finn gave me a sidelong glance. "Well, it's the only part of the house that's even remotely level and clear of rubble. At least, this area is. The rest of the place is overgrown with weeds."

"Looks like there's a lot of good places for Mab to hide her men around the courtyard," Xavier said.

"And a lot of good places for us to hide as well," Owen countered.

Xavier nodded his head in agreement.

I stared at the courtyard in the photograph. "How many bounty hunters do you think Mab has left, Finn? A dozen? Two?"

Instead of answering me, Finn pulled his cell phone out of his pocket and touched the screen a few times. "As of this morning, it appears there's about fifteen of them left in Ashland from the hotel records I was able to hack into. We took out five that night at Northern Aggression. Bria and I killed several more of them at the house last night, as well as the ones you took out in the woods. That thinned the ranks quite a bit. It looks like a few more have left town since last night, when Gentry turned in Bria and collected the bounty on her. Since you're turning yourself over to Mab, there's no use sticking around since there isn't any more money to be had from the bounties. Although rumor has it that Mab has paid some of the hunters to back her up tonight."

"But Gentry hasn't left yet," I murmured. "She'll be there with Sydney. I know she will be."

I'll take care of her as best I can until you come for her. The bounty hunter's words whispered in my mind. I wondered what she'd meant by them, what she was planning on doing. Gentry had already taken Bria to Mab, had already let my sister be tortured by the Fire elemental. What did the bounty hunter think she could do? Keep Mab from killing Bria outright? And why would she even bother trying? Gentry had gotten her bounty by now. Why would she care what happened to Bria after the fact?

Maybe it had something to do with my sparing Sydney that night outside Mab's mansion. Maybe Gentry thought she owed me something for not killing the girl when I had the chance. It didn't much matter what the bounty hunter was thinking or what she thought she owed me. If she stood between Bria escaping from Mab, then Gentry would die, just like the rest of the Fire elemental's men.

Finn continued with his count. "If I had to guess, I'd say that at least a dozen bounty hunters will be there, and Mab will have even more of her giants around the place as well. So let's say at least thirty men, total. Not counting Mab herself."

I didn't say anything. We all knew exactly how dangerous Mab was. I was the only one with even a remote chance of killing her, and I didn't think I could do it. Not really. I hadn't been able to stop her elemental Fire from burning through my Stone magic at the country club. Only the giant stumbling into my path at the last minute and being able to use him as a body shield had saved me from being burned to death.

Still, this was it—the final showdown—and I had to try, whether I thought I could actually take out Mab or not. So, game on.

Since my friends were determined to come with me, there was nothing I could do but let them—and hope I did everything in my power to help them survive it. Still, I wanted to give them all one more chance to reconsider, one more chance to back out and save themselves.

"You're all bound and determined to do this?" I asked, looking at each one of them in turn again. "Because you don't have to. You don't have to risk yourselves like this."

Warren cleared his throat, leaned forward, and stared at me with his dark eyes. "And you didn't have to risk yourself when you took on Tobias Dawson for me, Gin."

"Or when you helped me kill Elliot Slater to keep him from beating me to death," Roslyn chimed in.

"Or when you saved me from Jake McAllister at the Pork Pit," Eva added.

It went on and on from there, each one of my friends telling me how I'd helped them out at one time or another and how they were going to repay the favor now— whether I wanted them to or not.

Xavier. Roslyn. Eva. Violet. Warren. Jo-Jo. Sophia. Finn. Owen.

One by one, my friends and family all spoke up and offered to do something, anything, to contribute in some small way, even if it was just watching each other's backs. I'd once lost my family, once lost everything that I'd ever cared about, and their simple words meant more to me than any of them knew or could even guess.

But when they were through, I pushed my emotions aside, shoved them into the back corner of my heart, and let them ice over. Because now it was time to leave Gin Blanco and her friends, family, and lover behind. Now it was time for the Spider to come out and hunt once more—for the final time.

"All right then," I said, my gaze dropping back down to the photographs on the table. "Here's what we're going to do."

✳ 25 ✳

At exactly six o'clock, just as the weak winter sun was starting to sink over the western sky, I stood in front of the snow-covered ruins of my childhood home.

The last time that I'd been here had been seventeen years ago—the night that my mother, Eira, and older sister, Annabella, had been murdered. The night that I'd thought I'd killed Bria, when I'd used my Ice and Stone magic to destroy our house. The night that Mab had tortured me by melting my spider rune medallion into my palms. Even now, my scars itched and burned at the memory, so much so that I had to curl my hands into fists to keep them from trembling from the phantom pain.

Needless to say, given all that, I hadn't had any desire to return here since.

Our house had always seemed so large to me as a child, and now, standing here in the cold as an adult, I could see the ruined remains of the impressive mansion it had once been. I looked at the few walls that were still standing, even though everything else around them had collapsed and crumbled long ago. I didn't remember our having been particularly rich, but we must have been because the house stretched out and out and out. Or perhaps that was just because it had all been reduced to rubble.

My childhood home looked untouched by human hands, as if no one had been near the place since it had been destroyed. Maybe they hadn't, since Fletcher had bought the land so soon after my family's murder. Besides, not many people wanted to linger in a place where such atrocities had been committed. Even people without magic could sense those sorts of crimes, in the primal way that animals can sniff out fear, danger, and evil in others.

The mansion—or what was left of it—huddled in the middle of a dense section of the forest right in between Fletcher's house and Jo-Jo's beauty salon. Ridges covered with pine trees surrounded the mansion on three sides before rising up and rolling away into the rest of the mountainous landscape. Snow-covered rubble stretched out as far as the eye could see, rocks piled on top of more rocks. But the years had taken their toll, and the surrounding forest had made inroads into reclaiming the area. A few small pine trees had sprung up in what I remembered to be the downstairs living room, while weeds and winter wildflowers wound like ribbons through the black, jagged cracks in the stone foundation.

As I stood there, what little was left of the sun disappeared, replaced by heavy gray storm clouds. In less than a minute, twilight cloaked the land, and snowflakes started drifting down from the sky. They covered the mess in front of me in a fresh, white coat of snow, hiding what I could see of the ruins.

But even now, all these years later, I could still hear the stones.

They growled with dark, ugly, angry mutters, the remnants of my primal scream of elemental rage, pain, and fear. That one scream, that one burst of magic, had brought down the whole house. Even now, the stones still reverberated with the sound, so much so that it almost seemed to me like they were still vibrating, still ripping themselves apart one molecule at a time.

For some reason, the mutters comforted me.

Because the stones were still angry at what had been done to them, at what had been done to me, the elemental who felt such kinship with them, who had so much power and control over them. I closed my eyes and concentrated on the stones, listening to them, embracing their rage, letting it fill me up, and making it my own once more. It took only a moment for the stones' mutters to grow sharper, blacker, harsher. Stones never forgot when something traumatic happened on top of or most especially to them. Emotions, actions, and feelings might fade over time, but they never truly vanished. The stones sensed that I was near—the woman who had lashed out at them before—and that I was back now for a specific purpose. I reveled in the memory of their anger—because it was my anger as well, at everything that Mab had done to my family. And I knew that I would need it now even more than I had that awful night so long ago.

I walked forward, my boots crunching in the snow and scraping against the cold rocks underneath. I treaded slowly, carefully, making no sudden movements, not doing anything that would jeopardize Bria in any way.

Or give the bounty hunters who were watching me an excuse to put a bullet in my head.

I could see them, crouched here and there among the rubble. Men and women with rifles, crossbows, and other weapons, every one of them trained on me, ready to pull the trigger if I did anything stupid. Fools. They were the ones who were being stupid, because they all should have unloaded on me with everything they had the second that I was in range.

But Mab wanted to kill me herself and most especially wanted to gloat in my face while she did it. Her first mistake—and the one that might just finally lead to her own death.

It took me several minutes to pick my way through the rubble to the back side of the mansion. Along the way, I spotted more than a few broken bits of my childhood hidden in the snow and rocks. A half-melted doll's head. A charred teddy bear. Shards of glass and small figurines from my mother's snow globe collection. The ruination only hardened my resolve to do what needed to be done here tonight.

Finally, though, I stepped into the courtyard itself. It looked just the way I remembered it—the terrible, terrible way that it had appeared in my nightmares for so many years now. Truth be told, there was even less to see back here than there had been in the front of the house. Certainly nothing overtly menacing. Just piles of rubble everywhere.

It took me a moment, but I managed to pick out the

spot where our once-beautiful fountain had sat, until part of the house had fallen on top of it, reducing the stone to splinters. Farther back was another heap of rocks that had once formed a staircase with a secret chamber underneath it, the one where I'd hidden Bria. And over there—right over *there*—was the spot where I'd collapsed when I'd found blood on the stones and thought I'd killed Bria with my magic.

The memories rose up in me, the black emotions skimming the surface of my mind like shark fins. Somehow, I pushed the twisted feelings back down into the bottom of my soul where they belonged. I drew in a breath, pulled my eyes away from the rubble, and focused on the people in front of me.

Mab and Bria.

The Fire elemental stood in the middle of the courtyard in a flat, level area that was relatively free of debris—in the exact spot Finn had pointed out in the police photograph several hours ago. A bloodred evening gown hugged Mab's lush body, while a black velvet cloak trimmed with mink covered her otherwise bare shoulders. Her hair seemed to be as red as her dress tonight, the soft, curling waves of it just brushing the top of her cloak. I half-expected the expensive material to start smoldering, but of course it didn't. Mab had too much control over her magic to let that happen. Still, someone had dressed to kill tonight— literally.

As always, Mab wore her rune necklace around her throat. A sunburst. The symbol for fire. Even now, in the snow and fading twilight, the wavy golden rays flickered, and the ruby set into the center of the design seemed to glow, as though she were wearing a ring of fire around her neck.

I looked past Mab to where Bria stood. Dark circles ringed her blue eyes, and her blond hair was a mess around her face, especially since it had been singed off in several places. Bria wore the same clothes she'd had on last night during our run through the woods. Camisole, jeans, sneakers, coat. Only now they hung in tatters on her, and I could see where the fabric had been burned away completely in places—along with her skin underneath it. Puffy blisters and deep, bone-searing burns dotted what I could see of Bria's legs, chest, and arms through the flapping fabric. Mab had tortured her, burned my baby sister with her Fire magic, just as I'd feared that the cruel elemental would.

It was almost as though time had rewound itself and my worst fear had come to life once more. For a moment, I was back in the Pork Pit that long, awful night that Fletcher had been murdered, staring down at the old man's ruined flesh. Looking at the burns and blisters that dotted his body, staring at all the many places where Alexis James had used her Air elemental magic to rip his skin from his bones.

Once again, I'd failed to protect someone that I loved from being tortured. The only difference was that Bria was still breathing—for now.

I struggled to keep my emotions in check, to reveal nothing of what I was feeling, but I couldn't keep my nails from digging into the spider rune scars embedded in my palms. A small circle surrounded by eight thin rays. So similar to Mab's rune, but so very different at the same time.

Bria wasn't alone, of course. A giant stood on either side of her, their hands clamped on her arms, holding her upright and keeping her in place.

And Ruth Gentry was here, just like I'd thought she would be. The bounty hunter leaned against part of a wall about five steps behind Bria and the giants. The old woman's stance was casual, nonchalant even, but her hand hovered just above the pearl-handled revolver strapped to her waist. I didn't see Sydney, but I knew that the girl was here somewhere with her rifle, probably perched on one of the piles of rubble farther out in the courtyard.

Gentry saw me staring at her and gave me a respectful nod, almost like we were in on some kind of secret together. I didn't nod back. Still, I supposed that the bounty hunter had kept her word to me. She'd made sure that Bria was here in more or less one piece, despite the torture that my sister had endured. I would give Gentry the courtesy of killing her quickly for that.

Finally, I looked at Bria. Our eyes met and held across the snowy distance, and I could see the pain and fear and desperation flashing in her blue gaze—pain at her own injuries and fear for me and what Mab was about to do to me.

Jonah McAllister had also come to see me kick off to hell. The lawyer stood off to one side, a triumphant smile for once bringing a bit of emotion to his unnaturally smooth features. He wouldn't have missed this for the world. Oh, yes, McAllister was especially smug because he was finally getting exactly what he wanted—Gin Blanco, his son's murderer, fried extra crispy by his sadistic bitch of a boss.

As I stood there, surrounded by my enemies on all sides, a cold calm filled me. The sort of black, emotionless void that Fletcher had taught me to pour into my heart and coat every little piece of my soul with. I embraced the darkness, welcomed it, relished it even. For the very last time.

Because as soon as I'd stepped into this courtyard, I wasn't Gin Blanco anymore. I wasn't Genevieve Snow or the lost, terrified, thirteen-year-old girl I'd been the last time I was here.

No, right now I was the Spider. And I was here to finally destroy my nemesis—once and for all.

* 26 *

Behind me, the bounty hunters closed ranks, their footsteps crunching on the snow. In less than a minute, I was surrounded on three sides by both the bounty hunters and the giants Mab had brought along with her, with the Fire elemental herself directly in front of me. At least fifteen men and women made up the loose semicircle around me, and there had to be even more, like Sydney, hidden in the rubble I couldn't see.

But that was okay. Because I wasn't here alone, and I knew that my friends, my family, would back me up. They had come here tonight and put themselves on the line to give me a fighting chance. It was all that I could hope for. I'd do the rest myself—the way I always did.

"So here we are," Mab murmured, her silky voice slithering like a snake through the courtyard.

Perhaps the stones of my ruined house sensed the Fire elemental's opposing magic, or perhaps they knew she was the reason that I'd lashed out at them in the first place. Either way, the stones' mutters grew harsher and sharper underneath my booted feet. The raging sound made me smile. It matched exactly how I felt.

"Here we are." I returned Mab's de facto greeting.

The two of us stood there, staring at each other. The Fire elemental was twenty feet away from me, with Bria tucked another twenty feet behind her. No, Mab wasn't taking any chances that I could snatch my sister and escape with her.

"Now that this moment has finally arrived, I have to say that I'm at a loss for words," Mab admitted in a sly, satisfied voice.

I arched an eyebrow. "I wouldn't start crowing about your ultimate victory just yet. That's a good way to get dead, especially when I'm around. Just ask Elektra La-Fleur. Oh, that's right. You can't, because I killed her."

Mab's eyes darkened, a bit of fire flashing in her black gaze. The sparks seemed to suck up even more of the dusky twilight, instead of reflecting back the faint light.

"Your insolence is noted, little Genevieve, and it does not please me. Or have you forgotten that I have your sweet sister over here at my mercy? That I've had her at my mercy all day long already? I have to say, I'm actually glad things worked out this way. What fun I've had with her, especially in seeing how long and loud I could make her scream while I burned her with my magic. It's been most entertaining. After I kill you, I think I'll start on her face. Melt it right off and then put out her pretty little eyes with my thumbs. I might even let her live, keep her around as a sort of pet. Wouldn't that be fun?"

Rage filled me at her words—cold, black, unending rage. Whatever happened to me, Mab would not hurt my sister again. She would *not*.

But I didn't let any of what I was feeling show in my hard features, and I didn't look at Bria. If I did that, if I saw the fear in her eyes again, I might come undone, which was something I couldn't afford.

"Oh, no, I haven't forgotten that you have Bria. Kind of sad, though. That you needed a bargaining chip to catch me. But then again, you're not as young as you used to be, are you, Mab?"

Yeah, I was taunting her, but we both knew exactly how this was going to play out. Despite whatever empty promises she'd made to me over the phone, Mab wasn't letting Bria go or me walk out of the courtyard alive. Not unless I made her—not unless Finn, Owen, and the others made her. My part in this was to keep talking and taunting her. Every second I did that was another second that Finn and the others had to slip out of their hiding places in the woods, quietly take out the bounty hunters stationed on the perimeter, and get into position at the edge of the courtyard.

Buying my friends that precious time meant putting on a show for all those in attendance. So instead of staring at Mab, I turned around in a slow circle, looking at each one of the giants and bounty hunters gathered around me. My gaze drifted from one face to another. Most of them stared back at me head-on. After all, it wasn't like I was dealing with choirboys and schoolgirls here. These were professionals who were just as hard and ruthless as I was. But a few shied away from my eyes, while others dropped their heads entirely. Their reluctance to even look at me gave me some hope that my friends would be able to break their ranks and morale long enough to rescue Bria.

"I'm giving everyone here a chance," I said. "Walk away right now, and you can live. I won't come after you afterward. I know what Mab's like. How she's forced some of you to be here against your will. How she's threatened your wives, kids, whatever. I won't hold that against you, not if you leave right now and never look back."

My harsh words echoed through the courtyard, out into the remains of the ruined house, and even into the forest beyond. The stones under my feet muttered at my voice, recognizing it and the hidden elemental power in my words. The stones didn't want to negotiate, they didn't want to let anyone go. No, the stones wanted to lash out, to crush whoever came close and grind their bones into dust, just like I'd done to them once upon a time. Just the way I wanted to do to Mab right now. But some small part of me insisted that I give the others a chance first—which was more than they or the Fire elemental would ever do for me.

There were no takers, of course. Everyone remained where they were, weapons at the ready. Couldn't blame them for that. After all, I was the one seemingly twisting out here in the snow and wind all by my lonesome. Not for long, though. Not for long.

Mab let out a little peal of laughter when no one took me up on my offer. "Oh, please. You don't actually expect to walk out of here alive, do you, Genevieve?"

The sound of her saying my name again, my *real*

name, made that little primal voice in the back of my head start muttering the way that it always did whenever I was around the Fire elemental. *Enemy, enemy, enemy . . .*

I shrugged. "It seems to me like you're the one not expecting to walk out of here alive, considering all the men that you brought along with you. Admit it, Mab. You're scared of me. You always have been. Deep down, there's a part of you that realizes that I might be just that much better than you, that much stronger than you. That's why you killed my mother and older sister. That's why you tried to kill me and Bria. Because you've always been scared of us and what we could do to you. At the end of the day, you're nothing but a bully and a fucking coward."

Rage flickered in Mab's eyes, more rage than I had ever seen her show before. I'd hit a little too close to home with my words, but the Fire elemental would never admit it. Not even now, at the end.

"I killed your mother because I wanted to," Mab snarled. "Because she was an arrogant, pompous bitch who took everything that I ever wanted, including your father, Tristan."

I'd once heard Elliot Slater say that Mab had pursued my father because she'd wanted to pass his Stone magic on to any kids that they might have had together, even though that wouldn't have been a certainty. But my father had loved my mother and chosen her instead. Tristan had died when I was a child, supposedly in a car accident, and I barely remembered him.

"Our families have hated each other for years, Genevieve. We've been at war for decades," Mab continued.

"And why is that?" I asked, genuinely curious.

Mab smiled. "My family has always had certain . . . ideas about how things in Ashland should be run. And your family has always opposed us, being the goody-goodies that they inherently are. Ice elementals. Always so weak. But I was strong enough to make my family's ideas, our plans, a reality. I was strong enough to take my rightful place as the head of the Ashland underworld. But doing all that involved things that your weak, spineless mother didn't approve of, and she felt it was her duty to try to stop me, just as her mother thwarted mine for years before."

"Things like what? Murder? Extortion? Kidnappings? I wonder why Eira had such a problem with all that," I drawled in a mocking tone.

Mab waved her hand. "Please. Eira cared as little about me as I did about her, until one of her friends racked up a gambling debt to me that he just couldn't pay off. So I killed him, and then I killed his family, locking them in their own house and burning it to the ground."

I froze. Owen. She had to be talking about Owen's family and how she'd killed them. Somehow, my mother had known Owen's parents, and she'd started fighting Mab because of their deaths. Just when I thought that I knew everything there was to know about my past, something else reared up to surprise me once more.

"After that, Eira showed more gumption than I'd ever thought she'd had. Every time I made a move to gain power after that, she countered it, undercutting me. But I took care of her in the end."

Mab's eyes darkened that much more, and I got the sense that she was having her own flashbacks, remembering her own battles against my mother. I wondered if she was as haunted by them as I was by her. But the moment passed, and the Fire elemental stared at me once more.

"As for your being stronger than me? Please," Mab scoffed. "Says who?"

I straightened. "Jo-Jo Deveraux, for starters. For years, the dwarf has been telling me that I have more raw magic than any elemental that she's ever seen—including you, Mab."

Something almost like uncertainty flickered in her face. Around us, a few of her men shifted on their feet, the scrape of their shoes as loud as gunshots in the absolute quiet. They didn't know what to make of my threatening their boss—or the fact that she didn't immediately dispute my outlandish claims.

Mab stared at me, hate twisting her features. I wondered if this was how my mother had seen her. The two of them had grown up as part of two opposing elemental families. I wondered if this was what my mother had noticed in Mab that had made Eira stand up to her—the evil and hate that turned the Fire elemental into something small and black and ugly.

Mab snapped her fingers. I tensed, ready to reach for my Ice and Stone magic, expecting her to throw a ball of elemental Fire at me just like she had in the country club. But instead, a small red dot popped up on my chest, just level with my heart.

Well, well, well. Someone had a sniper rifle handy. I wondered if it was Sydney or one of the other bounty hunters. Didn't much matter, though. I'd taken the precaution of putting on one of my heavy silverstone vests before I'd walked into the courtyard. No mere sniper's bullet could get through the hard shell of the magical metal that shielded my chest.

"As you can see," Mab sneered. "I learned from my past mistakes. As you said before, I didn't come here alone, and now, it's your turn to die—for good this time."

I just smiled at Mab. "Wow, you really must be afraid of me if you can't even bring yourself to use your magic to kill me. Going to have one of your boys do it instead, are you? I was wrong before. You're no bully. You're nothing but a cowardly bitch."

Mab's eyes narrowed to slits, but she didn't respond to my taunt. "Good-bye, Genevieve."

Mab snapped her fingers again, and a shot rang out, shattering the silence of the falling snow.

* 27 *

The bullet ripped through the air on its deadly course—but not at me.

Instead, a sharp, startled cry sounded. A second later, a man rolled down a pile of rubble that he'd been perched on top of about thirty feet off to my left. His body came to rest in the base of the courtyard. For a moment, everyone was stunned. Just stunned.

Then Mab turned back to me, fury rolling off her in palpable waves so hot that the snow under her stilettos started to ooze and melt from the constant, invisible drip of her elemental Fire power.

"You didn't really think that *I* came here alone, did you, Mab?" I mocked her. "That's one down. Which one of your men wants to die next?"

Mab opened her mouth, no doubt to direct some other cutting retort at me, but I beat her to the punch.

"Now, Finn!" I screamed. "Now!"

Crack! Crack!

Two more shots rang out, and one of the giants holding onto Bria collapsed in the snow, thanks to the bullets that Finn had just put through his eye. One down, one to go.

Then the most surprising thing happened. Ruth Gentry pulled out her revolver and shot the other giant in the back of the head three times. He too dropped to the snow. Gentry reached forward and jerked Bria back, putting my sister behind her. Across the distance, the bounty hunter gave me another nod. For whatever reason, she'd changed sides. Hell, maybe this had been her plan all along. Let me and Mab duke it out, then sell Bria back to whoever was left standing at the end. Either way, she'd gotten Bria away from the giants and that much closer to safety. So this time, I nodded back at her.

Startled by the shots, Mab's head whipped around, wondering what had just happened to her two men, but everyone else was just as distracted as the Fire elemental. Except maybe Jonah McAllister. Out of the corner of my eye, I saw the lawyer staring at me, his face suddenly pale. He took a step back, then another one. What was McAllister up to? Running away? Or something more devious?

A giant off to my right charged me, his hands arching into claws like he wanted to wrap them around my throat and just *squeeze*. I had no more time to think about McAllister. I palmed one of my silverstone knives and turned to meet him. The blade sank into his chest before I ripped it out and used it to lay open his throat. He died with a gurgling scream, and I shoved his body back into the ring of men surrounding me. They scattered like the vultures they were as he thumped to the ground at their feet.

"Who's next?" I snarled, the giant's hot blood still dripping off my knife.

A couple of the bounty hunters on the far edge of the ring looked at each other and started easing away from me. Apparently, my words hadn't been enough, and it had taken more of a visceral display to make them see the light. However much Mab was paying them, the money wouldn't do them a damn bit of good if they were dead.

"Get her, you fools!" Mab screamed at her men. "Now!"

The bounty hunters exchanged another glance. They hesitated, then bucked up their courage and started toward me once more. My hand tightened around my knife.

Crack! Crack! Crack!

Three more bounty hunters went down, each one sporting a neat, round hole right between their eyes. Warren Fox, no doubt, helping Finn with his sniper duties, just like we'd planned. The old man had proudly claimed that he was a hell of a shot and would be more than happy to help Finn thin out the ranks a bit. He hadn't been lying about how good his aim was.

From outside the ring of men, back behind Mab and even Gentry and Bria, a low, guttural battle cry sounded, rising to a fierce bellow that reminded me of a Viking horn. A moment later, Sophia ran into view, swinging her fists into every single person that she could reach. And she wasn't alone. Owen charged into the fray right behind her, wielding his blacksmith's hammer, while Xavier and his massive fists brought up the rear.

"Get Bria!" I screamed at them, even though they were already moving in that direction.

Given a choice between me and the new people in the courtyard, the bounty hunters and giants decided to take the easy way out—they all rushed by Mab, heading for Bria and the others. But the Fire elemental didn't turn and follow her men. Not this time. Instead, she started walking toward me—and I toward her.

We met there in the middle of the courtyard, only five feet of empty air separating us from each other.

All around us, the courtyard was in total chaos, as Sophia, Owen, and Xavier fought the bounty hunters and giants, even as my allies slowly retreated and took Bria with them. This had been the plan all along. To make it seem like I'd come here alone, then let my friends sneak in behind and get Bria to safety while I battled Mab. I just hadn't counted on Gentry making things a little easier for us, but I figured luck owed me at least this much. So did the bounty hunter for my sparing her and Sydney that night outside Mab's mansion.

Nobody had particularly liked the plan, especially the part about leaving me behind to face Mab by myself. But we all knew that this was how it had to be. I was the only one with a chance of stopping the Fire elemental, the only one whose magic was strong enough. It was just—inevitable. Maybe it had been since the day the Fire elemental had murdered my mother and older sister just because I was some vague, nebulous threat to her. A threat she'd made a reality by her cruel actions.

Mab and I stood there in the middle of the battle, somehow untouched by all the blood and bodies flying through the air around us in the chaos of the courtyard. It was as if the rest of the world didn't even exist anymore, except for me and her and the snow slowly swirling in between us.

"Before we finally do this," I said. "There's one thing that I have to ask you."

"And what would that be?" Mab asked in a low, dangerous voice.

I stared at her, my gray eyes burning into her black ones, our mutual hatred writhing in the air between us like a living, pulsing, beating heart of darkness.

"Did you ever stop and think that maybe you brought all this on yourself?"

Mab tilted her head to one side, making her hair spill over her slim shoulders. The bright coppery color of her wavy locks reminded me of blood.

Everything about her reminded me of blood and death and fire and that horrible night when she'd so casually destroyed the people I'd loved, leaving nothing behind but dirty, crumbled ash and the hollow echo of my hoarse screams.

The spider rune scars embedded in my palms itched and burned at the brutal memories, the way that they always did. Or maybe that was because Mab was now fully embracing her elemental Fire magic. Her black eyes smoldered like coals in her beautiful face, fueled by her enormous power and her supreme satisfaction at finally arranging a face-to-face meeting with me.

"Whatever do you mean?" Mab asked in her low, sultry voice.

"Did you ever read about Oedipus? You know, the tragic Greek hero who was supposedly destined to kill his father and marry his own mother?"

"What's your point?" Mab snapped, more than ready to get on with the business of burning me alive.

I really couldn't blame the Fire elemental for her impatience. Seventeen years had passed since the first time she'd tried to murder me. A long time for anyone to wait to off her mortal enemy.

I shrugged. "It always struck me that Oedipus's parents went about things the wrong way. Instead of sending their son off to die, they should have kept him at home and loved him. That way, he would at least have known what his own father looked like. Then maybe he wouldn't have killed dear old dad when he met him on the road years later. But Oedipus thought that his father was just another stranger and not anyone important."

Mab frowned, not seeing my point.

"That's the thing that's always bugged me about the Greeks and prophecies in general. The more you try to prevent them, the more you hasten them along. Happens all the time in classic mythology," I said. "So I ask again. Did you ever think that if you hadn't come to my house that night, if you hadn't murdered my mother and older sister, if you hadn't tortured me, maybe we wouldn't be here today?"

Mab stared at me, the black fire burning even darker in her eyes now, sucking in even more of the twilight that streaked the wintry landscape in brooding purples and impartial grays. The snow fell silently around us, a steady torrent of fat, fluffy flakes that seemed at odds with the tension in the air. Despite the cold, I could still feel the intense heat radiating off Mab's body. Her Fire magic pricked against my skin like thousands of needles stabbing me one after another—a relentless wave of red-hot agony.

But I didn't reach for my Stone magic to block hers. Not yet. I'd need every ounce of power that I possessed if I had any hopes of defeating Mab, and I wasn't going to waste any of it now while we were still just taunting each other. No, I'd summon up my magic when she threw her elemental Fire at me—that's when I'd need it most. So I swallowed down the primal snarl that clogged my throat at the feel of the invisible, fiery needles against my skin and continued with my musings.

I figured that I could be forgiven my odd quirk of sentiment just this once. It wasn't like I'd ever get the chance to confront Mab again—as one of us would kill the other in another minute, two tops.

"Because let's face it. Me living on the streets, getting taken in by an assassin, becoming an assassin myself, becoming the Spider. That all goes back to one thing—you killing my family," I said. "If you hadn't done that, well, who knows what would have happened? I might have grown up to help people. Become a doctor or something. Learned how to save lives instead of being so very good at taking them."

"None of that matters," Mab scoffed.

"Of course it does—it's *all* that matters. Especially here in this place. Especially now."

Mab's eyes narrowed to slits, but the elemental Fire still burned in the smoldering depths of her gaze. "And why is that?"

"All the people that I've killed over the years? Yeah, I did most of them for the money, because being an assassin was a job and one that I was good at. But the biggies, all the folks that I've taken on in recent months, Alexis James, Tobias Dawson, Elliot Slater, Elektra LaFleur. You see, I've gradually come to realize something about them—and how they've each been different from everyone else that I've battled over the years."

"And what would that grand revelation be?" Mab asked.

This time, I tilted my head at her and smiled. "That they've all just been practice for you, bitch."

We stared at each other, the Ice and Stone magic in my gray gaze a perfect, natural enemy for the elemental Fire flickering in Mab's black eyes.

"Well, then," she said in her silky voice. "Let's see just how much you've learned, little Genevieve."

Mab brought up her hand and curled it into a fist. Fire spilled out from between her clenched fingers and dripped down them like water before falling away to the ground. *Plop-plop-plop*. The stones underneath our feet shuddered, snarled, and screamed as her Fire burned into them. The rocks' angry mutters blended in perfectly with the steady, evil hiss of the melting snow. Ribbons of steam twisted up into the frigid air between us, delicate ropes binding us together.

I never took my eyes from Mab's black gaze, watching her the way one gunfighter would another, waiting for that small twitch that would tell me that she was ready to draw down on me. I drew in a breath and got ready to reach for my own power.

Mab smiled at me a final time, confident in her magic, her strength, her unmatched, raw elemental power. Then she drew back her fist and hurled everything that she had at me.

A second later, the elemental Fire hit me, and the scorching flames engulfed my body, just like they had my mother and older sister before me.

And I screamed.

❋ 28 ❋

Mab's magic slammed into me with the force of a thousand infernos, each one blazing brighter than the sun, each one burning out of control, with the sole purpose of frying me alive.

She almost succeeded.

Despite everything I knew about Mab, despite all the long hours that I'd studied her, despite what I'd seen her do to my mother and older sister, despite the damage she'd inflicted on me at the country club last night, none of that prepared me for the raw elemental force of her Fire. The heat, the intensity, the sheer, unrelenting *strength* of it took my breath away like no one else's magic had ever done before. Not that of Alexis James, Tobias Dawson, or even Elektra LaFleur. Those other elementals had all been strong, incredibly so, when I'd battled them.

But Mab—Mab was just elemental Fire and flames

and fury herself. She was in a completely different league from all the others I'd faced before.

At the last second, I reached for my Stone magic, bringing all of it to bear, hardening my skin, head, hair, eyes, and every other part of me into an impenetrable shell, just the way I'd done so many times before.

And it saved me once again.

Mab's raging Fire didn't immediately kill me. But it still hurt, worse than any pain I'd ever experienced before, even the shocking jolts of LaFleur and her electrical elemental magic. Even through the shell of my Stone magic, I could feel Mab's flames licking at my skin, eroding my magic, burning through all the many layers of my Stone power. I staggered back from the sheer force of the blast, and the silverstone in my vest immediately liquefied from the heat. Sweat streamed down my face, and it was all I could do to hold on to my own magic, to not be overwhelmed by the deadly surge of Mab's power. She'd gone for the kill shot first, and I knew that I'd been lucky to survive it.

Mab had more raw power, more pure magic, than any elemental born in the last five hundred years, so she didn't stop her assault on me. Not for a second. Instead, she raised her hands, elemental Fire spewing out of her fingertips in a steady, unrelenting stream, every bit of her power, every bit of her fury, directed at me in a molten ball of heat, flames, and death.

My vision went red from the Fire crashing into me, and I flashed back to that fateful night when Mab had murdered my mother. I remembered in excruciating detail how her magic had just kept getting closer and closer to Eira, slicing through my mother's Ice magic, until the hungry flames had washed over and consumed my mother completely. Then Annabella. Both charred to ash in an instant.

That's how elementals fought—by flinging their raw power at each other until one elemental finally succumbed to the other's magic—and that's how Mab and I were fighting now. But I wasn't just an elemental—I was an assassin too. I was the Spider, trained by the best, trained by Fletcher Lane, the Tin Man himself. If there was one thing the old man had taught me, it was that it didn't matter how you killed your opponent, as long as she was dead and you weren't when the bleeding was done. My Stone magic wasn't going to save me from Mab, it wasn't going to help me kill her in the end. Not really.

Fletcher was—just the way that he'd always intended. The old man had trained me for this one moment, for this one fight, for years. Now, I just had to figure out a way to kill Mab and live up to the faith that he'd always had in me.

"Give it up, little Genevieve," Mab said in a mocking tone. "You're no match for me. You never were, just like your miserable excuse for a mother. One of the happiest days in my life was when I finally killed Eira. Today is going to rank right up there with it. Because not only will I get rid of you, but I'll burn that sweet little sister of yours to death too. Along with the dwarves, Owen Grayson, that shyster banker you call a foster brother, and anyone else who was stupid enough to come here with you. They won't escape me, Genevieve. None of them will.

Not a single one. Your charred remains won't even have to time cool before I send the rest of them to join you."

I screamed. Not in pain or fear or surprise this time, but in sheer, undeniable fury, in raw elemental force, pouring my magic into that one primal sound. The bitch wasn't killing anyone else that I loved. Not now, not ever. I didn't care what I had to do to stop her—or what I had to sacrifice.

Triggered by my scream, my Stone power tore through the rubble and rocks around us, pulverizing and shattering them instantly, one after another, just as it had done the night this had all started. It was like watching a row of dominos fall down on top of each other. The giants, the bounty hunters, my friends. All the people who'd been fighting in the courtyard stumbled and staggered as the stone foundation under their feet literally disintegrated out from under them. The few walls that had been standing collapsed with a collective roar, sending more piles of rubble crashing down, and shards of rocks zipped through the air, joining the angry swirl of snowflakes.

The elemental force of my scream surprised even Mab, breaking her concentration for the briefest second. The Fire streaming out of her hands flickered and dimmed for the smallest fraction of time, but it was enough to let me draw in another breath and focus myself.

But my magic didn't stop with the stones of my ruined house. It spread out farther and faster than it ever had before, leaping from one rock to another, until even the forest around us seemed to quake, mutter, and vibrate with it.

I'd never known that I'd had this much magic before.

The thought skipped through my head just the way it had the last time I'd been here—the night that I'd collapsed my own mansion on top of everyone who'd been inside it. Mab, her men, Bria, even myself. Before, back then, my magic had scared me, and with my guilt over thinking that I'd killed Bria with it, I'd spent years using it in only the smallest of ways. But now I gave myself over to it completely. I could feel the power inside me, the incredible magic running through me like a vein of the finest, richest silver imaginable. Stone, Ice, Ice, Stone—there was no separation anymore. It all mixed together in me until there was just sheer power, just raw, furious force over the elements themselves. So much power, so much force, that I went cold and numb from it. Fingers, toes, torso, I couldn't even feel them anymore. My magic was the only thing I was aware of, surging through me, building and building and building toward something spectacular—

My body burst into silver flames.

I didn't know how I did it or why it happened or even that it was possible in the first place. But something ripped open deep inside me, and a second later, silver flames engulfed me from head to toe, dancing around my body like all the ghosts of my past come back to life to haunt me one final time. But the curious thing was that the flames weren't hot—they were cold. Colder than Ice. And that's when I realized what they were. My Ice magic come to life, manifesting itself just the way that Mab's Fire magic did. A new quirk, a new extension of my elemental power in my most desperate hour. Jo-Jo had always claimed that one day my Ice magic would be the equal of my Stone power.

The dwarf had just never told me that the Ice would get *stronger*.

"Nice trick," Mab hissed, eyeing the silver flames flashing around my body with obvious disgust. "But it's not going to be enough to save you."

"We'll see about that," I muttered back.

And then we danced.

The two of us stood there in the courtyard, our hands outstretched, magic pulsing out of our fingertips in bright, continuous waves. Mab's magic burned red and orange and yellow and black, spitting, hissing, and crackling with ash and heat. My magic glinted like a stream of silver stars all strung together, whistling and whispering with cold and frost.

Fire and Ice.

Opposing elements in so many ways.

And now, the two of us finally engaging in this battle that had been so many years in the making.

Our magic crashed together, sending up sizzling sprays of red and silver sparks, fireworks of an impressive and most deadly sort. Steam rose in the air between us, wrapping around us like fog. Sweat poured down my face, until I could barely see what I was doing, but I didn't wipe it away—I didn't dare do anything to interrupt my concentration. I didn't move, I didn't blink, I didn't even breathe.

I don't know how long we stood there, the two of us just throwing our magic at each other, pushing, straining, and fighting with everything that we had.

But eventually, I realized that I was going to lose.

Despite all the magic I was holding on to, despite

all the raw power coursing through my veins, hell, despite the silver flames that coated my body, it still wasn't enough. Not enough to drive back Mab's Fire magic, not enough for my power to overtake hers and engulf her in Ice. All the rumors that I'd heard over the years were true. Mab did have more raw power than any elemental born in the last five hundred years—including me.

Now that we were dueling, I could sense the full extent of her power, and I knew that it was greater than my own. Not by much, but just enough to end me. Another minute, two tops, and I'd run out of juice. Then Mab's Fire would cut through my Ice, and she'd burn me to death, just like she had my mother and older sister. The fact that I was going to die the way they had wasn't lost on me. Hell, I would have laughed at the bitter, bitter irony, if I hadn't needed every bit of my strength right now just to keep standing.

Once again, I thought of Fletcher and what the old man might do in this situation. The truth was that he wouldn't have put himself in such a spot to start with. He would have found another way to kill Mab, something that didn't involve a face-to-face confrontation and an elemental duel. It was far too late for that now, of course, but what really irked me was that I was so close to finally beating her. All I needed was another burst of power, just another sliver, hell, another *fingernail* of magic—

And then I remembered.

My ring—the one Bria had given to me. A thin silverstone band with my spider rune stamped into the middle of it. She had poured her Ice magic into the silverstone last night before I'd gone to the country club to confront

Mab. With everything that had happened in the last twenty-four hours, I'd forgotten about the ring and the power that it contained—and that I was still wearing it on my right index finger. I concentrated, focusing on that sliver of power. Somehow, despite the magic that numbed my body, I could feel the silverstone resting against my skin, a cold, solid band of Ice wrapped around my finger.

And I knew what I had to do.

I gritted my teeth and forced my feet to move forward. The motion made my concentration waver, just for a second, but the lapse was enough to let Mab's Fire blast through my Ice magic. The flames licked at my skin like a sloppy lover, burning me down to the bone. I screamed again, in agony once more.

Mab laughed, thinking that I was weakening, thinking she'd finally won. Her delighted cackle only made me that much more determined to end this thing—forever.

Despite the searing pain and the stench of my own burning flesh, I kept moving forward, inching closer and closer to the endless Fire streaming out of Mab's fingertips. I wasn't able to push back as much with my Ice magic, wasn't able to completely block her attack, and I felt my skin begin to bubble, blister, and burn from the incredible heat. But I didn't care. All that mattered now was killing Mab.

Maybe it was all that had ever really mattered.

Five feet, four, three . . . I inched closer and closer to the other elemental. Through the flames, Mab's black eyes narrowed, as if she couldn't figure out what I was up to. She'd know soon enough.

I crept closer still, my silverstone knife still in my right hand. Despite Mab's magic slamming into me, I'd managed to keep my death grip on the metal. It felt soft and hot in my fingers, but maybe I could do something about that. Carefully, I reached for the Ice magic that Bria had stored in my spider rune ring. There was only a trickle of it, compared to what Mab and I were throwing at each other, but it was enough—more than enough for what I had in mind.

"Oh, do come closer, little Genevieve," Mab mocked in her silky voice. "It'll make your death that much quicker."

Only two small feet separated us now, and I felt my skin melting, melting, melting, dripping from my bones like candle wax under the fiery roar of her magic. Somehow, I managed to draw in one final breath, even though flames coated my mouth and throat like acid.

"You want close?" I rasped. "How's this for close, bitch?"

With my left hand, I reached through the wall of Mab's elemental Fire, grabbed her sunburst necklace, and used it to yank her toward me. With my right hand, I drove my silverstone knife all the way through her heart.

The Fire elemental's black eyes bulged in shock and surprise, and she screamed with pain and fury—all the elemental pain and fury that I had felt minutes ago. Flames exploded from the wound, along with blood, and spattered against my cheek, adding to my agony. But I didn't care anymore. My world had narrowed to one final thing—killing my enemy.

Mab jerked back, trying to get away from me, but I didn't let her go. Hell, I didn't even try to defend myself. Instead, I redirected all of my magic, pouring everything that I had into keeping my silverstone knife cold, solid, and sharp in her chest. I twisted and twisted and twisted it, driving it in deeper every single time, even as her Fire washed over me, consuming me.

Mab screamed again, or maybe it was me. Hell, maybe it was both of us shrieking with pain like a couple of harpies come to life out of one of my mythology books. Whoever was screaming, I knew I'd done my part. Mab wouldn't be coming back from the sucking wound in her chest. It was just too bad that I wouldn't be coming back either, not from the elemental Fire that had burned me to the core.

Then the silver and red flames engulfed us both, and I knew no more.

* 29 *

I hurried down the snowy street, my steps quick, sure, and purposeful. I was late, and I knew that he'd be waiting for me. He always waited for me after a job, no matter how long it took me to get here.

No one moved on the deserted downtown Ashland street except for me, and no cars crawled through the foot-deep snow. The flakes were coming down harder now, as heavy and wet as teardrops on my face, but I trudged on, eager to get to my destination. I turned the corner, and the familiar multicolored sign of the Pork Pit came into view, burning like a beacon through the dark night.

Home—I was finally home.

Light spilled out from the storefront windows, looking like pure liquid silver streaming down the snowbanks outside. I paused a moment and trailed my fingers over the cold, battered brick. The muted murmurs of clogged contentment sounded back to me the way they always did. I smiled and *opened the door. The bell chimed a single cheery note, announcing my presence.*

Inside, an old man with a wispy thatch of white hair leaned over the counter next to the cash register, reading a blood-stained book. Where the Red Fern Grows. *One of his all-time favorites—and mine too.*

Joy filled my heart at the sight of him, a burst of happiness so intense it was like I hadn't seen him in months, instead of just a few hours. After a moment, the feeling faded away, replaced by a darker, more ominous sensation.

And then I remembered.

He wasn't here anymore. Not really. No, he was dead, killed months ago in this very spot. Murdered in his own restaurant. I remembered crouching over his body, my tears dripping down and mixing with the blood on his ruined face. I remembered the pain of losing him, the pain that I still felt every time I woke up in his house and realized he was gone.

But here the old man was, and so was I—back together again. Or so it seemed.

He looked up at the sound of the bell chiming and used one of the day's credit card receipts to mark his spot in the blood-stained book. Then his bright green eyes met mine, and a grin creased his wrinkled face.

"About time you got here, Gin," Fletcher Lane said.

I stood there just inside the door, staring at the old man and struggling to make sense of this, of where I was and what was happening to me.

I remembered—I remembered—Fire. Mab's elemental Fire, washing over me, burning me to the core. My own Ice magic reaching out to hers, holding it at bay, and then finally, my driving my silverstone knife into Mab's chest as the flames consumed both of us.

I sighed. "So I'm dead then, right? This is heaven or hell or limbo or whatever?"

Fletcher didn't answer me. Instead, the old man moved over to the stove and came back with a plate of food. He set it on the counter, then picked up his book by the cash register once more, going back to his reading.

"Better start eating before it gets cold," he said.

I wasn't sure what was going on—if this was real or a dream or something else entirely—but I wasn't about to pass up a chance to be with Fletcher. Not now. Not after I'd spent the last few months missing him so terribly and feeling so guilty over his death—and that I hadn't been able to save him. Not from being tortured, not from being murdered.

So I took a seat at the counter and started eating the food. A half-pound hamburger dripping with mayonnaise and piled high with smoked Swiss cheese, sweet butter-leaf lettuce, a juicy tomato slice, and a thick slab of red onion. A bowl of spicy baked beans followed, along with a saucer of carrot-laced coleslaw. I remembered the last time that I'd had this meal—the night before Fletcher had died.

I dug into the food, a little hesitant at first, but soon I was relishing the play of sweet and spice, salt and vinegar, on my tongue. It was a simple, savory meal that I'd had hundreds of times before, one I'd cooked a thousand times more, but somehow it had never tasted as good as it did right now. It seemed like I'd barely started eating before my plate was clean. I pushed it back and sighed.

"*That was the best meal I've ever eaten,*" I said in a wistful tone.

"*I know,*" Fletcher said. "*Everything tastes better here.*"

I wasn't sure where here *was, and I sensed that he wouldn't tell me even if I asked. So I just sat there and looked at him, staring at the wrinkled face that I'd loved so much, that I'd missed so much. And I realized I had questions for Fletcher—all these burning questions I'd wanted to ask him for so many months now.*

"*Why did you give me that folder of information on Bria? Why didn't you just tell me that she was alive? Why wait until after you died? Why buy the land where my childhood house was? And did Mab really hire you to kill my family? Is that why you wanted her dead all these years? Because she tried to have you killed when you turned her down?*" *One after another, the questions tumbled from my lips.*

Fletcher marked his place in his book again, then looked up at me. His green eyes were sharper, clearer, brighter than I remembered and free of the rheumy film that had started to cloud them as he'd aged.

"*That's what you want to know?*" *he asked in an amused voice.* "*The murky, mysterious actions of an old man? Not the big stuff? You know, about life and death and if there's really a heaven or not?*"

I shook my head. "*I don't care about any of that. I just want to know about you, Fletcher. I want to know all about you.*"

The old man grinned. "*That's my girl, Gin, always focusing on the important things.*"

I crossed my arms over my chest and snorted. "*Only because you turned me into the same curious sort that you are. Or were. Or whatever.*"

His grin just widened.

Fletcher didn't ask me about killing Mab. He didn't have to. We both knew that I wouldn't be here if the job hadn't been done. Finally, finally done.

"Well," he rumbled. "I thought I explained it well enough in that letter I left for you in my office. But to answer your questions, yes, Mab did hire me to kill your family. At first, it was just your mother, but then Mab got greedy and wanted me to throw in you and your two sisters for free. And you know that I didn't kill kids—ever."

I nodded.

Fletcher shrugged. "Mab was a bit upset when I turned down her offer. She knew me only as the Tin Man, not as Fletcher Lane, but that didn't stop her from ordering some of her men to track me down and kill me. When I took the initiative and killed them instead, she sent a few more, but I took care of them too. As for why I bought the land, it was yours—yours and Bria's. Mab had already taken so much from the two of you. I didn't want her to take that too. You know everything else that happened. The rough outlines anyway. My trying to save your family that night but realizing I was already too late. My finding Bria roaming in the woods around your burning, crumbled house, giving her to her foster family, and then you, showing up at my back door . . ."

His voice trailed off, and his green eyes clouded over, lost in his memories, just like I was.

"But why keep me in the dark about Bria for all these years?" I asked. "Why even take me in? Why train me to be an assassin? You could have just shipped me off to Savannah to live with Bria and her foster family. That would have been the easiest thing for you to do. The simplest thing, for everyone."

"Maybe I could have, maybe I should have," Fletcher murmured. "I thought about it when you first came here."

"So what changed your mind?"

He looked down at the pages of his book, and for a moment, I thought that he wouldn't answer me. But he finally raised his gaze to mine once more.

"Do you remember the night that Douglas, that giant, came to the Pork Pit? He was one of Mab's men, one of those searching for me. He spotted me while I was out scouting another job, and he followed me back here to kill me. Do you remember that, Gin?"

Oh, I remembered, probably better than Fletcher did, because Douglas was the first person I'd killed inside the Pork Pit. I'd taunted the giant, lured him over to me, and then I'd stabbed him to death with the knife I'd been using to chop onions. The first time I'd ever used a blade that way—the first of many.

"When you killed Douglas, I realized how I could make things up to you, for your family being gone. I realized that I could train you to be an assassin, to survive. Even back then, you had that same cold, iron will you do now," Fletcher said. "I'd heard about Magda's prophecy, so I knew why Mab had wanted you and your sisters dead, because supposedly one of you would grow up to kill her. And I thought that maybe—that maybe this was what the prophecy was all about in the first place. That maybe you were meant to be with me, instead of with Bria. At first, anyway. Until you grew up. Until I could train you. Besides, by that point, I just loved you too damn much to let you go."

We fell silent. I thought back to what I'd said to Mab,

when I'd asked her if she thought that she'd brought all this on herself.

"It's all very Greek, isn't it?" I quipped. "Prophecies, tragedies, destinies. Just like in all those old mythology books we read over the years."

Fletcher shrugged. "Hard to beat the classics."

I nodded. "And what about all that talk of my retirement right before you . . . died?"

Fletcher shrugged again. "Being an assassin is all well and good, but I wanted you to start thinking about other things, to realize that there was more to life than killing people, no matter how good you are at it. I'd taught you how to survive. I guess I wanted to put you on a happier path before I died."

"The one that led me to Bria," I finished.

He nodded. We didn't speak. Outside the snow continued to fall, coating everything in its cold, wet embrace.

"So what now?" I finally asked. "Because Mab's dead. I made sure of that. And if I'm not already, then I'm probably on my way to join her—and you."

The old man snorted. "What now? That's up to you, Gin. Just like it always has been."

"So I can go back then? Back to being . . . alive? Or whatever?"

The old man stared at me with his bright green eyes. "You're Gin Blanco, Genevieve Snow, and the Spider all rolled into one. You can do whatever you want to, sweetheart."

I bit my lip and looked away. "I don't want to lose you again, Fletcher. I don't want to leave you behind. Especially since it's my fault that you died in the first place. My fault that Alexis James tortured you to death."

A hundred agonizing emotions tightened my throat, but for once, I forced out the words. "I—I failed you that night."

"And I failed you when I didn't stop Mab from killing your mother and older sister," the old man snapped right back at me. "We all make mistakes, Gin, even the best of us. I like to think that it all evens out in the end. Remember that, and you'll be fine."

"But what should I do?"

"I can't tell you that," Fletcher said. "But it seems to me like there are a lot of people out there who care about you. It would be a shame to up and die on them, especially when they're working so hard to try to save your life."

I thought about everything that I'd gone through in the last few months. Grieving over Fletcher's death, my messy affair with Donovan Caine, taking on bad guy after bad guy, finding Bria, connecting with her, and now with Owen too, and all the things I felt for him. Fletcher was right. I'd worked too damn hard to get through all of that, to build a real life for myself, to give it up now.

Still, I got to my feet with a heavy heart. I should have headed for the door, but I lingered at the counter. I breathed in, and the old man's scent filled my nose—sugar, spice, and vinegar all mixed together, with just a hint of chicory coffee. The caffeine fumes comforted me the way they always did.

"Well, then, I guess this is good-bye."

Fletcher gave me a sly smile. "For now."

I nodded, turned, and walked over to the front door. For a moment, my hand hovered over the doorknob, and I wondered once more if this was the right thing to do. It would be easy to stay here with Fletcher—so easy. But like the old man *had said before, I was Gin Blanco, Genevieve Snow, and the Spider.* Easy *wasn't in my vocabulary. It never had been.*

I twisted the knob, opened the door, and stepped out into the cold. But I wasn't ready to go—not yet. I turned and stared back through the storefront windows, looking at the old man.

Our gazes met and held through the glass. Green on gray. Our love and respect for each other glowing as bright as the neon pig sign above the door.

Fletcher raised his hand to me in a silent wave, which I returned. Then the snow swirled between us once more, and he was gone.

✳ 30 ✳

I shuddered in a breath and found myself staring into a pair of bright green eyes—eyes that were pinched tight with worry and fear.

"Fletcher?" I mumbled, my voice hoarse and raspy and broken. "Fletcher?"

I wheezed in another breath and wished that I hadn't. Pain flooded my body, snapping me out of whatever dream or limbo I'd been in. I was dimly aware of the agony coursing through my veins, of the sheer misery surging through me with every slow, erratic beat of my singed heart. But at the same time, I felt completely disconnected from myself, as though I were standing over my own body, watching my limbs twitch and writhe with pain with a dispassionate eye. I imagined the sensation probably had something to do with the fact that all of my nerve endings, hell, all my skin, had been seared off by Mab's elemental Fire.

But I'd gotten the bitch. I'd finally gotten *her*. I thought that I smiled then. I certainly wanted to, even as the blackness crept up on me again.

"No, it's Finn," my foster brother's familiar voice said. "Gin? Stay with me, Gin!"

Some indistinct murmurs sounded, and footsteps scuffled in the snow. But I didn't see anyone because my eyes were sliding shut again.

"She's alive!" Finn screamed. "Get Jo-Jo over here! Now!"

The world went black once more.

The next time I woke up, I felt like I was being stabbed with a hundred thousand red-hot needles—all at once. I cried out from the pain, screaming and thrashing. At least, I thought that I did. I certainly wanted to. Even Mab's elemental Fire hadn't felt as bad as all this, as painful, as agonizing, as brutal. It was like every last molecule of my skin was being ripped off and then stitched back on, one cell at a time. And there was no stopping it, no escaping it. Just pain, pain, and more pain.

"Hold her steady," someone muttered. "I can't have her thrashing around and tearing up what I've already healed."

It might have been my imagination, but I thought that the pressure on my arms and legs increased that much more.

"You're exhausted," someone else rasped in a broken voice that sounded vaguely familiar. "Help you."

"Me too," a higher, lighter, lilting voice chimed in. "I don't have Air magic, not like you do, but you can use my Ice power. I'll feed it to you however I can. Maybe it'll help. I have to do—something to help her. I can't—I can't stand to see her like this. So broken and melted—"

The voice cut off in a choked sob. After that, silence.

"All right," the first voice said, sounding more tired and weary than any person had a right to be. "Let's just hope that mashing all our magic together doesn't kill her outright. Because I'm running on empty at this point."

For a moment, the needles faded away. I sighed with relief. But I'd barely drawn in a breath when they returned, even sharper and hotter than before. More and more of them, stabbing me over and over again in an unrelenting wave of agony.

I threw my head back and screamed and screamed and screamed into the blackness.

A soft, cool hand stroked my forehead, and I felt the faintest trickle of Ice magic glide over my body, enveloping me in its cold, sweet caress. I sighed with relief and tried to lean into the touch, but something stopped me. My whole body felt like it was immobilized, wrapped, bandaged, and strapped down like I was one of the poor souls languishing away in Ashland Asylum. Maybe the powers that be had fitted me for my straitjacket already, as crazy and jumbled as my mind was right now. I didn't have the strength to fight against whatever was weighing me down. I didn't have the strength to do anything.

"Rest, Gin," that high, lilting voice murmured in my

ear, the same exhaustion that I felt coloring her words as well. "Just rest."

So I did.

The next time that I woke up, it was for good. I opened my eyes and found myself staring up at a cloud-covered fresco on the ceiling. I sighed with relief, and more than a few tears slipped out of my eyes. I was safe at Jo-Jo's house once more. Somehow, I'd done the impossible—killed Mab Monroe and lived to tell the tale. Wow. Sometimes, I surprised myself. I grinned. But in a good way.

Dark cloaked the room, although it was slowly giving way to dawn. A soft snore rumbled close to my left ear, and my eyes flicked over to find Owen asleep in the rocking chair next to the bed, a blanket covering him.

I wondered how long Owen had been sitting there, watching over me, waiting for me to wake up. He looked as exhausted as I felt. Deep lines grooved into his face, purple circles ringed his closed eyes, and a thick growth of black stubble covered his face, as though he hadn't shaved in a week. I couldn't see his clothes, but I imagined that they'd be just as rumpled as the rest of him.

Still, the sight of him sitting there, watching over me even when he was so obviously exhausted himself, made me happier than anything had in a long, long time.

But instead of waking him up, I carefully turned over onto my side. Blankets had been piled on top of me too, so I couldn't see what kind of shape I was in. Curious and a little afraid of what I might find, I lifted the covers.

White gauze covered me from head to toe, wrapped around my legs, arms, torso, toes, and everything in between. I'd never considered myself to be a particularly vain person, but my fingers trembled just a bit as I put my hand up to my face.

More gauze there too, although at least it wasn't an inch thick like it was on the rest of me. I felt like a mummy. Give me a pyramid and some dusty treasure to guard, and I'd be right at home in a horror movie. I looked like a monster too, given all the gauze and the ointment that I could feel underneath it soaking into my skin—or what was left of it.

But I wasn't too worried. I was still alive, still breathing when I shouldn't be. That was a victory in and of itself. Jo-Jo could fix the rest, no matter how long it took.

The small, slow movements took every bit of non-existent energy that I had, but I struggled against the blackness that threatened to swallow me. I wasn't going back down the rabbit hole—not until I told Owen how I felt about him. So I lay there and watched my love sleep. Seeing him here, knowing how much he cared, was the best medicine for me. Just his presence alone soothed me.

Time went by. Eventually, I heard others moving in the house. Doors opened and closed softly, and footsteps tread lightly, as my friends and family crept around so as not to wake whoever else was still sleeping. But I didn't call out to whoever was already up. Instead, I just lay there in bed and looked at Owen, grateful that I'd survived Mab's Fire—and more than grateful that Owen was here when I'd woken up.

I didn't know how long he slept or how long I watched him, but eventually his snores slurred, softened, and faded away. His head listed to one side, and I could sense that he was rising up out of the black void of exhaustion.

Owen's eyes fluttered open—his beautiful, beautiful violet eyes. The ones that never held anything but warmth and understanding and love and respect whenever he looked at me.

Owen rubbed his eyes, then ran his hands through his black hair, making it stand straight up. He let out a soft, tired sigh and looked over at me. Apparently he still expected me to be asleep because he frowned and blinked a few times, as if he wasn't quite sure whether I was really awake.

"Gin?" he asked, tremulous hope making his voice crack.

"Back from the dead, again."

I meant for my tone to be light, playful even, but my voice came out as a harsh rasp. I sounded—I sounded exactly like Sophia. Like I'd spent my life smoking, snorting, and drinking everything I could get my hands on. For a moment, I wondered why; why my voice would be this way, and then I remembered what Jo-Jo had told me. How the younger Goth dwarf had been forced to breathe in elemental Fire—just like I had.

My voice didn't bother Owen, though. He closed his eyes and let out a long breath. All the tension that had been coiled around him fell away, like chains being lifted off his arms and legs. Owen shuddered out another breath, and a tear tracked down one of his cheeks.

"Hey now," I rasped again. "Tears are a waste of time, energy, and resources. That's what Fletcher always used to tell me and Finn."

Owen gave me a crooked grin, although I could tell that it was an effort to be cheerful on his part. "That may be what you think. You gave us all quite a scare, you know."

"How much of a scare?"

He wouldn't meet my eyes. "From the fast and furious rumors that are going around Ashland, you could see the elemental flames from your battle with Mab from a half mile away. After you stabbed Mab, the two of you were just lying there in the courtyard. Just—burning. Bria used her Ice magic to try to smother the flames, and Jo-Jo and Sophia did the same thing with their Air power, but it took so long. By the time that we put them out, most of your skin was just—melted. Gone. Down to the bones. We didn't even think that you were still alive until you opened your eyes and spoke to Finn."

Memories of my conversation with Fletcher filled my mind. I didn't know if what I'd seen at the Pork Pit had been a dream, a vision, or just wishful thinking. Didn't much matter. I'd gotten to see the old man again, gotten some of the answers to my questions, even if it was only in my head, and that was what really mattered.

"I asked for Fletcher, didn't I?"

Owen nodded. "You did."

We didn't say anything. Owen moved over to the bed, sat down, and put his arm around me, as gentle and easy with me as if I were made of the most delicate crystal. Even then, I could tell that he was making an effort to touch me, to be close to me, though his every instinct must be screaming at him to get as far away from me as possible. I wasn't a pretty sight right now, which is why his devotion touched me all the more.

Even though I was still exhausted and close to sinking back down into the blackness, I forced myself to sit up and move deeper into his embrace. Then I leaned forward, put my head against his chest, and sighed.

"Is something wrong?" Owen stiffened in alarmed. "Am I hurting you?"

I laughed, although it wasn't a pleasant sound, given my ruined voice. "Of course not. I was just thinking that there was nowhere else I'd rather be than right here with you, right now."

"Me too," he murmured. "Me too."

"I'm glad that you were here when I woke up. More than you'll ever know."

His arms tightened around me. "I'm just glad that you woke up, Gin. More than you'll ever know. Because I just can't imagine my life without you in it."

This time, my eyes were the ones that filled with tears. The salty drops slid down my cheeks and soaked through the gauze covering my face, stinging my new, healing skin, but I didn't care.

"You know," I murmured. "You said something to me the night we made love before I went after Mab. Before all that crazy stuff happened in the courtyard. And I think it's past time that I told you I feel the same way. I love you, Owen. Completely, totally, irrevocably. I have for a while now. It's just that I've lost so many people in my life so brutally. My mother, my older sister, Fletcher. It's hard for me—to let people in. To let people—get close. I wanted to tell you how I felt before, but I couldn't. I just—couldn't . . ."

Emotion clogged my throat, cutting off my words. But

it was okay, because this time, I'd finally said all the things I'd needed to, that I'd wanted to for so long now.

Owen's arms tightened around me that much more. Underneath my ear, I could hear his heart beating in his chest, keeping perfect time with mine.

"I know, Gin," Owen rumbled in a soft voice. "I know. And I love you too. And now that I've got my arms around you, I'm never going to let you go."

"Good," I said. "Because I don't ever want you to."

✷ 31 ✷

I went back to sleep, safe and warm in Owen's arms. And when I woke up again, he was still there, still holding me. And I knew that he always would be.

It turned out that I'd given everyone more than just a little scare—I'd been unconscious for the better part of three weeks. I slept through most of the next few days, only waking up long enough to endure round after round of healing from Jo-Jo.

Slowly, the gauze was unwrapped from my body and replaced by new layers of shiny pink skin. My voice lost its harsh, grating rasp and went back to its normal tone once more. I could have left my voice the way it was, like Sophia had done after Harley Grimes had tortured her. But I had my spider rune scars to remind me of Mab—I didn't need anything else.

And that wasn't all that Jo-Jo did. I also got longer, thicker eyelashes and a new set of perfectly sculpted eyebrows, since my old ones had been singed off. Jo-Jo even grew out my hair an extra inch so she could layer it into a stylish shag.

"No reason not to do a little maintenance while we're at it," Jo-Jo chirped before letting loose with her Air magic again.

Once the dwarf had fixed the majority of the damage, I started receiving visitors. Of course, my friends and family had all been in and out of Jo-Jo's house ever since the night that they'd first brought me here. Still, I hadn't wanted them to see me weak, helpless, and disfigured. They'd seen the horror show the night I'd killed Mab. I imagined that one time would have been plenty for them to stomach—forever.

To my relief, everyone had survived the battle in the courtyard. Xavier had broken several bones in his hands, pounding on the other giants and bounty hunters, while Finn had taken a bullet in the shoulder from another sniper during the melee. Owen had been bruised and banged up, with two black eyes, several sprains, and a dislocated shoulder from swinging his hammer. Eva, Violet, Warren, Roslyn, and Jo-Jo had all been hanging back, out of range of the courtyard, so they'd been out of the frenzied fray. Sophia had come through without a scratch, and Jo-Jo had eventually healed everyone else.

Bria, well, Bria had been burned, of course. Although her wounds hadn't been as bad as mine, Mab had still horribly tortured my sister with her elemental Fire. Jo-Jo had healed all the outside damage. How much damage there was on the inside, only time would tell. But I thought that Bria would be okay. We'd survived the death of our mother and older sister, our long separation, and everything else. We'd get through this too—together. It would just take time, the way it always did.

Knowing that everyone else was okay was another burden off my shoulders. I didn't think that I could have lived with the guilt if one of my friends had been killed. But all was well that had ended well, I supposed. For once, luck had smiled on me and mine. About time that capricious bitch finally came through for me.

One sunny afternoon, Owen carried me downstairs, since I was still too weak to stand on my own. Jo-Jo, Finn, and Bria waited for us in the kitchen. Sophia would have been here too, but the Goth dwarf was busy keeping an eye on the Pork Pit until I could get back on my feet.

Since I was still under the weather, Jo-Jo cooked, whipping up homemade tomato soup loaded with sour cream and cilantro, along with ooey, gooey grilled cheese sandwiches on some of Sophia's soft, thick sourdough bread. It was one of my favorite comfort-food meals, and I felt my strength pick back up with every warm, cheesy bite.

While I stuffed my face, the others filled me in on what had happened on their end during the fight in the courtyard. I'd heard bits and pieces of it before, but Finn launched into a blow-by-blow account. My foster brother told me in bombastic, exquisite, and somewhat excruciating detail how Xavier, Sophia, and Owen had managed to heroically fight their way through the swarm of giants and bounty hunters and make it to Bria's side, while Finn and Warren had laid down cover fire for them.

"I, of course, never had any doubt that we'd rescue fair Bria, but I thought we'd have to go through Gentry to do it," Finn said. "But she handed Bria off to Xavier without a word, then vanished into the snow. She didn't put up any fight at all. I was still going to put a couple of bullets through her head, though, just for all the trouble she'd caused, but that's when I got winged in the shoulder by some sniper fire."

Even though Jo-Jo had healed his injury too, Finn rotated his arm, wincing with imaginary pain. He looked at Bria to see if she'd noticed, but she hadn't. Instead, my baby sister stared down into her half-eaten soup, a distant look in her eyes.

"I imagine it was Sydney who shot you, protecting the old woman's back just as usual," I said. "She might be young, but that girl knows what she's doing when it comes to guns."

"Why do you think Gentry helped us, Gin?" Owen asked. "Why do you think that she killed Mab's giant and turned on the Fire elemental?"

I thought of what the bounty hunter had said to me that night in the woods outside Fletcher's house. How she'd promised to take care of Bria for me until I could rescue my sister. And then how Gentry had nodded to me when I'd stepped into the courtyard. For whatever reason, the bounty hunter had felt she'd owed me something—

"She said it was because Gin gave the girl some cookies," Bria said in a soft voice. "That's why she helped me, not just in the courtyard, but with Mab too."

I stared at my baby sister, waiting, just waiting. After a moment, she looked up, meeting my eyes. Pain flickered in her blue gaze—pain at everything Mab had done to her that long, long night. Once again, my heart ached for my sister, for everything that she'd endured because of my failure to keep her safe. But there was no blame in her eyes, no angry accusation directed at me, which made it hurt all the worse.

"Mab tortured me, you know," Bria said. "She tied me down to a chair and used her magic on me—used her elemental Fire to burn my skin. She said she wanted to practice and make sure that she was ready to take on the Spider. And, of course, she enjoyed every second of it."

Bria stopped and stared down into her soup for several seconds. Finally, she continued with her story. "But Gentry was there too, the whole time, all through the night. And when Mab was really hurting me, when she was getting close to killing me, when I thought that I couldn't take any more, Gentry would distract her. Come up with some excuse to get the Fire elemental to back off, even if it was just for a few minutes. Mab left the room once, and I was able to ask her why she was still here. After all, Mab had paid her the bounty on me by that point. Gentry just looked at me. And then she said that she owed you for some cookies you'd given to her apprentice, Sydney. I didn't really understand what she meant. Do you, Gin?"

I thought of the hunger and the delight that had filled Sydney's eyes when I'd handed her the cookies—and the sadness that had etched Gentry's face at my small act of kindness. Whatever had happened to Sydney or maybe even to Gentry herself, I'd helped alleviate it, just for that brief moment at the Pork Pit. It had meant enough to the bounty hunter for her to return the favor.

"Yeah," I said. "I know exactly what Gentry meant."

We were all silent for a moment, before Finn launched into the second half of his grandiose story, which focused on watching the end of the elemental duel between Mab and me from a safe distance. According to Finn, several of the bounty hunters and giants hadn't been so smart. They'd gotten caught up in the elemental crossfire and had been killed instantly. Finn wrapped up his tale by telling how he and the others had retrieved my burned, melted body from the rubble and whisked me off to safety. He didn't linger on that part. Couldn't blame him for that. I didn't want to think too much about it myself.

"Anyway, the next time you go off and kill the ultimate evil, remind me to wear sunglasses," Finn quipped, taking a sip of his latest cup of coffee. "Because that elemental light show of yours almost burned out my eyes, Gin."

"Sure," I said. "I'll stop and do that very thing the next time I'm fighting for my life against a Fire elemental with unimaginable power."

"Well, that shouldn't be anytime soon," he drawled. "Considering that you killed Mab. Your Ice flames or magic or whatever they were did just as much damage to her as her Fire did to you. Once you were in Jo-Jo's hands, Owen and I went back to the courtyard to make sure that she was dead. All that was left of Mab were a few bones—and this."

Finn got up and retrieved something wrapped in a thick towel off one of the counters. He placed it on the table in front of me, and I carefully unwound the thick fabric, revealing Mab's sunburst necklace. The symbol for fire.

Somehow, the necklace had survived Mab's elemental

Fire and had come through unscathed. The wavy golden rays looked as bright and polished as ever, and the ruby set into the middle of the design gleamed like fresh blood. But more disturbing than that I could hear the gemstone's murmurs—its whispers of fire, heat, death, and destruction that were the essence of Mab herself. *Enemy, enemy, enemy . . .* that primal voice in the back of my head started muttering.

Emotion filled me then, terrible, terrible emotion that this piece of the Fire elemental had survived. I snatched up the golden rays and reached for my Ice magic. It took only a second for me to coat the necklace in elemental Ice.

And then I smashed it to pieces.

I slammed the frozen necklace down onto the table again and again and again, happily watching the rays snap off one by one, their golden glow choked to death by my Ice. Finally, all that was left of the design was the ruby. I grabbed the gemstone in my right hand, wrapped my fist around it, and blasted it with all the Ice magic that I could bring to bear.

The gemstone shrieked as it sensed what was being done to it, but I blocked the noise out and poured even more of my magic into it.

A second later, the ruby shattered with a tiny wail, the pieces zipping out between my hands like shrapnel. I listened to the broken shards, but I couldn't hear the ruby's murmurs anymore—only silence. Sweet, sweet silence.

Everyone stared at me, shocked by my violent outburst.

"Gin?" Jo-Jo asked.

"I'm okay," I said, breathing heavily. "I'm okay now that that thing is gone."

Everyone watched while I dusted the Ice-coated ruby shards off my hand. Without a word, Jo-Jo got the broom from the corner and cleaned up the mess I'd made destroying the necklace. Once all the pieces had been thrown in the trash, I felt myself relaxing once more.

It was over now—finally, truly over.

"We also found something else interesting," Owen said in a quiet tone when I'd regained my composure. "Something that I think you'll like a little better than Mab's necklace."

He handed me another towel. Once more, I carefully unwound the fabric, revealing a sharp, slender weapon. My silverstone knife—the one I'd used to kill Mab.

"I thought you might want it back," Owen said.

I nodded, staring at the metal. I must have done a better job of keeping it in one piece with the Ice magic than I'd thought, because the knife looked as solid and sharp as ever. My spider rune ring, the one that Bria had stored her magic in, had also survived Mab's elemental flames. Bria had slipped it back onto my finger the day I'd woken up for good, and I hadn't taken it off since. The thin band clinked softly against the knife as I picked up the weapon. To my surprise, the hilt felt cold in my hands—Ice cold.

"Your Ice magic is in the blade now," Owen said, seeing my confusion. "I can feel it in there, just waiting to be used. It's silverstone, after all. It must have absorbed your magic during your fight with Mab. Your other knives also contain your Ice power, although not as much as that one, the knife that you killed Mab with. "

"Well, I suppose that they'll all come in handy soon enough."

"What do you mean?" Jo-Jo asked.

I shrugged. "All of Mab's men, all of the bounty hunters—they all know that I'm the Spider now. It won't be too long before someone tries to collect on some kind of bounty or reward on me."

"Correction," Bria said. "The ones who lived know that you're the Spider, but there probably aren't as many of those around as you might think. You and Mab took out almost everyone in the courtyard with your magic. The coroner is still finding bodies out there. It'll be weeks before they identify them all—if they can even do that to start with, given how badly everyone was burned."

"And Owen, Sophia, Xavier, Warren, and I took care of some of the other stragglers we found out in the woods," Finn said. "So mostly, there are a lot of rumors going around the underworld, but there aren't that many people around to confirm or deny them. I'd say the damage and exposure to us is fairly minimal, all things considered."

Well, that was something to be grateful for. It wouldn't do any good for me to finally kill Mab only to have a dozen other people show up in Ashland looking to settle old grudges or create new ones. Still, despite the others' words, I knew that sooner or later some of the folks who weren't very happy with the Spider would track me down. But I'd be ready for them—the way I always was.

"The only one who might make trouble for you right now is Jonah McAllister," Bria said in a thoughtful voice.

I frowned. "You mean that bastard got away? How did he do that?"

Jo-Jo stared at me. "Jonah McAllister might be a pompous little weasel, but he also knows how to survive. Don't forget, he managed to keep his position as one of Mab's number-two men for decades, something that wasn't easy."

"Which makes him dangerous in his own way," I murmured.

"But even he's a little busy these days," Finn cut in. "McAllister is a follower, not a leader. Word is that he's trying to find himself a new boss to work for—without getting dead first. Last thing I've heard, he's gone into hiding until things settle down in the city. It's gang warfare out there on the streets. Almost a month after Mab dies, and every shark in the Ashland underworld is still going at it trying to grab as much power as he can."

Bria nodded her agreement. "I know. Xavier and I have been pulling double shifts for weeks now."

"So see, Gin? No one's really even noticed your absence," Finn said in a cheery voice. "They're all too busy killing each other off right now to think about coming after the Spider."

"Terrific," I muttered. "Just terrific."

But after a moment, I started to laugh.

"What's so funny?" Owen asked.

I shrugged. "Nothing much. Just the fact I killed the most unkillable woman in Ashland, the strongest, most unbeatable elemental around, and no one seems to care because they're all too busy mowing each other down in the street with machine guns. It's just—funny."

I laughed again, but the others exchanged puzzled glances. They didn't understand what was going on. I laughed until tears streamed down my face, and my stomach hurt from the force of it. And then I laughed some more.

Irony. What a bitch.

I managed to quit laughing long enough to finish eating. Jo-Jo went to check on something in the salon, while Owen stepped outside to call Eva and update her on how I was doing. Their departures left me alone with Finn and Bria in the kitchen. The two of them sat at the table across from me, not quite touching, but obviously wanting to do so. Being alive had put me in a rather generous mood, so I decided to make things easy for them.

"So," I said. "Exactly how long have the two of you been together? I assume that you've been going hot and heavy ever since that night at Fletcher's house when the bounty hunters interrupted you. Am I right?"

Finn and Bria didn't look at me or each other.

"Right," Bria mumbled. "Although if it makes you uncomfortable—"

"Then Gin's just going to have to deal with it," Finn cut her off.

Bria stared at him in surprise.

"What?" Finn said. "I worked too hard and too long to get you into my bed to just cut you loose now, cupcake."

Bria's eyes narrowed. "Cupcake?"

"Cupcake." Finn grinned at her. "Or would you prefer snuggle bunny?"

Bria's hand drifted down to the gun on her leather belt, as though she wanted to pull it out and shoot Finn with it. Well, it was good to know I wasn't the only one who occasionally had that reaction to him.

I looked back and forth between the two of them, surprised and more than a little pleased by the emotions I saw sparking in their gazes. Annoyance. Desire. Heat. And something a little softer and more promising as well. I thought they might have a chance of making it together—forever. Bria was serious enough to keep Finn grounded, while my foster brother was carefree enough to get my sister to lighten up. Something that she needed now more than ever to help her get over the horrors of what Mab had done to her.

"I'm going to have to agree with Finn on this one," I said in a mild tone. "Especially since I've had to listen to him tell me how fantastic you are ever since Christmas."

Bria stared at my foster brother with a little more warmth. "You think that I'm fantastic? I'm not just another conquest to you?"

Finn's shoulders sagged, and he gave me a defeated look. "Geez, Gin. Talk about kicking a guy when he's down. Now you've gone and done it."

I arched an eyebrow. "What? I've let the world know that there really is a heart underneath that slick suit and shiny tie? We've all known that for a while now, Finn. No matter how much you try to hide it."

"Curses," Finn muttered. "Foiled again."

I leaned over and rumpled his walnut-colored locks. "As for me, the two of you have my blessing—and then some. So go, get out of here and have some fun—together. You've been cooped up in this house long enough, worrying about me."

Bria stared at me. "But what about before? That night at Fletcher's house? Finn and I being, um, distracted was what led to this whole mess. My getting captured by Gentry, your almost being killed by Mab. How can you just forget about that? You were so angry about it before."

I thought of what Fletcher had told me when I'd seen the old man in the Pork Pit. "You're right. I was angry before. But we all make mistakes, even the best of us. I like to think that it all evens out in the end."

Finn gave me a strange look. "That sounds like something that Dad would say."

I just smiled at him. "Yeah, it does, doesn't it?"

Then I fixed them both with a hard stare. "Just don't ask me to take sides when the two of you go at each other. Okay?"

They nodded, then looked at each other. Finn waggled his eyebrows in a suggestive manner, and Bria snorted. But she couldn't stop a grin from curving her lips. Two minutes later, they both made excuses to leave. I only hoped they managed to make it to Finn's apartment before their clothes came off.

At that point, Jo-Jo strolled back into the kitchen and announced that it was time for me to go back to bed—whether I wanted to or not.

"I didn't spend the better part of a month putting you back together again for you to wear yourself out the first day that you're up," the dwarf announced.

Owen was still busy with his phone call, so I let Jo-Jo help me back upstairs. The dwarf stayed with me, even going so far as to tuck me in herself—something she hadn't done since I was a girl. She smoothed the covers down and stepped back. Jo-Jo stared at me with her clear, almost colorless eyes, and a soft smile creased her middle-aged face.

"I'm proud of you, Gin," she said. "So very, very proud."

"Why? Because I finally killed Mab?"

Jo-Jo shook her head. "No, not because of that. I'm proud because you finally believed in yourself, Gin. Because you finally fully embraced your magic. The way that the purest, the strongest elementals always do in the end."

For once, Jo-Jo's words didn't make me shiver with unease. Instead, I sat there and thought about them. The dwarf was right—and wrong too. Yeah, I'd finally embraced my power, finally used it the way that it had always been intended to be used, finally dueled and defeated Mab with it. But it wasn't just my magic that had helped me win—it had been Fletcher too. The old man's training, all the years of his molding me into the Spider, shaping me into a weapon—that was what had ultimately let me kill Mab. My magic had just been the means to the end. Fletcher was the one who'd prepared me to face the Fire elemental all along.

I told Jo-Jo as much, and she smiled again.

"Fletcher might have given you the tools, darling, but you're the one who used them. Don't ever forget that."

Something in her tone made me look a little closer at her. "What do you mean, Jo-Jo? It's over now. Done. Finished. Mab is dead. And if she somehow manages to crawl out of her grave, I'll put her right back down in it again."

The dwarf stared at me. "But your life isn't over, Gin. You're not through being an elemental just because you killed Mab. You're still growing, as a person, as an elemental, which means that your magic will keep on getting stronger."

My mouth fell open, and I struggled to come up with the right words. I'd never given much thought to what would happen after I killed Mab—mainly because I hadn't figured that I'd be around afterward.

"You mean—you mean that I'll have even more magic in the future? Even more than I did in the courtyard?"

My voice fell to a whisper. I'd been so busy just being grateful I'd survived, that everyone I loved was in one piece, that I hadn't thought about the future—certainly not about my magic, what it might do, or what I might be able to do with it.

Jo-Jo nodded. "You will. You're a very special person, Gin, in more ways than one. Your magic is strong, but so are you with that iron will of yours. It's served you well, and it will continue to do so."

I just sat there, digesting her words.

She hesitated. "But I have to tell you that I still see darkness ahead for you, darling, some dark days, some tough times."

I shrugged. "I figured as much. Because now, I'm not only the Spider, but I'm the woman who killed Mab Monroe too. Every elemental who wants to prove herself will be looking to track me down and take me out. In a way, it'll be even worse than the bounty hunters. They only wanted to turn me in—they didn't particularly care if I was dead or not."

"Yes," Jo-Jo said. "I suppose that it will be worse. But it's not just elementals looking to prove themselves. There are a lot of bad people out there with a lot of bad powers. And, darling, you seem to attract that sort of trouble like honey does flies. But we both know that you'll be ready for them—no matter what. And that I'll be here to help you, every step of the way. Me and Sophia and all the others."

I reached over and squeezed the dwarf's hand. "You'd better believe it."

❈ 32 ❈

I spent the next week recovering at Jo-Jo's. My friends all dropped by at one time or another to see how I was doing, and Owen spent more time at the dwarf's house than he did at his own. Finn was there too every single day, giving me updates about what was going on in the Ashland underworld.

Mab Monroe's unexpected but not unwelcome death had thrown the city's entire underworld into a feeding frenzy, as everyone sought to establish themselves as the new big bad on the block. Bria and Xavier told me some of it—all the murders, drive-by shootings, and other violence that soaked the city streets in blood. But there was nothing I could do to stem the tide or help the two cops—not when I was still so weak.

Jo-Jo made me spend two more days in bed before I convinced the dwarf that it was time for me to get back on my feet. I might have killed Mab, but that didn't mean that trouble wouldn't come looking for me sooner rather than later—and bite me on the ass when I least expected it.

Like right now.

The sword zipped by my head, close enough to part my hair, before I managed to duck at the last second. He raised the weapon for another blow, but I was already moving forward. I snapped my hand up and blocked his attack with my own sword before pivoting and slashing my blade at my opponent.

Clang!

Owen's sword met mine, smashing against my blade so hard that he almost ripped the weapon out of my hand. I growled with frustration. A month ago, before I'd taken on Mab, I would have already hit him a dozen times while we sparred. Now it took all the energy I had just to swing a sword at him for five minutes.

Owen grinned and rocked back on the balls of his feet. "Not bad for a woman who was at death's door a few weeks ago."

I paused a moment to catch my breath. "But not nearly good enough for me."

We stood in the depths of Owen's mansion in his private gym. Mats covered the floor, while mirrors lined three of the walls. The fourth wall was reserved for the rows of exquisite weapons that Owen crafted in his blacksmith forge in the back of the house. Swords, daggers, knives, maces, even an ax or two.

The two of us had been coming here and sparring ever since the day Jo-Jo had let me out of bed. It was hard—so fucking *hard*—but I worked myself to exhaustion every single day, then pushed a little harder. The Ashland underworld wouldn't stay in a tizzy forever, and sooner or later, folks were going to start looking in my direction. And I'd be damned if I wasn't ready when they did.

I used the sleeve of my T-shirt to wipe a bit of sweat off my forehead, and Owen frowned in concern.

"Are you tired, Gin? Do you need to take a break—"

I launched myself at him, whipping my sword through a series of moves. Owen parried the first blow, and even the second, but the third slipped past his defenses, and my blade just kissed his throat.

"Now that's more like it," I crowed.

Owen's eyes narrowed. "You cheated. You took me off guard."

"And you should have known better than to think that an assassin *wouldn't* cheat," I smirked. "Especially the Spider."

"Hmm."

Owen made a noncommittal grunt and used the tip of his own sword to gently push mine away. But instead of raising his weapon again, Owen put his sword on the ground and sauntered toward me. He was dressed in a T-shirt and sweatpants just like I was, but he wore them oh so well. The thin cotton stretched across his chest, highlighting his strong, firm muscles, while the sweatpants hung low on his hips, hinting at the hardness that was hidden under there as well. Mmm. A different sort of heat flared in the pit of my stomach. It matched the passion burning in Owen's eyes.

"You know," he murmured, tugging my sword out of my hands and lowering it to the floor. "I think we should move on to the hand-to-hand combat portion of today's workout."

I arched an eyebrow. "Really? What did you have in mind?"

"Oh, I don't know," Owen said, drawing me into his arms. "Perhaps something that will improve your flexibility."

"I happen to be quite flexible," I retorted. "You're the one who threw his back out in bed the other night."

Owen grinned. "Which is exactly why I think that you should be on top today."

He leaned forward and pressed a kiss to my throat, his hands already working their way under my T-shirt, just as mine were dipping below the waistband on his pants.

"So what do you say, Gin?" Owen said. "Care for a little one-on-one action? Think you can handle it?"

My hand slid down, closing around his thickening length. Owen's breath rasped against my neck.

"Oh," I murmured, turning my head to stare into his eyes. "I think that I can handle anything you've got, Grayson."

Our lips met, and we spent the rest of the afternoon engaging in a far more pleasurable form of sparring.

Another week passed. Every day I got a little stronger, a little tougher, until slowly, the old Gin Blanco emerged once more. Jo-Jo pronounced me fit to go back to work just as the last of the winter snow melted away in mid-March. One day, it was cold and frigid. The next, it seemed like spring had swept in with all her bright green glory trailing along behind her.

Six weeks after my fight with Mab, I walked through the front door of the Pork Pit. It was just after ten, and

I'd come in to open the restaurant for the day. I flicked on the overhead lights, even though the morning sunlight was already streaming in through the storefront windows.

This was the first time that I'd been in the restaurant since my battle with Mab. For a moment, I just stood there by the door, my eyes sweeping over all the familiar furnishings. The blue and pink booths, the matching pig tracks on the floor, the long counter along the back wall, the battered cash register. They all greeted me like old friends. I breathed in, and the scent of sugar and spices filled my lungs, smelling better to me than the most expensive perfume. The aroma would only intensify once Sophia and I started cooking.

I walked over to the cash register. For a second, it was almost like I could see Fletcher sitting on the stool there, wearing his blue work clothes and apron, just like he had in my dream, vision, or whatever that strange trip had been the night I'd almost died. My gaze went to the wall where the bloody copy of *Where the Red Fern Grows* hung in its usual spot, along with a faded photo of Fletcher and Warren Fox.

I might have only imagined it, but it seemed like the smell of chicory coffee suddenly filled the air. I breathed in again, and the aroma was gone, replaced by the usual swirl of spices. But I knew that Fletcher Lane would never truly leave me. I smiled and got to work.

All the waitstaff came in at their usual time, and everyone greeted me with enthusiasm, telling me how sorry they were that I'd had mono for the last six weeks. That's the story Finn, Bria, and the others had spun to explain my absence. I didn't think anyone really believed it, though. I wouldn't have. I didn't know how many of my employees knew what had really gone down between me and Mab, or even realized I was the Spider, but at least some of them had heard the rumors. I could see it in the way their eyes didn't quite meet mine. I supposed it would take some time for all the hoopla surrounding Mab's death and my part in it to die down—if it ever really could.

Thanks to Sophia's tender loving care, business hadn't suffered at all while I was gone. By lunchtime, the Pork Pit was as busy as ever, and I was happy to be back in the thick of things—back where I belonged.

My happiness lasted until about three o'clock that afternoon.

I was wiping down the counter when the door opened, causing the bell to chime. I opened my mouth to greet my new customers and then I saw who they were—Ruth Gentry and Sydney. With my right hand, I kept on wiping the counter. With my left, I palmed one of my silverstone knives. I still wore them, of course. One up either sleeve, one tucked against the small of my back, and two more nestled in the sides of my boots. My usual five-point arsenal, all stamped with my spider rune. I might have killed Mab, but that didn't mean that I had a license to do something as foolish as not have my knives handy.

"Sophia," I murmured. "We might have a situation here."

The dwarf, who was slicing tomatoes, grunted and looked over her shoulder. When she saw who had come to call, she moved to stand beside me, her black eyes as cold and hard as mine were.

Gentry didn't dawdle by the door. She marched over

to me, with Sydney trailing along behind her. Both of them had cleaned up considerably since the last time I'd seen them. Gentry had on a new stiff pair of jeans and a spiffy pink flannel shirt with what looked like real pearl buttons. They matched the handle of the revolver that she had tucked into the new holster under her matching pink jacket. As for Sydney, she wore a pair of expensive cargo pants, along with a sweater set done in a sky blue. Her face had also filled out since the last time I'd seen her, and her eyes were clear of that wounded, hungry, desperate look they'd held before.

"Ruth Gentry," I said in a pleasant voice, mindful of the half-dozen customers who were in the restaurant with us. "What can I do for you?"

Under the counter, out of sight, my thumb traced over the hilt of my silverstone knife. Gentry didn't look as if she'd come here for trouble, but you never knew. Just yesterday, Finn had heard a nasty rumor that Jonah McAllister was trying to put a new bounty on my head—literally. The lawyer wanted someone to bring him my head—without the rest of my body attached to it. Finn's sources claimed that there were no takers so far, despite the fat wad of cash McAllister was offering. Amazing how people tended to leave you alone after you killed the most powerful woman in town.

The bounty hunter stepped up to the counter, her pale blue eyes sweeping over me. Surprise flickered in her gaze, as if she couldn't quite believe that I was still alive. Sometimes, I couldn't believe it myself.

"Gin Blanco," she said, matching my pleasant tone. "You're looking well. All things considered."

I didn't say anything. Gentry could see just how well I was, and if the bounty hunter wanted to put me to the test, I'd be more than happy to oblige her.

"I just thought that I would drop by and see how you were doing," Gentry said.

"Really?" I asked. "You didn't come here to try to collect on anything else?"

Gentry gave me a sly, shit-eating grin. "I did that a few weeks ago. Cashed in my bounty on Detective Bria Coolidge first thing. Always get the money up front."

"That sounds like something my mentor would say if he were still alive."

Gentry's eyes narrowed, as if she wasn't sure whether I was mocking her, but she didn't respond.

"You know that I should kill you," I said in a mild voice. "Just for having the balls to show up in my restaurant, in my gin joint."

Gentry nodded her head. "Maybe you should, but I had to come here today. I had to give you my thanks."

This time, my eyes narrowed. "Your thanks for what?"

"For helping me and the girl. For not killing us both that first night when you had the chance in the woods outside of Mab's estate. For showing us that little bit of mercy." Gentry looked at Sydney. "And for giving a hungry girl a hot, decent meal, even though you would have been better off kicking us both to the curb that day here in the restaurant."

I shrugged. "I know what it's like to be hungry. That's all. Don't attribute it to any real kindness on my part."

Gentry smiled. "Oh, I think you're a bit kinder than you like to imagine, Gin."

"Don't count on it. The only reason you're not dead is because my sister asked me not to kill you. You helped her that night with Mab, kept the Fire elemental from torturing her to death. I'm grateful to you for that. You should appreciate your own kindness, Gentry. Because it's the only reason that you're still breathing right now."

There was more to it than that, of course. Finn had finally dug into Ruth Gentry's past for me and what he had found had made me see her in a new light. The old woman was a bounty hunter of some repute, with a reputation for being tough, ornery, and determined. Gentry was the kind of hunter who always got her man, until two of the bad, bad men that she'd collected a bounty on had broken out of prison, tracked her back to her remote Kentucky home, and burned it to the ground while Gentry was away on business. According to Finn's file, the bounty hunter had lost everything that night, except the clothes on her back.

And so had Sydney.

The girl and her parents had lived in the next house over, and when the men got through at Gentry's place, they went next door and started in on Sydney and her family. They'd decided to hole up there and wait for Gentry to return so they could kill her.

Sydney was the one who'd actually killed the men, somehow getting hold of one of their guns, but not before they'd raped and murdered her mother and killed her father. Finn hadn't been able to tell me what the men had done to Sydney herself during the time they'd held her captive—and I wasn't sure that I wanted to know.

Gentry had come home three weeks later to find Sydney living in the ruined remains of Gentry's home and half out of her mind with grief. Despite her own heartbreak, her own loss, Gentry had taken the girl under her wing. That had been more than two months ago, and the two had been inseparable ever since. I imagined all that was why they'd come to Ashland in the first place— Gentry had needed the bounty on Bria to get back on her feet and to provide a better life for Sydney.

Gentry nodded. "Fair enough. But what about the girl? Sydney's caused you quite a few problems as well."

"I don't kill kids—ever."

Sydney straightened her spine. "I'm not a kid. I'm sixteen years old."

I gave her an amused look. "Sure you are, sweetheart. Enjoy it while it lasts."

Sydney opened her mouth to protest, but one stern look from Gentry shushed her.

I gestured at their clothes. "Well, I see that you're treating yourselves to the nicer things in life, since you collected on your bounty. A million dollars can go a long way toward making life more comfortable."

Gentry winced a little at my pointed barb. "I don't care so much for the money myself. I've never needed much. But the girl here is a different story. Her parents came to an unfortunate end, and I'm looking after her. Now I've got enough money to take care of her—even send her to college so she can get a real job."

"But I want to be a bounty hunter like you, Gentry," Sydney protested.

Gentry gave her a fierce look. "You might be a fair enough shot for it, but a girl needs to know more than just how to shoot guns. There's book learning too, you know."

Sydney didn't say anything, but I could see the determination in her face. No matter if Gentry sent her to a dozen colleges, she'd always want to be a bounty hunter, just like the old woman. I stared at the girl, and, once again, I saw myself at that age. With a dead family and a strange new mentor that I didn't know quite what to make of. I wondered where Sydney would be in seventeen years. If our roles would be reversed, and I'd be in Gentry's shoes by then.

The thought made me smile.

Still looking at the girl, Gentry stuck her hand into her jacket pocket.

"Gently," I cautioned her. "I'm feeling a might twitchy today. So is Sophia here."

"Hmph." Beside me, the dwarf grunted.

"Of course you are," Gentry murmured.

She grabbed something in her jacket pocket and came out with it slowly, keeping her movements small and steady. Then she handed me a business card with a cell phone number on it. A rune was also stamped on the card in black foil. A revolver. The symbol for deadly accuracy. Fitting, given what I knew about the bounty hunter.

"Sydney and I have decided to leave Ashland behind for a warmer climate. If you're ever down in Charleston, give me a call," Gentry said. "Because based on what I saw in that courtyard, I'd sure as hell like to buy you a drink someday."

I probably should have ripped the card into pieces. Or better yet, stuck it on the end of my knife and then put them both through Gentry. After all, this was the woman who'd kidnapped my sister and carted her off to be tortured by Mab. But Gentry was also the reason that Bria was still breathing, which was something I just couldn't overlook. So I took the card and slid it into the pocket of my jeans.

"I just might do that."

"Well, Gin, I can't say that it's been a pleasure doing business with you, but it's certainly been an experience."

"I would say the same thing about you, Gentry. You certainly gave me a run for my money, and you earned every penny of that million that Mab paid you."

"Ah, now you're just flattering an old woman," she said, but a pleased blush crept up her leathery neck.

"That's something else you should know about me. I don't flatter people—ever."

A grin creased her wrinkled face. "Either way, Sydney and I need to be going. There's a bus that leaves for Charleston in an hour, and we plan to be on it. So you take care now, Gin. I hope we meet again someday."

"You too, Gentry, Sydney," I said and meant it. "You take care too."

Gentry nodded, before she and the girl turned and left the restaurant for the final time.

The rest of the day passed uneventfully. People came and went, eating, talking, laughing, gossiping, but no one entered the restaurant looking like they wanted to do me immediate harm. I enjoyed the calm, even though I knew it wouldn't last.

Finally, about six that afternoon, more customers left

than came in, and I thought about closing early. After being cooped up in Jo-Jo's house for the better part of a month, I found myself with a case of spring fever. I wanted to take a walk, do some yoga in the park, anything that would get me outside into the fresh air and sunshine. I'd just turned around to tell Sophia to shut off the stoves, when the front door opened, causing the bell to chime, and a young girl stepped inside.

I watched her, waiting for her mother or father to come inside after her, but no one did. After a moment, I realized that no one was going to. She was here all by her lonesome. She was twelve, maybe thirteen, far too young to be wandering around this close to Southtown by herself.

But what caught and held my attention was the puffy bruise on her face. It was blue, black, and every shade of green in between. There was only one way that you got a bruise like that—by someone planting his fist in your face. I stared at the girl, wondering who she was and what she wanted. There was a hardness in her face, a pinched set to her features that told me she'd already seen some bad things in her time. I knew that look. It was one I'd had ever since I was thirteen—the same one I saw every time I looked in the mirror.

The girl looked around carefully, staring at the other diners, as if she was measuring what kind of threat they might be. Apparently, she thought that she could take them, because she walked over to the counter. The girl hopped up on a stool close to the cash register and looked at first Sophia, then at me.

"Can I help you, sweetheart?" I asked.

The girl just stared at me. "That depends. Are you the Spider?"

Are you the Spider?

I'd been expecting someone to ask me that question all day long, but no one had. No one had dared to—until now.

I didn't answer the girl, but I didn't tell her that I wasn't the Spider either. If Jonah McAllister or someone else had sent her in here, I wanted to see what kind of game she was playing, and how I could twist it around to my advantage. If she had come in on her own, I still wanted to know what the hell she thought she was doing.

Some of the toughness in the girl's face melted under my hard, gray stare. She dropped her eyes from mine and drew in a breath, as if to bolster her fading courage.

"I heard that there's a lady here called the Spider who helps people," the girl said. "And I want to hire her."

Of all the things she might have said, that was one I'd never expected. I didn't help people, I killed them. The two were not necessarily one and the same. I looked at Sophia, but the Goth dwarf just shrugged. She didn't know what to make of the girl either.

"And who told you that?" I asked. "About the Spider?"

The girl reached out and fiddled with one of the silver napkin holders. "It was just something that I heard from some people."

She drew in another breath, then reached into the pocket of her jacket and came out with a wad of crumpled bills. She shoved them across the counter to me. I eyed the bills. It looked like she had maybe a hundred bucks there, total. Not exactly my going rate before I'd retired.

"There are some bad men who are hurting my mom," the girl said. "I want the Spider to make them stop. If you're not her, then do you know who she is? Do you think that she'll help me? Please?"

I should have told the kid no. Should have told her that there was no Spider here and to get lost. Maybe it was seeing the parallels between Sydney and Gentry, and me and Fletcher. Maybe it was this strange mood I'd been in ever since my ghostly talk with the old man, this strange feeling I had that I was at some kind of crossroads. Maybe it was because I thought being retired sucked. Hell, maybe it was just the damn *please* she tacked on at the end. But I didn't tell the girl no.

The truth was that part of me felt adrift now, restless and at loose ends. Mainly because my finally killing Mab wasn't turning out to be quite as fulfilling as I'd imagined it would be.

Oh, I was glad she was dead. More than glad. Ecstatic, really. But now that she was gone, now that my rehab was finished, I didn't quite know what to do with myself. Sure, I had the Pork Pit to run during the day, Owen to go home to at night, and the rest of my friends and family to fill in the time between. But so much of my life these past few months had been tied up in the Fire elemental, in killing Mab. Now that she was dead, I just felt . . . empty. Adrift, without purpose. Hell, bored, even.

Killing Mab had been my goal for so long that I wasn't quite sure what to do with myself now, what to say, even what to *feel*.

And now here was this girl, asking for the Spider, wanting me to pull out my silverstone knives and jump into the fray once more. Her simple words and the desperate plea in them stirred something in me, something I couldn't deny, something I didn't want to deny. Not any longer. For the first time, I realized how Fletcher must have felt. How the old man had realized that maybe there was another use for his particular skill set instead of just killing people for money. One that was far more satisfying in the end.

And I knew what I had to do. Maybe it was what I'd always had to do, what I'd always been doing. The path that Fletcher had set me on all those years ago, even if I hadn't realized it at the time or along the way. Even if I hadn't thought about it until this very moment.

"Put your money away," I told the girl. "There's no need for it here."

She stared at me, hesitating, before she scraped up the bills and stuck them back into her pocket.

"So you're her, then?" the girl asked. "You're the Spider?"

I slowly nodded.

"And you'll help me?" she asked. "And my mom?"

I nodded again. Out of the corner of my eye, I saw Sophia shake her head. I turned my head and winked at her. The dwarf grumbled something under her breath, but her lips turned up into a smile.

Meanwhile, the girl sat there and stared at me, the briefest glimmer of hope swimming up in the dark depths of her eyes. "But how will you help me? What can you do?"

I palmed one of my silverstone knifes and laid it on the counter in front of her. The girl's eyes widened in surprise, and maybe a touch of fear too, but I just grinned at her.

"My name is Gin, and I kill people."

Turn the page for a sneak peek at the next book
in the Elemental Assassin series,

BY A THREAD

Jennifer Estep

Coming soon from Pocket Books

* 1 *

"You need a vacation."

I looked up from the tomato I was slicing and stared across the counter at Finnegan Lane, my foster brother and partner in so many murderous schemes over the years.

"Vacation? I hardly ever take vacations," I said. "I have a barbecue restaurant to run, in case you've forgotten."

I gestured with the knife out at the Pork Pit. Most people wouldn't consider the restaurant much to look at with its blue and pink vinyl booths and matching, peeling pig tracks on the floor that led to the men's and women's restrooms. The long counter that ran along the back wall was older than I was, as were most of the cups, dishes, and stainless-steel appliances. But everything was clean and polished, from the tables and chairs to the framed, slightly bloody copy of *Where the Red Fern Grows* that hung on one wall. The Pit might not be some fancy, highfalutin place, but it was my gin joint, my home, and I was damned proud of it.

"A vacation," Finn repeated, as if I hadn't said a word. "Somewhere warm, somewhere sandy, somewhere where nobody knows your name, either as Gin Blanco or as the Spider."

Finn's voice wasn't that loud, but when he said *the Spider,* the words echoed like gunshots through the storefront. The folks sitting at the tables behind Finn immediately froze, their thick, juicy, barbecue beef and pork sandwiches halfway between their plates and lips. Conversation dried up like a puddle in the desert, and everyone's eyes cut to me, wondering how I would react to the sound of that name.

My assassin name. The one I'd gone by for the last seventeen years, when I was out late at night killing people for money and eventually other, more noble reasons.

My hand tightened around the long, serrated tomato knife. Not for the first time, I wished I could use it to cut out Finn's tongue—or at least get him to think before he opened his mouth. An elderly woman sitting two stools down from Finn noticed my death grip on the blade. Her face paled, and her hand clutched at her white silk blouse like she was about three seconds away from having a heart attack.

Sighing, I made myself relax and put the blade down on the counter. Fuck. I hated being notorious.

After a lifetime of being invisible, I was suddenly the most well-known person in Ashland. Several weeks ago, I'd done the unthinkable—I'd killed Mab Monroe, the Fire elemental who'd been the head of the city's underworld for years. Mab had murdered my mother and older sister when I was thirteen, and her death had been a long time coming, as far as I was concerned. I didn't know anyone who'd shed any tears over the Fire elemental's messy demise.

But now, everyone wanted their pound of flesh—from *me*.

Mab's death had left a vacuum among Ashland's legit and not-so-legit power players, and they were all scrambling to stake their various claims and position themselves as the city's next top dog.

Some of them thought the best way to accomplish that feat was by killing me.

Idiot after idiot had come to the Pork Pit in the last few weeks, either singularly or in small groups, all with one thing on their minds—taking out the Spider. The elementals came at me straight on, challenging me to duels and wanting to test their magic against my own Ice and Stone power. The humans, vampires, giants, and dwarves, well, most of them were content to try to get the drop on me when I was either opening up or closing down the restaurant.

Whatever their method, it always ended the same way—with the challengers dead and me calling Sophia Deveraux to come dispose of their bodies. I'd killed more people in the last month than I had in a year as the Spider. Even I was getting a little sick of the constant surprise attacks and blood spatters on my clothes, but the stream of suicidal lowlifes showed no signs of slowing down anytime soon.

The old lady next to Finn sucked in a breath. I looked

down and realized that I'd picked up the tomato knife again, rubbing my thumb over the polished hilt. It wasn't as nice or sharp as the five silverstone knives that I had secreted on my body, but the serrated blade would do plenty of damage. Most things would, if you put enough force behind them.

"What are you looking at?" I snapped.

The old lady's eyes widened. With a trembling hand, she reached into her purse, threw a fifty-dollar bill on the counter, and hightailed it out of the restaurant as fast as her white square heels would carry her.

"Another one bites the dust," Finn murmured, his green eyes merry in his handsome face.

I narrowed my eyes and made a slashing gesture with the knife. Finn, of course, ignored my glare and threats of violence. Instead, he raised his coffee mug and gestured to a dwarf who was chopping long, green ribs of celery to add to some macaroni salad she was mixing up.

"Sophia?" he asked. "If you please?"

Sophia Deveraux turned to stare at Finn. Sophia was the head cook at the Pork Pit, in addition to her side job of disposing of any bodies I left in my wake as the Spider. I'd inherited the dwarf's dual services when I'd taken over the assassination business from Finn's father, Fletcher Lane, the old man who'd been an assassin known as the Tin Man and had taught me everything he knew.

Sophia grunted and grabbed the pot of coffee that she always kept on for Finn, who usually dropped by the restaurant at least once a day. She refilled his cup, and the warm, chicory fumes filled my nose and momentarily overpowered the cumin and other spices that flavored the air. The rich caffeine smell always reminded me of Fletcher, who'd drunk the same chicory brew before he'd died.

Now, the Pork Pit might not be much to look at, but folks couldn't help but stare at Sophia. One by one, their eyes flicked from me to her. It wasn't the fact that Sophia was a dwarf that drew people's gazes; it was because she was Goth—seriously Goth. Sophia wore heavy black boots and jeans, topped by a white T-shirt that featured a black scythe slashing across her chest. Grim Reaper indeed. Her hair and eyes were black, too, making her skin seem that much paler, despite the crimson lipstick she wore. The lipstick was the same color as the spiked, silverstone collar that ringed her neck.

The good thing about standing next to Sophia was that it made everyone forget about me and the knife I still clutched in my hand. After a few more seconds, everyone went back to their sandwiches, along with the baked beans, coleslaw, steak-cut fries, and the other side dishes that went with them.

"Now, back to my vacation idea." Finn grinned, showing off his perfect white teeth. "Just think about it. You, Owen, me, and Bria, all happily ensconced in a swanky resort hotel. Bria in a bikini. You and Owen doing your own thing, Bria in a bikini. Did I mention Bria in a bikini?"

I rolled my eyes. "That's my baby sister you're talking about."

Finn's grin widened. "I know."

Along with everything else that had gone down when I'd been waging my final battle against Mab, Finn had finally hooked up with my younger sister, Bria, after a long, arduous pursuit. I wasn't sure how serious the two of them were, but they'd been hot and heavy for weeks now and showed no signs of slowing down anytime soon. I was happy for them—really, I was—but I could have done without Finn giving me the play-by-play of their sex life on a regular basis. Hell, I didn't even talk about that stuff with Bria, and she was my sister. But that was part of the sordid charm of Finnegan Lane. My foster brother loved talking about women as much as he did sleeping with them.

Finn opened his mouth to cajole me some more, but I'd had enough—enough of the stares, enough of the whispers, enough of everyone wondering if I was going to kill them for setting foot inside my restaurant. I just wanted to be left alone by everyone right now, including Finn.

"I don't need a vacation," I growled, stomping away from him and the curious customers in the front of the restaurant. "And that's final."

I grabbed a couple of trash bags, pushed through the swinging double doors, and walked through the back of the restaurant. I didn't stop until I opened another door and stepped outside into the alley that cut between the rows of buildings on the block.

It was after seven, and night had already fallen, wrapping the buildings in thick, coal black shadows that stretched all the way up to the sky. Wispy clouds flitted in front of the full moon, rolling over the bright silver orb like waves crashing onto a sandy shore and then retreating back out to sea.

My eyes zoomed in on a crack in one of the buildings, a tiny sliver of space barely big enough for a child. My old hiding spot when I'd been living on the mean streets of Ashland back before Fletcher had taken me in. For a moment, I wished that I was still small enough to fit into the crack and hide from all my worries—at least for a little while.

I'd thought killing Mab would solve all my problems, but instead it had just created a whole host of new ones. Sure, business was better than ever at the Pork Pit, but only because people came to gawk at me. Everyone wondered if I was *really* the notorious assassin known as the Spider and if I'd *really* killed Mab Monroe like some folks claimed.

Then there were the people who actually *knew* I'd taken out the Fire elemental—people like Jonah McAllister. He'd been Mab's lawyer and one of her top lieutenants before her death and had a number of reasons to hate me, especially since I'd killed his son, Jake, last year. McAllister had even gone so far as to offer a price for my head, sending a variety of bounty hunters my way, but no one had been able to collect—yet.

To some people, my taking out Mab had made me something of a folk hero, given how many people the Fire elemental had stepped on, hurt, and killed climbing her way to the top of the Ashland underworld. To others, I represented nothing more than a fat payday or the means to make a name for themselves.

Either way, I was the center of attention—and I *hated* it.

I breathed in, enjoying the peace and quiet after the tight, nervous tension that permeated the restaurant. It was early April, and the nights were still cold, although the warm days whispered of spring. I heaved the trash bags into the closest Dumpster, but instead of going inside, I lingered in the alley outside the back of the restaurant.

I skimmed my fingers over the rough red brick and reached out with my magic. As a Stone elemental, I could create, control, and manipulate the element in whatever form it took around me, from making bricks fly out of the wall in front of me to crumbling cobblestones to shattering the foundation of a house. I could even make my own skin as hard as marble, so that nothing could hurt me. I'd relied on that particular trick a lot these past few weeks.

My power also let me listen to the stone around me. People's actions and emotions sink into their surroundings over time, especially stone, as folks live, love, die, and more. Listening to the bricks that made up the Pork Pit was one of my favorite things to do because the sound was almost always the same—one of low, slow contentment, just like the minds, hearts, and stomachs of all the folks who'd eaten in the restaurant over the years. A good meal was one of the few things that could satisfy even the pickiest soul, and the Pit had served up its fair share of fine food over the years. I breathed in again, letting that soft sound fill me and soothe away all the stress of the day, all the stress and turmoil of the last few weeks.

Calmer, I dropped my hand and turned to go inside when the crackle of magic filled the alley.

In addition to dwarves, giants, and vampires, Ashland also had a healthy elemental population. Magic could take many forms, could manifest in all sorts of ways, which meant that elementals in the city and beyond had everything from the ability to shoot lightning out of their fingertips to being able to control the weather. But to be considered a true elemental, you had to be gifted in one of the four main areas—Air, Fire, Ice, or Stone. I was a rare elemental in that I was able to tap into not one but two elements, Ice and Stone in my case.

I focused on the other person's magic, which felt like red-hot sparks landing on my skin. A Fire elemental, judging by the way the scars embedded in my palms itched and burned. The marks on both my hands were the same. A small circle surrounded by eight thin rays. A spider rune. The symbol for patience. Something that I was getting real short on these days.

I sighed and turned around. Sure enough, two guys stood in the alley that ran behind the restaurant. One was a giant, judging by his seven-foot frame, while the other was human and an elemental. A ball of Fire flickered in the palm of his hand, gently bobbing up and down.

Ding, ding, Gin Blanco wins again.

"Let me guess," I drawled. "You're here to take out the notorious Spider."

The giant started to speak, but I held up my hand, cutting him off.

"I really don't care to listen to your blustering manifesto about what badasses the two of you are and how you're going to make me beg for mercy by the time you're done with me," I said. "I just want to say this—do yourselves a favor. Walk away now, and I won't kill you."

"Did you hear that, Billy?" the Fire elemental cackled. "The Spider's going to go soft on us tonight."

Billy, the giant, cracked his knuckles together, a grin splitting his face. "She doesn't look so tough to me, Bobby."

I rolled my eyes. People might not know for sure that I was the Spider, but you'd think that enough folks had disappeared in and around the Pork Pit by now for everyone else to realize that it might be a good idea to steer clear of me and my restaurant.

"Let's get her, Billy!" Bobby screamed.

The giant let out a loud whoop of agreement.

Apparently not.

They rushed me at the same time, and Bobby threw his elemental Fire at me. He was strong in his magic but compared to the blazing inferno that I'd faced when I'd killed Mab, his power felt as weak as a candle flame. Still, I ducked out of the way. I had no desire to have my hair singed off again this week.

I rolled to my left, came up on one knee, and grabbed the lid of one of the metal trash cans in the alley. I held the lid up over my head just in time for Billy to plant his massive fist in it. The sharp, ringing force of the giant's blow rocked me back for a moment. Billy drew his fist back again, and I lashed out with my foot, driving my boot into his knee. Billy grunted and stumbled forward, one hand going to the alley floor, putting him down on my level.

I looked him in the eyes, smiled, and smashed the metal lid into his face as hard as I could.

It took several blows, but eventually blood started to pour out of Billy's broken, bulbous nose and the deep, jagged cuts I opened up on his face. I hit him again with the trash-can lid, driving the metal into his square chin, and the giant toppled over onto his back. His head cracked against the alley floor, and he let out a low groan. Down for the count already.

Bobby looked stunned, just stunned, that I'd taken out his friend so easily. But his expression quickly changed to one of concern when I got to my feet and started walking toward him, holding the metal lid out in front of me like a shield. Bobby backpedaled, but he forgot to look behind him. He'd taken only two steps before he was pressed up against the side of one of the Dumpsters. Frantic, he snapped his fingers together over and over again, trying to summon up another ball of elemental Fire.

I didn't give him the chance.

Two seconds later, I slammed the metal lid into his face. I had only to hit him once before he crumpled to the ground.

When I was sure that neither man was going to get up anytime soon, I put the lid back on the trash can. The bloody dents in it matched the ones on all the other cans. More than one moron had jumped me in the alley this week. I eyed the two men, who were moaning and groaning and trying to figure out how things had gone wrong so quickly.

"Idiots," I muttered, and went back inside the restaurant.

A mirror with a cracked corner was mounted over one of the sinks in the back. I stopped there and washed the blood and grime of the fight off my hands. My hair had come loose while I'd been hitting the giant with the trash-can lid, so I yanked the elastic band out of my hair and shoved my dark chocolate brown locks back into a tighter ponytail.

The clink-clink and clatter-clatter of silverware and dishes drifted through the swinging doors, along with the savory smells and sizzles of grilled burgers and fried onion rings. All of the waitstaff had already gone home for the evening, so I was alone in this part of the restaurant. Instead of going out into the storefront and getting back to work, I put my hands on the sink and leaned forward, staring at my reflection in the mirror.

Wintry gray eyes, dark hair, pale skin. I looked the same as always, except for the blood spatters on my cheek from the alley fight and the purple smudges under my eyes. I wiped the blood off with a wet paper towel easily enough, but there was nothing I could do about the circles and the matching exhaustion that had crept over me these past few weeks.

All the stares, all the whispers, all the knock-down-drag-out fights. They'd all worn me down, until now, I was just going through the motions. Hell, I hadn't even pulled out one of my silverstone knives tonight and permanently sliced up those bastards in the alley like they deserved. Tangling with the Spider once was enough for most folks, but those idiots would probably be stupid enough to make another run at me.

I let out a frustrated sigh. Weariness was a dangerous emotion, especially for an assassin. If I didn't do something about it, eventually, I'd slip up and make a stupid, sloppy mistake. Then I'd wind up dead, my head served up on a silver platter to Jonah McAllister or whatever lowlife finally got the drop on me.

Much as I hated to admit it, Finn was right. I needed a vacation—from being the Spider.

I pushed through the double doors, stepping into the restaurant storefront. Once again, everyone froze at my appearance, as if they expected me to whip a gun out from underneath my blue work apron and start shooting. I ignored the fearful, suspicious looks, went back over to the counter, grabbed my knife, and started slicing tomatoes again.

"Took you long enough," Finn said. "I was beginning to think you got lost back there."

"Not exactly. I had another pair of unexpected visitors that I had to entertain."

Finn raised a questioning eyebrow. "Injured or dead?"

"Merely injured. What can I say? I was in a charitable mood tonight."

Finn arched his eyebrow a little higher at my sarcasm. Charity was one thing that assassins, even semiretired assassins like me, couldn't afford to have too much of. Especially not these days, when every wannabe hood in Ashland wanted a piece of me.

It took me the better part of a minute and two tomatoes to work up to my next words. "You know that vacation you were talking about earlier?"

"Yes?" Finn asked, a satisfied note creeping into his smooth voice.

I sighed, knowing that I was beaten. "When do we leave?"

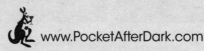

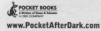

Desire a little something different?

Look for these thrilling series by today's hottest new paranormal writers!

The Naked Werewolf series from Molly Harper

The Daughters of the Glen series from Melissa Mayhue